The Death on the Black Rock

By

BRM Stewart

TP

ThunderPoint Publishing Ltd.

First Published in Great Britain in 2018 by
ThunderPoint Publishing Limited
Summit House
4-5 Mitchell Street
Edinburgh
Scotland EH6 7BD

Cover Image © Jevgenijs Scolokovs
used under license from shutterstock.com

Cover Design © Huw Francis

ISBN: 978-1-910946-44-2 (Paperback)
ISBN: 978-1-910946-45-9 (eBook)
Printed and bound in Great Britain by Clays Ltd, Elcograf S.p.A

www.thunderpoint.scot

Acknowledgements

I'd like to thank many people who have helped me on the journey with this book:

My wife Sally for her praise, edits, and helpful points for improvement; my beta reader Linda Douglas for her encouraging words and suggestions; and my brother-in-law David Fulton for helping me to get aspects of Police Scotland's work correct.

I'd also like to thank all those who read my previous books and told me how much they enjoyed them – that's what keeps a writer going! Also keeping me going is the Angus Writers' Group – thanks for your advice, friendship and support, guys.

Finally, big thanks to Seonaid and Huw at Thunderpoint for taking a chance on me and helping hone the book to its final form.

Thank you all.

Dedication

To my wife Sally for her constant support and encouragement, and my children Susie and Cameron (even though they find it hard to read their father's work).

To Stewart with best
wishes - thanks for
coming along!

Brian
October 2018 .

❧ 1 ❧
A year before

She couldn't believe she was falling. It had started as a stumble backwards when her fingers had slipped from the mobile phone. She had moved her legs to keep her balance, turning her body to try to recover. But she had tripped on a little rocky outcrop and her other foot had skidded on the wet grass, and the slope had steepened, and now she was falling forward, still tripping and sliding. Her balance went completely and she hit the ground and tumbled and rolled, faster and faster.

This was ridiculous! She gave something approaching a laugh, which turned to a gasp.

Then she was over the edge, past the point of recovery, and she gasped again, the sound whipped away from her. Her feet and hands scraped and scrabbled at the thick plastic mesh that had been pegged over the rock face to stop bits of it falling down to the road, but by then she had lost all orientation. She couldn't stop herself now.

This is stupid, she thought.

She rolled and tumbled, and finally hit the soft earth at the base of the Rock, before rolling onto the tarmac of the road, scraping her arms and smashing her face onto the hard wet surface.

She lay in silence, apart from her heavy rasping breaths. She was alive. In some pain – she daren't try to move – but alive. Thank god.

She tried to make sense of what had happened up there on top of the Rock, and wondered how long she'd lie here until help came. She heard the car coming and sighed with relief, until she realised it wasn't slowing down.

***

The cafe was on a corner, shaded and hemmed in by scooters and wheelie bins. It was off the main drag, and so generally avoided by the horde of tourists from the cruise ships, who swarmed over the city and up to the Moorish castle. So generally Craig Steele had it pretty much to himself.

He lit a cigarette and settled with his lager and his paperback at a table in the narrow alley, just a few feet across from a concrete and glass building. Ten minutes later he ordered another lager from the waiter, and lit another cigarette – effectively chasing away a couple who'd been about to sit at the next table.

When he sensed the presence near him, he thought it was just another tourist thinking of sitting down, but this person didn't move. He was standing quite close.

Steele looked up. The man was tall and fit, with hair tied back in a ponytail. He stood with a cocky smile on his young-ish face.

'Can I help you, pal?' Steele asked. In his accent, this was not a friendly offer.

The man sat down at Steele's table, leaning back. Steele tensed automatically and uncrossed his legs.

'*Puedo ayudarte?*'

'I'm the guy from Andy Robertson,' the man said. His accent was London, and his demeanour was cheery. He sat with his legs splayed, one hand reaching into his back pocket to bring out a folded, crumpled envelope.

Craig Steele looked round, but there was no one else taking any interest. He sat up in his seat, leaning towards the man. 'Oh aye?'

The man slapped the envelope on the table. 'It's all in there.' He signalled to the waiter and managed to indicate that he wanted two large beers.

Craig Steele put down his paperback, finished his lager, and reached for the envelope, ripping it open and reading the note inside.

Hi big man

The irritating cockney cunt that gave you this is Freddy Morton, and he's the real deal – he's got a track record and we're cool with him. I won't say you can trust the cunt totally, but you can believe him for now. The IBAN and BIC numbers are down below here. Whatever you transfer to us will come back trebled at least. We'll start small, just to show it's working, then we can build up. So go for whatever stake you want, big man. I suggest 10k to start with.

Once you've done it, burn this letter. It'll be a new account next time.

Give Freddy your account details, buy him a pint, and tell him to fuck off back here to Glasgow.'

Craig Steele re-read the letter, and folded it away carefully in the top pocket of his shirt. The lagers arrived, and the two men stared at each other. Steele was big, with vague traces of grey hair. He sat leaning on one elbow, his breathing shallow.

Freddy Morton sat grinning at him.

Craig Steele decided that he really didn't like Freddy Morton. And he didn't trust that easy smile.

❧ 2 ❦
A year later

Amanda Pitt and Pete McLeod saw Licker McGuire emerge from the doorway of the Station Bar and pause to light a very thin roll-up. He looked up, saw them, and did a double take. Then he shrugged and continued walking towards them, in the direction of Cowcaddens subway station, his body hunched against a stiff cold breeze, his free hand in the pocket of his leather bomber jacket. Amanda and Pete walked in that direction too, letting Licker catch up with them.

'Can we have a word, Licker?' Pete asked, not looking at him, trying not to appear like this was a conversation.

Licker lifted his head to the leaden sky, and took a big drag of his cigarette. 'Whit?'

Amanda smiled. He was the same height as her, and about the same age, but with a slightly hunted, scavenger look. Very short hair, a prematurely lined narrow face with a permanently aggressive stare.

Pete – slightly taller and only marginally less scruffy than Licker – looked around as they walked. He was looking for anyone paying too much attention to them, but there were dozens of windows all around in the low-rise flats, dozens of people walking about: any of them could walk past and double back without him noticing.

'We're still investigating those burglaries on Buccleuch Street,' Amanda said, nodding her head in the direction of that street, on the other side of the main road.

Licker sniffed, took the last drag from the cigarette, and looked down at his feet as he stamped it out. 'Oh aye?' His eyes avoided hers.

'But mainly we're interested in the Robertsons. What are they up to these days?'

They reached the mouth of the underpass, near to the entrance to the subway station, and they had to stop to continue talking.

Licker's nose twitched, and his head gave an involuntary sideways jerk. His shrug was unconvincing. 'Couldn't say, Sergeant Pitt.'

'We've heard they're shifting a lot of MDMA pills. Es.'

He lifted his eyebrows and the head twitched again. 'Aye?'

'Anyway, back to those burglaries…'

His breath hissed in through his teeth and he started looking around, just like Pete was. 'They've cornered the market, like, since big Craig Steele fucked off a few years ago. They're the go-to guys for Es nowadays. In Glasgow anyway.'

'And the supplies come from…?'

He shook his head. 'Don't know. Down south. England. Somebody said London, somebody said Manchester. Don't know.'

Amanda nodded. 'If you happen to hear of a delivery coming then do let me know, Licker.'

'Aye sure.'

'By the way, we've got photographs of the laptops stolen from those flats, and the serial numbers – they'll be unsellable. And we've got the IMEI numbers of the stolen phones – they'll be unusable.'

He swallowed and blinked.

'So we're just waiting for them to turn up. We pay for information, remember.'

'Aye, I remember.' He turned away from them, heading towards the door of the subway station.

They watched him go.

'So that's three people have given us Manchester,' Pete said. He shivered in the cool, damp breeze. 'Right, what now, boss?'

She checked her watch. 'Ramesh wanted to see me. I'd better get back. I'll tell him what Licker said – he can pass it back to OCCTU W.' This was Police Scotland's Organised Crime and Counter Terrorism Unit – the 'W' referred to the Glasgow section, covering the west of Scotland. OCCTU's duties included the drugs trade. Local detectives – like Amanda and Pete – were sometimes asked to use their local contacts to provide intelligence. They knew the Robertsons, just as they'd known Craig Steele – and Ken Talbot, Sandy Lomond and the rest. Talbot was dead, but Lomond and Steele had managed to slip away, leaving a vacuum that had now been filled.

'What do you want me to do?'

'Come back to the station with me and see if they want us to do anything more on this. Until then you can carry on getting through your emails.'

'Haud me back.'

They walked the short distance to their police station on Stewart Street, contained by those low-rise blocks of flats. Pete went to his desk, while Amanda went to find Ramesh.

Chief Inspector Ramesh was free. Amanda knocked and went in, closing the door behind her and sitting opposite him, knowing that there were never any formalities, or small talk, or offers of tea or coffee. The room was sparsely furnished and quiet.

Ramesh was a big tall Sikh with dark skin, and saggy, baggy dark brown eyes. He made Amanda look and feel even slimmer than she was. He nodded at her and pushed two full ring binders across the desk towards her.

'We've had a complaint,' he said.

She frowned, feeling her heart-rate increase.

'Not about you,' he added.

Amanda relaxed.

'There was a death just over a year ago in Clachdubh.' He pointed in the general direction of north, and Amanda nodded: the name was familiar. 'A young woman fell down a hill there, landed on the road, and was hit by a passing car. She died, sadly. It was all fully investigated by Inspector Jones, the local man, and his team. The Fiscal ruled it was an accident because there was no evidence to the contrary.' He held up his hands. 'Case solved, no problem.'

Amanda was nodding: she remembered it now from the papers. No major story, just a sad footnote to all the rest of the deaths in the world. A waste of a young life.

'Until the woman's mother decided that it wasn't accidental. She thinks her daughter was murdered.' Ramesh turned down

5

the corners of his mouth. 'Murdered by person or persons unknown, for reason or reasons unknown – but the mother's prime candidate is the FBI, or GCHQ, or whoever. And of course, all police forces were complicit in the cover-up.'

'Any basis for that?'

Ramesh sighed. 'The woman and her husband are Syrian immigrants – from twenty-five years ago, not from the recent crisis. The father's name is Salah Khalaf, the mother is Dina Khalaf. The dead woman was their only child, Rima Khalaf. She was born in this country. The mother thinks her daughter was murdered and she is threatening to make a fuss if we don't re-investigate.' He pushed the folders slightly further across the desk towards Amanda, so that they were in danger of over-balancing onto her lap. She reached to steady them. 'She wants a fatal accident inquiry at the very least. Talking about hiring an investigative reporter.'

Amanda looked at the folders. 'You want me to investigate her complaint? Shouldn't the Fiscal Service be the ones to investigate?'

Ramesh pursed his lips. 'We've been asked to look at how the investigation was handled first.' He coughed. 'You are not investigating the death, you are investigating the investigation. Clear? If you find it was all done perfectly competently, then we tell Mrs Khalaf that, and let her grieve. Or make a bigger fuss, whichever is her choice. Whatever: we spike her guns. However, if you find there were gaps in the investigation…Well, we will make a judgement call on how important those gaps are, and we will probably have to take it back to the Fiscal who may ask for a re-investigation of the whole case. But I've skimmed through the stuff and it certainly looks to me like the death was accidental. And I certainly do not have the resources to re-open the whole investigation. But you must investigate the complaint thoroughly.'

Amanda nodded, already hoping to hell she would find nothing amiss.

Ramesh coughed. 'For the purposes of this investigation – and this investigation only – you will be given the rank of Acting Detective Inspector.' He looked unhappy. 'This will give you status in Mrs Khalaf's eyes. HR will sort out your pay for the week you will spend on this.'

'A week?'

'Yes. I can give you the rest of this week for fieldwork, and then next Monday afternoon you give me your report.'

'And I can...'

'You must obviously go to Clachdubh. Normal procedure would be to speak to the original investigating team and the original interviewees – wherever practical, of course. And with Mrs Khalaf. I have telephoned her, and she is willing to come up to Clachdubh this Wednesday to meet with you.'

'How about Mr Khalaf?'

'He has not been involved at all – he is very busy with his business, apparently.'

'What does he do?'

'He's a pharmacist – owns a shop in Manchester.'

Amanda nodded. 'And I'm alone doing this?'

'I can't spare anyone else. You need to brief DC McLeod on his duties for the time you are away, and then you go.'

'We've had another confirmation about the Robertsons and the MDMA pills, by the way – and about manufacturing in England, possibly Manchester.'

Ramesh nodded. 'I'll pass that back. They'll say if they want us to assist any more.'

There was a silence, and she realised the meeting was over, so she stood and picked up the two heavy folders. 'Thank you, sir.' She tried to say that without sarcasm.

Outside, she told Pete what had happened, and they started sketching out a plan for him to work on during the rest of the week.

'Do you know this place Clachdubh?' she asked him, once they'd finished.

He nodded. 'Up near the Trossachs,' he said. 'Never been there, I don't think. You going to travel?'

'Think I might just stay over, saves dragging through the city morning and night.' Her flat was on the south side of the city, so a daily commute to Clachdubh would waste hours each day. She automatically started searching online for hotels.

'No offence, but I think this is a shit job you've got, boss.'

'How do you mean?'

'If you find out nothing, this woman will be pissed off, and if you find out something Ramesh and Police Scotland will be pissed off.'

She nodded. She had already worked that out.

'Still, Acting Detective Inspector Pitt, eh?' He grinned and gently punched her upper arm.

'Ouch.'

❧ 3 ❧

Gary sat at the till and swiped his card while the supervisor lifted away the *Sorry Till Closed* sign and swung the gate open. An old woman began to unload her trolley. As he waited, Gary spotted that attractive red-haired woman with her basket, looking up and down the till queues, and finally deciding that Gary's was the best option. He saw she was wearing a scoop-necked top, and hoped she'd be doing a lot of bending over when she got to him.

He took a deep breath and shifted in his seat. 'Would you like any help with your packing?'

The old woman pursed her tight, wrinkled lips and shook her head, and Gary started scanning her items. Lives alone, he thought. Money's tight – all 'value' products. Sad. But she looks like a miserable old cow. Or did she just become that way…

She packed, paid and moved away, and the redhead was there, giving him a smile as he offered her help with her packing, her hair bouncing as she shook her head. He scanned her items, his eyes flicking to her cleavage as she leaned to pack. She's beautiful, he thought. Fit, in every sense. Not married. He sighed deep inside.

A bottle of rosé wine. Chicken thighs. Garlic, ginger. Peppers. Spring onions. A bunch of coriander. Packets of biscuits. Pack of ground coffee…

As he scanned, he conjured an image of a romantic evening with her, chatting over the curry she'd made, drinking wine, making love all night until the sun rose.

'That's twenty-seven pounds fifty-four, please. Have you got a club card?'

'No – sorry.' Her voice was soft – Scottish but cultured, not rough like his.

He watched her lean over the card reader, shielding her PIN, and then he handed her the receipts as they spooled out. He pointed out the petrol offer. 'And your shop today has been fifty-four pence cheaper than Asda,' he said.

'Thank you.' She smiled. 'Every little helps!'

She lifted her bag-for-life, and his eyes stayed focused on her as she walked away. He'd seen her before in the store over the past month or so. A lot. He liked her. He shifted again in his seat.

'Hi, Gary.' The two huge plastic bottles of cider rolled sideways along the conveyor belt. It was Jill and Jasmine, who'd been in his year at school.

'You workin here all the time, Gary?' Jill asked. She was short and dumpy, contrasting in every way with Jasmine.

He nodded. 'Yup.'

'*All* the time? Is it no borin as fuck?'

He shook his head. 'I like it.' It's mindless, but I see people, he thought. I see people like the redhead; I get to talk to them. And I put them in my stories. 'Can I see your ID please?'

'For fuck sake, Gary. You know us.'

The couple in the queue behind the girls were frowning, their lips moving.

'It's the rules. No ID, no service.' He knew they were nineteen, of course, same age as him, but he also knew the rules – and he knew this would annoy them. Jasmine McCallum in particular. She thought a lot of herself, he thought – though with good reason: she had long black hair, an artificial tan, and a figure that turned heads. Big eyes and full lips.

'Come on, Gary,' Jasmine said, in a seductive voice, eyelashes fluttering.

He shook his head.

'Aw, fuck this,' Jill said. 'Come on, Jasmine. Leave this sad wanker to it.'

Jill almost dragged Jasmine away, but she turned to give Gary a smile, and then stuck out her tongue, making a fast licking motion with the tip. He knew she was teasing him, but it still unsettled him. He knew that she was unattainable but he'd get even with her, one way or another.

He lifted the bottles of cider off the conveyor belt and put them aside. He smiled at the couple in the queue who were still frowning and tutting. 'Sorry about that. Do you need any help with your packing?'

***

9

We had ridden for two days, following the thieves who had taken our cattle. And during the night we'd crept into their village, and we had exacted a terrible revenge on those men. They screamed and begged for mercy as we dragged them out in front of their womenfolk and we sliced them from neck to groin and left them in the open.

Most of the women were scrawny, dirty and bedraggled, but my men pulled them aside anyway and took their satisfaction. I entered one hut, my sword still dripping blood, and saw the young dark-haired woman. She was not yet twenty, but I could see she was a woman.

'No – please!'

I stood over her and told her to disrobe. She crouched there shivering, the fire flickering shadows across her young body. I pushed her onto her back and lifted my kilt. Her eyes grew wide. 'No, no,' she cried.

Soon she was moaning with pleasure as I…

'Gary!'

Gary saved the document and closed the window, and then closed the browser behind it. He was breathing quickly, his erection almost intolerable.

'Gary – you up there?'

He stood up and opened his bedroom door, shouting back down: 'I'm here, Dad. What is it?'

'What are you up to?'

Gary made his way down the steep narrow staircase to the small lounge where his father was turning on the TV and flicking through the channels. 'Want to get me a beer, son?' He selected a film channel and started rolling a cigarette.

'Aye sure.'

Gary's father was barely forty, and short, thin and muscular. He accepted the open beer can without looking away from the television. 'What have you been up to?'

'Just doing some writing.' Gary sat down. The programme on the TV was a film involving cars: cars being driven very fast and crashing into each other.

There was a snort. 'You and your writing. What is it now?' He lit the cigarette and inhaled deeply.

'Still that historical epic. Scotland in the eleventh century.'

'Oh aye? Loads of sex?' He laughed.

'It's based on fact.' But there *was* plenty of sex, he thought. He'd taken care of that haughty bitch Jasmine in this evening's work, and there was a long-term storyline for the redhead somewhere in his head.

His last main female character had been thrown from Dumbarton Rock, the centre of the Scottish empire a thousand years before. He wasn't quite sure how to dispose of Jasmine McCallum just yet.

And the redhead would be next, he thought.

❧ 4 ❧

In another small bedroom in a small council house in Clachdubh, a former classmate of Gary's lay back on his bed, smoking a roll-up, Beats headphones clamped over his ears, the sound still loud enough to be clearly audible to anyone else in the room.

But there was no one else in the room. The driving beat – faster than resting heart-rate – echoed from the walls, and threw itself out of the open window.

Jamil smoked and thought. He thought about fighting and death. He thought about women and sex. He thought about women and death.

Specifically he thought about Jasmine McCallum. He knew she had a fascination for him, and sometimes gave him a come-on, but she always ducked away whenever he got too close.

He hardly saw her nowadays. She had a job at that place in the business park, on reception. He had nothing. No money, no hopes. Jasmine was as unattainable as could be, unless…He smiled, and the cigarette smoke that rolled from his parted lips was sucked into his nostrils. Yes, she might respond to danger, the threat of death.

A new track played and he impatiently skipped it, then another, till something harsh and angry burned into his head and he let go of the ancient iPod. He dropped the end of the roll-up onto the plate on the floor by his bed. He wanted another, but he couldn't be bothered making one.

He switched on the iPhone he had, and started the Telegram messaging app. He had to lean under his bed to peel off the post-it with his password so he could log on.

There was a message from B: 'We need you to look for targets. Big scare coming. You up for it, man?'

He messaged back. 'Yeah. Fuckin bored here. Need action.'

A few seconds later: 'Stay cool, brother. Wait and watch. Your time will come.'

Jamil smiled to himself, and he stretched and yawned. His heart was beating a little faster now. He wanted to tell Jasmine McCallum about this, get her excited. Get her wanting him. He logged out and powered off the iPhone. They'd told him to use it as sparingly as possible; he thought that was bollocks, but he pretty much did as he was told – unless he wanted to impress someone with it.

He stuck the post-it with the password back under his bed, and gave another yawn.

His other phone buzzed, the old heavy HTC. He lifted it and stared at the cracked screen. It was a text from Rose. 'Sorry I woz angry about what you asked me to do. Forgive me?'

He waited for a full two minutes before texting back. 'One way you can make sure of that.'

Five minutes went by. 'Maybe. I'll think.'

'Good girl. Love you babe.'

'Love you.'

Now his grin was a mile wide. Jamil had met Rose at the youth club a month or so before. She was in fourth year at school. She was skinny, shy and reserved from years of neglect by her mother. She was now with foster parents, who kept a tight rein on her. Jamil had shown an interest in her, and she'd gradually responded. He'd been barred from the club after that fight, but by then they'd exchanged mobile numbers. Their relationship, such as it was, had been carried out mainly by texting since then.

He was slowly working towards getting her to send him pictures of herself. It looked like it was working.

He closed his eyes and pushed one hand down under the waistband of his jeans as the music pounded in his head.

❧ 5 ❧

'I'm Acting Detective Inspector Amanda Pitt,' she said, and held up her warrant card. 'I phoned yesterday.'

The man who had answered the door was big: tall, wide and heavy-set. He looked down at her, his eyes crinkled and lips tight. He nodded and stepped aside, holding out an arm towards the interior of the bungalow.

'Can I get you a tea or a coffee?' His voice was a growl, its tone mid-way between friendly and aggressive, as if he wasn't sure what tone to strike.

'A coffee would be great,' she said.

'You take a seat in there. I'll get your coffee.'

'Just black,' she said.

One of the leather armchairs was obviously his, so she sat on the sofa. Retired Inspector Gordon Jones could only have been about twenty years older than her at most, but this lounge – cluttered with china and fussy little tables – looked like it was two generations away from her flat in Glasgow. She looked round: photographs, many of Jones in uniform, some in teams – rugby and football – wedding photographs of him and his wife, and what must be his grown-up children with their families. She heard the kettle boil, and the clatter from the kitchen. She waited patiently, still looking at the photographs, Jones's life laid out there.

'There you go.'

He set her mug down on a coaster on the small table by her, and went over to sink deep into his armchair with his own mug. His back was to the window; the late afternoon was bright outside so she found it impossible to make out his features.

'Thanks for agreeing to see me,' she said, pulling her notebook from her large handbag. She had the case folders in the car.

'No problem.' He blew across his coffee and sipped at it. 'You said it was about the Khalaf girl.'

'Yes. I'm investigating how the case was handled. The mother has made a formal complaint. You were the Station Inspector – the senior officer investigating the death of Rima Khalaf.'

'So she's still insisting the girl was murdered by person or persons unknown,' he said.

'Yes she is.' She took a drink of her own coffee. It tasted very strong. 'You investigated, and the Fiscal ruled it was accidental death.'

He scratched at his chin. 'Yes. The mother couldn't accept it. Had to believe someone had robbed her of her only child rather than blind chance. I can quite understand it, of course – ' he gave a genuine, deep sigh – 'but there was no evidence.'

'I've been through the files.'

He let the pause build in the air. 'And?'

'You found no forensics suggesting she'd been pushed off the hill – they call it the Rock, don't they?'

'No forensics. It was really bad luck, in fact. If that car hadn't come along just when it did, with that half-blind old fart driving, she'd have been OK. But he ran right over her.'

'And there was no suggestion of anyone with a motive to push her off the Rock?'

'None.'

'You didn't ever establish why she'd gone up there?'

He put his coffee mug down and clasped his hands on his lap. 'Didn't need a reason. It was late Saturday morning, turning into a fine day – the rain had just stopped. No reason for anyone not to go up there for a walk.'

'No one came forward to say they'd been up there at that time?'

'No one. Nobody saw her, nobody said they were with her.' He gave a shrug.

She scribbled notes, and looked at the questions she'd come prepared to ask. 'How about the boyfriend? You interviewed him. He was a work colleague. Married.'

He took a deep breath. 'He was her boss – head of the science faculty at the school. And yes, married. He came forward straight away: told us he'd been with her the evening before – quick rendezvous at her house after school while her housemates were down the pub – and he'd phoned her on the Saturday morning to arrange a meet that afternoon. He was devastated – both by her death and by the fact that his wife was going to find out all the details of the affair. Poor bastard. Mind you, if he hadn't come forward, and we'd found out about him, then he'd have been firmly in the frame.'

'But you don't place him on the Rock, giving her a shove to end the affair.'

'No. He was obviously getting what he wanted from her – she was a young, attractive woman – and he said she had never talked about prising him away from his wife to set up home. She seemed happy just being his bit on the side. Her housemates confirmed that. She wasn't the possessive type.'

That struck Amanda. She could see how the boyfriend would be happy with the arrangements, but why was Rima? It jarred with her, and she wondered whether a female investigating officer would have pursued the point. 'You spoke to the wife too, but she knew nothing about the affair.'

'She had no idea.' He gave a grunting laugh. 'That was a difficult interview. Went through a box of tissues that day.'

She put her notebook down on her lap. 'And you're quite satisfied you investigated the case thoroughly?'

Jones gave his grunting laugh again. 'I was a few weeks away from retirement, and I wasn't about to leave with some unfinished case locked in my drawer. But I didn't rush through it. No, I investigated everything fully. No one disagreed that it was an accidental – and unlucky – death.'

'Except the mother.'

'Except the mother. What's the basis of her complaint? What does she say I didn't do properly?'

Amanda drank the last of her coffee and put the mug down. She hadn't particularly taken to him in these few minutes, but that was neither here nor there. 'They've nothing specific, just a general accusation that you didn't investigate thoroughly enough. I'm meeting her later. You were happy with your interview with the boyfriend?'

'Like I said, he came forward of his own accord, and we questioned him for two hours. Then we brought him in the next day and went through it all again. And again two days later. His statements matched: not perfectly, because that suggests a memorised story, as you know. But in all substantial detail. He was telling the truth.'

'You didn't follow up on any potential Islamophobic dimension.'

He snorted. 'There was no Islamophobic dimension. We went through her Facebook posts and her tweets.' He paused there, and then shook his head. 'Nothing untoward.'

'You didn't think she was being watched because of any Islamic issues?'

'The mother thought the head teacher had done her in because some kid's parents complained about some science lessons.' He shook his head. 'We found no evidence out there.'

'So, looking back – and remember, I'm not investigating the case, I'm investigating the investigation. Looking back, in your heart of hearts, is there anything you think you could maybe have gone deeper into? You're the only one who would know.'

'No,' he said after almost a full minute. 'There's nothing.'

She wished she could see his features clearly. She wished she'd taken longer talking to him before asking that key question. She wasn't perfectly sure she really believed him.

❧ 6 ❧

Her next stop was the Rock View Hotel, which turned out to be a misnomer. Amanda went through the big front door into what still looked like the hallway of an old house, but with a reception desk – just a shelf really – at the side, and rang the bell. She could hear voices, and one sounded familiar.

The woman who appeared was middle-aged and blousy, well dressed, made-up and coiffured, flaunting gold everywhere. She gave an over-dramatic gasp and pointed – 'Inspector Pitt?'

Amanda nodded.

'I'm Joan. Please, please come in – Mrs Khalaf is in here, waiting for you.'

Another woman had followed Joan out of the room. 'Amanda – hi!'

Amanda did a double take. 'Nicola. What are you doing here?'

Nicola McGregor smiled. 'Joan is one of my IIP clients.' She looked back into the lounge and her voice dropped to a whisper. 'I've just been speaking to Mrs Khalaf about her daughter. Terrible business.'

Amanda nodded.

'You two know each other!' Joan said. 'How exciting.'

Nicola gave a half-smile. 'I'd better leave you to it. I have work

16

to do.' She gave a mock frown directed at Joan. 'See you back in Glasgow some time, Amanda.' She headed for the stairs, holding a full glass of wine in one hand and a briefcase in the other.

'Nicola's advising me on the business,' Joan whispered. She showed Amanda into the small lounge where an elegant woman got to her feet.

'Inspector Pitt.'

'Mrs Khalaf. Thank you for coming all this way to see me.' They shook hands.

Joan was fussing around, lifting away a wine glass and an empty cup. 'Mrs Khalaf, do you want anything more to drink? Tea? Coffee? Wine? No?'

Mrs Khalaf gave a patient smile and a shake of her head. She was a very attractive woman, Amanda thought, with a young-looking face. She wore a pale pastel coloured headscarf, and a very modest jacket and long skirt that matched the headscarf, and she looked self-contained and well off.

'Nothing for me,' Amanda said. She didn't want to give Joan any excuse to hang around. She sat on one armchair, while Mrs Khalaf sat back down on hers. They waited, looking at each other, while Joan made a noisy fuss of trying to slip away quietly.

When Joan was out of the room and the door closed behind her, Amanda took a folder out of her briefcase and balanced it on her lap. She took the notebook from her handbag and set it precariously on the arm of her chair.

'Mrs Khalaf, before we start,' she said, 'I must make it clear to you that I am not investigating the circumstances of your daughter's death as such. I am investigating your complaint that the investigation was not conducted fully and properly.'

'And if you decide in our favour,' Mrs Khalaf said in a soft but firm voice, with only a slight foreign accent interleaved with a polite English one, 'you will reopen the investigation.'

'That would have to be determined by my superiors. But, there's a possibility that could happen, yes.' She didn't want to raise her expectations, which were probably already too high. 'Your husband is still in Manchester?'

'Yes. He is very busy. He felt that I would be able to conduct negotiations with Police Scotland alone.'

Amanda raised an eyebrow. Negotiations? Maybe that was an

accident of translation: Mrs Khalaf's English sounded perfect, but it was still her second language.

'So in what way are you investigating our complaint?' Mrs Khalaf asked, before Amanda could explain.

'I am reading the case files – the transcripts of interviews, contemporaneous notes, forensic evidence. I have spoken with the senior investigating officer from the time, I am obviously speaking to yourself, and I will also interview key witnesses, someone from the Fiscal's office, and the chief forensics officer. As I say, my purpose is not to investigate the case: my role is to check some of the evidence, and to test the thoroughness with which that evidence was gathered.'

'Inspector Jones told us it was an accident. Right at the start he told us that. And at the end he told us that all the evidence pointed that way.'

Amanda swallowed. She doubted whether Jones had said it in quite those terms, but he may well have suggested at the start that it was *probably* an accident. Which was a stupid thing to have said before gathering any evidence – but that didn't mean he'd got it wrong.

'He interviewed you and your husband. Together? What did he ask?'

Mrs Khalaf clasped her hands loosely on her lap, still sitting very upright. 'He asked about Rima's life. He asked about any boyfriend: we said we knew she had one, but we'd never met him. We only knew he was a teacher at the school. When the man came forward, and it turned out that he was her superior and married, Inspector Jones started asking about Rima's past loves.'

She kept her voice calm, but Amanda could see she was upset that her daughter had been in an adulterous relationship. Amanda knew very little of the Muslim religion, but she knew that adultery was a pretty serious sin. In Christianity too, she supposed, as an afterthought, but not so much maybe.

'And what did you say?' Amanda glanced at the file in front of her – the transcript of the interviews with the Khalafs.

'We told her Rima had many friends at University. She was a popular girl.'

'Any serious relationships?'

There was hesitation and doubt in her voice. 'Nothing serious.

She concentrated on her career. She always wanted to be a teacher. She was a dedicated teacher.'

Amanda ignored the denial. 'Were any of her boyfriends at University married?'

Mrs Khalaf's hands now clasped each other more tightly. 'Of course not.' Her voice was controlled.

OK, Amanda thought. Was there anything in her past? Had she brought consistent shame on her family, so much so that the *father* had arranged to have her murdered?

She shook away that particular conspiracy theory. Of course the parents hadn't murdered their child – she thought back to the files: yes, their *only* child. Why would they insist on trying to reverse a closed accidental death case if they'd actually murdered her? Keep it real, Amanda.

'I don't want to intrude on your grief. I assume Inspector Jones asked about all of this.'

'No. Not really.'

Amanda nodded. She planned to speak to former housemates of Rima later, and maybe they could tell her more about past boyfriends. Maybe they had a story about Rima that the parents knew nothing of – after all, children were good at keeping secrets from their parents. Had Inspector Jones been thorough with *them*? Already little threads were unravelling, and she was growing annoyed at Jones.

'So,' Amanda said, 'do you think any previous friends from University, or the teacher, would have had a grudge against your daughter?'

Mrs Khalaf looked straight at Amanda. 'I don't know. Someone murdered her, though. Someone hated her.' She took a deep breath. 'They did not investigate the political angle.'

Amanda looked at her. 'What do you think they missed?'

'They did not look at her emails, Facebook.'

As politely and gently as she could, Amanda said: 'The police went through her Facebook posts – and her Twitter feeds. There was nothing there.'

'They were watching her.'

'*Who* was watching her?'

'GCHQ was monitoring everything. IS was monitoring everything. The FBI. The NSA.' Her voice was growing more tense.

19

Amanda's voice was still gentle as she asked: 'Have you any evidence for this?'

'They did not investigate properly,' Mrs Khalaf said. 'She was writing a novel. None of this was investigated.'

Amanda flicked through the file. She wondered about the social media accounts: had something been missed there? And she also thought that no one had mentioned bank accounts: not that money seemed to be a motive anywhere, but surely they would have been checked. And how exactly did you get GCHQ to admit they were monitoring someone?

Had Jones really been thorough on the social media side of things? He'd been vague when mentioning it.

And…something…Something else…

It slipped away.

'You said she was writing a novel?'

'Historical fiction, she said.'

'Do you have a copy?'

'No. It is undoubtedly on her laptop but she has a password and we do not know what it is.'

'Did the police try to get information from the laptop?'

'They took it away for two weeks and then they gave it back to us and said there was nothing there. I asked how they had got past her password and they said they could not tell me. It was a secret. I do not believe they looked at it.'

Amanda sat up. She imagined Jones trying to get IT forensics to examine the laptop, and time running out as no evidence of any crime being committed came to light; it would have been way down their list of priorities.

Yes, she thought, there were gaps in the police investigation. But ultimately this girl had fallen off the Rock and been hit by a car: there was no suspect, no one who wished her enough harm to have murdered her. It was just very bad luck.

Conscious that Mrs Khalaf was staring at her, she said: 'Where is the laptop now?'

'Upstairs in my room.' She pointed to the ceiling. 'Could you take it and get your people to open it?'

Amanda shook her head. 'Definitely not, I'm afraid.'

Mrs Khalaf seemed not to hear. She stood up. 'I will fetch it for you.'

❧ 7 ❧

Pete checked his watch. 'Fuck sake,' he said. 'I need to get home.' He lifted his pint and started to neck the final third of it.

'One more,' Roy said. 'C'mon.'

Pete's mental tussle took all of three seconds. 'Aye, OK.'

As Roy shoved through the dense bodies to get to the bar, Pete sat back with his near-empty pint glass and looked around the pub. He was in Patterson's on Byres Road. Roy thought they were out for a pint and a catch-up – with strictly no talk about police work or teaching or religion, only football and politics – which was the cover Pete needed.

But he was looking around. This was one of the pubs that had been whispered about as being a conduit for the Robertsons' business. Pete didn't know if that was true, but he'd seen small deals going on.

There was a barmaid named Taylor, a young, pretty lassie who looked sixteen but must have been twenty-one at least. When she went round the tables, all eyes were on her, and often remarks were made, to which she would give a resigned smile and sometimes a quick retort. But now and again a whispered remark was met with no apparent response. Pete had watched what happened next. She would go behind the bar again, and she would say something to the lean, ponytailed man who'd been there for the past two hours but had only had two pints. Pete had heard his voice: he was a Londoner.

The ponytailed man would then take an old tobacco tin from his pocket and make himself a roll-up, then head for the door. On the way, he'd meet the eyes of the man who had whispered to the barmaid Taylor, and a minute or so later this man would also go through the door. Five minutes later ponytail was back, closely followed by the man. Pints would be finished, and the man would leave with his pal.

The men buying the presumed Es were always young, and Pete guessed most of them were students.

Roy was back with the pints. 'Cheers, mate. Now, where were we?'

'Firhill,' Pete said. 'As fuckin usual.' They touched glasses. Who was ponytail, Pete wondered.

❧ 8 ❧

The head teacher of the school was a small woman with tightly curled black hair. She wore a matching jacket and skirt, and several gold bracelets. She took Amanda into a small, stark meeting room and made her a tasteless black coffee that Amanda wasn't sure was really coffee.

Amanda opened her folder and her notebook. 'I'm not investigating Rima Khalaf's death as such,' she said. 'I'm investigating how the investigation was carried out. As part of that process, I need to check with some witnesses. I'm partly cross-checking on their memories with what they said at the time, but mainly I'm forming a view on how thorough they feel the investigation was.'

The head teacher smiled and nodded. 'I was interviewed twice.' Her voice was proud.

Amanda shuffled the papers to get to the statement.

'Once here at the school, and then I was asked to go down to the police station to make a formal statement.'

Amanda scanned the sheets. 'You said Rima Khalaf was an excellent teacher.'

'Indeed. She was knowledgeable about her subject, she understood how science should be taught – not a succession of facts and formulas, but as a way of thinking – and she got on well with the pupils. Not that many here give staff a hard time, but she got everyone on board. Well, a couple of the girls didn't like her, but they didn't like anyone.'

'Did they give her a 'hard time'?'

'They tried. She followed our behaviour policy, and didn't ever take it personally. She didn't let it get her down.'

'The only issue seems to have been her personal relationship with her head of faculty, Scott Anderson.'

The head teacher looked like she'd bitten into something sour. She fiddled with the bracelets on her wrist as she spoke: 'Yes, she turned his head rather. All the men on the staff fancied her to some degree, I heard, but it was Scott she went for. Such a pity he was married. You always sensed there was a lot going on under the surface with Rima. She had a vulnerability about her. She was enigmatic, I suppose.'

'Did his marriage survive the affair?'

'It seems to have, but it will never be the same. It couldn't be.' She looked momentarily distant.

'So you're happy that the police went into Miss Khalaf's background pretty thoroughly?'

The head teacher's expression froze for a second, then she smiled. 'Yes.' And more firmly: 'Yes I am.'

'Did Miss Khalaf express political opinions – on Islam for example?'

Again there was the fiddling of the bracelets. 'Some parents complained.'

'About what?'

'Rima had a bee in her bonnet about the world's current view of Islam, and the focus on extremism. She was keen to put it into historical context.'

'Which was?'

'She referred back to the original Muslim invasion of the West, from the eighth century onwards. She spoke about the advances in science, medicine and mathematics – and art too – that were made by them. She spoke about how, under Muslim rule, all faiths and beliefs co-existed happily, and great strides forward were made.'

'Is this all true?'

'Apparently. She went a little too far when she said that the ignorant Christians drove the enlightened Muslims out of Western Europe before going on to ransack the Holy Land during the Crusades. She said that set back civilisation by at least a hundred years. Without that there would have been no Dark Ages, we'd have reached the moon in the mid eighteenth century.' The head teacher gave a little laugh. 'Some parents complained, and I asked her to be careful of what she said. With all that's going on in the world, one doesn't want to excuse it through events a thousand years ago.'

'Indeed. Did the police pursue this during the investigation into her death?'

'No. Not really.'

A bell started ringing, and there was a rush of footsteps in the corridor outside. 'That's the bell. I've asked Mr Anderson to come along – he's free just now. Give him a minute.'

They waited until there was a tentative tap at the door, and the head teacher shouted: 'Come in!' in a surprisingly authoritative voice. The door opened. 'This is acting Detective Inspector Pitt, Mr Anderson. I'll leave you both to it – I'll be in my office.' She pointed in the direction of next door.

Scott Anderson sat opposite Amanda. He was tall and thin, good-looking she supposed, but looking very serious, and almost gaunt and hunted. He wore a pinstriped suit, and a chunky steel and gold watch. His hair and beard were dark and neat. He pushed the chair back a little way from the desk and crossed his legs. He looked her up and down, and then focused on a knot in the wood of the table, a fingernail reaching to scratch at it.

'Good morning, Mr Anderson. I'm Acting Detective Inspector Amanda Pitt of Police Scotland. I'm here to investigate how the investigation into the death of Rima Khalaf was conducted – I'm not investigating the death itself. As part of that process, I'm speaking to witnesses. I'm trying to check with them whether they feel the investigation was thorough – '

He interrupted her in a quiet voice: 'It was thorough.' He didn't look up.

'You were in a relationship with Rima, so you knew her well.'

'I'm not sure that I really did.'

She wondered what he meant by that. 'How did your affair start?'

He left off picking at the table-top, and clasped his hands on his lap. He looked up, but beyond her, not meeting her eyes. 'We were together a lot, because she was a probationer in my faculty. So we spoke, and she'd stay on after school and I'd help her research lessons. I observed her teaching, of course, and we'd discuss that. And one evening we went for a drink, and she said she wasn't in a relationship and she was actually quite lonely. And she looked at me, and I could tell she wanted me. And one day after school, when we were about to leave, I just gave her a hug because she'd done a brilliant lesson with her National 4 class – I'd observed it – and she kissed me and I started stroking her.' His eyes looked at Amanda.

'She broke off after a while, and went home.'

Amanda swallowed.

'That Friday she said her two house-mates were away for the weekend, leaving right after school, and did I want to go round. I told my wife we had a faculty heads' meeting, and I went round to Rima's place, and we made love. When I got home, I was sure my wife would suspect, but she didn't. Says a lot for my marriage.'

Amanda tried not to frown. 'And you continued in that vein.'

'Yes. Opportunistic sex, I suppose – slipping out of school during a free period, after school in my classroom.'

'Did you ever speak of leaving your wife?'

'Never. I thought Rima would make demands on me, and I wasn't sure what I'd do if she'd asked – I think I probably would have left my family for Rima – but she seemed happy the way things were. Some companionship and sex, a lot of texting.' He gave a shrug.

Amanda almost snapped her fingers: texting – mobile phones – *that* was the thought that had slipped away yesterday. There was no mention of Rima Khalaf's mobile phone in the files. She parked the thought. 'So you came forward when you heard she'd been killed.'

'I knew they'd check her phone records and everything, so I just told my wife what had been going on, and I went to the police station.'

Amanda scribbled a note about the mobile. 'Do you think they ever suspected you of murdering her?'

He gave a frown and a grimace. 'No.' Then he thought: 'Why would they? No, they told me she'd accidentally fallen off the Rock and been hit by a car at the bottom – really bad luck. But they had to investigate, so they were interviewing me.'

'They questioned you a few times.'

'Twice more after that first time. Three times in all. But it wasn't threatening – not good cop bad cop stuff. They were just checking. They knew it was an accident.'

OK, thought Amanda. Inspector Jones had gone straight to a theory of accidental death, and had pretty much told everyone he'd interviewed that this was his theory. The investigation had looked thorough, but he hadn't been critical enough.

Though it was hard to see that he'd missed anything significant.

'Rima had strong views on Islam,' she said.

Anderson frowned. 'She just felt they'd had a bad press historically – their contribution to the development of science and maths had been largely ignored. She certainly didn't condone any of the extremism going on at the moment. She wasn't attempting to excuse it – she just wanted to put it in context. Perfectly valid, I thought.'

'But some parents didn't think so.'

'A few of our parents have connections with the armed forces – one had a son, a former pupil of ours, killed in Afghanistan. So feelings ran high amongst some people. Irrational feelings. Well, understandable feelings I suppose. Rima was young, committed – inexperienced. She got it a wee bit wrong now and again.'

'Did she tell you she was writing a novel?'

'Yes, but she never showed me any of it. Historical fiction, she said. She was in a writers' group here in Clachdubh. Someone there might know about the book.'

Amanda bit her tongue. Was it all about the sex with him, she wondered. Did he really pursue Rima's interest in writing at all? 'Do you have a note of her mobile number?' She had hoped he would answer without thinking, but he frowned, obviously thinking that she should have known the number.

'I can't remember it.'

'Isn't it still on your own mobile?'

He looked away from her, down at the table, up at the corner of the room. 'I – er – '

Of course, she thought. 'You bought yourself a pay-as-you-go mobile to call her from.' So the wife wouldn't accidentally see the texts and the calls.

'Yes.' The voice was small.

'And...'

'I got rid of it. After...'

Amanda let her silence do the accusing. As is often the way, he felt obliged to fill that small void, thinking she suspected what he was about to say. 'And I bought her one. As a present. Hers had got lost – well, stolen, she thought.' When she still didn't speak, he added: 'An iPhone.'

❧ 9 ❧

I am Ali Ibn al-Lukuh. I live in a street near the middle of the city we call Toledo, perched on a mountain in the very centre of Iberia, with deep gorges protecting us on three sides. I am twenty-four years old. It is the year 438AH, but my Christian friends call the year 1016AD. It is early in the morning, but the sun is already climbing into the clear blue sky, its merciless heat on us – there is no shade here. In my robes, I and my Arab brothers are cool, but my Christian friends dress stupidly and are always too hot.

I am walking through the town to where my master, Ibn al-Wafid, the pharmacist, works and studies. I am eager to discuss my latest research on plants with him – for he is the expert: no one in our world knows more than he does.

As I turn the corner I see two young Christian men approaching me. They are scowling, and I feel uneasy. I duck down a side alley to escape them.

I reach my master's pharmacy, and gratefully enter the shade of the shop, and through to the smells of his workrooms at the back. There is a door open to the garden, but the air is still overpowering with scents, and my master is coughing.

"I'm sorry I am late," I say.

"No matter – you are in time for prayer. What happened?"

"Two Christian men blocked my way. I had to go around."

"Hmm. Their arrogance grows with their ignorance. We have been at peace for over a hundred years, and most of us live together, learning and studying. But there are dark clouds. I pray that I do not live to see the loss of so much knowledge."

We kneel to pray.

Amanda looked up from the iPad, and reached for her gin and tonic. The bar of the Clachdubh Hotel, where Amanda was staying the night and where she'd eaten earlier, was crowded and noisy. Crawford Ballantine took a long drink of his beer and stared moodily at her.

'This is all she gave you?'

'First I heard about her novel was when she read out a passage at one of our slam nights – that's where everyone does a reading – and I said I'd be interested in looking at more. That was what she sent me. I've no idea if she actually wrote any more.' He lifted his pint again.

Amanda folded the cover over the screen of the iPad and handed it back to him.

'She was trying to set the record straight on this whole Christian versus Muslim thing, where all the Muslims are the scary hate figures,' he said.

'Did anyone from the police interview you at the time of her death?' she asked.

He shook his head. 'No.'

'So, was anyone in the writers' group particularly interested in Rima? Was she particularly interested in anyone there?'

'She kind of hung close to Fergus Watson. He published a book last year – historical thriller. I don't know if she fancied him or just wanted his help in getting to his publisher. Anyway, he's very happily married and too busy with his writing.'

Amanda digested that. Rima had slept with her boss at the school. Would she have slept with this Fergus Watson to get on with her writing career? She suddenly saw Rima in a particular light.

'Who else is in the group?'

'We're a loose mix of people. A few teachers – like Rima. Another solicitor like me – she writes crime thrillers. A social worker, a nurse, a young guy who works at Tesco. Some retired folk. Various others.' He shrugged. 'Apart from her trying to suck up to Fergus – sorry, bad choice of words maybe. Apart from her palling up with Fergus, she just listened. She sometimes gave her views on Islam after a couple of gins, but never too loudly.'

Amanda finished her drink.

'Want another?'

'Yes – but it's my shout.' She found her purse and handed him a note. 'Same again for me.'

She thought about what she was going to have to do. Yes, she had to tell Ramesh that the enquiry had been compromised from the start because Inspector Jones had set out with a particular view. Understandably. But she didn't really believe the investigation had missed anything significant. Any Islamophobic dimension just didn't hold water, though it was, of course, perfectly possible that Rima had been flagged as someone who needed to be watched because of her expressed views, which might be construed in today's paranoid Western world as making her a threat.

Perfectly possible. Her emails could be monitored, her online activities tracked, her phone calls intercepted.

Her phone…

But so what? Why would the authorities have killed her? She hadn't done anything, hadn't been near any terrorist outrage.

Crawford was back. He put down her gin and a small pile of change. 'What do you think?' he asked her. 'Cheers, by the way.' He took a long pull at his fresh pint.

'I don't know,' she said.

She'd found Crawford on the writers' group's website, had emailed him, and had met him here for a drink. She liked him, and she felt that somehow she now knew Rima Khalaf a bit more, even if that meant she was starting to dislike her as a person.

'So,' he said. 'What do you get up to in Glasgow when you're not fighting crime?' He smiled over his pint.

'Oh, my partner and I live quietly. She works for a computer company.' She glanced at him over her glass, and almost grinned at his crestfallen look. 'Sorry.'

He gave a rueful grin. 'So what next with this case?'

'I don't know,' she said. 'It's not for me to decide.'

The only thing that would really work would be a full reopening of the enquiry. Jones had missed out on the political dimension. No one had followed up properly with the writers' group. After a solid day, Amanda had just one more interview tomorrow – Friday – and then it was back to Glasgow to compile her report. And nobody there wanted to start an expensive and embarrassing enquiry that would find nothing.

But there was Rima's mobile phone. That seemed to be a big gap.

❧ 10 ❧

She'd packed and checked out of the Clachdubh Hotel, and driven to the Rock with the vague idea that she had to see the scene of the death of Rima Khalaf. She had an hour or so before going back to the school to meet Rima's housemate Mary – also a teacher there, but who hadn't been available the day before.

There was a small car park, and then a path than zigzagged up the hill. Calling it 'The Rock' made it sound more impressive than it really was, thought Amanda. It was less than two hundred feet or so high, and an easy climb. It was almost all grass here, and mounds of dog dirt were evident all the way up – some on the path, and some wrapped in poop bags and then left for posterity.

But at the top, the view was good. She could look back over the town to the remaining high-rises of Glasgow in the distance, and in all other directions to the mountains, some still with scatterings of snow in shady corners. She looked round, wishing she knew the names of those mountains, and then stepped to the edge.

The north side of the Rock was steep, and had apparently been made more so by the need to widen the road down below. There was no barrier, only a line of warning signs. Amanda looked over the edge. The grassy slope fell away, steeper and steeper, and then there was the drop to the edge of the road. Plastic mesh coated the side of the rock face.

Amanda could see how you might slide and then simply fall. But surely you would be aware of it right at the start. You'd catch hold of one of the many rocky outcrops and stop yourself, then pull yourself back up.

OK, late at night if you were drunk, you wouldn't manage to retrieve the situation. Or if you were old or had poor balance.

Or if you'd been given a good, hard shove in the first place.

Amanda looked down. A van appeared on the road and drove past at speed. Amanda frowned. And waited for the next vehicle – a blue car, also going fast.

She found a small stone, waited till the next car appeared in view, and lobbed the stone underhand away down the grass. It bumped and jumped, and fell off the edge. Amanda didn't see it reach the roadway – and tensed in case in smashed into the car, but nothing seemed to happen. She reckoned it hit the road pretty much at the same time as the car reached the spot.

Give or take, a body would probably do the same. So, bad luck that Rima Khalaf had fallen at just the right time to land on the roadway as a car was about to be at that spot? Or had the person giving the shove known that would happen?

She shook the thought away. She wasn't here to investigate the death, she reminded herself. There were gaps in the investigation, but nothing material.

'Careful,' said a man's voice behind her.

Amanda turned: he was an older man with a Jack Russell on a lead – one of the few breeds of dog she recognised.

'A couple of young lassies have fallen over the edge here. Careful.'

He stood while his dog had a pee on the grass beside the path, and he shivered inside his waterproof jacket.

Amanda stepped back from the edge. 'I was just wondering how long it would take someone to fall down the slope.'

'Well,' he said. 'We're fifty metres above road level – free-fall would take…let me think. Call it square root of ten, so just over three seconds.' He noticed her expression. 'I was a physics teacher at the high school.' She smiled, and he went on: 'It's not free-fall of course, not remotely. Even though it looks steep, it's still more rolling very quickly rather than falling – no one could survive a straight fall of that distance. So it would take someone maybe ten seconds to get to the road, and their injuries would depend on exactly how they landed – on the verge or on the road.'

'And how far would a vehicle travel in ten seconds? Down there.'

'At sixty miles an hour…something like nine hundred feet. I apologise for mixing SI and imperial units. Bad form.' He smiled widely.

She stepped closer to the edge again and looked down. Maybe it was around nine hundred feet or so from where a vehicle became visible and when it was right where a body would hit the road after a fall, but the timing would be ridiculously tight. If someone had pushed Rima Khalaf, they would have picked a time when she was off-guard, off-balance. It was very unlikely that the person could have chosen a time when a vehicle was going to hit her body. That had been just bad luck.

She turned and smiled again at the man, then her smile faded. 'You said two girls had fallen.'

'Yes. That Khalaf lassie – the Muslim teacher – last year. And Karen McKechnie – oh, three years ago now.'

'What happened with Karen?'

31

'End of session after-party. Crowd of fourth-years came up here after the school dance, drinking and playing music. Happened every year, and the cops turned a blind eye – they were happy they knew where the kids were. Some time during the night, as they were packing up, someone apparently noticed Karen was missing. The kids all stumbled about shouting for her, they said, called her mobile. Her body was found in the morning down at the side of the road. She'd smashed her head off the rocks on the way down, but they reckon the poor bitch took a few hours to die.' He realised he sounded ungracious. 'I taught her. She was a pretty wee lassie, but a bit on the dim side. Bit of a tease too. Wanted to be a model.' His mouth screwed up and he shook his head.

The Jack Russell was sniffing at Amanda's feet and looking up at her expectantly. She ignored it. She thought there were too many dogs in the world.

'Hasn't anyone ever thought of fencing-off this edge?'

'Oh aye. It's been done a couple of times, but the fence got vandalised and they said that made it more dangerous than not having a fence at all. So they stuck the warning notices up instead.'

'Rima Khalaf fell over during the day,' Amanda said. 'She must have noticed the drop. She'd lived here for a few months.'

'Aye, right enough. It's a bit strange.' He shrugged. 'The cops were happy enough, though.'

'Yes,' Amanda said. 'Yes, they were.'

He gave a brief laugh. 'Mind you, Jonesy was about to retire: he wanted it all sorted as fast as possible.'

Yes, Amanda thought. I rather think he did. 'When did you retire?'

'Couple of years ago.'

'So you weren't in the school when Rima Khalaf worked there.'

'No. I know people who worked with her, though.' His voice tailed away.

'Any gossip?' She smiled.

'I heard she was good – passionate about the historical Muslim agenda, and quite rightly too. It's amazing how the West thinks everything started with the Renaissance, apart from a bit of Euclidean geometry. She was right to try to set the record straight.'

'Any particular relationships…'

'You're talking about Scott Anderson. Silly boy. Lovely wife and two wee girls, and he risks it all for that.'

'I should maybe tell you that I'm a police officer,' Amanda said.

'Aye, I know.'

She smiled again. 'I'm looking at the police enquiry – following up on a complaint that it wasn't handled thoroughly. I'm not investigating Rima Khalaf's death.'

'But you are really, aren't you?' His eyes met hers. 'Because you think there's something odd about it. And you think Jonesy glossed over some of the evidence. You think Jonesy arsed it up.'

She realised she was nodding, and tried to turn it into a shake of the head. 'I don't know. Why would anyone want to murder her, though? She was good at her job, she was popular, she was passionate about teaching. Why would anyone want to murder her?'

⊱ 11 ⊰

'Look, she wasn't that popular, and she wasn't that good a teacher really.'

Mary Liston was tall and heavily built, with short spiky hair and a mass of earrings. She sat opposite Amanda, in that same stark office as the day before.

'You shared a house with her.'

'Yes – the council organised it. Three of us female probationers together, low rent. Part of a recruitment drive – trying to get us to love the place.'

'And did you?'

'I stayed on – and I hate to say it, but if Rima had still been here I'd have left, like Diane did.'

'You teach biology. Scott Anderson is your head of faculty.'

Mary's mean mouth tightened. 'Yes.'

'Mr Anderson was having an affair with Rima Khalaf.' She made it sound half like a question, half like an assertion.

'Yeah. She got all his time and all his attention, and all his help. All because she was shagging him.'

There was real anger there, thought Amanda. 'Do you think she slept with him because of her career?'

'Yes.' The word was almost a shout. Then more softly: 'Of course I do. She did it at Strathclyde too – slept with a couple of the lecturers during her time there. I asked her about it once, and the bitch told me she'd let a science teacher at her school shag her so she could get good marks on her assignments.'

Amanda looked at Mary. Anger certainly, at the unfairness of what Rima had done, and who could blame her? But Amanda thought she detected jealousy too. Mary Liston had fancied Rima.

Amanda shook her head. 'I'm not here to investigate Rima Khalaf's death,' she said, as much to herself as to the young woman opposite. 'I'm here to investigate a complaint arising from the enquiry. Were you interviewed by the police in the aftermath of the death?'

'Yes.'

Amanda knew that, of course. It was the follow-up question that mattered. 'How long were you questioned for?'

Mary screwed up her face. 'Five minutes?'

That explained why the transcript was so brief, then. 'Did they get to the heart of your issues with Rima?'

'What do you mean?'

'What you've just told me. Did you tell them that you hated her?'

'I didn't hate her. That's too strong.'

'But you didn't like the way she got all the attention from Mr Anderson.'

'No.'

'And you thought she had an unfair advantage over you in the department.'

'Yes.' She spat the word out. 'Look, I had to work bloody hard to prove myself here. All my life I've had to work hard to prove myself and get anywhere. And she has this little-girl-helpless look and a nice wee pair of tits and a pert bum and she opens her legs and off she goes. There was no way *she* was going to fail her probation.'

Amanda closed the file with the notes of the interview with Mary. 'Did you get the impression that the police wanted the whole issue of Rima Khalaf's death sorted out quickly?'

'Oh yes.'

Amanda hesitated before asking: 'Do you think she was pushed off the Rock?'

Mary thought for a minute. 'No, I can't see how that could have happened. It was a Saturday, broad daylight.'

'So how did she manage to fall over the edge by herself?'

'I really don't know.'

'You say you didn't 'hate' her. Did *anyone* hate her?'

Mary thought again, looking over Amanda's shoulder at the far wall. 'No, not that I can think of.'

'Did she talk to you about the book she was writing?'

'Yes. We got on OK when we first arrived here, sharing the house, and she showed me a few pages. I thought it was shite. I didn't say anything at the time, but she didn't ever mention it again to me.'

'You didn't know any of the people at that writers' group she went to?'

Mary shook her head.

'OK. Thank you, Miss Liston. Just to summarise, you think the police interview of you was a bit superficial, but you don't have any material evidence about Rima Khalaf's death that was missed at the time.'

'That's right.'

'Do you still have Rima's mobile phone number?'

Mary looked taken aback at the question. 'Oh god. Maybe.'

When she didn't move, Amanda prompted: 'Can you check for me?'

Mary took out her mobile – almost like a reluctant pupil – and unlocked it. 'Have I still got it…' She scrolled down with a fat thumb with a big metal ring round it. She stopped scrolling and seemed to hesitate.

Amanda reached over and slipped the phone out of Mary's fingers. 'Let me.'

Mary looked like she was about to protest, but subsided. Amanda wrote down the number of Rima's mobile and handed Mary back her phone. 'Thank you.'

Mary put her phone away and sat scowling.

Amanda stood up and reached for Mary's hand as she stood up also. 'Thanks for your time.'

The handshake was firm. Mary was strong. She'd disliked Rima, and maybe – if she'd been there that day on the Rock – that dislike could have boiled over and Mary could have shoved her. Not intending to kill her, of course, but that shove would have been enough to send her tumbling down the Rock, and by blind chance a car was coming along at the time she landed.

But Amanda wasn't here to investigate the death, just the enquiry. It was full of holes, but none of them mattered. She wondered how she was going to have to explain it to Mrs Khalaf, to give her closure.

Home to Glasgow, she thought. Dinner with Claire, a few drinks, and an early night.

But there was still the issue of Rima's mobile phone. And Rima's laptop, which was now in the boot of Amanda's car at Mrs Khalaf's insistence.

❧ 12 ❧

The basement restaurant on Bath Street had been very busy, but two large parties of women of a range of ages abruptly upped and downed large glasses of Prosecco, and headed out the door. They cackled and shouted, and started roaring 'Don't stop me now!' as they went up the outside steps to the street, hips swaying.

'Last night of 'We Will Rock You' at the King's,' Nicola said as they grabbed the sofa and armchair and pushed empty glasses aside. She indicated Martin. 'He didn't fancy it.'

'And how right I was.'

Amanda and Claire smiled at each other, and Amanda touched Claire's thick red hair.

Claire worked for Martin at his company B&D Software Solutions. Martin had had dealings with Amanda professionally in the past, both working with her and keeping activities hidden from her. The four of them had met in various combinations several times before, but this was only the second time they'd all been out together for dinner. The first had been after Martin and Nicola's wedding a year before. Amanda thought they were a lovely couple, but she wasn't sure whether Martin deserved such luck.

'That was sad about that business at Clachdubh,' Nicola said. 'Mrs Khalaf.'

'Yes,' Amanda agreed. She knew she shouldn't talk about it, but

Clachdubh was mentally far away from here, and she'd had rather a lot of wine to drink. On Monday, she was going to have to write her report and present it to Ramesh, and tell Mrs Khalaf what she'd found. And that would be the end of the matter. She already knew that no one wanted to reopen the enquiry: too expensive both in terms of manpower and money, not to mention Police Scotland's reputation. There were gaps in Jones's investigation, she thought, but there was nothing material missing from the enquiry. 'Have you told Martin about it?'

Nicola smiled. 'Yes, but I never know how hard he's listening.'

'I *was* listening,' he protested. 'But remind me.'

Amanda looked round but no one was paying them any attention. She took him through the story.

'So,' he said. 'Case closed.' And he noticed the look on her face. 'Or is there some kind of problem?'

'Oh, I don't know,' Amanda said. 'I've just got this feeling…' She shared a look with Claire, whose eyes urged her to speak. 'Well. The police retrieved all this girl's Facebook, Twitter and emails,' Amanda said. 'But there was nothing significant there. I was just…'

Martin was frowning at her. 'How did they manage to get all of that?'

Amanda couldn't understand his doubt. 'I imagine they put in a request – a court order maybe.'

'Did they? Did you see what they found?'

'Well…no.' She realised she'd finished her gin.

'My shout,' Claire said. 'Same again?' They all nodded.

A small band had assembled in a corner by the bar, and were tuning up and checking their PA system. Amanda had to lean across the table to speak to Martin. 'You sound sceptical.'

'It's just that Facebook are in charge of what they release to the authorities. They get thousands of request from UK police every year, but it's not routine for them to hand any information over. They check each case.'

'What percentage get through?'

'More than seventy per cent at the last count, but it's not a given.'

'This case must have been accepted by them. They got all her Twitter stuff too, of course.'

Martin was shaking his head.

Amanda frowned: 'What's wrong with that?'

'Twitter almost never release information on users to the UK police, even in extreme cases of trolling.'

'Why the difference?'

'Facebook has staff in Ireland who can deal with the UK police, but Twitter has all its staff in the States. It's too difficult for them.'

'So somebody's lying to you,' Nicola said.

Amanda was frowning.

'Did you say they got her emails?' Martin asked.

Jones hadn't mentioned emails. 'I'm sure I saw something in the reports. I think they said Hotmail – I'd need to check. I'm sure it said they'd checked her emails.'

He was shaking his head again.

'Oh come on, Martin!'

'I'm sorry, but Microsoft is very secretive about all of that. And law enforcement agencies are very secretive about information they get from Microsoft. Now that the 'snoopers' charter' is in force, we can assume government agencies will soon be hoovering up anything they want – they're already freely getting stuff from Yahoo. But this was last year, you said. I doubt if some cop in a town in Scotland could just have phoned up and asked for all that information. Not in the real world.'

Claire was back with the drinks, setting them down and squeezing onto the sofa beside Amanda. 'Have you asked Martin about the Islamophobia stuff?'

Martin almost choked on his drink, but the band started up and conversation was impossible for a few minutes. Martin looked accusingly at Nicola, and she mouthed: 'I told you that!'

When the song finished and the applause died away, Amanda said: 'Does that make a difference?'

'You know it does. Was she outspoken at all?'

'Yes, she was. Everyone at her school knew she was committed to giving a place to Muslim history. But she wasn't a religious fanatic.'

'But she had a profile. She would be known. *Somebody* would be watching her.'

Amanda lifted her fresh drink. Had Rima Khalaf been pushed off a hill by an undercover security agent because she was a dangerous fanatic? No. She wasn't a fanatic, and she wasn't dangerous.

The band started up again and played a different song but with the same rhythm as the first, and pretty much the same arrangement and tune. After it, Amanda said: 'If you had the girl's laptop, could you find out what was on it?'

'We've discussed this before: it's not like the movies. What kind of laptop did she have?'

'It's a MacBook.'

'Right. Is it password protected?'

'Yes – the parents can't get into it, they said. The police investigation had it for a few weeks and then gave it back, said it was OK. I've no idea if they really got past the password and looked at it.'

He grimaced. 'It's not like the movies! OK, we can take out the hard drive or the solid state drive, whichever it is, and get data off it and probably make sense of it all. But if she has encrypted the drive, then we're totally stuffed. Apple themselves couldn't help, even if they wanted to. The FBI is trying to get Apple to create a back door, just for them – as if they could then keep it private. Did she have a cloud service for backups? Did she have a backup drive?' He shrugged. 'It's not like the movies,' he said again.

'If I got you the laptop, could you try?'

'That would be illegal – and a police officer should not be asking for such a thing. But yes, I could give it a go – like I said, if the drive's not encrypted then it's easy. But you've got forensic IT people. Why not use them?'

She thought about what to say. 'You know how stretched they are. And I think my request would be refused, or the laptop would be taken away and forgotten about.'

The singer announced the next song and the band started up again. 'Oh good,' Claire said. 'I like this one.'

❧ 13 ❧

The house was a modest semi-detached bungalow, built in the 1960s perhaps, with small windows and thick walls. In the driveway was a car, and it was hers: a white Polo. He'd spotted her getting into it at Tesco, when he'd been out collecting trolleys.

Since then he'd searched the private housing estates in the town.

And now he'd found her.

Gary grinned as he cycled past. Saturday evening, getting dark, and there were lights on inside. She hadn't gone out, which was sad in a way for someone so beautiful. Of course, she might have company.

He doubted it. She'd been shopping that morning: only a few items at the basket checkout. She had her hair tied back, and she'd been wearing running clothes, the Lycra tight on her form. There was no sign of a romantic dinner for two. She was home alone.

He went home to write more of his novel, constructing fantasy from brief web searches, but resisting the urge to visit any porn sites. His father was out, visiting some woman whose husband was offshore at the moment.

After ten o'clock, he thought the time was right. He cycled close to where the redhead lived, and chained his bike to a lamppost. The street where she lived was silent, the street lights were old, pale orange. No one was about. His bike was black, with no lights.

He walked slowly past the bungalow, and saw the light go off in the lounge. He glanced around, and steeled himself, his mind thrilling with his fantasy. He clutched his mobile, the camera ready.

He walked down the drive, past her car and through the open gate, looking around all the time, moving slowly. A path led round the side of the house, and there was a frosted glass window, a light on inside. He moved as close as he dared. Was she having a shower before bed? Would he see her naked silhouette, and perhaps more?

The light went out.

He waited till his eyes adjusted to the darkness again, and he moved on round the back of the house. Another street of similar-looking bungalows backed onto this one, with the Rock View Hotel – converted from a mansion in whose grounds this private estate had been built – sitting high and dark. There was a black expanse of double gardens to conceal him. There were no gates.

The back of the house had a large patio, and he worried that the darkness could hide garden furniture, so he was cautious as he stepped. He reached with his hands and feet, like a blind man stumbling. The night air was cool, the sky cloudy.

After a few steps he was quite disorientated, until a light came on inside the house, shining from behind a gap at one side of the curtain. Gary stood motionless, focused on that gap. He stepped towards it.

He could see a tiny part of a room.

He moved closer.

There was the briefest glimpse of a pale form and the curtain was tugged, closing off the gap. He almost trembled. It had been her, just there, a matter of inches from him. He closed his eyes, his imagination building massively on what he had actually seen.

He moved left. Away across two gardens an outside light came on, and a door opened. There was a scraping of feet on concrete and a solitary bark. Gary froze, but the door closed again and the dog fell silent.

The outside light was easily enough to show him the back door now. He reached out and touched the handle. Dare he risk it? And what if the door was unlocked, what would he do?

His mouth was dry, his heart thumping.

And a light came on beyond the door. The pale form moved right up to the glass panel behind the door, fractured by the vertical patterns of glass, and a curtain was pulled across the glass closing off the view. The key rattled in the lock, the door handle was checked, and the light went out.

It had been her. Naked. Her body had been distorted by the glass, but he'd seen it all. Inside him, nerves screamed.

***

We creep towards the edge of the cliff high above the lochan. It has been a difficult climb, and one of my men slipped – he did not cry out even as a bone cracked in his leg. I cannot have broken cripples in my army, so I dispatch him quickly to ease his suffering. We lie flat and look down.

Two soldiers stand, their backs to the water, their arms folded. Two handmaidens hold up long swathes of cloth behind Rebecca.

I watch as Rebecca shrugs off her dress and her underclothes. The late afternoon sun shines on her perfect white body as she steps into the water, shuddering with the cold. She wraps her arms around herself and wades into the water, gasping and then throwing herself in. She shrieks as she rolls and splashes in the water, then stands up and stretches.

My hand reaches for my sword. I could kill the guards, I

could take Rebecca. My man could have the handmaidens.
But no. Not yet.
Her time will come.

❧ 14 ❧

The party was at Jill's house: she had an empty. Jamil had passed
her in town that afternoon and she'd invited him, probably
because she thought he might stir things up.

He didn't bring any drink, because he had no money. He simply
helped himself to others'. At one point he forced open Jill's parents'
drinks cabinet and pulled out a bottle at random: Lidl vodka.

He hardly knew anyone at the party. There was the residue of
classmates from school – a few sad bastards were still pupils there
– but he didn't know the others. He didn't want to.

He spent the time swigging from the vodka bottle, turning the
music way up, doing some kind of dancing that involved bumping
very hard into people and looking aggressively at them if they
looked like they might complain.

Jasmine wasn't there, which was annoying. Rose couldn't come:
she hadn't been allowed out. That was a pity.

Which left Jill. She was short and dumpy, but she'd made an
effort tonight, he thought, watching her breasts squeezing out of
the top of her dress. He danced with her a few times, and pulled
her close and whispered into her ear: 'I could show you a good
time, girl.'

She laughed and danced away. 'As if!'

Eventually he needed the toilet, but the downstairs one – the
one Jill had insisted they all use – was occupied, so he went
upstairs to a big plush bathroom. Afterwards, he opened doors
at random, hearing the thud of the music away below. Maybe
neighbours would call the cops. He could start a fight with them.
That would be fun.

But he'd been told to stay cool, and wait for the word.

He walked into one bedroom, and lay back on the bed in the
darkness – just a glow from the hall light leaking in. He sniffed
perfume in the air. He checked his phone, took a selfie, and
messaged it to Rose. 'Big double bed, babe. Would look great

42

with you in it.'

She messaged back a smile.

He tried again. This time he unbuttoned his shirt. 'My chest, babe. Your turn.'

His heart pounded. Then: 'I don't know.'

'Just for me, babe. No one else.' Not strictly true. He'd probably share it with Gary in return for the ones he sent him.

And then it was there, a picture of her standing in front of the mirror, her blouse and bra pulled up to her collar bone.

'Gorgeous, babe.' He sighed and smiled. This was going really well. The next stage…

'What the fuck? Jamil! Get the fuck out of my mum and dad's room!' Jill stood in the doorway, hands on hips.

He grinned, still excited by the message from Rose. 'Give us a kiss first.' He stood up and grabbed Jill lightly, pulling her into the room and trying to nuzzle into her neck.

She pushed back at him. 'Get out of here, Jamil.' Her voice was slurred and didn't sound seriously angry.

'Oh, come on, babe. Just a kiss.'

She stopped pushing him away and turned her face up to him. 'OK. Just a kiss. And then you get the fuck out of here.'

The next moment, she was under him on the bed and his hand was on her left breast, trying to lever it out of her bra, his groin thrusting against her thigh, his other hand forcing up between her legs.

She kicked and squirmed and pushed him back, but he had her pinned down. He kept up his thrusting and rubbing, her hands trying to fight his away. 'Jamil! Jamil, for fuck sake – stop it!'

Then he came with a loud groan, and he stopped moving, and just lay on her, panting for breath.

'Fuck sake,' she said. 'Jamil!' She pushed at him. 'Jamil!'

He grinned. 'Enjoy that?'

'Get off me, Jamil.' Her voice was stern now. She was angry. Scared.

As he rolled over and she stood up, adjusting her bra and her dress, checking for stains, he murmured: 'You're a jihadi's bride now.'

'Fuck off, Jamil. Jesus Christ. Get up! Get the fuck out of here!'

❧ 15 ❧

By Monday lunchtime, Amanda had finished her report, re-read it twice, and done a final edit. She was due to meet with Chief Inspector Ramesh at one o'clock. They'd discuss the report and then she'd go over it again incorporating any suggestions from Ramesh, and someone would contact the Khalafs to tell them the original investigation into the death of their daughter had been thorough and no further action would be taken by Police Scotland. If they were unhappy still, there was the Ombudsman, and perhaps their MSP if they so wished. They'd spend a lot of time and a lot of money, and they'd get nowhere. Maybe they'd go to the media, and maybe someone there would grab at the story as another excuse to try to rubbish Police Scotland: they'd worry about that when and if. Police Scotland would stand by her report.

But Amanda knew that the report contained lies by omission.

She phoned retired Inspector Jones in Clachdubh.

'I'm heading out to golf,' he said. 'Can you call back later?'

'It's just a courtesy call,' she said, her voice neutral, no courtesy there. 'I've finished my enquiries.'

'And you're satisfied that the investigation was thorough?'

She chose her words carefully. 'My report will say that no material evidence was overlooked during the police enquiry into the death of Rima Khalaf.'

He said nothing for a few seconds. 'That's fine then.'

'It's not really,' she said, knowing she was speaking out of turn. 'You know how the investigation was conducted, and so do I.'

Again there was silence, until: 'But my team missed nothing material.'

'It seems not.'

'Good. Thanks for your call, Miss Pitt. Now, I need to go.' He put the phone down.

Amanda found her fists were clenched, and she took a deep breath. She had wanted to tell Jones she knew he'd been superficial: he'd made assumptions straight away and worked on that basis. OK, he'd been right, but that fact didn't excuse casual police work. But telling him would have been pointless. Even dropping hints like she'd done hadn't helped anything, and had maybe just made a retired colleague feel bad – and for what? She should have asked him about Rima's mobile phone, and her laptop: get him to admit he hadn't bothered with either. But again, what would have been the point?

Amanda checked her watch and started on another read-through of her report. Afterwards, she emailed a copy to Ramesh, telling him she'd bring a hard copy along for him but that he might want to glance at it if he'd time before they met. She printed off two copies.

Pete McLeod was out, and she hadn't had a chance to catch up with him. Unable to concentrate on anything else until her meeting, she did some searching online. The retired teacher with the dog on the Rock at Clachdubh had spoken of another girl who'd fallen to her death: Karen McKechnie.

Many of the news items from the time had been taken offline under data protection, but there were still some photographs of Karen that had been gathered from her Facebook profile. Amanda looked. The teacher had said she aspired – if that was the word – to being a model, and certainly she was posed and pouting in her selfies and other photographs. A pretty girl, Amanda thought, and yes, she liked to be looked at, that was for sure, and there was plenty of young push-up cleavage and leg on display there.

The news reports were all comments from her Facebook news feed, about how wonderful and precious she had been: 'a light has gone out in our lives'.

The police notes were thinner and more factual. There was a list of the fellow pupils who'd been at the after-party on the Rock that midsummer night. Amanda scanned the list, but none of the names meant anything to her: Jill, Jasmine, Gary, Henry, Jordan, Jamil, Shirley, Wendy, Danny…There were statements from all of them. They'd all admitted to drinking a lot, but denied drugs – and none had been found in Karen's bloodstream, just far too much alcohol. They'd got the drink from parents' houses, and those parents had all been cautioned.

Karen's death was judged not suspicious and hence accidental, and the file was closed. The mother had been heartbroken, but hadn't made a fuss, not like Mrs Khalaf.

Amanda scrolled through what she could find, but there was nothing remotely suspicious about Karen's death. Just a stupid drunken girl falling off a hill. Such a waste.

Her desk phone rang: Ramesh was ready now if she was. She locked her computer and went along to his office.

He stood and shook her hand and indicated that she sit down. He always looked intimidating because of his size and his dark eyes, but particularly so today.

Amanda sat while he slowly read her report from the hard copy she'd brought. He didn't offer her tea or coffee. He just sipped from his own glass of water, and didn't offer her any of that either. She wished she'd remembered to bring some: her throat was dry.

Finally, he put the report down and gazed at her. 'Exactly the report we needed – congratulations.'

She wasn't sure what he was getting at, so she just gazed back at him.

'The police investigation was thorough,' he went on, 'and Inspector Jones missed nothing. The girl's death was accidental, and anything said to the contrary by the parents is the result of grief. Understandably. But there is no conspiracy, no cover up.'

She gave a small nod.

Ramesh sat back, crossing his legs and clasping his hands on his lap. 'Do you think the family will accept this judgement?'

'No, sir, I don't. They'll take the complaint further.'

'But they won't get anywhere.'

'No, sir, they won't.'

He nodded. 'Good.'

She thought that was the end of the meeting, and almost got up to leave, when he added: 'So tell me what's not in your report. What else did you find? Off the record – this conversation is not happening.'

'OK, sir.' She collected her thoughts. 'Retired Inspector Jones seems to have formed the view immediately that this was an accidental death, rather than collecting the evidence and *then* forming a view. Some of his interviews were less than thorough: once he got something that confirmed his view, he wasn't interested any more. He had a bad habit of telling interviewees up front that he thought the girl's death was accidental.'

'So what did he miss?'

'Well that's just it, sir – I don't think he missed anything material, which is why I'm happy to sign off on my report. But he didn't go into any investigation of the dead girl's religious issues.'

'What were they?'

'Her family is Muslim – '

'Sunni or Shia? Ba'ath?'

'Eh – I don't know. I didn't ask.'

'OK. Go on.'

'Anyway, she does not seem to have been particularly religious herself, but she was interested historically in the Muslim legacy – she brought it into her science lessons, and she was writing a book about it – historical fiction. She shared some articles online. Now, retired Inspector Jones maintains he checked her Facebook newsfeed and her Twitter feed and found nothing untoward – nobody trolling her, nothing inflammatory.'

'What do you mean 'he maintains he checked'?'

'My understanding is that these companies don't release information readily to law enforcement agencies.'

He nodded. 'Have you tried looking at her online activity?'

'I briefly tried her Facebook page, but I can't see anything there – her security settings were really tight. I can't find any Twitter feed, because I don't know her user name. It's maybe been deleted too.'

Ramesh was still nodding. 'So Jones did not investigate all that thoroughly, but you have no evidence of anything odd there.'

'No, sir.' She took a deep breath. 'At least, I don't think so. I can't be sure. And there was another accidental death a few years ago in Clachdubh – a school pupil fell off the Rock, just like Rima Khalaf did.'

'Sounds like a dangerous place.' He raised his hands, fingertips together, touching his lower lip.

'Indeed. Now that incident involved a crowd of pupils drinking very late on a summer night, and one was very drunk and fell off the edge. I haven't checked *all* the files, but it looks clear-cut.'

'However…'

'However, I'd have thought Retired Inspector Jones would have cross-referenced. I'd have thought he'd have run a check on the people around at the time of the schoolgirl's death and those around at the time of Rima Khalaf's death.'

'But she was on her own on the Rock – how big is this Rock anyway?'

'It's less than two hundred feet. Hardly Edinburgh Castle.'

He gave a rare small smile. 'But Rima Khalaf was on her own on this 'Rock',' he said, 'so there was no one from the previous accident to question in connection with this one.'

'School kids move on and some stay. Jones didn't even check which of that original crowd was still around in the town at the time of Rima Khalaf's death.'

Ramesh let the silence fall, until he finally said: 'Jones was a good man by all accounts. In the job for thirty years. He doesn't deserve anything souring his retirement. He lost his wife last year, just as they were preparing to spend time together now he was retired.'

Amanda hadn't known about Jones's wife – she wished Ramesh had told her at the start. It made her feel sad for Jones. 'I've no intention of souring his retirement, sir.'

'Are there any loose ends at all that may come back to bite us?'

'There's the dead girl's laptop, sir. The parents can't get into it – it's password protected. I wondered whether…'

'That's not going to happen. I don't have the resources or the time. Leave it with the family.'

'Yes, sir.' That confirmed what she thought would happen. She was glad she had decided to give it to Martin McGregor, and see what he got. 'And there's no word of the girl's mobile phone.'

'None at all?'

'None.'

'That is very odd. But not suspicious in itself.'

'No, sir.' She wondered whether to tell him she had the number, whether to ask for permission to search Rima's phone records…And while she wondered that, the opportunity slipped away.

Ramesh was nodding. 'Thank you for your report, DS Pitt. You can return to your normal duties now.'

He didn't stand up, didn't offer to shake her hand. And it seemed she was no longer an acting inspector.

Above the coffee shop Roasters on Byres Road was the West End Hackers' Makerspace. Martin McGregor's company paid the rent and supplied equipment, and Martin himself turned up some evenings after work to help and keep an eye on things. His old school friend Davey Collins, wheelchair-bound after a serious road accident many years before, was there almost every afternoon. A schoolteacher, George Webster, with long hair and a straggly beard, cliché corduroy jacket and elbow patches, came along after school when he could. Between them all they organised workshops and seminars from business people and academics, or just let everyone get on with things.

The attendees were mostly older pupils from nearby schools, and a few university students, including Michael, whom Martin had known for a few years now. And a group of pensioners who kept coming along, giving and seeking help.

There were a dozen young people there this evening – including three girls – and a couple of the retirees. Many were on laptops, two were observing a 3D printer with its head whining, the base plate darting back and forth and then pausing – and darting again. A couple had wheeled robots, and others had small Raspberry Pi and Arduino boards with piles of LEDs, resistors and motors.

In one corner of the big room, Martin stood with Michael and Amanda Pitt; Davey Collins was in his chair beside them.

'This setup is impressive,' Amanda said, sipping from a cardboard coffee cup. 'What are all these people trying to achieve?'

'Just practising their skills,' said Davey in Stephen Hawking's synthesiser voice.

'Hacking and building,' Martin said. 'Designing apps, improving systems. The world needs people with those skills.' He took a deep breath. 'And testing security of systems and websites. Michael is ostensibly employed to check my company's security.'

'Do I want to know about all this security stuff?'

'Probably not. And you probably wouldn't understand it if I did tell you.'

She handed over Rima Khalaf's MacBook. Michael had a power

lead for it, and now he attached it and opened the lid. They had to wait a few minutes before the screen lit up, with a small picture of an expressionless pretty girl that Amanda recognised as Rima Khalaf, and the password field.

'So, tell Michael the story,' Martin said. 'He's going to be the one looking at this.'

Michael stared at the MacBook, then simply pressed the return key. The password field box shivered. 'Ah well,' he said. 'Worth a try.' He stroked his full, black beard as he stared at the MacBook.

Amanda thought he looked older than his years; dark skinned and black-haired, he was dressed in jeans and a checked shirt, the sleeves turned back to show slim, hairy wrists with no watch.

'Right,' Amanda said. 'This laptop belongs to a young woman who died just over a year ago. The death has been judged to have been accidental: she fell down a rocky slope and was hit by a car on the road at the bottom. Very sad and unfortunate. Her name was Rima Khalaf' – she spelt it out for them – 'She was writing a historical fiction novel set in the time of Muslim rule in Europe, over a thousand years ago. She was a science teacher, and she was very keen to make sure that kids understood the Muslim contribution to science, maths and medicine – in order to balance the current view of them as barbaric, murdering, religious fanatics. A thousand years ago, apparently, it was the Christians who were barbaric, murdering, religious fanatics. She didn't seem to be particularly religious herself, but she shared some articles online.'

Michael leaned over the keyboard again. He typed 'Rima' in the password field, then 'rImA', 'RIMA', 'RiMa', 'rima' and 'rIMA', but got the shiver each time.

Martin folded his arms. 'Your mission, Michael, is to get into the machine and find what you can: emails, documents, social media stuff, whatever.'

'Did she have a middle name?' Michael asked.

Amanda tried to remember the files. 'I'll find out.'

'Mother's maiden name too. Parents' names. Any pets? Boyfriend? And I'll need her email address and her date of birth – if I ever get that far.'

'Her novel was set in Toledo a thousand years ago.'

Michael typed 'Toledo', 'toledo', 'TOLEDO', 'ToLeDo,' and 'tOlEdO', 'Toledo123', but none of them worked. He tried 'password' too, and '12345', but that got nothing.

'Do you know if she had a backup disk for TimeMachine? Or did she just use iCloud? Dropbox?'

'I don't know. Not sure I can check with the parents: I don't want to let them think I'm going to magically come up with something. Do you think you can get into it?'

He looked at her with one eyebrow raised. 'Easily. All Macs have a way of bypassing the log-in screen and resetting the password. But if she's used FileVault to encrypt the drive, or Disk Utility to create an encrypted sparsebundle disk image, then I need her original password or key – and I'd rather try it out from the logon screen. How urgent is this?'

Amanda shook her head. 'It's not urgent at all.'

'I'll give it a couple of hours when you give me those names, and if nothing works I'll bypass the password and hope FileVault is not enabled. If it is and we don't have the password, well...' He shrugged.

'It is not like in the movies,' Davey's electronic voice said.

'What do you expect us to find?' Martin asked. 'You said the investigation was closed.'

'I know what I said, Martin. Yes, the investigation is officially closed. I don't know what I expect to find there – I suppose I'm trying to help the parents.'

Michael stared at the screen. 'It's like chasing a ghost,' he said.

Amanda turned away from them and looked around the room again at the bizarre assortment of people, all focussed on their technology. There was also a young girl in a Roasters tabard – her name badge read 'Taylor'. She was petite, with short dark hair, and Amanda thought she was very pretty.

Taylor came over to them, and gave Amanda a smile. 'Hiya.' Her accent was very broad Glasgow.

Amanda smiled back, and handed Taylor her own empty cardboard cup.

'Aw this technology,' Taylor said.

'Boys toys. Do you do this sort of stuff at school?'

Taylor gave an exaggerated frown. 'Ah've left the school.'

'Oh, sorry.' Amanda had thought the girl was maybe around sixteen, but now she revised that upwards: eighteen – twenty at most. A smoker.

Taylor was staring at Martin and Michael, then at Davey in his chair. She reached through the group to retrieve another couple of cups, and then smiled again at Amanda. 'Better get back.'

Amanda watched her go.

❧ 17 ❧

Martin sat by Davey Collins and Michael. He'd been there for an hour, watching Michael patiently try combinations of middle names and character names and maiden names that Amanda had supplied them with. They tried her date of birth, and different combinations of lower and upper case. They tried her lover's name.

Each time, the password field box shivered, but the computer didn't unlock.

Finally Michael looked at Martin, and Martin nodded: 'Bypass it.'

Michael clicked on the Apple menu and selected restart. As the MacBook booted up and got to the chord, he held down the option, command and R keys, and the machine booted into recovery mode. He clicked on the menu bar at the top of the screen and opened a Terminal window, then typed 'resetpassword' into it. The reset password dialogue box opened up, and Michael typed 'michael' as the new password, checked that they'd all seen it, and saved it

They all waited while Michael re-started the MacBook again, then unlocked it with his new password 'michael'. Then they held their breath while he tried to open a random document: if the disk was encrypted, they wouldn't be able to access anything without the original password.

The document opened, and they all released their breath.

'So that was an hour wasted,' Davey Collins said in Stephen Hawking's voice.

'Yeah,' Martin said. 'But we had to try it.'

Michael pointed to the clock at the top corner of the screen. 'I haven't got much time, Martin – I need to…well, I need to get home.'

'Oh.' Martin had planned to let Michael do all the investigation.

'OK, Michael. That's fine: I'll take the MacBook home and have a look at it tonight, and I'll give you a go next time you're down.'

Michael shut down the computer he was working at and picked up his man-bag. They watched him go, head bent and face expressionless.

When Martin got home, Nicola was already there, making dinner. 'Prawn curry,' she said. 'Seems stupid with so many good Indian restaurants around, but I like it.'

He kissed her. 'I wasn't arguing.'

'How did you get on?'

'Michael unlocked it and it turns out the disk wasn't encrypted, so we could just have done it yesterday. He's gone home. I'll text Amanda and tell her. Wine?'

'We're supposed to be having an alcohol-free week. Yes please.'

He poured her a glass of Sauvignon Blanc, and a beer for himself, and stood beside her in the kitchen while she gave the curry a stir and checked her watch. The prawns – previously stir-fried to an all-over pink colour – were waiting in a dish beside the cooker.

'You met the mother of the dead girl, didn't you?' Martin said.

'Yes.' She turned the gas down a notch and stirred again. 'Nice woman. Her and her husband are Syrian originally, but have been living in Manchester for years – the dead girl, Rima, was born in this country.' She sipped her wine. 'Five minutes, then the prawns go in for a microsecond and we serve.'

'What do you want me to do to help?'

'Sit down out of my way.'

He took a drink of his beer and sat at the kitchen table.

'So what was the theory about the dead girl?' He took out his mobile and texted Amanda to tell her they'd got into the files and he would have a good browse at them later.

Nicola shrugged. 'Police are convinced it was an accident, parents are convinced she was murdered for her enlightened Muslim views. Possibly by GCHQ or the FBI. She wasn't that religious it seems, but she was expressing a particular view on Islam – that it used to be enlightened and great and now it's viewed as being repressive and crap – so she could have been killed by anyone: Sunni, Shia, or Christian. Or it could have been her married lover – or his wife – or it could have been some random nutcase who just happened to be about in the middle of the day on a weekend.' She shrugged. 'Right – prawns going in.'

There was hissing and bursts of steam, and she stirred and then turned off the gas after a couple of minutes. She spooned it out and brought the plates to the table, where they touched glasses. 'Sweet and sour prawn and mango,' she said.

His eyes opened wide. 'Delicious. Spicy!'

'You know I like it spicy, darling.' She smiled and sipped her wine. 'Shit – the naans.'

She dashed to the oven, releasing a cloud of smoke, and with much ouching she got the naans onto a plate and brought them over. 'Burnt round the edges – sorry.'

'They're fine. Ouch!'

His mobile pinged and he glanced at it: Amanda – 'Thanks. Speak tomorrow but call me if anything interesting pops up.'

'You got work to do tonight?' he asked.

'I've got Joan's stuff. If she didn't have so much money from her divorces, she'd be bankrupt. I need to get her sorted out. She undercharges and goes for holidays in peak season. It's like a hobby to her. She could afford to get someone to run the place properly and still make money. You going to play with the laptop?'

'Yes. Nothing I might find there would constitute evidence, of course.'

'She's maybe just interested for her own sake.'

'And in many ways she must hope I don't find anything.'

After dinner, he settled down to browsing the dead girl's laptop, feeling slightly odd at intruding into her life. He scanned the documents and checked some, and tried to find the ghostly traces of her online life.

'Listen to this,' he said eventually, his finger on the MacBook's trackpad.

'Listen to what?' Nicola looked up from her own laptop, reaching to scribble on her notepad. 'What?'

'It's emails from the dead girl's MacBook.'

'Who to?'

'Here's a thread from her deleted items. It's hilarious.'

He read aloud (including the exclamation marks):

> *To: rimakhalaf1016@hotmail.co.uk*
> *From: garymcallister798@hotmail.co.uk*
> *Subject: writers' group*
> *Hi Rima!*
>
> *Great to see you at the group last night, and I was really interested that you're doing historical fiction! I didn't get a chance to speak to you, but so am I!! I'm writing a novel set in Scotland in the mid-11th century, around the same time as yours! What a coincidence!!!*
>
> *It would be great if we could chat about our work! And maybe you could read some of my stuff? I'd love your comments!! And I'd like to read more of your stuff too – loved what you read out!!!*
> *Gary*
> *(I was the one in the black jeans and the black sweatshirt).'*

'So who is this Gary?' Nicola asked.

'Don't know – Amanda didn't mention him. But listen to the rest of the thread.'

> *To: garymcallister* – blah blah blah –
> *Gary*
> *Thanks for your email, but I'm afraid I haven't time to meet up. I also don't have time to read any of your work.'*

'How very supportive of her. What was Gary's reaction?' Nicola was leaning over to see the screen of the MacBook.

'He sent her some extracts anyway, and she didn't reply. Then he pestered her for a reply, and I can't see any response. Then this from him:

> *Rima*
> *I'd have thought you'd have been more supportive of a struggling writer like yourself, but you're just a self-centred bitch. Read this extract, and fuck you.'*

'So he was a bit annoyed then,' Nicola said.

'Damn right.'

'Have you read any of his extracts?'

'Not yet.' He slid his finger on the trackpad and pressed, opening up a document. 'OK – here we go:

> *The English lord stands in my great hall by Dumbarton Rock with his five knights. I sit on my throne, with my men at the long tables, drinking ale. A huge fire burns in the hearth, and serving maids walk amongst us, serving food and drink, and submitting to my men's caresses.'*

'Oh for fuck sake,' Nicola hissed.
Martin continued:

> *My attention is taken by the young maiden the lord has brought. She stands confident and proud, her wrists manacled behind her. Her face is dirty and sweaty but I can see she is beautiful.*
>
> *'This woman was brought from the East by traders,' the Lord says. 'She is young and proud. I offer her to you as a gesture of peace between us.'*
>
> *I look at the girl and she looks straight back at me. 'Let me see my prize,' I say.*
>
> *The Lord signals and one of his men steps forward with his large knife. Within moments, the girl's clothing is at her feet. She does not flinch, and her eyes are still on me.*
>
> *Her body is young and curving, her skin olive and smooth. I take it all in, but when my eyes return to her face, she still stares at me.*
>
> *I turn to my chief handmaiden. 'Have her washed and taken to my chamber. Tie her wrists to the bedhead. I will be there presently.' I will have her, I think, and then, when I tire of her, I will have her cast from Dumbarton Rock.*
>
> *An hour later, I conclude my negotiations with the English lord and go to my chamber. She lies there, spread naked, her olive skin glistening, her eyes on me, her breasts heaving. I disrobe and kneel on the bed – '*

'Stop right there,' Nicola said, her mouth screwed up.
Martin closed the file and resumed his search through the laptop.
'So, Game of Thrones set in Dumbarton,' she said.

'Indeed. I did a quick bit of research. There was a lot of power play going on at the time as Malcolm the Second tried to unite Scotland, but the Kings of Strathclyde were having none of it. And the Vikings still pretty much ruled the islands.'

'What was the girl's novel about?'

'It was set in Toledo, Spain, a few years earlier. Something of a golden age, apparently. The Muslim empire ruled different caliphates and taifas, and science and mathematics – and medicine – flourished. Toledo welcomed anyone and everyone, regardless of religion. The only threat was from the Christian world. Eventually the Christians re-invaded Spain and Portugal, drove the 'heathen Muslims' out, and plunged Europe into the Dark Ages. And then the Crusades of course. A couple of hundred years later came the Renaissance, and a bit of airbrushing of Muslim influence out of history. Her novel seems to be talking up the Golden Age bit, and I couldn't make out any particular plot-line.'

'So how do we end up with the current world situation, where so much of the Muslim world is effectively in the dark ages?'

Martin yawned and stretched. 'I guess it's complicated, and it's also perception. Lots of Muslim countries are enlightened and open-minded, just as lots of Christian countries – or parts of Christian countries – are repressive. It's not black and white. And don't forget that most of the problems in the Muslim world have been generated by the West interfering.' He shrugged. 'It's complicated, despite what many people want us to believe.'

They sat in silence for a few minutes. Outside, the night had gone dark.

'How's work?' he asked.

'I think I have to go back to see Joan in Clachdubh. She needs to sort out her target market. Are you going to call Amanda about all of this?'

He sighed. 'I suppose I should.'

'And what are you going to do with it now?'

He closed the lid of the computer. 'I'll text Amanda.' And, he thought, maybe Michael too. Michael had connections to a group called 1794. Martin knew almost nothing about them, except that they were good. Very good.

At times too good.

Amanda and Claire had been at the GFT. On the way back to their flat on the train, Amanda read Martin's text. Once home, she called him.

'I haven't found anything crazily important,' he said. 'I take it you know about this guy Gary McAllister.'

She sat on her couch, hearing Claire in the kitchen filling the kettle. 'No. Who is he?'

'There are emails between him and your dead girl. They met at some writers' group, and he wanted her to read some of his stuff – I think he fancied her. But she was having none of it.'

'She rebuffed him.'

'Firmly. And he wasn't best pleased.'

She was trying to think, but the name meant nothing to her. It certainly hadn't figured in retired Inspector Jones's investigations.

'He was writing some historical stuff – set in Scotland. He sent her one passage which seemed to be a fantasy whereby his main character – who is probably him – has sex with an eastern slave girl, who is probably her.'

'Sublimating his desires into his fiction. I suppose all authors do that.' But it had got her thinking. This Gary had been rebuffed by Rima Khalaf, and it seems he'd conjured a fantasy rape to get his revenge on her. Had that satisfied him, or had he gone on to enact his fantasy?

No: Rima had not been sexually assaulted before she died. Nobody had mentioned 'Gary'.

'In this fantasy,' she asked, 'what happens to the girl?'

'He doesn't write that, but he talks of throwing her off Dumbarton Rock once he's 'finished' with her.'

Amanda felt cold. Claire set down her mug of green tea, and she reached for it to warm herself, mouthing 'Thanks darling,' to Claire.

'You still there?'

'Yes – yes I'm here. It's just the parallel with Rima Khalaf falling off the Rock in Clachdubh.' And another girl called Karen McKechnie, two years before.

'Was there any mention of this 'Gary' being around at the time?'

'None. Rima fell off on a Saturday, during the day, but there was no one around and there were no witnesses.'

'Nobody? Nobody out walking their dog even?'

'Apparently not. Quite a risk for anyone to be up there banking on being alone with Rima. How could they be sure they weren't seen? No emails arranging a meeting, I suppose?'

'No. Do you want me to forward these emails to you – with the attachments?'

'Yes please, Martin. Is there anything else on the laptop?'

'Her novel, loads and loads of teaching notes and lesson plans, bookmarked websites, downloaded resources, video clips.'

'Anything suspicious?'

'In what sense?'

She sipped her tea, trying to fight away that chill. 'The parents think she was being targeted because of all the Muslim stuff she was working on. They think the UK security forces were targeting her.' She gave a laugh.

'It's perfectly possible,' Martin said. 'Someone who obviously thinks Islam is great – despite the fact she's talking about a thousand years ago rather than the current world situation – might be a target for investigation, assuming something triggered their interest.'

'How would that happen?'

'A website visit, an email subject line, an email or message from another person who is being targeted.'

'Is there any way we could find out?'

'GCHQ don't publish their list of suspects.' He gave a short laugh. 'I don't know whether there is a way of knowing if a person is of interest to the security forces. And I don't think it really matters. She was writing historical fiction – her book isn't nearly finished, and it probably wouldn't ever have been published anyway. And if she self-published then only a handful of people are going to read it. She's hardly a major threat that needs to be 'taken out'. Anyone who thinks so is fantasising.'

'The mother is trying to find a reason for her daughter's death. And a purpose to her life, I suppose.'

'I'll pass it over to Michael when I see him,' Martin said. 'He has time to investigate. There might be stuff hidden away.'

The search of the girl's computer was not authorised, and none of the material there could in any way be used in court: there was no chain of evidence. So there was no harm in letting the investigation of it carry on. 'OK, Martin.'

She hung up, and smiled across at Claire, who was leafing through a magazine which was perched on her knees. She was beautiful, Amanda thought, and her heart gave a sigh at how lucky she was.

'Fancy taking these to bed?'

Claire looked up, and smiled.

Later, Amanda cradled Claire against her shoulder, hearing her breathing slow to normal, feeling her drift into sleep. Amanda was still breathing heavily, her body giving after-trembles. She almost slipped into sleep, but then the thoughts tumbled through her head. Who was Gary McAllister? Had Jones missed him, or had he been well below the radar? Was he even in Clachdubh any more?

There was no way she could get Ramesh to re-open this. She'd given her report and he'd said he was happy with it. The whole thing was buried.

What would she tell Mrs Khalaf? Now that Martin had unlocked their daughter's computer, and after Michael had had a look, she would give it back to them so they could sift through it at leisure – and they'd find nothing there.

Would that appease them? Or would they go to the press, try to find someone who had it in for Police Scotland and would want to use this to create a story?

Was there a story?

She closed her eyes. She had too much work to do right now – manpower was being cut, expectations under the new Chief Constable were high. She couldn't carry on investigating this...

Or *could* she go to Clachdubh for a weekend, ask around some more? She could take Claire, go for walks?

No, she thought. Stupid.

Her heart and her breathing slowed, and she slept. Until something in her brain fired and she was wide awake.

Gary. That had been the name of one of the school kids at that after-party on the Rock when Karen McKechnie had fallen to her death.

❧ 19 ❧

Amanda was at her desk early Wednesday morning, busily ignoring her emails, trying not to catch Ramesh's eye as he walked around clutching pieces of paper.

She checked again the details of that schoolgirl who had fallen from the Rock, but there was little to see. Inspector Jones had investigated, although it looked like he'd worked towards a pre-conceived idea of accidental death. And who was to say that wasn't the truth of the matter? But hadn't he even considered the second death could be more than coincidence?

The list of school pupils who had been at the drinks party on the Rock that night was there, but she now checked second names. Yes, Gary McAllister. He still lived in Clachdubh, with his father Robbie. No other children. No other person at the address, so no wife or partner. No convictions for either of them.

She called Crawford Ballantine and got his voicemail. She left a message for him to call her back whenever he could. She simply wanted to check what she knew, that Gary McAllister was in that writers' group. But she also wanted to know more of what he was like, if he had seemed especially interested in Rima Khalaf.

The only other thing that was hanging over her was the Khalafs themselves. Ramesh hadn't mentioned that anyone else would call them, so she felt she should. It was only fair. Eventually she decided to get it over with. She phoned the number she had.

Mr Khalaf answered, and she said who she was. 'One moment.' There was some conversation in the distance, and then there was silence around him. 'Inspector Pitt.' His voice was more heavily accented than his wife's, and sounded urgent and unfriendly. 'What have you found?'

She would rather have been speaking to his wife, whom she'd met. She couldn't picture this man, didn't know what he was like. 'I'm afraid we've found nothing, Mr Khalaf. There was nothing wrong with the investigation into your daughter's death.'

The silence shouted disappointment. Then: 'You must find something.'

'I'm afraid not. We managed to get into your daughter's laptop,

61

but found nothing incriminating. I will arrange to get it back to you in the next week or so.'

'You found nothing of the British government monitoring Rima?'

'No trace of that at all, but there wouldn't be. If such a thing were going on, they'd be monitoring her emails on the server, not on her laptop. And they'd be monitoring her mobile phone calls. But that wasn't happening.'

'She did not have a mobile phone,' Mr Khalaf said.

Amanda wondered why he thought that. 'How did you communicate with Rima? Did you call her house when you wanted to speak to her?'

'Yes of course. And she called us here. She had no mobile phone.'

Amanda wondered whether Rima maybe had just not wanted her parents pestering her, phoning at inconvenient times. Or were they quite estranged for some reason?

'Right, Mr Khalaf. I will return your daughter's laptop to you – we have your address on our files. You can continue trying to search it, but we cannot commit any more police time.' She'd send him a note of the new password too, but had no idea what he would make of anything there.

'Cover up,' he said.

'What?'

'You are all the same. Fucking cover up. You fucking bastards.' He disconnected the call.

Amanda's mobile rang almost immediately. 'Hi – Inspector Pitt? Crawford Ballantine here. You wanted to speak to me.' His voice was flat, as if he was still hurting a little from her rebuff.

'Yes – thanks for calling back.'

'I don't have long – I've got a client to see in ten minutes.'

'Just one question, Mr Ballantine. The writers' group. You have a member called Gary McAllister – is that right?'

'Yes – Gary. Works in Tesco. What about him?'

'He had emailed Rima Khalaf, and I wondered whether you noticed them together at club meetings.'

'Not particularly. She was popular, I suppose, though she didn't actually contribute much.' That rebuffed tone sounded worse, and Amanda wondered whether Ballantine had asked Rima out too and been rejected: he wasn't influential, so he'd have been of no use to her. 'She had lots of hangers-on, and Gary probably just listened in.'

'No particular connection then?'

'Not that I saw. Is that it?'

Amanda gave a deep internal sigh. 'Yes, Mr Ballantine. Thank you for your time.'

❧ 20 ❧

Mark Grosvenor limped up Charles Street under the soft glow of the street lights, and in through the doors of the Seven Seas bar, his glasses steaming up as he hit the noisy, moist air. He paused to take them off.

The young barman was there as he reached the counter. 'How are *you* today, sir?'

'Scotch and water.' Grosvenor didn't do Massachusetts politeness: he was from Brooklyn.

He scratched at his thick white beard and gazed around. There were empty seats along the counter, and space at a table in this long, busy bar.

'Would you like to see the menu, sir?'

'No thanks.'

'You take a seat, sir, and I'll bring your drink right over.'

Grosvenor grunted and dropped himself onto the bench seat at the vacant table, struggling out of his jacket. He cleaned his glasses on a tissue from his pocket, put them back on, and found his phone. There were no messages from Natasha Lavery. If she'd decided not to show then she wasn't telling him.

He took a deep breath and thought again how he was going to play this. But he was never one for following a plan, not even his own one, so he decided on the mood he was going to strike and left it there.

He sipped his scotch and water when it came, and he waited. She was late now, and getting later. Eventually he waved at the barman for another scotch, and passed the time by watching the clientele, assessing them and making decisions, the way he would have done in the old days.

There was a woman at the bar with a large glass of white wine. She looked like she was in her late thirties, wearing a nice dress and jewellery, and manifestly alone. Two chairs away was a man sipping a Sam Adams lager. He was a similar age to her, and looked like a businessman out for the evening, killing time in a strange city. They had struck up a conversation.

As Grosvenor watched, she adjusted her dress, checking her cleavage. The man was checking it too. They spoke some more, and then she shifted to the empty seat between them. They leaned closer, and laughed at what each other were saying. He bought another round of drinks. Grosvenor grinned. He reckoned that she was a professional, and she'd found a potential customer.

The door had been opening and closing regularly with people coming and going, but now someone had come in and paused before coming over to drop onto the seat beside Grosvenor.

'Hi,' he said. 'Double espresso?' He signalled to the barman and mouthed his order, including another scotch for himself.

Natasha sat staring down at her feet. She was in her mid-twenties, tall and uncomfortable in her skin. He thought she was maybe sitting a little more upright than he remembered from two years before, but still with her toes turned in and her knees tightly together.

Their drinks came and she knocked back her coffee in one mouthful, then replaced the tiny cup in its saucer.

'So,' he said. 'How's it going?'

She looked to his eyes briefly, then away. 'Well still the same fine I guess.' As ever, her words tumbled out without any change of pace or inflection.

'You didn't go back to MIT?'

She shook her head.

'And you're still with 1794?'

'Why did you want to see me Mr Grosvenor is this an FBI check-up I thought you did that all online.'

He sighed. 'We've had a bit of a change of heart at the top,' he said. 'With all the growing threats in the world that can't just be bombed away, even the Federal Government has begun to realise that we need to work with people, and not fight everyone. That's why I'm here. We're not hunting down 1794 any more, we're not judging what you do. We want to work *with* you.'

She lifted her head and looked into his eyes. 'I'm not sure we need your help.'

'Oh yes you do. With respect, we can do a lot more surveillance than you can.'

'So what is it you think we can work together on Mr Grosvenor?'

He took a deep breath. This was going a bit better than he'd hoped: she was here and was listening and she was staying. 'Before we get to that joint project stuff, how about we do a trade? Just to show faith. I'll ask you to help with one of our investigations, and I'll offer to help with one of yours.'

'You show me yours first.'

He nodded. He'd met Natasha a couple of years before, when he'd been trying to recruit MIT dropouts for the FBI. It had seemed like a good idea to him – still did – but none of them were interested. MIT people by and large hated the Feds, and Natasha certainly shared that view. But she'd been part of an online group – 1794 – who were chasing, amongst others, a cybercriminal known as Gregorius. Grosvenor had given her some information he had, hoping it would help her. It had. She'd blown open a Gregorius operation, but wrecked an on-going FBI sting in the process.

That had somewhat influenced the FBI's opinion of 1794, but there had been no other conflicts of interest since then, and 1794 had managed to close down some ISIS online resources. So Grosvenor had suggested making friendly overtures and his bosses had said OK. He could be the go-between: she didn't trust him much, but she would trust anyone else even less.

Up at the bar, the woman was resting her hand on the man's and was leaning very close to him. He was staring into her eyes and her cleavage, and grinning away.

'Dimitri MacDonald,' Grosvenor said. He shrugged: 'Russian mother apparently. Anyway, he moved to Vancouver four years ago, married a Canadian. He's working for West Coast Logic in North Vancouver.'

'You seem to know all about him.'

'Apart from his name and location and his company, we know nothing about him.' That was stretching the truth, but it would do for now.

'The Feds don't usually have a problem monitoring people,

following them electronically.'

'This one's tricky for us.'

'Is it a test for me?'

'It's a test for our relationship.'

'May I have another coffee, Mr Grosvenor?'

They waited till the barman caught his eye, and then till it was served. At the bar, the woman now had her hand on the man's shoulder, one breast touching his upper arm, and was giggling at every word he said.

Natasha drank the coffee in one mouthful, and he sipped at his scotch. 'Rima Khalaf,' she said, and spelt it while he keyed it into his phone. He shouldn't do that, she thought: notes from his iPhone automatically uploaded to iCloud, and could be vulnerable depending on how strong his password was. Somebody from the FBI should really know this.

'Who's...she? He?'

'She. She was a schoolteacher in Scotland and she's dead she fell off a hill and it was almost certainly accidental and there's no suspect but her parents think she was being tracked by GCHQ and maybe the Feds because of who she was.'

'So who was she?'

'Her parents came to England from Syria. She wasn't strongly Muslim but she had views about Islam about how great they were a thousand years ago and how that contrasts with everyone thinking they're Stone Age monsters and all terrorists and shouldn't be allowed to go anywhere especially not the US. Her parents think that security forces thought she was dangerous and monitored her and maybe killed her.'

'That's one hell of a conspiracy theory.'

'Doesn't mean it's not true.'

'Suppose. OK, I'll try to check.'

She stood up. 'Goodbye, Mr Grosvenor.'

He watched her walk out in her long-legged awkward way, and noticed her speak to someone outside the door, then go on up the street with him. So she'd had a minder, Grosvenor thought. She didn't trust the Feds – and who could blame her.

He flew back from Logan to New York the next morning and spent the day checking Rima Khalaf on FBI databases and by calling contacts. He found out what Natasha had asked him to find out, but decided to wait a couple of days before calling her, to make it look harder than it really was.

She used a Blackphone, of course, so her communications were secure, no location data leaking out when she was on a call, all texts encrypted.

'Well, you were sort of right,' he said. 'Rima Khalaf was on an FBI 'watch' list because of her background and her social media activities. But it was a very low priority, because there was no link from her to anyone else on any watch list, no indication that she was part of a network. It seemed she was just a loner, doing what she did. There was a negligible risk of her of being radicalised because she was in her twenties, she was intelligent, she was thoroughly Westernised, she was educated. But her work might have been useful for propaganda purposes, so she stayed on the list, and I'm not sure what would have happened if she'd tried to enter the US. Nobody's security forces would have bothered to have had her killed, that's for sure – if that's your conspiracy theory.'

'Thank you,' she said. Her voice was flat, and he thought that she probably didn't wholly believe his answer.

'How are you getting on with my request?'

'Nothing yet. We're working on it.'

'OK. Keep in touch.'

She finished the call, and he put his phone in his pocket. Outside, the weather was dry. He felt like a walk in City Hall Park.

❧ 21 ❧

Over a period of a few nights, he'd discovered that the street where 'Rebecca' lived was quiet, but not too quiet. There was a small Co-op down at the corner, and a pub a couple of streets away. People seemed to come home after work or whatever and stay in, with occasional forays out to the shop or the pub or to walk their dog. It was a through-road but there was little traffic.

The neighbours didn't seem too nosy either. When he stopped on his bike, no curtains twitched. When the odd person went past, there was eye contact and a greeting, but no suspicion. There was that hotel in the street behind, though, and any guest in a room at the back could look out and see Rebecca's house.

Gary reckoned that he wouldn't be noticed: his clothing was dark, his bike was an old, cheap black mountain bike, the maker's name on the down tube obliterated. He wore a black helmet.

So he became bolder, cycling past several times, lurking near her house when he saw she was in. Dusk was a good time: the lights would be on inside her house, but the curtains wouldn't be drawn until it got really dark. He would catch glimpses of her walking about inside, sitting on her sofa with the TV on and an iPad on her lap.

As he grew even bolder, he'd stop to take pictures on his phone, and look at them later in his room. He got one or two with her in shot.

She was beautiful, he thought. She was alone. She needed someone, someone like him – the age difference wouldn't matter. He wondered how he might approach her.

Then, that Friday evening, someone stopped their car outside her house. A man driving. She had been at the window, looking out, and now she waved. The curtains closed, and a couple of minutes later she was out of the front door – checking it was locked behind her – and trotting down the path in her heels, pulling on a coat. Her face was smiling. She was wearing a dress, a short scoop-neck dress. Dark tights – maybe stockings.

Gary quickly snapped her on his phone, then watched as the man got out to briefly hold her, give her a peck on the cheek, help her into the front passenger seat. Gary saw her coat fall back, got a glimpse of her thighs. Then the door was closed, the engine started, and she was gone.

A black Audi A4, Gary noted, and recited the registration to himself. And then he realised he had seen the car and the man before. It was him! He pedalled after them, enraged.

He spent an hour or so cycling round the town, but there was no sign of the car, so he went home.

She is a queen of her own empire and she owes nothing to any man, but she has her needs and her desires. The man Duncan has travelled to her from the kingdom of Moray, with offers of allegiance that they might challenge the Kings of Strathclyde and this upstart Malcolm who would be king of all Scotland.

*She meets with Duncan, and they talk. He is young and
strong, and she finds him appealing. He tells her tales of the lands
in the north, of the bounteous harvests, of the plentiful seas.*

*She lets him stay for a few days, and they continue talking.
They ride together, out into the forests of her lands, and over to
the flat plains of the meandering river. He makes her laugh, he
makes her feel happy, he makes her feel not alone.*

*One day they ride to the hills, and she shows him the pool at
the base of the waterfall where she likes to bathe. Between the
two of them they decide that the day is hot, they are sweaty and
dusty from their ride, and so a bathe would be good.*

*They stand as far apart as they can and undress. He sees her
run the few steps to the water, and the sight of her naked body
catches his breath. She throws herself into the pool and she
shrieks and giggles.*

'Come on!' she shouts.

*He steps toward the water, and she sees that he is erect. She
laughs when his erection vanishes as the water reaches his knees,
and he swims towards her. 'What's so funny?'*

She turns and swims away.

*Later, they leave the water, and they stand together, side by
side, on the bank, their arms spread as they let the sun dry
them.*

*He takes her hand and leads her to the longer grass, and he
kneels before her. He pulls her to him and his mouth travels
down, seeking her out...*

Gary squirmed and had to stand up, walking away from the
computer.

'Gary!' came the shout. 'Gary – you up there?'

His breathing was hard, and his fingers shook on the mouse as
he saved the file and closed the window. 'I'm here, Dad!'

He headed down the narrow, steep staircase. His dad was in
the lounge, hissing open a can of beer as he swapped channels
on the TV.

'You eaten yet?' his dad asked, not looking round.

'I got a pizza – haven't cooked it yet. You?'

'Naw. Gonna get a carry-out curry later, go round to a mate's
house.'

69

When his dad didn't specify the name of his 'mate', Gary knew it was almost certainly the woman whose husband was away offshore. Or maybe another woman. But he thought his dad was being reckless: the woman's neighbours would see him coming and going – and staying – and would surely tell the man. But maybe she didn't have neighbours. Maybe she didn't care – maybe the husband didn't care.

'What are you up to?'

'Just working on some stuff. Going to do a reading at the writers' group next week.'

His dad didn't react, just sipped at his beer.

Gary cooked his pizza and ate it in the lounge while watching some medieval drama. His own book was better, he thought. When the credits came up, he noted the production company. He could maybe do a screenplay of the early chapters of his book, send it to them. Judging by what he'd seen, they'd like the sex and violence. Maybe he'd have to tone down some bits.

He washed his plate and the pizza cutter, and stood in the kitchen. The man who had seduced Rebecca was going to turn out to be evil, he knew. She would have to be rescued by the main character, and she would be very grateful. Very grateful indeed. He squirmed again, and adjusted the front of his jeans.

He went out on his bike, past Rebecca's house. The black Audi was there. The lights were on in the lounge, the curtains shut tight.

Should he lock up his bike and go round the back of the house? Would he catch a glimpse of them having sex?

He went home. He didn't, at this moment, want to see them together. In his mind, she was still his.

He hated the man in the black Audi, the man who was yet again stealing his woman.

❧ 22 ❧

Jamil, alone in the silence of his bedroom, smoked his roll-up and stared at the wall.

Rose had left ten minutes before, in floods of tears. He'd tried to keep her there until she calmed down, but she'd thrown on her clothes and run down the stairs and out of the front door. He could feel the cold draught: she hadn't fully closed it.

He smoked and stared.

It wasn't rape, he said to himself. It was his right as a warrior. To be honest, he hadn't even done it properly. She'd fought him, and he'd come, but it wasn't what he'd imagined it would be. And it wasn't even that great, he thought. She was too scrawny and pathetic.

But he'd *liked* the way she'd fought him. He'd enjoyed it.

He'd text her later, calm her down, win her back. Or maybe he'd focus on Jasmine McCallum, set his sights higher than Rose or that fat dog Jill. Had Jill spoken to Jasmine about that night at the party?

Yes, Jasmine. She was a stunner. He would have her. It was his right as a warrior. It was part of the preparation for the big event.

❧ 23 ❧

'OK,' Pete said. 'Are we still helping out OCCTU W, boss?'

'Yes, yes of course.' She wheeled her computer chair over to him, and looked at his monitor. 'Why?'

'I spoke to Licker McGuire again yesterday. He says the Robertsons are setting up a deal to ship Es up from England. Various people have been offered buy-ins. It's been done this way before.'

Amanda nodded. 'So somebody major underwriting it then parcelling it all out. Has he got any names?'

Pete shook his head. 'No names, no locations. But Licker reckons the deal is pretty big, so there's going to be big money washing around. Rumour is they have someone abroad financing them.' He shrugged.

'Probably a spate of burglaries to raise money too. Any idea of timescale?'

'He's saying next weekend or maybe the weekend after.' Pete shrugged. 'Sorry, that's the best I've got.'

'OK. Good work, Pete. I'll tell Ramesh and he'll feed it back to OCCTU W.'

'I've been round a few pubs too, checking things out.'

'Must have been awful for you, Pete.'

'Ha ha. Anyway, I reckon Patterson's on Byres Road and the Scarba on Dumbarton Road are where most of it is happening in our area.'

'Did you spot anyone in particular? Anyone known?'

He shook his head. 'There's a skinny guy – tall, late thirties, long ponytail. He's dealing, but I don't know if he's a main man.' He watched her face as she thought about that. 'Want me to keep hanging round the pubs?'

She nodded. 'I'll check. We don't want you spoiling things for the surveillance team.'

❧ 24 ❦

Martin and Nicola were due to be at friends' for dinner at their flat just up Highburgh Road. Michael had phoned as they were nearly ready to head out: he'd taken over the job of exploring Rima Khalaf's MacBook from Martin, and now he reckoned he'd pretty much finished.

So Nicola had gone on ahead to the dinner party while Martin had gone to the computer club above Roasters to discuss it all with Michael, hoping it all wouldn't take too long. On the way, he called Amanda to tell her what he was doing. She said she was free and would come over too.

There were four teenagers and two of the pensioners, and the schoolteacher George Webster, at the club. The 3D printer was hard at work, its base plate moving in all four directions, the plastic wire feeding down through its print head. Martin looked at the layers building up on the plate.

'Chassis for a robot,' George said. 'And the wheels.'

The two pensioners were helping the teenagers with circuit boards, tiny breadboards, and various LEDs, resistors and small motors. A soldering iron sat in its dock.

'So, we need the motor shield with its own power supply on top of the Arduino. We can connect LEDs to show which way it's going – it's a good indication of how the program is working.'

Martin tuned out and went over to where Michael sat at his computer with the two monitors.

'How's it going?'

Martin caught sight of a name on the screen – Dimitri MacDonald – just before Michael minimised a couple of windows and turned to him. 'University? Oh, it's fine.'

'How's your mum getting on?'

'Fine.' Michael turned back to the computer, opened a window full and minimised it again.

Martin knew Michael's mother was on her own. She worked in a pub, and Michael had no siblings, but that was all Martin knew. Whenever Martin asked about Michael's family life, the questions were answered minimally or deflected. But recently, Michael's reactions had been accompanied by a twitch of his eyes, a passing look of worry. Martin knew something was going on there, but couldn't think of how to find out – and didn't know if he wanted to. Nicola had told him to ask Michael outright, but he felt he couldn't.

After a couple of minutes of awkward silence, Amanda arrived with a coffee from downstairs. She sat down beside Michael.

'So,' she said. 'Have you found anything more?' She glanced over at the other kids, but they were as far away as they could be, and didn't seem interested in this. 'Apart from Martin's stuff about those emails from 'Gary'.'

Michael took a deep breath and blew it all out in a sigh. 'I haven't found anything significant on the computer at all. Nothing tucked away or encrypted. No signs of any small programs intercepting information. All I've got is what was left over from her Facebook and Twitter feeds: all activity stopped around the date of her death.' He pursed his lips. 'The usual rubbish posts and then nothing.'

'So what sort of stuff did *she* post?'

'Links to news items, historical papers. Almost all on that theme of the Golden Age of Islam. She liked to contrast the present with the past. No personal stuff at all that I can see. She seems to just have had the one account for Facebook and Twitter. She wasn't on Tumblr or Pinterest or Instagram or anything else. I suppose she might have used WhatsApp on her mobile – it's end-to-end encrypted, so that's one of the things you would use if you were communicating securely with someone. She didn't seem to use TOR for anonymous browsing.' He gave a shrug.

'Anything else about those emails you mentioned?'

Martin shook his head. 'No other contact between Gary McAllister and Rima after she rebuffed him.'

'No sign he was stalking her?'

'If she was careless about her Facebook settings, he might have been keeping an eye on her. But that's very difficult to find out. Have you got her mobile? We might find things on that.'

Amanda shook her head.

'Don't you have it?' Martin asked.

She took another sip of coffee. 'No I don't. It was never found.'

Michael and Martin shared a look. 'That could be significant,' Michael said.

'She was having an affair with a married man,' Amanda said, 'and he bought himself a pay-as-you-go mobile and her an iPhone, just to keep in touch between the two of them. I've got the number, but I've no official way of finding her call records.' She grimaced. 'I've no unofficial way either.' She looked at Michael.

He pursed his lips. 'There's any number of ways to locate a phone,' he said in a soft voice, almost to himself. He turned to the computer and opened a browser window.

'There's a website that can do this?'

'Not exactly, but I can find the phone if it's switched on. What's the number?'

She told him the number Mary Liston had given her from her phone, and he typed it in. She watched as he created an account. 'Can I have a credit card number please?'

Martin fished out his wallet and handed Michael a credit card. 'How much will this cost me?'

'Nothing – it's just to get a free trial. I'll try to remember to cancel…'

'It's not a scam, is it?' Martin knew all about those.

'No no…There you go.' He handed the credit card back to Martin, and typed more, opening his email client, clicking on a confirmation email, going back to the website.

Google Maps opened up on one of the monitors, showing a street and a marker. Fonthill Road.

'Good god,' Amanda said. 'That phone's been missing for a year. How is it still functioning?'

'I guess somebody found it and started using it,' Martin said. 'Or – '

'Can you zoom out?'

Michael zoomed out. Fonthill Road was in Aberdeen, not far from the city centre. 'That address is a bit approximate,' he mumbled.

Martin was looking at Amanda. 'Where did you expect to find the phone?'

'I don't know what I expected. I suppose I thought that if someone had killed her then they would have taken the phone and binned it.' Amanda looked at the map. 'But maybe they thought an iPhone was just too valuable.'

'So…' Martin said. 'How did it end up in Aberdeen?'

Amanda shook her head. 'Somebody moved there, after finding the phone? Or sold it on to someone?'

'Any other mobile numbers for her?' Michael asked. 'She might have had two phones.'

Amanda pondered that. 'I wonder if a previous married lover also gave her a mobile.' Then she repeated: 'I can't just go asking for phone records.'

'There are people who can do this sort of thing for you,' Michael said.

Amanda shook her head firmly. 'Have you found anything else?'

Michael clasped his hands on his lap. 'Rima Khalaf was being monitored by the FBI.'

She felt cold suddenly. 'And?' How did he know this? Scratch that thought: she didn't want to know.

'She came to their attention because of her social media activity: the links she shared, the websites she visited. But it was very low-level monitoring. They didn't think she was a real threat. She had no links to other suspects, she didn't really fit the profile of someone who could be radicalised – she was too intelligent, too mature. So, that conspiracy theory is wrong.'

'And your information is reliable?'

Michael just gave a shrug in response.

Amanda turned to Martin. 'What do you think?'

'Either Michael's contact has been fooled, or this information is accurate. She was being monitored, but she wasn't an active threat. Now, just before her death, something may have happened that escalated that and they decided to push her off a hill, but it's pretty far fetched.'

She nodded. 'I think you're right.'

A mobile beeped and Martin pulled his out of his pocket, and read the text. 'I'm on my third gin. Get here soon, nerdy. Xxxx'

'I'd better go,' he said. 'Remember to cancel that mobile tracker account,' he said to Michael.

'Yes I will, Martin.'

'I'd better go too,' Amanda said. It was going to be a Friday night in with Claire, while Pete was out in pubs pretending he was working and trying not to get in the way of unknown undercover colleagues.

She left Martin on Byres Road. He headed across at the lights, and she walked up to Hillhead underground, her mind working away.

Rima Khalaf's flatmates, she thought. That girl Mary had told her had left after her probation year – Diane was it? Had she maybe gone to Aberdeen? Had she stolen Rima Khalaf's iPhone before she left? Had she pushed Rima from the Rock and taken her phone?

❧ 25 ❧

Amanda had hoped to grab a cheap hotel room for the Saturday night in Aberdeen, and a cheap train fare to get there. It seemed that neither existed, so she drove Claire to a place on Beach Boulevard. They checked in and walked out towards the city centre.

For all the downturn in the oil industry, and the general austerity in the country, Aberdeen still seemed to be busy and full of drunks. They had a couple of large gins in Ma Cameron's, and managed to get into the nearby Italian for dinner with a bottle of wine.

'Where to now?' Claire asked sleepily and drunkenly afterwards. 'Back to the hotel?' She held Amanda's hand, pulled her close.

'Let's go for a walk,' Amanda said. She got out her phone and checked Google Maps. 'This way.'

They headed down and diagonally off Union Street, then left at a big roundabout. They walked through the dark, cold evening along the uniform grey granite of Fonthill Road. Amanda looked at the house numbers, and then stopped.

'What are you doing?' Claire shivered in her coat, and stamped her feet to warm them. She pushed strands of red hair under her fur-lined hood. Her breath steamed slightly in the air. 'God, it's so bloody cold here!'

Amanda wasn't quite sure what she was doing. She took out her mobile and dialled the number she had for Rima Khalaf, realising immediately that she should have had Michael standing by to update her on the phone's location. But she was here, and that mobile had been near here, so let's just see what happened, she thought.

The mobile rang, and then there was a woman's voice, the tone a mixture of caution and boredom. Presumably she thought this was a cold call. 'Yes?'

'Hi. Is that Diane?' This was a guess.

An even more cautious 'Yes?'

'I need to talk to you about Rima Khalaf.'

There was dead silence, and then: 'I don't know...Oh god...Who are you?'

'I'm standing outside your house right now, so would you like to come down and talk to me?'

Amanda kept her eyes on the houses, scanning the other side of the road too. A brightening in one window as a curtain was pulled back, two doors to the right. Amanda quickly sidestepped and gave a wave up to the window. The curtain fell back.

'Or do I have to come up there?'

'Are you the police?' The voice was frightened.

'Yes. But this doesn't have to go any further – not if you talk to me now.'

A pause and then a reluctant, nervous: 'OK. I'll come down.'

Claire was staring at Amanda. 'What's happening?'

'That woman has Rima Khalaf's phone. Martin's pal Michael traced it to here.'

'So this isn't a romantic weekend away?' Claire pouted.

Amanda smiled. 'It will be once I'm finished with this.'

Claire leaned her head into Amanda's shoulder briefly.

A door opened and slammed, and footsteps came down to the street. The woman looked around. 'This way,' she said.

The three of them walked down the street and then round to

the left and up the driveway of a hotel. Inside, the place was packed solid. Amanda bought drinks – gins and tonic for her and Claire, a double vodka and tonic for Diane, and they squeezed themselves into a corner. Around them were couples, old and young, and some singles. Men looked across at Claire as she took off her coat, her top straining, and then clocked Amanda, and leaned closer to whisper and laugh loudly.

'You're Diane,' Amanda checked.

'Diane Strong,' she said.

She was in her mid-twenties, quite short, shoulder length black hair and a pale face, slim-built. Her lips were tight, and her eyes looked hunted. Her fingers trembled as she drank her vodka.

'You did your probation year at Clachdubh High.'

'Yes. Got a permanent job up here afterwards.'

'What do you teach?'

'Modern Studies.'

'You shared a house with Rima Khalaf and Mary Liston.'

'Yes.' The vodka was already almost finished, and Amanda and Claire were matching her pace.

'I'll get them in,' Claire said, and squeezed into the mass of bodies.

'I've interviewed Mary,' said Amanda. 'She didn't get on with Rima.'

'No.'

'Why do you think that was?'

The look from Diane was almost contemptuous. 'Mary fancied her, and that turned to hate when there was obviously no chance. And Mary also hated Rima for having an affair with her boss – screwing her way to the top.'

'How did you get on with her?'

'She was all right, I suppose. She could be annoying because she'd cancel on you at the last minute if *he* was available suddenly. But she was OK.'

'There's a theory that Rima was pushed off the Rock.'

Diane seemed to think about that, but Amanda couldn't tell whether she was genuinely considering the idea, or about to deny it outright – for whatever reason.

Claire was making her way back – she always managed to get the attention of male bartenders. She also got more unwelcome attention: Amanda saw her turn and speak to a young man who had said something to her, and he blushed then laughed with his mates.

Amanda finished her first gin and took the fresh one, managing to find a gap on a nearby table for the empty glass. She raised her eyebrows at Claire, who shook her head and gave a confident smile.

Diane was saying: 'No way. Nobody hated Rima *that* much.'

'But a lot of people didn't like her.'

'Mary told me she'd shagged a couple of the lecturers at Uni to make sure she got good grades. And one drunken night she confessed she'd shagged one of her teachers at school.' Diane shook her head.

'Any what you would call normal sexual liaisons?'

'Not as far as I know. Maybe – I thought there was at one point. Probably not. She didn't do sex just for fun, I don't think.'

'So tell me about the phone.'

Diane was reluctant. She closed her eyes, and then told them the story. 'She'd left it in the house – she often did. So that Saturday morning it was in the lounge, and my credit had run out, so I used it to phone a friend of mine – I knew Rima's PIN. Then when it all kicked off and the police were round, I realised I still had the phone in my jeans. By the time I realised the police would want it, I couldn't tell them I had it: I'd used it, it might look bad. Turns out the cops weren't interested anyway.'

Amanda looked her in the eyes and was inclined to believe her.

'So I found I could top it up, and I had a charger that fitted it, and it was newer than mine, so I wiped the memory and I just kept it…I'm sorry.'

'Can I see it?'

Diane rummaged in her handbag and produced the mobile, which she handed to Amanda. 'Look, you said this wasn't official. I need that phone – all my contacts are on it. If you need to take it away, can you give me a chance to get everything off it?'

Amanda wasn't listening. She was staring at the smartphone. 'This isn't an iPhone,' she said. She kept reading the name Samsung above the screen.

Diane was frowning and looking at Amanda like she was stupid. 'No…'

'Rima Khalaf was given an iPhone by her lover. This isn't it.'

'Oh – *that* phone.' Diane looked relieved. 'Yes, I knew she had another phone. We'd hear it ringing at times when this one was lying about. She kept it very much to herself. I never even saw it, I don't think.'

'So what happened to it?'

Diane was shrugging and looking at her empty glass. 'I've absolutely no idea.'

'And you don't know the number?'

'No. This was the number I had for her. The Samsung.' She tapped it just to make sure Amanda understood which phone she was talking about.

Amanda was trying to think. Diane had said she'd wiped the memory on the phone, and Amanda knew enough about such things to know that it could be undone unless the memory had subsequently never been written to. But Diane would have filled this phone with photographs and new contacts and all sorts of stuff. Rima Khalaf's world had been deleted and over-written. It was gone.

Diane looked at her. 'I don't know where the other phone is. Look, can I have another drink?'

'Buy your own – we're leaving.'

'I need that phone!'

'Here. Take it.'

Diane only just managed to catch it when Amanda lobbed it to her.

❧ 26 ❦

'Hi, Mikey boy. What you up to?'

Michael hated being called that, but he fought the urge to retort and simply grunted. 'Just university work.'

The man was called Freddy Morton. He was a Londoner, and Michael's mum had first brought him home a couple of months before. He was now a regular – albeit infrequent – guest, who stayed over a couple of nights a week. Michael wasn't sure how genuine the whole cockney geezer persona was, but it irritated him. He also wasn't sure how genuine Freddy's affection for his mother was, beyond the loud and enthusiastic sex.

Michael watched Freddy roll a cigarette, looking ridiculous in his mother's pink dressing gown, skinny hairy legs sticking out, the gaunt stubbled face with long hair tied back in a ponytail. The cigarette was rolled and lit, and the lounge window opened fully. Freddy stood in front of it, blowing smoke into the night air, oblivious of it blowing back into the room on the cold breeze.

Michael focused on his own MacBook, the one Martin had bought him as a present for passing his Highers and Advanced Highers and getting to university. He'd been in his bedroom working on it, but the sound of Freddy and his mum through the thin wall had grown too much for him, so he'd come downstairs.

'You doin' all that Internet stuff, Mikey? Hackin' and all that shit?'

'Something like that.'

He was helping Shala – his contact in 1794, but whom he'd never met – find out about a man called Dimitri MacDonald. Many government and company databases had vulnerabilities, and some of those had been hacked by organisations like Anonymous and 1794, and records extracted. Sometimes Anonymous simply published all the email addresses, contact details, and bank details on the web. For customers of companies like Madison, the dating site for adulterers, this had been really embarrassing, because people could search for anyone they knew. But mainly the information from hacked databases was simply tucked away for later use, for so called 'zero-day' attacks. Sometimes the owners of the databases didn't even know they'd been hacked till much later.

Michael was helping Shala search, but he was also searching for traces of Rima Khalaf, just out of interest. Shala had checked again with her main contact in the FBI, and other contacts she had, but the story there hadn't changed: low-level monitoring, but no real threat identified from her, so no need for any action.

Michael had been searching randomly, but a thought suddenly popped into his head. A few years before, the communications company TalkTalk had been hacked by a pair of teenagers from Northern Ireland, and customer records downloaded. The case had hit the papers, and the teenagers had been arrested. TalkTalk had told everyone to change their passwords, 'just in case', and said that bank details were safe.

But Michael knew that TalkTalk had been hacked again a few months later, only this time there had been no publicity. The customer details were simply sitting out there for people who knew where to look, and Michael knew where to look. And, as it happened, Rima Khalaf had apparently been a TalkTalk customer.

She'd bought a SIM-only plan with TalkTalk – 1000 minutes, unlimited texts, 3GB data, one year contract – in the January of the year before she'd died. The number was there, and Michael noted it.

'You OK, Mikey?'

He looked up at Freddy and nodded. 'Fine.'

'How's uni? Loads of drugs and sex?' Freddy chuckled and flicked the end of his cigarette out into the darkness, then pulled the window shut. A mobile started ringing – a full volume Clash song – and Freddy scooped it up and dropped into an armchair.

'Hey, Licker, you mad old cunt. What you up to?' Freddy laughed.

The conversation went on for five minutes or so, with Freddy laughing like a drain. Then he got more serious. 'Nah, nothing in yet. Next Saturday we're thinking, Licker. I'll give you a bell. OK. Cheers, mate. You muppet. Daft cunt.'

Freddy stood up and yawned, putting the mobile down on the side table. 'Right, better get upstairs. Once more into the breach, eh Mikey?' He chuckled again.

Michael closed his MacBook. He was tired, but there was no point going to bed now, not with Freddy and his mum up there.

He folded his arms and closed his eyes. Then his phone pinged with an alert, and he opened the MacBook again.

It was Shala, wondering if he was still investigating Rima Khalaf. He said he was. She said she had done a search on Rima's father, who had emigrated from Syria before she was born. 'He's on a watch list too, but at a higher level. He's a pharmacist, and the Feds worry about people with those skills.'

'Any specific alerts on him?'

'No. But they're monitoring him – everything he does.'

Michael passed the message on to Martin, via WhatsApp, which was encrypted and secure – as far as he knew. He closed the MacBook again and folded his arms, staring at the window and the street lights beyond – Freddy had forgotten to close the curtains.

So, he thought, the conspiracy theory was still live.

He looked across to Freddy's mobile, and stood up. He leaned over to pick up the mobile and stood facing the door. He'd seen Freddy unlock the phone many times, knew the sequence of swipes. Michael unlocked the phone now and browsed through it.

There had been a lot of calls over the past few days, including Licker – whoever he was – Michael's mum, 'Robertson1' and 'Robertson2', 'Tommy', and 'Taylor'. There had been texts between Freddy, Licker and the Robertsons too, with cryptic discussions about delivery dates and pickups, references to 'the supplies'. Michael got the number of Freddy's phone and saved it to his own phone.

There were no emails on the phone – no accounts set up. A messaging program looked promising but needed a password, so Michael left it alone. He scanned the browser history, but there was just news and cars.

Michael locked the phone and put it down exactly where he'd got it. From upstairs came a male roar and a near-scream from his mum. He closed his eyes tight and pressed his fists against his ears.

❧ 27 ❧

Gary was due to start work at ten that Saturday morning, but he got up very early. His dad had come in at three – loud and drunk, sitting for another hour to watch the TV at high volume.

Gary cycled through the morning, light rain falling. He didn't like cycling in the rain and then having to sit in wet trousers all morning, but today he had to.

He went down her street, his heart thumping in anticipation, and there it was. The black Audi still on the street outside her house. He stopped at it, and had an insane urge to kick it or scratch the paintwork.

She'd been unfaithful to him. She hadn't waited for him. She'd gone with that man – *him*. It was just like before.

He wiped a tear from his cheek and stood upright on the pedals, speeding away from the scene. At work, he was silent, his face impassive, hardly bothering to ask if anyone wanted help with their packing.

And to compound it all, *they* came in: his Rebecca and *him*, the man who had spent the night with her, the man who had *had* her. She looked happy. They held each other as they came in with their trolley, and laughed and joked as they went through the self-service – even pausing in their scanning for a kiss. He saw the bottles of wine scan through – the red light flashing for a staff check – and then they were off, their trolley with its two hessian bags, his arm round her waist, fingers splayed and reaching over her tight jeans for her bum.

Gary felt the fury in himself. He decided he would re-write that section of his novel, to reflect his new anger.

*

The summer sun is high in the sky. Sweat runs down into my eyes. It is slow work creeping through the trees to the edge of the pool at the base of the waterfall. The dry summer has slowed its flow to a muted splashing, not like the wild roar from the winter snow melt.

I know she'll be here. I remember the day I saw her, swimming naked with her handmaidens guarding her. I wake at nights with that vision in my head, the sight of that perfect body, the red hair and the red bush. I have scoured my kingdom for young redheaded wenches, and I have had them all. And some have been exceedingly pleasant and eager to please. Some fought and scratched and had to be taught obedience, of course: the young are often disobedient – they have no respect these days.

But always I wake with the longing for her – Rebecca. She will be my queen.

I creep closer. I hear splashing – the splashing of a body in water. And laughter.

But what's this? A man's voice?

I move forward. The man is in the water with her. They cuddle and cavort and splash each other, and she giggles and laughs. On the shore are their clothes, and a flagon of wine and two goblets. I watch as they emerge from the water, hand in hand, laughing, and a rage builds up inside me. I see her naked body, but my eyes are on him, the water dripping from his muscular chest.

I get to my feet, my sword in my hand, and I run towards them, roaring.

They both stop, stunned. I am close to them before he realises what is happening and raises his arm, pushing her away with his other hand.

He raises his arm. Hah! My sword swings down, right though the arm and into the side of his neck, almost severing his head. The blood gushes from the wounds and he collapses, his eyes still surprised but glazing over. He is dead before his body splashes into the muddy earth.

I turn to her. She stands facing me, her fists clenched, her splendid body shaking, her face full of horror.

'I have come for you,' I said. 'You shall be mine and mine alone.'

'Never,' she says.

'On your back, woman,' I command, pointing my sword. 'On your back and I will show you what a real man can do.'

'Never.'

She arches her back defiantly. 'You will need to kill me before I will let you have me.'

'On your back!'

'Never,' she screams. 'You will never have this body while I am alive.'

The rage surges inside me, washing back and forward. My eyesight clouds. I have never been so angry. I have killed people on a whim, murdered women with whom I have finished, murdered women who were unable to please me. But this is different. This is the woman I want, the one I must have.

'On your back!'

'Never!'

And one thing becomes clear. If I cannot have her then no one else will.

❧ 28 ❧

Amanda sat at her desk, knowing she really did have to concentrate on the Robertsons' case, really did have to push thoughts of Clachdubh away. Pete McLeod interrupted her as he arrived. 'Good weekend?'

'Romantic break in Aberdeen,' she said. 'Cheap hotel – just getting away. How about you?'

'Quiet. TV and a carry-out curry, few beers.' He yawned and logged on to his computer. 'It was Clachdubh where all that business was, wasn't it? The thing you were investigating.'

'Yes, why?' She turned to him.

'You not seen it?'

'What?' She ran her eyes down the latest alerts. 'Oh fuck,' she said.

'Murder in Clachdubh,' he said, exaggerating his accent and rolling the 'R's. 'Came in a few minutes ago.'

There was only the basic detail on the Police Scotland site: a body had been found, the death officially unexplained but suspicious.

'No no no,' she murmured, and stood up. 'Not another one.'

Ramesh was obviously very busy, and he frowned and winced when she knocked and pushed his door open, but he beckoned her in without too obvious a sigh.

'Yes?'

'There's something on the news – Clachdubh, a suspicious death.'

'Yes. What of it?'

'My report – it's background – context – I need…'

'Close the door and sit down,' he said.

When she'd done that, she went on: 'I should be on the MIT.'

He shook his head. 'The major investigation team will have been set up and be on site. They'll ask if they need more manpower.'

'Who's senior officer?'

He tapped at his computer. 'DCI Paige.'

Amanda knew Paige, had worked with her on a murder investigation before. 'I need to at least talk to her about the background – my report.'

'What makes you think the previous death – the *accidental* death, fully investigated – has anything to do with this?' He tapped the computer again. 'This is a stabbing.'

She sat back. A stabbing. Not someone being pushed off the Rock, then. Nothing like Rima Khalaf's death, or Karen McKechnie's. Her brain stalled.

This death wasn't the same…

'Our investigation shows that Rima Khalaf's death was accidental,' Amanda said, 'but Paige should know about it. And she should know more than is in my report and the original investigation. Just in case.'

'Just in case what?'

She took a deep breath. 'You know there were gaps, and we both believe they are unimportant. But what if I'm wrong?'

His frown was deep, his eyes sinking into the bags under them. 'And if it turns out that you are?'

'I'm sure you'll work out how to deal with that if it happens, sir.'

She wasn't sure exactly what she meant by that, and Ramesh's face showed that he didn't understand either.

'OK,' he said. 'I'll call DCI Paige and tell her that you'll be in touch to give her an informal briefing on a previous death in Clachdubh, which has nothing to do with this murder but may furnish her with useful contextual information. Then you arrange to go up there and brief her. Give it till this afternoon before you call – she'll be busy getting the investigation moving.'

Amanda fought down her impatience. She went out with Pete to continue their part in the investigation into the Robertson brothers: finding who was bringing the MDMA pills into Glasgow, where they were coming from, who was making them. They spoke to a few people in cafés and on street corners, and then in pubs. They were listening for snippets of information, trying to build up a pattern.

They spoke to people who said they'd heard there was a deal going on and supplies coming in 'soon'. No one said that the Robertsons were involved, though.

They found Licker McGuire in the semi-darkness of an almost empty Wyatt's Bar in Partick.

He glowered at them, and then: 'Any progress with thae burglaries, Sergeant Pitt?' he asked, with a sly grin.

'No progress yet, Licker. I'll be sure to tell you. Tell us about the Robertsons – the Es they're bringing up from England.' They'd agreed not to ask Licker about the guy with the ponytail, not yet, not till he'd given them more information: they didn't want him warning the guy off.

Licker's face fell. 'Don't know much,' he whispered. 'But if I find anything out…'

'Aye right,' Pete said.

They got back to Stewart Street just before three, and Pete sat down to write up all the tentative information they'd got and feed it back to OCCTU W.

'I hesitate to ask, boss, but how did Licker get his name?'

She grinned. 'I was told that he got it at school. Some party he was at, and an older woman got him to…well, I'll leave the details to your fertile imagination, Pete. There was an appreciative crowd watching, apparently. He's been known as Licker ever since. Didn't play too well in prison, however. I heard he had a very bad time there – six months he did, and every day was hell apparently.'

'Yeuch.'

'Strangely enough, one of the big guys who was in with him was mysteriously stabbed soon after he got out. Gangland violence, it was said.'

'Licker?'

'We never solved the case.'

Amanda was dialling Paige on her police mobile, and recognised the clipped, slightly harassed voice that answered: 'Paige. Yes?'

'Hello, ma'am, it's DS Pitt from Stewart Street.'

'Good afternoon, DS Pitt. What can I do for you?' The words were spoken fast.

'Has Chief Inspector Ramesh been in touch with you?'

'No. Why?'

Shit, Amanda thought: thanks, boss. 'I don't know if you're aware of a death in Clachdubh a year ago.'

'I wasn't. A suspicious death?'

'No, ma'am. Well – not really.'

Paige spoke to someone to the side, finishing with a terse 'Just get on with it,' and then spoke into the phone: 'What do you mean?'

'It would be best if I spoke to you in person, ma'am. It's a delicate situation.'

'Delicate for whom?'

'Police Scotland.' Amanda didn't want Paige to think that Amanda was covering her own back here.

'OK. You'll need to come here. I have a MIT meeting at five.

I'm staying over in Clachdubh – a hotel called Rock View. Meet me there at…eight o'clock this evening? If I'm out, call me and come find me.'

'Should I stay over, ma'am?'

'Up to you. Depends how long you want to talk to me for.' She hung up.

Pete had been on a call too. 'That was Tommy Johnston,' he said. 'The Robertsons are going to be in Patterson's this evening at eight. He's not sure what it's about but he says there's a wee bit of excitement.'

She nodded. 'Can you go yourself tonight?'

'You got a hot date?'

'I have a live-in partner and every night with her is a hot date, Pete.' She loved the effect she had on him when she talked like this, and wondered why exactly men got so excited by a relationship between two women. 'But I need to go back up to Clachdubh, speak to Paige – she's senior officer.'

He nodded, obviously not sure what she wanted to speak to Paige about but understanding that she would have said more if she'd chosen, and would not respond to questions.

'I might stay over,' she went on. 'I'll let you know.'

She remembered the journey: an hour and a half at least, plus the traffic getting in and out of Glasgow. She could get back, and it wouldn't be stupidly late. But if she stayed over, she might get a chance to speak more to Paige, perhaps even find out something about the murder. She checked her watch, and got back to her proper work.

❧ 29 ❦

Amanda arrived at the Rock View Hotel at seven, to be met by an over-excited Joan. She checked in and ordered dinner. Joan stayed at her elbow throughout, drinking wine, even while she ate. When Amanda declined to order a glass of wine, Joan simply poured her a glass from her own bottle. There were three other guests, Joan said, but they were all out. Amanda suspected that this was some of the MIT.

'So how did you come to know Nicola McGregor?' The

bracelets rattled on her arm as she lifted her glass, and her perfume wafted across the table.

Amanda wondered whether Joan was permanently half-sozzled, or whether she was under some particular stress at the moment. There was no way she was giving Joan her whole back-story, so she said: 'Nicola's husband owns a computer company, and my partner is his secretary.'

'Unusual to have a male secretary, but I suppose equality works both ways these days.'

'My partner is called Claire. She's a woman. We live together.'

Joan's eyes widened, and then she relaxed and smiled, and her free hand rested on Amanda's wrist. 'Modern times indeed. Never tried that myself. Not many things I didn't try, though.' She raised her glass for a drink, her eyes gazing into the distance. 'Had a threesome once. Didn't like it. I was drunk. What a mess!' She shuddered. 'Never tried bondage either – that's quite fashionable these days.'

Amanda finished her meal, declined coffee, and tried to escape through to the guest lounge with only a brim-skimming top-up of her untouched wine. But Joan followed and sat on the sofa near her.

Rather than be quizzed about her own life and work, Amanda asked: 'How's the business doing? Nicola helping?'

'Nicola comes out every year and tells me the same thing: establish your market, identify your unique selling point.' She lifted the wine bottle. 'Sure you won't…?'

'No thanks.' She covered her glass with her palm – not that there was room for any more wine.

'I'm not broke, of course, but my investments are sliding – bloody Chinese economy, and the oil prices!' She gave that shudder again, and sat back, crossing her legs, showing extravagant amounts of thigh: she had good legs. 'But this place keeps going, despite my poor business skills. There's talk of a Premier Inn being built just on the edge of town – that'll hurt me.'

Before Amanda could get in another question, Joan added: 'So, you were investigating that poor girl's death. And now there's been a murder. Such excitement!'

Amanda eyed her, and asked: 'And what's the gossip about the murder?'

Joan looked round theatrically and leaned sideways over the arm of the sofa towards Amanda, her voice dropping. 'Young woman – lives just over the back from here – Hill View Road. I can see her house from the back bedrooms upstairs. Dentist. Only arrived in the town a couple of months ago. Stabbed!'

No match at all, thought Amanda again. Not like Rima Khalaf's death in any way. Not like the schoolgirl who fell off the Rock years before. This was different altogether. A sudden wave of tiredness and a feeling of pointlessness swept over her.

'Stabbed!' Joan repeated.

Amanda always wondered how such information leaked out. Not that this was worthy of being kept quiet: it wasn't an unusual way to be murdered in Scotland. But there might be aspects that were being kept quiet.

'Any suspects?' Amanda asked. 'Off the record.'

Joan puckered her lips. 'The boyfriend,' she said, nodding and taking a drink of wine. 'He stayed over the night it happened. Must be him.'

Amanda heard voices outside in the entrance hall, and Joan got to her feet unsteadily. The lounge door opened, and DCI Paige was there in a severe dark suit. 'Ah, you're here.'

Joan winked at Amanda. 'I'll leave you to it.' She teetered out.

Paige sat beside Amanda. Amanda thought she looked tired and drawn, stressed. But she knew Paige could cope with that. Paige glanced pointedly at the wine glass on the table.

'It was forced on me,' Amanda said.

'You staying over?'

'Yes. I'd be getting back very late.'

'So what's your story?' Paige sat back, looking hard at her. No preamble.

Amanda took her through the initial investigation into Rima Khalaf's death, and pointed out the gaps in it. 'But I don't think anything was missed,' she said.

'So why have you come all that way to tell me this?'

'There was the previous girl.'

'What previous girl?'

'The one who fell to her death from the Rock a couple of years before – a schoolgirl.'

'And was that suspicious?'

'Not at all.'

Paige gave an exasperated sigh. 'I don't know what you're getting at, DS Pitt.'

'Can I speak off the record?'

'A police officer cannot speak to a senior officer off the record, especially during a major investigation. You know that. If you have any information that may be relevant to my enquiry then you must tell me. I'll judge how to handle it.' She looked at her watch. 'Talk to me.'

'The mother of Rima Khalaf asked me to check the girl's laptop – they couldn't get into it. I found someone – Martin McGregor: you remember him?'

Martin had helped on a previous case, and Paige had met him. His evidence had never formed part of the official evidence base of that case, because of how it had been obtained. But Amanda could see Paige saw him as a credible source. 'Go on.'

'He got into the laptop, and one of the things he found was an email from someone called Gary McAllister to Rima Khalaf. They were both in a writers' group together. He had asked her to read some of his stuff. She refused, and he sent her an extract anyway. A rather sexually explicit and violent extract involving an Eastern slave girl who is raped and then thrown off Dumbarton Rock. Rima died falling off 'The Rock' here in Clachdubh.'

Paige sensed Amanda wasn't finished. 'And?'

'When that schoolgirl fell off the Rock two years before, it was during a drinking session. One of the boys there was called Gary.'

'OK. Have you checked on him?'

'I haven't been able to. My investigation is closed. What I did with the laptop was unofficial. Possibly illegal.' She winced.

'OK. I'll get someone to check. But I don't think it's likely. This young woman was stabbed, and we have the boyfriend at the scene at around the time.' She looked at Amanda. 'But I'll get someone to check.'

'Thanks, ma'am. How is it all going?'

Paige sighed. 'It's going. We've kept him in custody because of the prima facie evidence, but he denies everything. No other fingerprints inside the house, DNA tests being run. He confirms a sexual relationship, confirms they had sex that evening and again during the night. They'd both been quite drunk so he says he walked into town in the morning to get a few things for breakfast – it was her day off and he was taking the morning off. When he got back she was lying in the hall, just outside the kitchen, stabbed. She was wearing a dressing gown, which was open, exposing her. We're not sure whether she was on her way to or from the bathroom, or the bedroom. There's no sign of forced entry to the house. There was a bag of fresh croissants on the floor by her. He called it in round about the time of her death, so it looks like no tidying up or staging had been done. I think he has to be guilty.'

Paige sighed again. 'But he denies it. Back door closed but unlocked. No prints at all on the handle of the knife – big kitchen knife, found just inside the kitchen door, a few feet from the body. She was stabbed through the dressing gown – below her left breast – and it had been subsequently pulled open.'

'Was she raped?'

Paige grimaced. 'He admits the multiple sexual encounters they had during the night were pretty enthusiastic. Condoms used and in the bedroom waste basket. Contact trace evidence from her body will confirm whether another person was there.' Again a sigh, and Paige was staring past Amanda, like she was thinking aloud. 'At the moment there are questions over the blood patterns. He's got her blood all over him because he knelt over her, tried to resuscitate her. We're looking for a cast-off pattern, from the actual stabbing, but we can't see it. It's probably under all the other blood, but there ought to be detectable traces. Unless it was just one deep stab into her heart – not a frenzied attack.'

Amanda nodded.

Paige looked at Amanda. 'It looks like a straightforward crime, but there are loose ends. Particularly the lack of any motive.'

❧ 30 ❦

Paige went back out to work on the investigation, and Amanda went up to her room. The curtains had been drawn when she'd checked in, and she'd simply dropped her case on the bed and gone down for food. Now the curtains were open and someone was standing there at the window.

When Amanda clicked on the weak overhead light, the figure

turned abruptly, almost spilling the wine in her glass.

'Joan, what are you doing here?'

'Sorry, sorry! Couldn't resist it. Turn out the light! Come see!'

Amanda switched off the light again and went over to the window. She found herself looking across to the back garden of a semi-detached bungalow, the whole surround to the house taped off. A tent had been erected over most of the back of the house, including the back door. Small floodlights illuminated the back garden, and two officers were carrying out a slow, systematic visual search. Amanda could see floods at the front of the house too.

'So that's the murdered woman's house,' Amanda said.

'Yes. Fascinating watching the police at work.'

'Do you often look out?'

Joan laughed shamelessly. 'I'm afraid I do. I'm not getting much these days and I wondered whether she was. I saw her at the dentist's, you know. Lovely girl. Just lovely.'

'How about the boyfriend?'

'Kevin Baker. He runs a software company from a unit on the business park. I've seen him but never spoken to him. Divorced, I heard. Good looking bugger, I must say. I don't trust men who are too good looking. Do you? Of course – sorry. Forgot.' She took a slurp of wine. 'I've had my share of men who were too good looking. Cost me dear.' Her tone was wistful.

Amanda suspected that Joan had exactly the same intentions as those good-looking men. She was a handsome woman, running to fat with the vast number of alcoholic calories she was consuming, but still showing signs that she would have been beautiful in her youth. And her sexual appetite was obvious.

'Do you think he could have murdered the woman?' Amanda asked. She hoped Joan would never be in any witness box: 'So, to sum up, you were led by a police officer who was not officially on the investigation team into saying that the accused was guilty. And you repeated this around the town.'

'Oh, men will do anything, in my experience. Absolutely anything. But if he was sleeping with her then why kill her? I saw them together in Tesco the other day: they were clearly infatuated with each other.' She shook her head. 'Such a waste.'

Amanda's mobile rang and she answered: 'Hang on.' To Joan, she said: 'I need to take this.' It took a couple of moments for

Joan to realise that this meant she was to clear off.

Once she'd gone, Amanda said: 'Yes, Martin.'

'We've done a bit more research through Michael's contacts. The girl's father was being monitored, and at a slightly higher level. He's a pharmacist and a refugee, which apparently gives him more points on the scale of US paranoia.'

'Interesting. But I'm not sure of the implications of that.'

'Neither are we. Maybe someone threatened him through her, and he didn't budge so they killed her.'

'Doesn't sound likely. His demeanour is all wrong. They wouldn't ask for a more detailed investigation if that were the case.'

'That's all we have right now. I'll let you know if anything else comes up.'

'Thanks, Martin.'

Amanda stood watching her colleagues out there in the glare of the floodlights, the unmistakable sight of Paige moving around, directing things. There would be people moving from house to house, getting statements and then collating and cross-checking them. There would be a roadside check tomorrow first thing to catch people passing by: were you here yesterday morning, what did you see? The trace evidence from the body would go for DNA profiling, looking for matches and looking for unidentified traces. There would be a fingertip search of the garden and the surrounds. All the slow, painstaking police work.

Would they find evidence to convict the boyfriend? And was he really guilty?

Amanda phoned Claire, and then went to bed.

In the morning, she found Paige there talking with a female DI and a male DS over coffee, always looking round to check that Joan wasn't hovering around listening to their quiet conversations.

Amanda joined their table and was introduced. A young girl – looking like she was still at school – came through and took her order: coffee and toast. The cereals were on a big sideboard at the side of the room. Amanda fetched some muesli and semi-skimmed milk, and sat with the team.

'We've checked that name you gave us,' Paige said, glancing round. 'Nothing against him. He works at Tesco. Haven't interviewed anyone about him, but he looks OK.'

They fell silent as Amanda's toast and coffee arrived, and the others were asked if they wanted anything. They declined.

Amanda finished her muesli, listening to the others talk about the organisation of the team for the day. Then she buttered a slice of toast, spread some marmalade thickly on it, and sipped her coffee. It tasted strong and burnt.

'How's it shaping up for the boyfriend?' she asked in a whisper.

'Not looking good,' said Paige.

The DI nodded, her face grim. 'His ex-wife. The divorce told a story of mental cruelty, and assault. He kept calling her when they split and she had to take out a restraining order against him. She finally divorced him for cruel and unusual behaviour. The assault charge never made it to court, but he didn't fight it.' She gave a shrug. 'It's a pattern. He's clearly prone to violence.'

Amanda held her coffee cup in both hands and drank from it. 'How long had he been seeing the murdered girl?'

'Not long.'

Paige nodded at Amanda. 'I know what you're thinking: the abuser usually only comes to the fore after a bit of time, and it builds up gently so that the victim is almost unaware of it until she's locked into hell. This is unusual.'

'The landlady here says she saw them together just the other day – they looked blissfully happy.'

'In public they often do,' the DI said.

'The landlady says he runs a software company.'

'Yeah,' the DI commented. 'So probably borderline autistic, can't express his feelings, bottles things up, then it explodes. It all fits.'

Amanda thought of Martin McGregor and Michael, and partially agreed with the DI. But Paige caught Amanda's eye.

'We'll be thorough,' Paige said. And then, to the DI: 'Nobody's jumping to conclusions here.'

✒ 31 ✒

Martin looked up from his iMac as his mobile rang. 'Hi, Amanda.' He sat back in his chair and swivelled to look out at the Glasgow sky – blue this morning.

Her voice was clear with a car engine running but no road noise.

'Hi, Martin. I wonder if you could do me another favour.'

His voice was cautious. 'If I can.'

'There is a man in Clachdubh who runs a software company – it's on the business park here apparently. His name is Kevin Baker.'

'And?'

'I wondered if you knew him.'

'Never heard of him. What's the name of his company?'

'Don't know: no one told me.'

After a moment's silence, he realised it was his turn to speak. 'Anyway, what about him?'

'I wondered if you could find out about him?'

'Find out what about him?'

'Find out anything about him.'

'Why?'

She hesitated. 'Because he may be charged with murder soon.'

He scratched at his cheek and his face set in a frown. 'But your lot will be investigating him. What do you expect me to find out?' He'd seen the news of the suspicious death in Clachdubh, and guessed this was what Amanda was involved in.

She gave a frustrated sigh. 'I don't really know, Martin. They'll be searching his premises and his computers, but I just wonder…' She took a breath. 'I just wonder whether he's really not guilty at all and somebody else…'

He picked up that she was genuinely anguished about this, so he did the only thing he could. 'Look, I'll spend some time on it and tell you if I find anything that looks interesting.'

'Thanks, Martin. I appreciate that.'

He stood up and went through to the main office, and made himself an exotic coffee from a mixture of pods in their silver coffee machine. He made small talk with Claire, then he went back to his computer and started researching Kevin Baker.

After half an hour he'd built up a reasonable picture. The company was Rock Software and Design, which specialised in designing websites and publicity material. It had only been running for two years or so, but already had a long client list. Martin checked on a couple – they were genuine and had long client lists themselves, so Rock Software looked sound and successful. Baker had worked for a big design company in London before moving up to start his own business.

It all looked real, and Martin wondered whether that was what Amanda hoped or feared. No suspicions of dodgy clients, no hint at money laundering – things that Martin knew about only too well. Of course, they would need some forensic accountancy to make really sure.

Martin looked up at the clock. He had other things to be doing, but he turned his attention to Kevin Baker's personal life.

He was on LinkedIn of course, and other business networking sites. All seemed normal.

Twitter was for his business: tweeting about delivery of products, retweeting tweets by clients, publicising corporate events and launches, occasional news items about the design and software markets including mentions of his own company.

Facebook. Recent posts were selfies of him and a very pretty red-haired woman who wasn't tagged in the pictures. Baker himself was handsome, Martin thought, every inch the successful entrepreneur. There were some company staff photographs. The small number of employees were young and good-looking too, Martin thought. One was of a very young, very pretty brunette woman at a computer – 'Jasmine, our trainee receptionist'. Visible in the picture was a short skirt and a scoop-necked top showing cleavage. There were three other photographs of her, from slightly different angles, all with her leaning forward slightly and staring up at the camera, or sitting with her thighs crossed showing lots of leg, shot from below. Martin thought the photos were rather creepy.

Further back on Baker's timeline – and Martin was wondering why the guy allowed just anybody to see his stuff. Had he missed all the chat about changing security settings? Or, despite his job, was he actually not that knowledgeable about computers? He was the designer and manager, not the programmer.

Anyway, another woman appeared. Another redhead. Selfies again, with exotic backgrounds: tropical beaches, cityscapes, airport terminals. Holding flute glasses full of sparkling white wine with Uluru behind, deep shadows cutting into the red rock.

She was tagged as Cordelia Baker. Martin scrolled back through their lives together, and then forward again. Then back and forward, trying to bring what he was noticing into focus.

The early days – seven years before – showed them grinning

and wrapped round each other. The ones on beaches had her in a tiny bikini, him in budgie-smugglers. One had them in bed, duvet pulled up to their shoulders, hair tousled. But later, things changed. He still looked very happy, but her smile was more forced. She looked thinner: one bikini shot revealed very thin thighs. She almost always wore sunglasses. He had his arms round her, but her arms were straight down by her side.

So the marriage had fallen apart, Martin thought. The new girlfriend looked uncannily like the ex-wife, but a bit younger. Had the brunette receptionist been a waypoint in his story?

And what was the story?

Reluctantly he called Michael and gave him the name of the man, and the name of the company. 'I've checked all his social media activities, and done a quick check on his company activities, and it all looks fine.'

'What do you want me to do, Martin?'

'I'm not sure. Maybe there's a link to something dodgy, but I can't see it.'

'I'll do a quick search, see what I come up with.'

Martin called Amanda.

'What did you get?'

'Nothing,' he said. 'The guy looks very happy with his new girlfriend. He was married but that obviously fell apart.'

'It turned into an abusive relationship, apparently.'

Martin thought of the photographs on Facebook. 'That figures. Nothing else looks odd, but there were some creepy photographs of a very young and very pretty brunette trainee receptionist at his company Rock Software and Design. Her name is Jasmine. I've no idea whether something happened there.'

'OK.' He could tell she was thinking about that. 'Anything else?'

'Nope. The company seems genuine. What were you thinking?'

'I don't know. The red-haired woman was murdered, and he's the main suspect.'

'Hmm. They looked very happy together. One of the selfies was just the other day. I can't imagine a happier-looking couple. She does look quite like his ex-wife, I have to say.'

Amanda said nothing.

'So what are you going to do?'

'I've no idea. I'm not on the investigation team. I don't know what I can do, Martin.'

Half an hour later, Michael phoned him back.

'Hi, Michael. What's up?'

'I – er – was wondering – ' Michael slid to a halt.

Martin frowned. Michael was usually clipped and concise on the phone, a bit like himself. 'Wondering what?'

'Can you ask Amanda to find out about somebody for me?'

This was unusual. 'Who – why?'

'His name is Freddy Morton, Martin. He's – eh – well, he's my mum's lover at the moment.'

'OK. Why do you want Amanda to check on him?'

'I think he's dealing in drugs.'

❧ 32 ❧

Pete McLeod phoned her as she sat in the small room by Reception in Clachdubh High School. 'Where are you, boss? Ramesh was asking. I said you were out chasing the Robertsons.'

She bit her lip and ducked the question. 'How did last night go?'

'I got pissed in Patterson's. It looked like there were a few deals going down in the toilets and out the back, but no sign of the Robertsons or any of the big players. Just low-lifes and students buying and selling. Duff info, I guess. I got chatting to one guy – name's Lighthouse because he's over five foot eight. Didn't get anything really. The ponytailed guy came in for a wee bit, chatted up the barmaid, then went off. I haven't been able to find Licker.'

'Right – thanks, Pete. Look, give me today and I'll get back on the job tomorrow. If Ramesh asks just cover for me – if it comes to it he can call me and I'll bluff it out.'

'So what exactly are you doing, boss?'

'I've no idea, Pete. There's something I can't put my finger on. I'll give it today in Clachdubh and then I'll just have to leave it.'

'You spoke to Paige?'

'Yes. The case against the boyfriend is pretty strong but it's not watertight and he's not confessing.'

'You got an alternative idea?'

'That's the trouble, Pete – I don't.' The school bell started ringing. 'Look, I better go.'

As the sound of the school bell died away, and the sounds of hundreds of school pupils surged and ebbed, Amanda wondered where she was going with all this, and how soon it would be before somebody put in a complaint about her.

She was here to speak to Mary again. She was still pursuing Rima Khalaf's iPhone.

Mary came in, suspicious and surly like one of her own disengaged pupils, and closed the door. She sat down, looking at Amanda.

After noting the lack of any greeting, Amanda said: 'I promise this is the last time I'll bother you, but I need to know some things. I've tracked down Rima Khalaf's phone – the Samsung, the one you had the number for. She left it in the house the day she died, and your housemate Diane took it. I assume you knew that.'

Mary looked like she might try to deny it, but her mouth twisted into something like a sneer and she said nothing.

'But Rima had another phone – an iPhone. Scott Anderson gave it to her so they could keep in touch. I need to know what happened to that phone.'

'I've no idea where it is.'

The words had come out in a rush, and Amanda couldn't be sure whether Mary was being honest. She moved on to the other line of questioning: 'You said she'd had an affair with a lecturer at Strathclyde.'

'Two affairs.'

'OK. Who was the second one with?'

Mary was reluctant, but she finally said: 'Dr Sinclair West. Chemistry department.'

Amanda noted that. 'Thank you. Now, tell me about Rima's writing.'

'I told you: she showed me some and I thought it was rubbish. She never showed it to me again.'

'She was in a writers' group in town. She must have spoken about some of them.'

A glowering silence.

'Come on. When you were all in the house and having a few drinks, the times when Scott Anderson couldn't get away from his wife to give Rima a seeing to. You must have spoken.'

'There was a guy Crawford who was hitting on her quite a bit.' The words were slow and stilted. 'She said he finally got the message.'

'Anyone else? A young kid?'

'Oh – Gary. Yeah, she said he was writing some historical porn epic, had sent extracts to her. She'd told him to get lost. Rima only really had time for Rima, and for anyone who could help her career. Gary works in Tesco, I think.'

Amanda nodded. This all told her nothing new, but it confirmed the picture of Rima's life.

'Why was Rima on the Rock that Saturday?'

'I don't know. Maybe she was out for a walk. Maybe the boyfriend had arranged to meet her and he didn't show up. I don't know. What does it matter? She's dead. She fell off the Rock and she's dead. That's it.'

Yes, thought Amanda. That's it indeed. So why was she wasting her time pursuing it?

'Do you know anything about a company called Rock Software and Design in town?'

Now Mary shifted in her seat and she crossed her arms, her eyes flicking away. 'No.'

'The owner is called Kevin Baker.'

'Don't know him.'

This sounded like an honest answer, so Amanda went back a step: 'But you know somebody who works there.' After allowing the pause, she went on: 'Did Rima know someone there?'

A shake of the head and a 'No' spoken firmly.

'So who do *you* know?'

'Just somebody.' She fidgeted and squirmed in her seat. 'It's difficult.'

'I should tell you that my colleagues will be investigating Rock Software and Design, so I suggest you get in the habit of telling all you know.'

'I can't.'

'You need to.'

'She was a pupil here. I could get in a lot of trouble.'

'Did you have a relationship with her when she was in school?'

'No – I didn't have a relationship with her at all. She was a tease

102

at school – gave me the come on from time to time. Gave everyone the come on. I ran into her in a pub one night, after she'd left school. I was pissed, depressed. I bought drinks for her and her pals. Her pals left and she stayed on, with me. She gave me the come on again, and I really thought she was interested in…trying that out. But it was all fake, just for a laugh. So nothing happened, but I could still get in trouble. She was eighteen, had left school, but the publicity – I could lose my job.' The confident, aggressively challenging young woman was suddenly looking very vulnerable.

'Tell me her name.'

Mary's face fell, and she wiped a tear from under one eye. 'Jasmine McCallum.'

'And is there anything more you want to tell me about Rima? Did she know Jasmine was leading you on?' *Jasmine*, she was thinking; the name had cropped up somewhere else. Martin had mentioned 'Jasmine' the day before – the trainee receptionist at Baker's office – but there was something else…

Mary's words were almost inaudible: 'One night Rima told me about her affair, and I told her that Jasmine had seemed quite interested in me and that I really fancied her.'

So, Amanda thought, Rima was a threat to Mary, and maybe that gave Mary a reason to give Rima a shove off that Rock. But had she?

But Jasmine needed following up. As did Dr Sinclair West. She checked her watch and grimaced. She had to get back to her proper work soon. She'd checked out of the hotel after breakfast, but she was strangely reluctant to leave Clachdubh for Glasgow.

❧ 33 ❦

Sitting in her car with her phone, Amanda found Dr Sinclair West on the Strathclyde University website staff list, and emailed him asking him to call her as soon as possible to arrange a meeting: *she needed his help.* She was deliberately vague about what, but she signed the email Detective Sergeant Amanda Pitt.

She'd been tempted to drive round past the crime scene and try to speak to DCI Paige again, to tell her what Martin had found out about the prime suspect Kevin Baker, but that would have been pointless: Paige would find out all of that for herself soon enough. But she followed signs to the business park, and found herself on a road in a collection of identical modern units. It wasn't hard to find Rock Software and Design: there was a police car outside.

Amanda stopped, turned, and drove away. She had to get back to Glasgow, back to work.

The bypass went round the north side of the Rock, and she couldn't help but imagine the impact of a body tumbling down and landing on the carriageway.

Her phone rang through the car's Bluetooth.

'Hi – is that Detective Sergeant Pitt?'

'Yes. Doctor West?'

'Yes.' His voice was Received Pronunciation, low and rich. She had almost expected him to be American with that name. 'You wanted to meet me. I'm strangely intrigued.'

'Yes. I'm on my way back to Glasgow. Can I meet you somewhere near the University?'

'Ah – yes – I suppose so. Can I ask what it's about?'

'It's in connection with a police enquiry. I'll tell you when we meet. It's quite a delicate matter.'

'Even more intriguing. My my. I'm free after five. I suggest we meet at five fifteen. Pub or cafe?'

'I'm driving and working, so either would do but I won't be drinking.'

'Ah well – you have to uphold the law, I suppose. Do you know Café George – on Cochrane Street, just east of George Square?'

'I'll find it. I'll meet you there at five fifteen. Do you still look like your official staff photograph?'

'I'm afraid I've aged a little since it was taken. But I should be recognisable.'

She found a space in the NCP on Montrose Street, and got to the café on time. She saw him in the queue ahead of her. She waited, watching him as he collected his drink. Very tall, slightly stooped, good physique. A handsome tanned face topped with close-cut silver hair. He wore a white jacket and jeans.

She waited to get served, seeing him checking his phone and replying to messages, and then she joined him at a tiny table by the window. 'Dr West?'

'Detective Sergeant Pitt? Splendid. Delighted to meet you.'

He wore a wedding ring, and she saw him glance at her fingers and register the lack of one there. Then his smile was turned up and he leaned slightly closer. 'Good health,' he said, and they clinked coffee cups. His eyes swept up and down what he could see of her as he lifted his cup to his lips.

'So, Detective Sergeant Pitt, what can I do for you?'

'Just Amanda will do.'

'Amanda.' He briefly touched her hand and the smile glowed. He had perfect, very white teeth.

'I'm working on an enquiry into the death of a young woman.' OK, she thought, it's almost true. 'You knew her when she was a chemistry student at Strathclyde. Rima Khalaf.'

The smile faded and the light dropped out of his eyes. He looked older suddenly. He held his coffee cup in front of his lips.

'I know you had an affair with her when she was a student.'

Now his face sagged. 'So what more can I tell you? You've just said it all.'

'You knew about her death last year?'

'I saw it on the news.'

'How did you feel?'

'How did I feel? What a strange question.'

'You were close. You had slept with her. How did you feel about her death?'

'I felt sad, of course. Sad for her family. She had a lot of potential.'

'Did part of you think she deserved to die?'

'What an extraordinary thing to say.'

Amanda looked into his eyes. 'Rima Khalaf used people. She slept with people in positions of power and influence to get on. She had an affair with a lecturer before you, she had one with a teacher at school, and she had one with her head of department where she was teaching. She used people, and when they were no more use to her, she moved on. You know she used you.'

His voice was resigned: 'Of course I do.' He took a long drink of his latte. 'She let me enjoy her young body, she made me feel young again – made me feel alive.' The light burned in his eyes again. 'And then, when she graduated, she was gone. She didn't return my calls. She never ended the relationship – she just...went.'

'Did you ever have other affairs with students?' She wasn't sure why she asked that: it was a potential distraction to the interview.

He grinned at her, and at that moment she decided she detested him. 'One or two, I confess. If it happened it happened – I never chased them, never put pressure on them. That sort of thing is frowned upon.'

'Did Rima Khalaf chase you?'

'She placed herself close to me, got my attention. And then one day, in my office, she was asking my advice about her project, and she was right next to me. Her right breast was pressing into my arm, I could feel her breath. We kissed, and then we – well, I almost said 'made love', but it was sex. We *fucked* on my carpet. Dangerous, unprotected fucking. It was fantastic. Her skin was so smooth, her body firm. She was a wildcat.'

Amanda pushed the mental picture away. 'What exactly did you do to help her in return for all that sex?'

He hesitated, pursing his lips. 'When she submitted projects and write-ups, I'd comment and then let her re-draft and re-submit. I'd give her ideas.' He shrugged. 'Nothing hugely unethical. I didn't actually write it for her. And I don't think we actually fucked that often, you know. But when we fucked, we really fucked. I remember one time – '

'You gave her a phone.' This was a shot in the dark.

He snapped away from his memory. 'She said she only had a crappy old pay-as-you-go mobile, and she really fancied an iPhone. So I bought her one, and she said it would always be so special because that would be the one I called her on when I had a chance to meet up with her.' His eyes flared and then dulled again. 'She kept it after she graduated.'

'Can you remember the number?'

'I still have it.' He opened his phone and found the number, then read it out to her, and she keyed it into a note on her own phone.

'When you tried to call her after she left, did it ring?'

'It rang and rang, but she never answered. After a time I gave up – I knew it was over.' He looked wistful now, and old and sad.

Amanda wanted to smash her coffee cup into his face. But Rima Khalaf had used *him*. And the bitch *had* had a third phone. For fuck sake.

She called Martin the following afternoon, when she had a break from normal work. 'I've got another line of enquiry,' she said. 'Another iPhone.'

'I'm tied up at work,' he said, 'but Michael said he'd be at the club this afternoon. He mentioned something about a phone too.'

Somewhere along the line there had been a tacit agreement that Michael would not contact Amanda directly; they would not have each other's mobile number. She felt that Michael was probably slightly paranoid about a police officer having his number.

She looked around at people working. Pete was out. 'I'll go over,' she said, and logged off her computer.

She negotiated the busy afternoon traffic out to the West End, and eventually found a meter.

She walked down the hill to Byres Road, and along and into Roasters, indicating to the young brunette girl – Taylor – that she was heading up to the hackers' club; Taylor clearly recognised her and just nodded. Amanda went through the door marked 'Staff Only' and up the open wooden staircase to the big room with its wooden tables and chairs.

The place was quiet. There were two lads who looked like students there, and an old white-bearded man helping with one of the 3D printers. 'This will take over an hour to print,' he was saying. 'Sure you've got the time?' The students nodded.

Michael was in the corner with his dual monitors. Amanda sat beside him, and he briefly registered her presence before minimising some of the windows on one screen.

'I have a phone number belonging to Rima Khalaf,' she said. 'Another one.'

He looked bemused.

'This is an iPhone which a previous lover gave her and which she kept once he was of no further use to her.' She opened the note on her phone and showed it to him.

He still looked bemused, and Amanda thought he murmured: 'It's different,' but that didn't make sense to her.

He clicked the mouse, and Amanda recognised the number

tracking website from the other day. She watched him type in the number Sinclair West had given her.

Michael turned to her briefly, then back to the screen. 'It isn't on.'

'Oh.' She thought about that. 'So it may have been destroyed.'

'Or jailbroken, set up with a new number. Or maybe the owner just keeps it switched off.'

Amanda frowned. Nobody switched their phone off, except when they were flying, and not even then any more. And it wouldn't simply be lying somewhere with a dead battery – not an iPhone. No. The phone Sinclair West had given Rima Khalaf was gone.

Michael was now typing something else.

She was reluctant to ask, because she knew she wouldn't understand the answer. 'What are you doing?'

'I'm writing a program in Python that will periodically scrape this website and check if there is any activity on the phone. It'll email me if there is. So we can detect the phone when it's switched on.'

'Oh. Right.' She watched him type until he sat back, satisfied with his work. 'Martin said something about you having a number…'

'Rima Khalaf took out a SIM-only contract seventeen months ago, with TalkTalk.'

She took a breath to ask how he knew that, then stopped herself. She watched Michael on the tracking website, typing in another number.

He sat back. 'Here we go. We've only got cell tower location, so it's not very precise. And it seems to be away from the city, so the cells are larger.'

He zoomed the map out. The location was Clachdubh, around the business park on the edge of town. Amanda stared at the screen, trying to work out a logical explanation.

'Can you find out anything about the phone?'

He shook his head.

She looked at the map on the monitor and tried to think of her options, tried to line up the facts. Rima's own phone had been taken by the housemate Diane, to Aberdeen. The iPhone from her university lover was gone. The one from her lover at the school was unknown, but maybe this was it, somehow. Were there any others?

If this had been a legitimate enquiry, Amanda could have got the phone records: she knew the name and at least one of the person's numbers. But it wasn't.

She'd gone to Aberdeen to find that first phone, believing it would lead to some kind of breakthrough for her, but that had turned out to be a complete waste of time. She'd just come back from Clachdubh the previous afternoon – could she face driving up there again?

They sat in silence for a minute, and tiredness tugged at her. Could she really drive up to Clachdubh on what would in all probability be a dead end, like the Aberdeen trip had been? She tried to control a yawn.

'You could try calling it,' Michael said, with a shrug, as if sensing her dilemma.

She prevaricated, trying to think. Would the person with Rima's phone know she was dead? Yes, of course they would – they were in Clachdubh.

So she stepped away from Michael into another corner of that big room, and dialled the number. A cautious female voice, that sounded young, said: 'Hello?'

Amanda put on a breathy salesperson voice. 'Hello, is that Miss Rima Khalaf? This is Amanda from Vodafone here.' She saw Michael frowning across as he typed at his keyboard.

'I'm not on a contract. I'm pay-as-you-go.'

She hadn't denied she was Rima. She knew she was using Rima's phone.

Amanda gave a light laugh. 'Yes of course, you haven't been with us for a few years. But we're wondering whether we could tempt you back. We've got some fantastic deals on the new iPhone at the moment, or one of the Androids. Fantastic deals.'

'Eh – no – sorry.'

'No worries, Miss Khalaf. Now, if you could just bear with me for a couple of seconds, I'd like to just check we've got your details right.'

'Eh – why?'

'Just for our records, Miss Khalaf. So it's Rima – ' she spelt it – 'Khalaf – ' and spelt that too.

'Eh – yes – '

'And you work at Clachdubh High School, is that correct?'

'Eh – yes – yes, that's right.'

'And your home address is – ' Amanda made up a street and number.

'Yes, that's right.'

'Fine.' Amanda had reached the end of the line with her fiction. She dropped the singsong tele-sales voice and used her flat bad-cop one. 'What's your real name?'

'What do you mean?' There was a tremble there.

'You're not Rima Khalaf. Rima Khalaf is dead.'

'Oh fuck – oh god. Who *are* you?'

'You don't want to know.' She responded to Michael's concerned look from across the room with a smile. 'What's your real name?'

'My name is Jasmine. Jasmine McCallum.'

'And where do you work, Jasmine?' Jasmine!

'I'm on reception at Rock Software and Design in Clachdubh. I've not long left school.' The voice was close to tears. She sounded very young now.

'And how did you get this phone?'

'I found it.'

'Really?' Amanda loaded her voice with sarcasm.

'Really. Honestly. You've got to believe me. I found it.'

'When did you find it, Jasmine?'

She hesitated. 'Couple of months ago.'

Amanda didn't believe this at all. 'Look, Jasmine. I need to have a look at that phone. I'm a police officer.' She carried on talking over the sobs. 'You might just avoid getting into serious trouble if you give me that phone.'

'I've got twenty pounds credit on it!' she wailed.

Amanda sighed. 'I'll pay you back. Now, I'm going to drive up to Clachdubh right now. Where can I meet you? I assume you don't want the police turning up at your house or at your work. It'll take me a couple of hours to get there.'

'Just come to my house – mum's out tonight. Phone me when you get here and I'll come out. Thirteen Portal Road.'

'And I'm not driving all that way for a pack of lies, Jasmine. I want the truth when I get there.'

The voice was a sob modulated by a whisper. 'Yes. I promise.' Amanda hung up. 'Thanks, Michael.'

He seemed to be about to say something to her, but didn't as she stood up and left.

❧ 35 ❧

It has been a month since I slew the woman Rebecca, the one who had stolen my heart and betrayed me before I could win her body. I should be content: I had her. I had her as she breathed her last.

I have her jewelled ring as a memento of that day, and I look at it every night, remembering.

I should be content, but she is lost to me now…

'Gary! You up there?'

He jumped, then quickly saved and closed the file, and the private browsing window behind it, and put the computer to sleep.

'Hi Dad!' he shouted back. He stood up, realising he was shaking slightly. His face reflected in the mirror as he stood up, and he could see he looked pale.

He headed downstairs to see his father opening a can of beer and switching on the TV.

'I thought you were out all night,' Gary said. He stood fidgeting, restless, then sat down on the sofa.

His father clicked channels. 'Fuckin switch in shift patterns. Three on and three off.' He shook his head. 'Fuckin three weeks,' he muttered. He flicked past a news channel, cutting off a report about a murder in Scotland. He looked up at Gary. 'You eaten, son?'

'Aye. Got a lasagne from work. You?'

'Naw. I'll get chips later. You OK?'

Gary shivered. 'I'm just cold. Can I put the fire on?'

'Go and put your jumper on.'

'Cannae find it.' Gary crouched and put on the gas fire, then stood in front of it.

'What dae ye mean ye cannae find it?'

'Lost it.'

'Where?'

'Don't know.'

That'll have to do for now, he thought. He'd get himself some new clothes from work when they changed seasons. And trousers and trainers. He'd had to throw them out after that morning, biking out to the recycling centre and throwing the bag into the landfill skip.

He sat back down on the sofa, watching as some fantasy swords and sorcery drama played out on the screen and he thought about his own novel. The hero couldn't go on like this in his story. He needed to find happiness and salvation. Rebecca hadn't worked out obviously, but someone would come along.

As those initial hours of panic left him, he thought of the experience, how it would feed into his writing. The smell, he thought; that overpowering smell of blood.

He watched the TV as two handmaidens undressed each other and started to kiss and caress. His dad was clearly aroused by this, but Gary thought it tame. There were much better lesbian scenes on the Internet. Much better scenes of every kind of sex on the Internet.

But the very best was inside his head.

❧ 36 ❧

Jamil lay on his bed with a roll-up dangling loosely from his lips, his eyes half-closed against the smoke. One arm was behind his head, the other raising a long knife towards the ceiling.

He was alone in the house, as ever. His mother was out at her cleaning job at the local primary school. Later she'd be at her cleaning job at the veterinary practice. And tomorrow she would be out with the agency, cleaning people's houses.

She never spoke of Jamil's father, and he couldn't remember ever having one. They never saw any aunts or uncles or grandparents, and she never spoke of them. He was alone in the world, and that suited him just fine.

He made pretend cutting strokes with the knife, then stabbing motions.

With this knife, the warrior brings death, he thought. The

message from B was promising: 'Soon, brother.'

He hoped so. Rose was ignoring his messages, or maybe she had blocked him. On Saturday he'd bumped into Jasmine in the Co-op with Jill: Jill had totally blanked him, but Jasmine had given him a curious look. Maybe she fancied some rough, he thought. He'd got a feel of her tits that one time, when he'd given her the iPhone – he could remember every detail…

He felt angry and frustrated. He swished with the long knife again.

Soon, brother.

✿ 37 ✿

On the journey back to Clachdubh, Amanda called Joan at the Rock View hotel and found she could get a room for the night – in fact, the same one she'd been in before was available. She could have driven back to Glasgow after seeing Jasmine McCallum, but this would give her another opportunity to get near to Paige, ask more about the enquiry.

She phoned Pete to say she'd not be able to catch up with him that evening, wouldn't be able to help with the surveillance on Patterson's Bar.

'Is my beer on expenses, boss?'

'You can try it, Pete.'

Finally, as her SatNav led her through a neat council estate in Clachdubh, she called Jasmine. 'I'm just pulling up outside your house now.'

She kept the engine running and saw a rectangle of light, and a slim figure trot down the path. Jasmine got in the car. Amanda noticed the short shift dress and leggings, and the make-up.

'Where can we go?'

'There's a pub I know. I'll show you. Left at the end there.'

Jasmine seemed much more relaxed and confident than she had been during the phone call, and Amanda wondered what had caused this.

'Oooh – I like this one.' Jasmine reached to turn up the car radio, and started doing a little dance as she sat there, her arms waving.

She's pissed, Amanda thought.

The pub was on the edge of town, a bland cuboidal slab of harled concrete. The car park was empty apart from a pimped-up Corsa and a couple of other old cars, but the large open lounge bar had around twenty people in it, many gathered round a pool table at the far end. TV screens covered the walls.

'Vodka and tonic for me,' Jasmine said, and skipped off to an empty table, eyes following her, then switching to Amanda, and back to Jasmine.

The young barman didn't blink when Amanda ordered the vodka and tonic and a coke. She wondered whether he knew Jasmine and that she was over eighteen, or whether he didn't care.

Amanda went over to the table where Jasmine sat almost twitching, her fingers tapping the arms of her chair.

'Is this where you came with your ex-teacher Mary Liston?' Amanda asked.

Jasmine almost flinched, then turned it into a grin. She crossed her thighs and leaned forward. 'Yeah. Liston the lezzer. She was hot for me all right.'

Amanda wanted to go down that road, tell Jasmine she was a manipulative bitch who could have cost Mary her job, but she had a bigger agenda.

'Do you enjoy working at Rock Software?' Amanda asked.

Jasmine took a drink of her vodka, and then stared at the glass and the condensation running down. 'Yeah. Suppose. I'm trying to get into modelling.' She sat upright, arching her back, then slumped a little. 'But I haven't got anywhere.' His eyes stared, unfocused, and Amanda wondered what she was thinking.

'So, tell me about Rima Khalaf. Did you know her at school?'

'Yeah, I saw her around. Wasn't in any of her classes, though. Didn't ever speak to her.'

'Could I have her phone now please?' Amanda held out her hand.

Jasmine pulled it from a pocket in her dress and handed it over with a show of reluctance and a sigh. 'I've got thirty pounds credit on it.'

'You said twenty earlier.'

'I made a mistake.'

Amanda looked at the iPhone: she didn't know enough to guess at the exact model, but the case was a bit scratched, so it was older. 'Tell me how you got your hands on it.'

'This guy I know. Got talking to him in here – he was chatting me up, fancied his chances. As if. Offered me the phone – said he'd bought it cheap off someone and I could have it if I gave him a kiss. I said fair enough. He felt my tits during the kiss, of course, but an iPhone's an iPhone, yeah? I didn't let him go any further.'

'And the name of this guy?'

'Jam – Jammy – Jimmy. Honestly, that's all I know. I only ever saw him in here. And he's not been in for months now.'

And the guy 'Jimmy' had bought the phone from would similarly be only known by a first name and would likewise be long gone. Amanda looked round the pub, at the old men playing dominoes, the young guys playing pool, the loners sitting at the bar nursing a half-finished pint of lager. She didn't fancy quizzing them all about 'Jimmy'.

'When was this?'

'Oh – about a year ago.'

This sounded true. 'When you were still at school?' Before Rima Khalaf's death? Or just after.

'Yeah.'

'So what state was the phone in?'

'Well it was locked, wasn't it. Bastard didn't know the passcode.'

'So what did you do?'

'I was in Glasgow one weekend, with my mates. Went into a shop. Guy unlocked it.'

'Clever. So what's your PIN now?'

'4444.'

'Genius.' Amanda thumbed that in and the phone opened. She looked in the call history, showing the phone to Jasmine.

'Those are all my calls,' Jasmine said.

'OK.' She looked at contacts and scrolled down.

'Those are my contacts.'

And into emails.

'Those are all my emails.'

'So when this guy unlocked the iPhone…'

'It wiped everything on it.' Jasmine shrugged, wide-eyed, and finished her drink. 'I just do top-ups.'

Amanda stared at the phone, angry with it. Another wasted

journey. Unless Michael could do something with it.

She looked at Jasmine. 'Look, you knew this phone belonged to Rima Khalaf. So how did your pal Jimmy find it? How did he explain it to you?'

'He just said he found it.' She shrugged.

'He didn't explain exactly where he found it?'

Jasmine was wide-eyed, painting a picture of innocence. 'No.'

Amanda knew Jasmine was lying to her, was missing out things. Jasmine knew that the phone had belonged to Rima Khalaf so she knew exactly how this mate of 'Jimmy' had got it. But she couldn't see a way in, and she shouldn't be here in the first place. 'I need to take this phone away with me. Can you survive without it?'

'Suppose. I've got my old crappy Sony in a drawer.'

'I'll make sure I don't lose any of your stuff.' Actually she didn't care whether it was lost or not.

'OK.' Jasmine was staring at her empty glass. She looked up at Amanda, who shook her head.

'I'm taking you home.'

As she drove, she remembered where she'd seen the name Jasmine before. 'You were around when that schoolgirl fell off the Rock. Karen.'

'Yeah.'

'Did you know her?'

'Yeah.'

'Were you at the party on the Rock?'

'Yeah.' Jasmine was looking away now, out of the side window, subdued.

'Shame.'

'Yeah.'

'Do you know Gary as well?'

Jasmine turned to look at her. 'Gary? What about him?'

'He was there.'

'Loads of us were there. The whole fourth year was there.'

'You have much to do with Gary?'

Jasmine snorted. 'He's weird. He stares at you, you know? Trying to look up your skirt when you're sitting down, or down your top. He watches a lot of porn, and he writes stuff too.' She sniffed. 'He works in Tesco.' She said that like it was the most demeaning thing about him. 'I wind him up now and again, give

116

him a pretend come on. He's weird.'

'The teacher Rima Khalaf – she was heavily into Muslim history, wasn't she?'

'I heard that. My pals thought it was boring. Danny's mum came up to complain she was doing too much of that stuff, wasting his time.'

'What did your pals think of her?'

'Couple of the boys were hot for her. As if.'

'Was there anybody who was really interested in what she had to say? Anyone who got worked up about it?'

'I suppose.'

'Who?'

She hesitated. 'Jamil. Jamil Sabry.' She looked away, and Amanda could feel the tension in her.

'I take it his family is Muslim.'

'Yeah.'

'Do you know where he lives?'

'Number seventeen in my street.'

They pulled up at Jasmine's house and she held the door handle. 'Have you been interviewed about Kevin Baker?' Amanda asked. Jasmine nodded.

'Did he ever try it on with you?'

There was a fractional tightening of her jaw muscles and then the door handle was pulled and she was out of the car and away. Amanda watched her walk up the path like she was on a catwalk, short dress swinging. Amanda drove slowly further down the road, past Jamil Sabry's house – realising she should have got the parents' names.

Jamil. Jammy. He was Jasmine's 'Jimmy'. And if he had found Rima's iPhone, then where…

Amanda felt cold suddenly. Had he found it where Rima Khalaf had dropped it – on the Rock, just as she'd fallen over? Or had he grabbed it from her and pushed her over. Or fought with her over it and she'd overbalanced and fallen. Jamil Sabry.

She parked at the Rock View Hotel and phoned Martin to tell him what Jasmine had told her.

'Yeah, unlocking erases all the data – which is what you would want, otherwise what's the point of having a PIN in the first place? In the movies they guess the password or bypass it. All rubbish. Even Apple can't get into it, though the FBI are pushing for software changes to give them a back door, and they claim to have managed to get data from terrorist iPhones. Touch ID is better security, of course, because – '

'Is there anything I can do?'

'Is there a backup?'

'Where would that be?'

'Either on iCloud – and you'd need the password to log into that – or in iTunes on that laptop, which might need a password too if it's encrypted. Or it could be somewhere else.'

'Can you check?'

He didn't suppress his sigh. 'Will do. Oh – before you go, Michael wants a favour from you.'

'Michael wants a favour from *me*? What kind of favour?' And why hadn't he mentioned this earlier?

'Apparently his mum has hitched up with some guy called Freddy Morton and Michael obviously doesn't like him. He wants you to check on him.'

'That sort of thing is very much frowned on, Martin. Lots of officers have got into trouble for using police resources to check on potential partners or their daughters' boyfriends.'

'Hmm.'

'So is Michael worried about this Freddy Morton for any particular reason?' She thought back to earlier, when Michael had been about to speak to her.

'Michael thinks he's dealing drugs.'

'Ah. That's different.'

↢ 38 ↣

Joan's chef at the Rock View had gone home, and the best Joan could offer Amanda was the carryout menu from the local Indian.

'They'll deliver by taxi if you want – it's just four pounds extra.'

Amanda felt exhausted suddenly and couldn't be bothered going out to try to find the place, so she phoned them and asked for a delivery. She couldn't even be bothered reading the menu Joan had for them, so she went for the classic: 'Chicken tikka masala, rice, one chapati.'

'Twenty minutes.'

She yawned and sat in the lounge of the hotel. Joan brought her own glass of wine in and poured one for Amanda. 'I hate to drink alone.'

Amanda raised her eyebrows at that, but accepted the glass. 'So what's been happening?' She sensed Joan was desperate to talk to her.

'Well!' Joan sat beside her. 'They've been all over that house all week, taking away boxes and boxes, and a computer.'

'And what's the up-to-date gossip about the boyfriend?'

'He beat up his ex-wife. Nearly killed her. So this isn't a surprise.'

Joan prattled on about the theories about Kevin Baker's private life and his relationships, until the doorbell rang and the taxi delivered Amanda's curry.

She ate it in the dining room – which was already set up for breakfast – and Joan continued with her theories. Amanda was only spared when DCI Paige and her DI arrived back, both looking more drawn and exhausted than before. Joan asked if they wanted anything. 'Pot of tea, please.' Joan slipped away.

'What are you doing back?' Paige asked Amanda, tiredness probably making it sound more aggressive than she'd meant to.

'The girl Rima Khalaf.' Amanda tidied up the remnants of her curry, and they all moved through to the lounge. Joan appeared with a tray, and set out the pot of tea and the cups, milk and sugar.

'Thank you,' Paige said, and waited pointedly until Joan had closed the door behind her.

'What about the Khalaf girl? Sugar?'

Amanda and the DI shook their heads. Paige spooned sugar into her own cup and stirred it.

'I'm checking on her phones. She had three phones, apparently.'

Paige frowned at her. 'Three phones?'

'Two of her married lovers gave her iPhones. I've traced one but can't find the other. She also had a Samsung, which I've traced.'

'And have these yielded any useful evidence?'

'No,' Amanda said. 'No they haven't.'

'Why would you have three phones?' the DI was saying. 'Why did they give her phones?'

'Presents. Rewards for great sex? Useful for the lovers too.' She remembered what Scott Anderson had said now: he'd primarily

119

bought Rima the iPhone because she'd lost a previous one…in fact he'd said it had been stolen. So had Jamil stolen it from her? Nothing to do with her death on the Rock at all? No, the timing didn't work…

Her own mobile rang at that moment, and she excused herself. She stood outside the lounge, by the front door. 'Martin, hi.'

'Hi. Michael says there is one iPhone backup in iTunes on the MacBook, but the settings say it is encrypted, so no use. And it's dated five months before her death, so probably no use to you anyway. He's tried to log onto iCloud but it's asking for her password – which we don't have.'

'So it's a dead-end.'

'Not necessarily. There is some data which has been synced with iTunes separately from the complete backup – he might get something there: he's exploring.'

Total waste of time, she was thinking. Why couldn't these tech geniuses just crack things? Why was it so hard in real life? 'OK, thanks, Martin. Will Michael be at your club tomorrow evening?'

'Should be.'

She put her phone in her trouser pocket, and went back into the lounge where Paige and the DI were muttering together.

'How's it going with your murder, ma'am?' She sat down and drank the last of the wine Joan had poured for her earlier. Paige was yawning, and it was infectious.

'Still looking at forensics. There are a couple of footprints down the side of the house, and we've lifted recent fingerprints from the back door handle, which don't match the boyfriend. That could be anybody and is not suspicious in itself. But it's a loose end, and the defence could use it if we don't explain where it came from.'

'How about your blood spatter?'

'We're not really worried about that now: death was caused by a single stab wound that penetrated the heart – possibly not intended to kill her at all. So there is technically no need for there to be any cast-off, but it gives the defence another opening. I'm sure it's him, but the case could fall apart on us if we're not careful.'

'And he's not confessing.'

'No – he's weeping and wailing, and I have to say that if he's lying he's the best liar I've ever come across.' She gave a sigh, and it turned into another yawn.

'How about his ex-wife?' Amanda asked.

The DI shook her head. 'Not as good as we thought. She says the marriage just fell apart. She could see it happening. She says that with hindsight she was happy for it to end: she just didn't love him any more. But he couldn't accept it, and he kept fighting. Her divorce story about the cruelty isn't really true – though the final assault is. She looks very like Kirstin Grainger, I have to say.'

Paige nodded and smiled grimly.

'So did the wife have an affair?' Amanda guessed.

The DI gave an ambiguous twisted grin. 'Yes she did, and our man flipped and hit her. She then went on to build the case of cruel and unusual behaviour stretching back over some years, and took out a restraining order. This was all down in London. She's told us now that he wasn't normally violent: he just flipped. She feels sad about how she treated him.'

'Poor guy.'

Paige gave her a warning look. 'That doesn't make him innocent of this murder.'

The DI added: 'And if there was any sign that history was about to repeat itself, then he might very well have flipped again.'

'And was there any sign of history about to repeat itself?' Amanda asked.

Paige and the DI exchanged glances. 'No,' they both said at the same time.

From her room, Amanda phoned Claire to say goodnight and apologise for another night away from her, and then phoned Pete. He didn't answer – which she'd expected, because it was late by now – so she left a message: anyone mentioning someone called Freddy Morton?

❧ 39 ❧

She left Clachdubh very early in the morning, skipping breakfast. She hadn't slept well. In her dreams Paige's case kept overlapping with her own. She'd forgotten to ask whether they'd investigated Gary McAllister any further, but she assumed Paige would have checked anything and everything: she was nothing if not thorough.

Amanda drove back down to Glasgow, hitting the morning

rush hour. She phoned Claire as she sat in traffic, edging forward, cursing the people who deliberately took the wrong lane and then forced themselves in at the head of the queue. Everything was fine with Claire and work. Martin was in the process of appointing an operational manager to take some of the load off him. He'd be 'more strategic'. Amanda guessed that would mean he would simply do less work, but why not.

She arrived at Stewart Street police station in time for a case conference with Ramesh and Pete on the Robertson brothers. As she desperately tried to catch up with events that she was supposed to know all about, Ramesh said that there was intelligence from OCCTU about 'big consignments of ecstasy' becoming available soon, and he reckoned the Robertsons would almost certainly have booked a slice – confirming what Pete had heard. They were being asked to keep up casual questioning of contacts – anybody – and try to glean absolutely any information. All over the city, local CID were doing the same, feeding it all back to OCCTU.

'Won't the Robertsons be alerted by all this activity?' Amanda asked.

Ramesh pursed his lips. 'Be very discreet.' He looked at Pete. 'As discreet as you can be.'

So Amanda and Pete headed out into the mild day and knocked on some doors, and visited some café. As more and more pubs opened, they went in there, talking to people they'd come across professionally in the past.

It quickly became obvious that the intelligence was accurate: supplies were expected that weekend. A few with previous cautions for possession said that things had been tight just at the moment but were going to pick up 'soon'. One or two mentioned that people were going around with wads of cash, ready to buy.

Answers to questions about where the supplies were coming from separated into two strands: one that it was coming in from abroad, and two that 'abroad' meant England, where it was being manufactured.

Amanda and Pete decided to take a break from late afternoon till late on in the evening, and then visit some more pubs and clubs and see what they got. Pete went home, and Amanda went to Byres Road and Roasters, with the iPhone she'd got from

Jasmine in her handbag.

Michael wasn't there, so she went back downstairs to get herself a latte and a panini by way of dinner. She called Claire from the queue, apologising yet again for a no show. She took the latte and panini upstairs.

She sat watching the teenagers, the three old men and the schoolteacher working away, building circuits, 3D printing something or other, tweaking the program for their little wheeled robot.

There was a sudden gasp and a cheer as four circles of multi-coloured light sprang up, the colours changing and spinning and flashing. Amanda couldn't help but grin.

Michael arrived carrying a man-bag. He walked past Amanda – he must have seen her but gave no acknowledgement – and sat down at his computer, switching it on and putting in the password. Then he took Rima Khalaf's MacBook from his man-bag and laid it on the table.

'Have you got the iPhone?' he asked, still not looking at her.

Amanda thought he looked tired, jaded, distracted. He was normally focussed, but today he was different. Something was bothering him. She suspected it was his mother's boyfriend, Freddy Morton.

'Here it is.' She handed it over. 'It would be polite to take the data off it, I suppose, in case you accidentally wipe anything.'

She watched while Michael attached the phone to his computer, and opened a terminal window. He started typing, waited while text and numbers filled the window, then typed some more.

This went on for ten minutes, while Amanda drank her cooling latte and ate her panini, until he finally sat back. 'I can see the stuff on the phone, but there's nothing remotely relevant. Is this some schoolgirl who has it now?'

'Yes,' Amanda says. 'Well, just left school.'

'She likes taking selfies.'

He showed her some of the pictures from the iPhone: all of Jasmine, some with other people, and a couple of them showing her smiling with an older man – late thirties, maybe – very handsome and well-groomed. Amanda peered, trying to make out more of the background of the photo. It looked like a room in a house, and there seemed to be a camera on a tripod.

She heard footsteps behind her, and Martin McGregor was there, wearing his suit. 'How's it going? Found anything interesting?' He pointed at the monitor. 'Ah – Jasmine and Kevin Baker?'

So that was Kevin Baker. Why was Jasmine in a room with Kevin Baker? She couldn't make sense of that. 'We've found nothing,' she said.

'What were you expecting to find?'

'I don't know.'

'The backup is encrypted,' Michael said. 'I can see some pictures in iTunes, but no texts.'

'Any suspicious apps?'

Michael said: 'Only WhatsApp.'

Amanda turned to look at Martin. He said: 'Loads of people use WhatsApp, of course, but it is encrypted end to end, so bad people like it.'

'But Rima Khalaf wasn't a bad person.'

Martin merely gave a shrug. 'We'll never know.'

Amanda was tired, and feeling angry and frustrated. She'd gone to great lengths to get her hands on these phones, but she'd found out nothing. Nothing at all. Her fists clenched.

'Anything from Twitter or Facebook?' Martin asked.

Michael shook his head.

'The girl who had this phone mentioned a name: Jamil Sabry. She wasn't happy talking about him.'

'Who is he?' Martin asked.

'He was at school with her – he'd still be a teenager.'

Martin looked at Michael. 'Can you do anything with this?'

Michael nodded. 'I'll try. Unlikely.' He got Amanda to make a guess at the spelling for him, but didn't write it down.

Amanda looked at her watch. 'I need to contact Mrs Khalaf again.'

Martin in turn looked at his watch. 'I need to go.'

Her mobile rang: Pete. 'Where are you, boss?'

'I'm on Byres Road in a café'

'I'm in Patterson's bar – across the road. Can you get over here?'

'I'm coming, I'm coming.'

She realised Martin had gone, and Michael was looking at the floor by her feet. She looked down, saw nothing, then made to stand up.

'Amanda,' he said.

She halted. 'Yes?'

'Did Martin talk to you about…?'

'Yes he did,' she said. 'I said I'll see what I can find out.'

He nodded, and went back to his computer and started typing again.

She found Pete in Patterson's, said hi and went up to the bar to get him a pint and herself a coke. The barmaid turned out to be Taylor, the girl who also worked in Roasters during the day.

'Hiya,' the girl said in her broad Glasgow accent. 'Huvnae seen you in here before.' But her glance across at Pete told that she recognised him.

Amanda froze and then thought fast. Very fast. This girl had seen her in that room above Roasters with Martin and Michael. Had anything been said when she had been around? Any mention of police work? Did she have suspicions about Pete? Had she overheard any chat in Roasters? Sometimes she materialised out of nowhere…had she *seen* anything?

She unfroze. 'No, I've never been in here before,' she said, giving a laugh. 'I live on the south side. But my boss lives on Hyndland Road.' She leaned forward, whispering: 'He's trying it on, but he's wasting his time. That's why I'm sticking to coke.'

Taylor gave a grin. Amanda thought she really was very pretty when she smiled.

Amanda took the drinks across to the table, and spoke softly into Pete's ear: 'You're my boss, trying to get into my pants. I'll explain later.'

Pete smiled, and leaned closer to her, putting his arm round the back of the bench seat behind her and reaching a hand under the table.

She smiled back at him. 'Touch me and you're a dead man.'

He gave a soft mocking laugh.

Nothing seemed to be going on in the pub that evening, so they drank their drinks and got up to go. Amanda gave Taylor a mock grimace as they turned towards the door. A man was coming in and he held the door open for them. 'Thank you.'

They walked up to where Amanda had parked.

'She works in Roasters during the day,' Amanda said, pointing to the café 'The barmaid – Taylor. She's seen me there before.'

'And she's seen me in Patterson's before,' Pete said. 'Shit. Do you think she's suspicious?'

'I'll talk to her when I see her next.' Shit indeed, she agreed: she hoped they hadn't screwed up the surveillance operation.

'That guy who came in as we were leaving, the guy with the ponytail? He does the dealing and Taylor tips him off about customers who are asking. His name is Freddy Morton, the name you were asking about.'

'Freddy Morton,' she repeated, looking back at the pub door.

'How did you get his name?'

'Someone mentioned it to me.' She smiled at Pete to reassure him. 'Can't remember who.'

'We need to log it.'

'I'll do that.'

❧ 40 ❧

Friday morning they met with Ramesh in his office.

'The general consensus is that people are being told "get back to me on Sunday"', he said, 'so the guess is that a supply is coming in on Saturday – tomorrow. Just how, when, where from and where to…well, I don't know, and I don't know whether anyone knows, but several people are confirming Manchester. OCCTU is linking to HMRC, NCA and the Met.'

Pete and Amanda looked at him, trying to think what they might do, or be asked to do.

'They're looking at previous patterns, known vehicles, all the usual.' Ramesh leaned forward across the desk. 'We're all assuming the Robertsons are buying a chunk of this shipment and bringing it to Glasgow. You two know the Robertsons. So go and get yourselves a supply of coffee and sit in a dark room for two hours and come back to me with your best guesses on how it would be organised to bring it to them.' He glowered. 'I know you can do this.'

They didn't sit in a dark room: they went out, down to Buchanan Galleries and sat in the Costa on the ground floor there, watching the people on the long escalators and keeping well away from anyone else. They talked in quiet voices, brainstorming.

'Do they own a private aircraft?' 'No!' 'Do they know someone who does?' 'Not sure.' 'Boats?' 'Maybe. Trucks?' 'Van hire?'

After two lattes, they went back to Stewart Street with a to-do list, and sat at their computers. They searched and talked and searched again. Finally they went in to see Ramesh.

'Andy Robertson is linked to Hugh Johnson, who runs a van hire business in East Kilbride.'

Ramesh waited for more but it didn't come. 'Is that it?'

'It's our best guess,' Amanda said. 'In fact, it's our only guess.'

'OK. What size of van would they need?'

'Depends how much is coming. A big van gives scope for concealment amongst other merchandise, a small van is nippier.'

Ramesh pointed at Pete. 'Call them and ask what their availability is for the weekend, what different sizes they have. See what happens. Don't actually book anything though.'

Amanda sat by Pete as he dialled from his mobile, withholding his number, and she listened to his vague conversation. He was thinking of a big van – any available? The weekend? Plenty. Not sure about driving it though – would a wee one be better maybe? Two of them? I've got a mate – he could drive one. Nothing really Saturday or Sunday? OK. I'll think about the big one and get back to you.

Ramesh was impressed. 'I'm impressed, Pete,' he said. 'I'll pass this back and see if it's any use.'

'Pete came across a name,' Amanda said. 'We've checked our files but there's nothing. Freddy Morton.'

Ramesh frowned at Pete. 'You think he's big?'

Pete frowned back at Ramesh and at Amanda. 'He's doing little deals in Patterson's on Byres Road, selling Es and grass to students and locals. I don't think he's – '

Amanda interrupted him: 'But we wondered whether HMRC or NCA or the Met had him on a list anywhere.'

Ramesh shrugged and nodded. 'I'll ask.'

Amanda and Pete went back to their desks and sat looking at Google maps on their respective computers. If the drug shipment *was* coming from Manchester, the empty vans would most likely traverse from East Kilbride to the M74 and down, and then similarly coming back.

'Though they might turn off at Dumfries and go the back roads coming up,' Pete suggested.

And then they played a game of bluff and counter bluff. 'They would expect the police to think they were going the back roads, so they'll stick to the M74.' 'But they'll expect us to work that out, so they'll go the back roads after all.' And so on.

'The motorway cameras will track them there anyway,' Pete said. 'We'll need cars at the border.'

'And the cops in Manchester better be ready.'

'If that's where they're really going.'

Ramesh called them in. 'We're being asked to supply a surveillance team for the car hire place.' He pointed at the two of them.

'Isn't that risky?' Amanda asked.

He pondered that. 'OK, could you monitor the exits from East Kilbride?'

Amanda sensed Pete suppressing laughter, and quickly said: 'There are dozens of routes out of East Kilbride, sir. We can't possibly monitor them.'

'What's the most likely route, then?'

Amanda turned to Pete, who said: 'Probably A726 and cut across at some point. But they might go up on the A725 and over to get to the motorway faster. Or their sat nav might have some crazy idea about a cross country trip.'

Ramesh sniffed. 'OK – you'll operate surveillance on the van hire business from early tomorrow morning. You'll need to check the place out this evening and plan the deployment of your team.'

Amanda did a double take: it was 'her' team now? 'How big is my team, sir?'

'Four.' When she nodded, he added: 'Plus you two.' He looked down at his desk, then back up at them: 'Plus our surveillance teams on the way down, and our English colleagues in Manchester.' After allowing a short silence, he finished with: 'It's a big team in total. Off you go.'

Amanda and Pete shut down their computers and left the police station, planning to check out the van hire place now and then simply go home. So they both took their cars to East Kilbride.

They negotiated the million roundabouts and the rush hour, and finally parked at the big shopping centre just off Queensway. The air was cold and damp as they walked down. There was low-rise social housing on the other side of the dual carriageway, and some businesses tucked away behind trees on their side.

Pete looked around and sniffed. 'Nearly ended up living here,' he said.

She didn't know the place at all, and was careful to avoid any clichéd views about Scottish new towns and the attempt to clear the overcrowded Glasgow slums: those attempts hadn't been thought through properly, and had often given rise to bigger problems than the ones they'd claimed to solve.

'The original village is still here – ' he turned as he walked, looking round – 'somewhere. Like the Monty.' In answer to her frown he said: 'Montgomerie Arms. Pub.'

'Naturally.'

They loitered near a small queue at a bus stop, keeping up their pretence of just looking round. They could see Easy Wheels Car and Van Hire beyond the trees: a sign and a gate with white vans parked beyond. But nothing else.

'We'll need to do a drive by,' Amanda said, as they headed back to the shopping centre.

'Looking for what?'

'Somewhere we can park and see vans coming out, get their registrations. We need two cars here, on top of them, because once they're out and onto these roundabouts, they're gone. We'll use the team in shifts for forty-eight hours.'

'All four of us.'

There wasn't really anywhere suitable for surveillance. The access road that ran parallel to the Queensway was double yellows, so any vehicle parking there would look very suspicious, especially when no police turned up to move it on. There was a small group of offices with its own car park, and the only solution was to ask permission and park there tomorrow. It was almost empty now, and they identified an angled parking bay that would show anybody coming from the van hire. The shopping centre car park would have to do at the other side: again, they'd need to get there early to bag the most suitable bay.

They drove past the van hire in Amanda's car, and went on and back to the shopping centre.

'What time tomorrow?' he asked.

'I think we meet the team at Stewart Street, organise the rota, and get on site here for seven in the morning. They might do their trip to Manchester in one day or they might leave in the afternoon, stop overnight, load up in the morning and come home.'

'*If* it's Manchester,' Pete reminded her.

She was on the phone to Stewart Street, to find the names of her team and their contact details.

ঌ 41 ঌ

The night air was cold, blowing the smoke from Freddy's roll-up round the small lounge. Michael focused on his MacBook as his mum sat watching TV, yawning, a cup of tea in her hand. She checked her watch, then the clock on the wall, and grimaced. She was in her late thirties, with a classic blonde, blousy barmaid look: short skirt, and a low-cut top that revealed the huge swell of her breasts.

Freddy's mobile rang. 'Hey, Grunter, you fuckin' wanker. How are you, mate? Any word?' He flicked the end of the roll-up out into the evening and went out to the hallway, closing the door behind him. His voice was still perfectly audible.

'Tomorrow, yeah?…Fuckin' right, mate…I'm in for two grand…Right, give me a bell when you get back.' He opened the lounge door and gave a small war dance of pleasure.

Michael's mum reached for his hand, smiling. 'What is it, babe?'

He bent over and kissed her, and one hand cupped her full left breast, his thumb stroking her nipple. Michael cringed with embarrassment, trying to concentrate on his work.

Freddy stood upright, still holding her hand. 'Tell you tomorrow. Let me walk you down to the pub.'

He stood chuckling while Michael's mum went to the toilet and then got her coat on.

'OK, son.' She kissed the top of Michael's head. 'See you later, darling.'

'Cheers, Mikey boy.'

The front door closed behind them. She was off for her shift in the pub. Michael had no idea what Freddy would do all evening till he picked her up and walked her home.

Michael sat back, closing his eyes briefly and enjoying the silence in the house.

Freddy used his phone for everything, and never let it out of his sight – except for that one occasion when Michael had managed to look at it. He didn't own a computer or a tablet. Michael's mother was infatuated with him, and it seemed to be reciprocated. She'd occasionally come home from work with men like Freddy – but things usually never lasted more than a week or so. And often just the one night.

She'd never talked to Michael about Freddy, never asked for his permission or his understanding.

Michael was beginning to think he shouldn't be living here at all, he didn't belong any more. But he couldn't afford anything else – unless Martin could help, but Martin had been generous enough.

He messaged Shala. They were both still working on the investigation of Dimitri MacDonald, though she hadn't told him why. He had come up with nothing – actually, suspiciously nothing.

He wondered if Amanda was taking his request to check up on Freddy seriously, and what he could possibly do with whatever information she gave him.

In bed later he was woken by Freddy and his mum coming home. He checked the time: one o'clock.

He lay listening to them getting ready for bed and talking loudly, then going to the bathroom, and then the lights going off.

'Need to get up early, babe.'

'Do you? I think you're up now.' She giggled.

He laughed: 'Ah, fuck it. Get down there, gal!'

And for the next twenty minutes the bed creaked and the headboard bashed against the wall. Michael sent his text to Martin, telling him about Freddy's phone call and asking him to pass it on to Amanda.

∂ 42 ∂

She'd taken the early shift in East Kilbride, with a young cop called Scott Millar beside her in the shopping centre car park, and Pete with another guy on the other side of the van hire place. At nine thirty, three lightweight white vans, with the company name Easy Wheels on the side and two men inside, went past, and round onto Queensway. Amanda got the registrations and relayed them to their admin at Stewart Street, who would share them with the main surveillance teams.

For the next three hours, nothing happened except that the shopping centre got busier and busier. Another two cops arrived to relieve Amanda and Pete, who went back to Stewart Street.

They heard the white vans had been spotted on the M74, heading south towards England.

'That looks like that then, boss,' Pete said.

'Hope so.'

'Should we stand everyone down till they're on their way back?'

'No,' she said at once. 'Just in case.'

She got some routine work done, some tidying up of paperwork and emails, and archiving cases. She and Pete went out to a Subway for baguettes and coffee. Martin texted to say that Michael had overheard a call from Freddy Morton to someone called Grunter: some kind of drug delivery was happening today. She was non-committal, but quietly reassured. She had no idea who Grunter was.

They killed time, watching everyone else in the world out enjoying their Saturday.

When the time came, Pete drove her down to East Kilbride and its roundabouts in silence. She was dropped off discreetly, and the young man from the morning got in with Pete, leaving the woman who had relieved Amanda earlier. Pete drove away to take up his post.

Amanda's new companion was PC Patricia Morrison. She talked and asked questions, and asked questions and talked. She wanted to be in CID. How had Amanda managed it? She had been brought in from Falkirk for this job. What was it like policing in Glasgow?

Amanda answered her questions, tired and distracted but not wanting to kill the girl's enthusiasm. But a large part of her mind was in Clachdubh.

Ramesh called, his voice weary. 'DS Pitt, you've to stand down your operation.'

'What's happened?'

'The vans got to the location for the suspected drugs pickup, and Manchester police rushed them.'

'I thought they were supposed to follow them back here to the Robertsons.'

'No idea what went wrong. But look on the bright side: you get your weekend back.'

She got out of the car to avoid PC Morrison's questions, and waited till Pete pulled to a halt behind them. He was angry, and she held her hands up to try to placate him.

'It's a cock-up, Pete. Nothing we can do.'

Nothing but enjoy the weekend, she thought. And think about Clachdubh.

❧ 43 ❦

The folder Natasha had brought lay on the table of the restaurant on Fisherman's Wharf. It was much more secure to print such information rather than email. In this modern world, people were actually writing letters to keep their communications safe: computers couldn't open envelopes and read the contents, though they could read addresses and do basic traffic analysis.

'That's everything you asked for,' she said.

Grosvenor nodded. 'Thank you.'

'He's too clean too shadowy and too vague we think he's not a real person.'

Grosvenor nodded again.

'Have you anything for me, Mr Grosvenor?'

'How's 1794 doing, by the way?'

She stared at the floor. 'Have you anything for me, Mr Grosvenor?'

He scratched at his thick white beard. 'Your name – Jamil Sabry. Just a kid. We're not picking up any IP address that could be him watching the jihadi videos, no comms to his location. He hardly ever leaves his home town of Clachdubh. I don't know how you're supposed to pronounce that.' He had pronounced it Clack dub. 'He's never travelled to the Middle East. Goes to Glasgow a few times.' He shrugged. He'd pronounced Glasgow properly: he'd been there.

'So he's not a threat.'

'No suspicious pattern. And there's only him in that town.'

'Did you look at Mr Khalaf any more?'

'Yeah. Nothing else. He's got some criminal connections, but nothing for us to be worried about. We're watching him online.'

'Criminal connections?'

'He's a pharmacist, and his house is way too big for his take home pay. He's operating something, but not with any contacts we have.'

'Have you told the British police this?'

He pursed his lips. 'I've no idea.'

'Anything more on Rima Khalaf?'

He shook his head. 'I don't think your investigation is going anywhere, Natasha.'

❧ 44 ❧

Amanda was beginning to know the road to Clachdubh very well. The post-mortem into the abortive drugs raid was no doubt going on somewhere at a high level, and she'd asked for the Monday off in lieu of the Saturday surveillance.

She had called ahead to the school and got an appointment with the head teacher. Once again, with her visitor's badge on, she was met and taken up to the small empty meeting room.

'Coffee?'

Amanda remembered it from before, and declined.

'Such a lot of police activity in the town these days,' the head teacher said, shaking her head, her tight curls unmoving

'I'm still following up on the death of Rima Khalaf.'

The head teacher sat back, her eyebrows raised. 'Oh? Still?'

'There's a couple of things have come up and I'd like you to clarify them for me.'

'If I can.'

Amanda was pleased to have slipped past any questions about what authority she had to be here. 'You told me about Rima Khalaf's teaching and what some saw as an over-emphasis on the historical Muslim dimension.'

'Yes.'

'And you told me one of your parents had objected.'

'Yes.'

Amanda nodded. 'I had assumed that if there had been any threat to Rima, then it would have come from someone objecting to her line – showing how enlightened Islam was a thousand years ago. But I'm now wondering if someone objected to it for the opposite reason.'

The head teacher sat forward, her face screwed up. 'I don't understand.'

'Was there any tension from anyone in the Muslim community who felt she actually wasn't radical *enough*?'

The head teacher gave a patronising smile. 'Detective Inspector Pitt, look around. There is no Muslim community in Clachdubh.'

'But there are a few Muslims.'

'Well yes – one or two. But that's hardly a community.'

'Do they feel valued as part of the wider community?'

'Of course they do. I mean, I can't see why they wouldn't.'

'Do they take part in everything that's going on?'

'Of course. Except that they can opt out of religious festivals in school, naturally.'

'Do they have their own religious festivals?'

The head teacher's patronising smile turned to a patronising laugh. 'There's only one or two of them. They can hardly have a festival of their own.'

Amanda found herself getting annoyed by this attitude. She remembered her schooldays when she had belatedly – and disastrously – discovered her own sexuality. There had been nothing for her to relate to about that, and no doubt the overall view would have been 'there's only one or two of them'.

But she pulled herself back from personal annoyance, and kept her voice as friendly as it could be. 'Can I ask about Jamil Sabry?'

'He's left.'

'Yes I know. Can you tell me about him?'

The head teacher put her elbows on the table and clasped her hands in front of her face. She didn't look at Amanda. 'Disaffected, disinterested. Caused trouble wherever he went. Stole from his fellow pupils – and occasionally from members of staff. Left here with no qualifications whatsoever – and that's not easy to do. We tried to get him into an apprenticeship, but he wasn't interested.'

'Do you know what he's doing now?'

'No idea, and frankly I couldn't care less. I know that's bad of me, but Jamil was one of our failures. One of our rare failures.'

'What was he like – I mean apart from the hassle he caused you.'

'He was usually rude and nasty. And threatening. He was always on a hair-trigger. Some members of staff called him 'feral'. I was glad to get him out the door. I never interviewed him alone in my office – I always brought in Mr Cornwall. One of my deputes. Used to be in the army.' She gave a shudder. 'We had one or two confrontations where Jamil had to be restrained.' She looked at Amanda now, almost daring her to challenge. Then she shrugged grudgingly. 'But, he could also be charming and persuasive when he chose – charismatic almost. Some of the girls went totally la-la over him, the silly creatures.'

Right, thought Amanda, this looks clear enough. Jamil was bad news. He'd been rejected by a society he'd hated – and understandably so, perhaps. He was ripe for recruitment to any cause which included him and allowed him to use his talents, which probably included intimidation and violence. Maybe Rima Khalaf was a target for his wrath and an imagined jihad.

But what to do now…

'What are his parents like?'

'We only ever saw the mother when Jamil was being readmitted after an exclusion. Oh, I think she came to the first year parents' evening but obviously wasn't happy with the messages about her son.' She shrugged. 'And if you can't get parental support, well…' She shrugged again.

Amanda, with a forced smile, thanked the head teacher, who took her down to reception to hand back her badge, and walked her to the entry door. This was done in silence, because Amanda had nothing to say to her – she was still seething about the 'only one or two of them' remark – but they found themselves face to face at the door.

'Do you think Jamil could be a threat to anyone?' the head teacher blurted out.

Amanda looked her in the eyes. 'He's got nothing to lose, has he? He's got no stake in all this.' She indicated the school environment outside the doors: the rows of private houses, the line of neat council houses, the clear air. 'And he doesn't think he owes you anything. People like that are always dangerous.'

She drove to the Rock and parked her car, then climbed out. The early afternoon was cool – the wind picking up, rain threatening, the sky getting darker. She fastened her coat, headed up the winding path, and stood at the top. She looked at the view, and then she looked around in detail at where she was standing.

Rima Khalaf must have been standing about here, she thought. Nobody else was in sight. It wouldn't take much to propel her over the edge to her death, but where had her attacker come from?

It was maybe just possible he'd come up the hill behind her and stayed low, not breaking the horizon – just possible. Or it was just possible he had stayed behind that clump of rock there, and it was just possible she hadn't been aware of him at all until he leapt up and pushed her, then ducked back down. He'd have seen that nobody was around at the time.

But he'd been very lucky to get up and down in the middle of the day without being seen. Very lucky.

Or had he walked up with her, somehow unnoticed, and then pushed her over? No – impossible.

'Hello there again.'

It was the man from the week before, with his Jack Russell.

'Still trying to puzzle it out, I see.'

She turned up her collar and sank her hands deep into her pockets, and smiled at him.

'It can't be done,' she said. 'Nobody can get up here and back down without being seen.'

'You can come up the side there and back down the same way. Look.'

He took her to the left-hand edge of the hill. There was an easy-looking rock climb, and it looked like anyone doing it wouldn't be seen from the car park. Then a scramble, hugging the ground, behind the rock, a hard push, a scramble back, and down.

'Still very lucky not to be seen. How can you tell no one else is up here?'

'Maybe it didn't matter to them. They took their best shot, and it paid off. Your colleagues never asked about suspicious people hanging around here on other days.'

'Were there any?'

'Just a few kids. Always racing up and down the Rock, 'accidentally' bumping into people, swearing at them. Real pests. Haven't seen any recently, right enough.'

Amanda looked down at the Jack Russell, which came over to her and looked back up at her, cocking its head.

'Did you teach Jamil Sabry?' she asked.

The man's lips tightened. 'I tried. Believe me, I tried. Don't know what was wrong with that boy. His mum was nice enough – worked hard – a cleaner I think. But he hated the world. He was a right pest.'

'I heard some girls found him attractive.'

'Aye, well. Teenage girls, eh?' He sniffed. 'Some found him fascinating – usually the vulnerable ones.'

Amanda nodded, thinking about her own teenage years as she stared out across the view.

❧ 45 ❧

Amanda called Jones on his home number, and when it wasn't answered she called his mobile. It was answered after several rings with a cautious: 'Hello?'

She could hear voices all around him, and laughter. 'It's Amanda Pitt.'

He didn't attempt to conceal the irritated sigh. She heard him walk away from all the noise, and he asked: 'What do you want now? I thought that was all over.'

'Officially it is,' she said. 'But I need to speak with you again. There's a few things I want to get straight.'

'I really don't have time for this.'

'If you don't talk to me then I go to my boss and I persuade him to reopen the investigation. There have been three deaths in Clachdubh now: something's going on.'

He didn't say anything for almost a minute. She could still hear the voices in the distance, didn't know whether her complete bluff would work.

Finally: 'I'm at the golf club. Drive over and park here and I'll come out and talk to you in your car.'

'I'll be five minutes.'

She assumed he meant the nearest golf club, which she found in her sat nav's POI. She found a space in its big car park, close by a Fred Perry tour minibus. The clubhouse was big and ageing, and looked busy. She watched people manoeuvre trolleys and golf bags into or out of their cars.

She called Jones again, told him roughly where she was in the car park and what colour her car was, and after a couple of minutes she saw him walk stiffly down the steps, looking round. She flashed her headlights, and he re-commenced his stiff walk towards her, and got into the passenger seat.

'Regular game?' she asked.

He looked at her, knowing she was making conversation and not interested at all. 'The seniors. Good crowd. My group took the money. Eighty four points – not bad in this wind.' He sniffed and stared ahead. 'What do you want from me?'

She looked ahead also, giving up any chance of reading his expression as she spoke. 'My investigation into the complaint by Mr Khalaf about the police investigation concluded that the investigation was fair and thorough.' Her eyes glanced to the side to see him give a slight nod. 'Which is what my boss is very happy about. But we both know it wasn't thorough.'

'I missed nothing.'

'You missed a lot. But none of it seemed relevant, so we let it go.'

An old man walked past the front of her car wheeling a trolley with a golf bag on it. There was a glance of recognition, a wave, and then a frown as he noticed Amanda. Jones waved back and then gave a thumbs up. The man with the trolley laughed and walked on.

'Let's talk about Rima Khalaf's online activities.'

'I told you: her social media accounts were clear.'

'No they weren't. You looked at her Facebook timeline as an outsider, but you didn't see her Twitter feeds and you didn't get any response when you asked Facebook and Twitter for access.'

His silence was deafening.

'And what about her mobile phone?'

'We didn't ever find her mobile.'

'Which is interesting, because she had three of them. I've tracked down two of them but one is still missing. You interviewed the married lover at school – '

'Of course.'

'But you didn't pick up that he had given her a phone to use just between the two of them. He could have given you the number then and you could have searched for the phone and got important information from it. But you didn't, and he got rid of his phone soon after and there's no trace of the number now. You lost that evidence.'

She heard him try to swallow, and then cough.

'And her laptop.'

'We couldn't get into her laptop. It was password protected. We didn't have the IT resources to access it.'

'And it didn't strike you as relevant.'

'We couldn't get into it. We gave it to the parents.' His voice was weak and dry.

She wanted to tell him how easily Martin and Michael had got into it, but that might have backfired on her. 'You were aware of her activities at school.'

'She was an Islamic apologist,' he said, hardly making an effort to conceal his distaste.

'So you didn't investigate who might have wanted to murder her for that.'

'Oh, come on, *acting* inspector!'

'What do you know about Jamil Sabry?'

Jones gave a sigh. 'He's a wee bastard. He'll do something some day that will get him locked up, then it's the slippery slope. Seen the pattern before. Even you must have too.'

'So you're not aware that he hated Rima Khalaf for her views.'

'Doesn't matter. Gutless little shit wouldn't have done anything. No way he could have been on the Rock and pushed her off. It was the middle of the day – a Saturday.'

'You don't think he could have come up the side of the Rock, pushed her off, then gone back down the same way?'

'Oh for fuck sake.' His breath hissed out in a long sigh. 'Honestly.'

Hearing herself formulate that theory made it sound crazy even to her own ears. 'How about Gary McAllister?'

'Who?'

'He knew Rima. He had a grudge against her.'

140

'Who is he?'

'Young lad – a couple of years out of school. Works in Tesco in the town. Fancies himself as a writer – violent historical fiction, with a lot of non-consensual sex. He emailed Rima.'

He was shaking his head. 'Never came up on our radar.'

'Yes he did.' She gave him a few seconds of confusion then went on: 'The school after-party on the Rock, when – '

'When Karen McKechnie fell to her death.'

'Gary was there.'

'I remember now. Most of fourth year were there. You think Gary is a serial pusher-offer?' He snorted.

'What did you find on *that* investigation? Any history between Gary and Karen?'

'I don't remember Gary, but he certainly can't have been a boyfriend. She was very pretty, so I assume he'd have fancied her.' He sniffed and repeated: 'But he wasn't her boyfriend. Hadn't ever been her boyfriend.'

'My guess is that he did fancy her. And he fancied Rima too. And my next guess is that they both rejected his advances – probably laughed and told him to piss off.'

'So that fuelled his fantasies and he pushed them off the Rock? Rather than, say, sexually assaulting them to get some gratification? Come on!'

Amanda bit her lip. She didn't know how adolescent boys thought. At her school, no boy had seemed infatuated with her. She'd had a few 'boyfriends' but relationships hadn't ever gone far, and eventually the school as a whole had seemed to realise that they wouldn't ever go far, not with her. She guessed most assumed she was frigid, but she definitely wasn't. She just wasn't into boys.

'Is that it?' He turned to her, his hand on the door handle. 'Is that all your theories? Is that all you've got to try to rubbish my entire career in the police? Is that how Police Scotland rewards long service these days?'

'Of course not,' she said. She didn't want to rubbish his career, but she thought that the last few years of his career had *been* rubbish. He should have gone before then, to devote his life to golf with his mates. 'Who do I talk to about interviewing Jamil Sabry and Gary McAllister?'

'There isn't a full-time inspector any more in Clachdubh. They share one, but she's on this MIT. If you go to the station you'll find Sergeant Craig Torrance. Talk to him.' He pulled the door handle, and, with a rush of cold air, he was gone.

She watched him walk stiffly back to the clubhouse, his legs almost bowed. Dare she cut across a murder investigation? Would DCI Paige be receptive to her theories?

❧ 46 ❧

The Major Investigation Team was based in a large Police Scotland caravan in the car park of the local police station, which was a small brick-built building, looking like it dated from the days before the big private estates and the business park had dramatically extended the town.

Paige beckoned Amanda in and indicated a small plastic chair in the corner. She was with the DI and DS that Amanda had seen before at the Rock View Hotel, and another two detectives that Amanda didn't know. At the end of the room were display boards: photographs and names. The biggest photograph was of the murdered woman, lying back on a carpeted floor, her dressing gown open, blood pooling under her breast and running off to the side.

Paige looked even more tired and harassed than before. 'We can't hold him any longer without charging him,' she was saying.

'It's a solid case.'

'It's a circumstantial case.'

Paige sighed as her team lobbed in different views, then she sighed again and leaned back. 'We have no other suspect, and there's a lot of evidence against Kevin Baker.'

'No cast off blood from the weapon.'

'We've dealt with that.'

'No prints on the weapon. No sign of gloves.'

'And those fingerprints on the back door outside handle – not his.'

'Forensics say it was a single deep incision, knife in and out, pretty much instant death. He may not have waved the knife around. No cast off.'

142

'Should be some blood on his face.'

'He's clever.'

Paige held up her hands. 'He may be clever, but our hypothesis is that he lost it somehow and killed her, and that doesn't fit with any carefully planned cover-up.'

She lifted a pen and tapped it against her teeth. 'Look, we've got three more hours. Check the door-to-door again, ask about anyone suspicious lurking about.'

'We've got the mysterious figure on the bicycle,' the DI said.

'Any confirmation of that?'

'A couple of people saw him – assuming it's a him – for a few days before the murder, but not on the morning of the murder and not since.'

'On the night before the murder?'

'No. And no meaningful description.'

Paige threw her pen onto the table. 'Just go check.'

They squeezed themselves out of the space through the narrow door, letting much needed air into the room. Amanda watched Paige close her eyes and fight a yawn.

When she opened her eyes, she looked straight at Amanda. 'He has to be guilty. There's no other suspect.'

Amanda didn't move.

'Sorry. What did you want, DS Pitt?'

'I'm not supposed to be here,' Amanda confessed.

Paige looked baffled. 'What?'

'Have you investigated Gary McAllister? I told you about him.'

'I checked but there is nothing linking him to this investigation. He didn't know the dead woman. There's no history.'

'He knew Rima Khalaf. His correspondence with her shows quite violent sexual fantasies. If he was fixated on this woman in the same way, then he may have – '

'Gone from pushing people off hills to stabbing them? All without leaving any trace evidence?'

'Maybe he's the one on the bike, watching her. Maybe it's his fingerprints on the door handle at her house.'

Paige knitted her eyebrows. 'I've no basis for questioning him. None at all. I can't just pull people in randomly.'

'There's someone called Jamil Sabry in this town.'

'Are you now constructing a jihadi plot against your dead girl?'

'He's violent, uneducated.'

'So it could be him on the bike and his fingerprints on the back door.'

Amanda stared back at Paige.

'So you still think your girl was pushed off the hill, in broad daylight, despite the official police investigation and your own investigation finding otherwise. By either a fixated school kid or a wannabe jihadi. Someone who then progressed to a savage stabbing.' Paige shook her head. 'It doesn't work, DS Pitt. I've seen you in the past with good analyses, good ideas, but this isn't that. And don't you have work to do back in Glasgow?'

Amanda was still looking steadily at Paige. 'I think this kid Gary McAllister warrants investigation.'

'He's got no record.'

'No.'

Paige sighed a few more times. 'Does he have a bicycle?'

'If he doesn't have a car and if he lives a good bit away from Tesco where he works, then yes, he'll have a bicycle.'

Paige picked up her pen again, clicked it a few times, then dropped it and sat back. 'Kevin Baker is still denying everything, so either my interview technique is getting worse or he's innocent. We have some circumstantial evidence against him, but not a watertight case. I'm not saying you're correct about this Gary McAllister, but I am inclined to think that we need to spread the net. I'm prepared to put out a public call for information regarding a cyclist – possibly a young male cyclist – who was seen in the vicinity of the dead woman's house in the days leading up to her murder. I don't like doing that, because it can compromise the court case later: solicitors say it's planting suggestions in witnesses. But I've no other option here.'

Amanda nodded at her. 'Anything I can do to help?'

Paige raised her eyebrows. 'You're not supposed to be here at all, remember.' She reached for papers on her desk and looked at them.

Amanda was dismissed.

She went outside and knew she really had to get back to Glasgow. She wondered whether Paige would tell her if they found out anything about Gary McAllister.

And what to do about Jamil Sabry?

Her phone went. It was Martin. 'Michael says he has got a trace on that mobile – the third mobile, the second iPhone. It was on for a brief period about an hour ago and now it's off again, but he got the rough location. Clachdubh. Near the Co-op in Portal Road.'

'Thanks, Martin.'

She checked her watch: she really did need to get back to Glasgow. But Jamil Sabry and Jasmine McCallum both lived in Portal Road.

❧ 47 ❧

Amanda found the Co-op on Portal Road, then drove back to park near Jamil Sabry's semi-detached council house. The houses here were well kept with neat gardens. Further down the street were a couple that had fallen into disrepair, the gardens neglected and overgrown, but by and large it was a nice estate, she thought.

She'd asked Martin to text her any updates from Michael, but nothing had come in.

She sat looking at Jamil Sabry's house, wondering if she was being stupid to assume he was connected to this phone. He wasn't linked to the murder in any way, so if she talked to him she wasn't going to compromise that case. But on what basis could she speak to him? Would she end up on the end of a complaint? And what could she ask him?

Her dilemma vanished of its own accord. She saw what must be him coming in her direction, crossing the road diagonally towards his house, holding a big bottle of Coke. He saw her car, and saw her. And he saw her looking straight at him. His face curled in anger and he altered direction to come straight to her, thumping the bonnet of her car and then standing at her door.

'Who the fuck you lookin at lady?' The accent was Scottish, but he was copying lines from an American cop show. He was tall and lean, a long face topped by curling black hair. Despite the anger, there was something magnetic about him, something primeval. Amanda could see that he might be compelling to some young women.

She wasn't sure what to do. She turned the ignition half way round so she could lower the window. 'I'm sorry?'

He jabbed his finger in the direction of her face. 'What you fuckin lookin at?'

She focused past the finger, at his face. He was angry, and most of it was spontaneous: this kid probably got angry at anything and everything. But part of it was put on too: this was a weak defenceless woman – he could do what he liked.

'I'm lost,' she said, in a weak defenceless woman's voice. 'I was checking my sat nav but it seems to have packed in. Can you direct me to the bypass?'

His face was screwed up still, and he licked his lips. 'No fuckin sense of direction you women.'

She smiled and nodded. 'Has your phone got sat nav in it? I can't find mine.'

He stepped back, looking up and down the street, then stepped to her window again. He gave a big sigh and pulled his phone from his trouser pocket, waving it in front of her face. It was an iPhone. She stared at it, hardly hearing his next words, spoken softly: 'You show me your tits, yeah?'

She blinked. 'I beg your pardon?' Was he being serious?

His voice was stronger: 'I give you directions, you show me your tits.'

She tried not to laugh at the outrageous request – had this *ever* worked for him before? Then she made a show of looking round the empty street. 'I don't know,' she said. This was ridiculous, but she wanted him to switch on that iPhone.

Now his attitude was aggressive. 'Fuckin MILF – show me your tits. Not much there, but let me see them anyway. Then I'll give you directions.'

She sighed, as if some internal struggle was going on. 'Give me the directions first.'

He turned on the phone and they both waited for a minute or so while it started up and he keyed in his passcode: she watched his thumb fly across the screen – she saw the pattern. That was all she needed. If this was Rima Khalaf's missing third phone, then Michael would be getting a location. It was highly unlikely that this phone had been switched on at exactly the same moment as the target.

'Bypass, yeah? Got those tits ready for me?' He was pinching and zooming the maps app but glancing at her, the big bottle of Coke tucked awkwardly under one arm.

She looked down and arched her back. 'They're ready. Are you ready?' She stroked the gear lever suggestively, pressing the clutch and slipping the car into first.

'I'm ready, MILF.' He licked his lips and grinned.

'OK. Here we go.'

She started the engine and slipped the clutch, her front wheels giving a brief slide till the traction control kicked in. As she rolled up her window she heard the shout from him, and in the mirror she saw him gesticulating and screaming with anguish. He ran a few yards down the road after her then stopped.

OK, she thought: teenage men were pathetically easy to distract.

She drove on down the road, round a slow bend till she was out of sight of him, and stopped, and called Martin. 'Yep, text from Michael: phone was on – same location – still on now.'

OK, that was Rima Khalaf's third phone. Just how Jamil had got it was another issue.

But what to do now?

Her amusement slipped away, and she thought of other women that Jamil Sabry may have harassed, frightened or actually assaulted over the years, and would do again, and she turned the car and drove back to his house, parking right outside it. There was no sign of him. She waited, trying to control and focus her anger.

Sure enough he came out, waving his arms. 'You come back to apologise, MILF? You want to apologise properly? Give me a blow-job?' The iPhone was in his hand.

She climbed out of the car and stood on the pavement with a sweet smile on her face as he came closer and closer, till he was pointing at her with his right hand, the one holding the iPhone. She took a deep breath, pushing away doubts about what she was about to do, thoughts of what would happen if she got this wrong.

She grabbed his wrist and turned, pulling him off his feet onto his knees on the rough concrete of the pavement, then forward as she twisted his arm up his back. She had judged his strength correctly, which was just as well: this boy looked fit enough but he wasn't particularly strong and she had totally surprised him. As she put her foot against his neck – not too hard – and ignored his shouting, she was able to prise the phone from his fingers.

'Hey, you steal my fuckin phone, MILF?' His voice was muffled.

She put the phone in her pocket. 'I'm a police officer, Jamil,' she said. His protests stopped as he realised how wrong he'd got this situation. 'I'm confiscating Rima Khalaf's phone from you.' Still stunned, he didn't deny it. 'How did you get it?'

'A mate found it,' he said.

'Oh come on!' She increased the pressure of her foot, giving a glance up and down the street, but no one was in sight.

'He said he found it. Honest.'

'Did he steal it from her?'

'Don't know. Nothin to do with me. Honest. I bought it off him.'

'Oh come on.' She increased the pressure on his arm, hoping to hell that nobody was watching: she was seriously out of order.

'Fucking hell – OK OK! He nicked it.'

'From Rima Khalaf?'

'Yes.'

'How did you unlock it?'

'Another mate knew the code.'

'How did he know the code?'

'He used to hang out with her. Watched her unlock it, worked out the code.'

'Was this Gary?'

He paused, and said: 'No,' very unconvincingly.

'OK,' she said. 'And you just carried on using it?'

'Nobody blocked it,' he said. 'After a couple of months an email came in saying the direct debit hadn't worked so I put in details of a credit card.'

'Your credit card?'

Again the very obvious lie: 'Of course.'

It sounded plausible to her: Rima's father really hadn't known about the phone and it had slipped through all the legal procedures after her death. And retired Inspector Jones had totally failed to consider the possibility. Jamil might very well have managed to continue paying for a SIM-only contract after Rima's bank account was wound up.

'And the other phone? The one you gave Jasmine McCallum in return for a feel of her tits?'

His voice was muffled. 'A mate gave it to me. He found it.'

'Found it where?'

'Just lying about.'

She was getting tired holding him down, and could feel him flexing his muscles, fighting her grip. She had to go soon, and she needed to ask Martin for advice.

'I'm taking this phone, Jamil, and you're going to do nothing to stop me. Are you?'

A muffled: 'No.'

She tentatively released her grip on him. 'Stay down!' She stepped over to her car and climbed in, watching him all the time, ready for his attack. But he stayed down. She started the engine and locked the doors. As she drove off quickly, he leapt to his feet, gesticulating shouting and swearing after her. She drove out of the town towards the bypass.

She was both excited and appalled by what she'd just done. It was totally out of order, and could get her into a lot of trouble if Jamil thought straight and put a convincing story together, or if there had been a witness.

As the adrenaline subsided, she felt almost sick at her own stupidity. That could all so easily have gone completely wrong, and she had no legality behind her.

She stopped in a lay-by, and looked at the phone she'd taken from Jamil. She pressed the home button and swiped to get the unlock screen – this wasn't the latest iOS. She looked at the keypad, and rewound the sight of Jamil unlocking it, the way Gary McAllister must have watched Rima Khalaf unlock it at the writers' group meetings. Top left, right-then-left, bottom. Probably 1650. She tried it.

The phone opened up, and she let out her breath and locked it again. If there was evidence here, then she needed someone else to witness it with her, and it was best if that witness was an IT expert.

❧ 48 ❧

Gary reflected that it was a very odd kind of day. He'd seen that haughty bitch Jasmine McCallum in Tesco with her fat little pal Jill, but they'd gone to the self check-out even though there was a queue there and his till was clear.

A young red-haired woman had been in the next checkout down, and Gary had done a double take. But of course it wasn't

Rebecca. Rebecca was dead. And this woman was older, surlier, flat chested.

Gary looked round, but there was no one to focus on. No one for the next chapter of his book, no mysterious princess or slave girl.

As business ebbed and the day dragged, he was sent to make up some online orders, then some shelf-stacking, and then out to get the trolleys rounded up. He was always annoyed by the people who just abandoned their trolleys, when the trolley park was maybe just feet away.

As he manoeuvred a long line of them – twenty, but that wasn't the store record by any means – he saw the police car parking, a uniformed man and woman getting out, putting on their caps and walking towards the store and inside. His first instinct was fear. Then he noticed how the woman walked, her athletic strides, and she turned as something caught her eye: a round, beautiful face, stray light brown-hairs escaping from her hat. Gary's eyes followed her.

He went back inside after he'd rounded up all the trolleys, nearly at the end of his shift and wondering whether to keep out of the way or whether to act willing.

The police officers were with one of the assistant managers, Charlie, pinning an A4 poster up on the small-ads board. They sellotaped another three onto the doors. Then the police officers left, Gary's eyes following the woman.

Charlie smiled at him. 'OK, Gary?'

'Nearly finished my shift.'

Charlie checked his watch. 'OK. See if anybody needs a hand then get off home.'

Gary nodded. He could make out the poster. The police were looking for someone who had been seen in the vicinity of the murdered woman's house in the days before her death. Someone on a bicycle. A young man on a bicycle. A black bicycle.

Gary swallowed. He'd been seen. He'd thought nobody had spotted him, but he'd been seen. Fuck. He felt the blood drain from his head, and he was almost dizzy.

He looked round, momentarily ready to run. And then he took a deep breath and forced himself to relax. There were dozens of people out on bikes in this town – which, with the obvious exception of the Rock, was a pretty flat area. Why should anyone pick *him* out? Nobody could have got a good look at the cyclist. The description was really vague.

He realised he was shaking.

He wandered the aisles, asking if anyone needed help, then drifted away into the staff area. He took off his badge and his overall, and – his heart in his mouth – he went outside to unlock his bike, and cycle away through the car park towards home. As he went, he passed in front of the police car, which waited for him, then overtook him and sped off.

He grinned as the shaking stopped, and shook his head. The cops were stupid. He was a cunning and wise leader.

❧ 49 ❧

Martin yawned and Nicola reached to touch his hand, then went back to her folder. She was still trying to make sense of Joan's business plan, and was close to a belief that there was actually no 'plan' and might soon be no 'business'.

Amanda was on the armchair, almost falling asleep with the drone of some American cop show on Netflix, which Martin was half-listening to as he looked through the phone she'd taken from Jamil. Outside, it was dark now.

'Well?' Amanda asked.

'There's some odd stuff, but I don't know what you're hoping to find.' He stopped Netflix and mirrored Rima Khalaf's iPhone on the TV. Amanda shifted her position to look at the big screen.

'Phone calls,' Martin said. 'Local numbers, a couple in Glasgow. Other calls are to contacts with inscrutable names – again, local. Incoming spam calls – I recognise the codes. Nothing from before when you say the girl died.'

Amanda nodded. 'So he wiped it all, like before with the other phones?' Another pointless dead end.

'Looks like he wiped most of it, certainly. But if he knew the PIN, like you say, he may not have done a factory reset. Texts: same contacts and random incoming spam texts.'

She nodded again, seeing on the TV as he scrolled through them that he was correct.

'Emails – none. Cleared out. No Twitter app. No Facebook app.'

'That's odd.'

'Her account would have been cancelled by the parents or the family lawyer after she died, and it looks like your guy Jamil didn't set one up.'

'I thought kids couldn't get by without Facebook.'

'Apparently they can. But this looks like he's using some other social media – or trying to. He's got Telegram Messenger, which is used by ISIS amongst others. It's encrypted. But Anonymous has been targeting this, and Telegram Messenger themselves have been closing terrorist accounts.'

'So this kid is a jihadi?'

'How did he seem to you?'

'Just an angry teenager. Uncontrollably angry at times. Sexist, misogynistic undoubtedly.'

'Michael said that he's being tracked by the FBI but they don't think he's a real threat. He's a fantasist.'

'They've been wrong before,' Amanda muttered.

'You going to tell somebody?'

'Anything else on the phone?' she asked, turning again to the TV. 'Anything of Rima's?'

'There is some stuff that he didn't wipe. Notes: ideas about lessons, references to books and TV documentaries. Photos. None of him. This must have been the phone Rima actually used a lot.'

'Again,' she said, 'strange that he didn't take selfies. Or sneaky pictures of girls.'

Martin scrolled through the photographs taken by Rima, working back in time. Amanda found the experience strangely sad, like she was behind the eyes of the girl who had died.

They were mostly views – many from the Rock in Clachdubh, including some from the edge of the slope that had killed her, looking down. She had also taken some selfies, with the Rock in the background, or the town in general. Many were obviously from her first few weeks in the place: pictures of the school, pictures of the surrounding streets. It seemed like she had really liked the place. She'd had all that potential, all the possibilities for her life. All gone.

Martin swiped through the photos till Amanda shouted: 'Stop! Back up.'

He swiped the other way till she said 'Stop!' again.

It was a view of a late evening sky, the high thin clouds tinged with red. Because of the lightness of the sky, the ground was very dark. But visible there at the junction was someone on a bike, one foot on the ground, the handlebars turned sideways. The person was looking straight at the photographer.

Nicola had stopped her work and was looking at the screen. 'Who's that?' she asked.

'I think that's a kid called Gary McAllister,' Amanda said. 'I think he's watching Rima. I think he may have pushed her off the Rock.'

Martin was frowning. 'Bit of an extrapolation, isn't it?'

She shook her head. 'There was another girl fell off the Rock a couple of years before, when she was a pupil. Gary was there that night too. Rima must have spotted him watching her – maybe she confronted him. Maybe…'

'Why would he do such things?'

'I don't know. I'm trying to get the MIT to investigate him in connection with the murder of a young woman in Clachdubh last week.'

'The woman who was knifed?' Nicola asked. 'That's a big step, going from nudging them off a hill to stabbing.'

'Yes,' Amanda conceded. 'It is.'

Nicola exchanged looks with Martin, and they both shrugged. Amanda saw them out of the corner of her eye and ignored them – after all, they were right.

'So what are you going to do?' Nicola asked, as Martin continued to rummage through the iPhone's contents and they all looked at the mirroring of it on the TV screen.

'I've got other work,' Amanda yawned, looking at her watch and groaning. 'I'm sorry, I've out-stayed my welcome.'

'Oh, Michael texted me, asking if anything happened about Freddy Morton…'

'He's down as a suspected drug dealer,' Amanda said. 'He might have paid into a big deal that was planned for the weekend – that may have been what Michael overheard. The drugs didn't arrive though, so Freddy won't be able to do anything for while. Is

Michael worried about his mum?'

'I don't know. It's hard to tell what Michael is really thinking.'

Nicola and Amanda shared a look, then a grin that almost turned into a laugh.

'This isn't Jamil's only phone,' Martin said, staring at it and thumbing away. 'I think he has this as his flashy "look at me I've got an iPhone" but he hardly ever uses it – as we know. I think you're right: the lack of content is wrong. The texts are innocent, and he couldn't have lived without email and social media. Telegram Messenger could just be there for show too. I can't open it, though, so maybe it is an active account. Don't know.'

He kept sliding and pressing, then: 'Here's another album of photos. Oh dear.'

They were a random collection, all of people, mainly young women and teenage girls. It looked like they were all photographed surreptitiously. Certainly the ones where the iPhone had been held low to get a view up someone's skirt were surreptitious.

'Oh god,' Nicola said. 'What a pervert.'

Amanda agreed, but she was staring at the screen. 'Keep going, Martin. Not too fast.'

There was what looked like a school party on the Rock, raising cans in a toast to the photographer. Then a couple of teenagers in a clinch on the ground, kissing. The next picture had the boy with his hand up the girl's dress, and the next two saw him progressing further.

'Christ,' Nicola said.

'Keep going, Martin.'

A teenage girl in a party dress, high on the Rock, lit by the phone's flash, laughing and lifting her dress high on her thighs in a tease. In the next picture the dress was even higher, and in the next she was turning away, one foot lifted like she was ready to run.

Amanda was frowning. 'These pictures were taken before Rima Khalaf arrived in Clachdubh.'

'So someone uploaded them to this phone for Jamil to look at in private.'

Then pictures of Rima Khalaf. In the street, in her house, in a car with a man, in the back seat of a car – just a blur of limbs as Jamil must have sprinted past.

A slim red-haired woman. Shopping on her own. Out running.

Greeting someone at her front door. Pulling curtains closed upstairs in her house.

Amanda found she had almost stopped breathing, and gasped air into her lungs.

'You OK?' Nicola asked. 'Do you know who these women are?'

Amanda nodded. 'That red-haired one is the woman who was stabbed. The previous ones were Rima Khalaf. And I think the early ones were the girl who fell off the Rock during the school after-party: Karen McKechnie.'

'So this nutter was stalking them,' Martin said.

Nicola asked: 'Do you think *he* killed them all?'

'Could be.'

'But what about the other boy you mentioned – Gary McAllister?'

Amanda sat back in the armchair, suddenly in need of a gin and tonic, but she was driving. 'I don't know,' she said. 'Maybe Gary took these photographs and gave them to Jamil.'

Oh fuck, she thought. They were in it together.

'Uh oh,' Martin said.

The final pictures were of a very young, skinny girl, in various stages of revealing herself. The last picture had her pulling her top up to her shoulders.

'Grooming?' asked Nicola.

Amanda felt almost physically sick.

❧ 50 ❧

In the week since the murder, the days had grown noticeably longer. This meant that Gary could get out on his bike with no lights but still with almost no chance of being seen. The few posters round the town were growing tattier by the minute – the ones in Tesco had half-fallen off the windows while they were being cleaned and had then been taken away and binned.

That evening, Gary went out as it was growing dark, reckoning he wouldn't be spotted. It was a time when people had their lights on but maybe hadn't yet shut their curtains, ideal time to catch glimpses into private lives.

Twice in the past he'd been able to watch people who didn't

realise that net curtains were no barrier when lights were on inside. One couple – probably newly married, in their twenties – had been kissing and fondling, before getting up to go upstairs, leaving him almost quivering. Another couple had just gone for it, on their sofa, like in one of his Internet movies.

But that had been a year ago. Nothing since then had lived up to that, and he'd been left purely with his imagination, especially the redhead Rebecca. He'd imagined what she had been doing, and he'd imagined she had been doing it with him.

He cycled around the town, sticking mainly to the nicer parts, but staying away from where Rebecca had lived. Now and again he left his bike against a wall and tiptoed through a gate and up to a window. But he saw nothing.

Then the worst-case scenario happened. A police car turned into the street he was cycling down, its headlights in his face, the luminous chequered paintwork screaming at him. The car stopped, and two policemen got out, one holding his hand up for Gary to stop.

He made a split-second decision, and came to a halt in front of them, putting on the guileless expression he so often wore. It was the right decision, he thought: he couldn't turn and run, and if he'd cycled right past them then the street light would have caught him. It would have raised their suspicions: a young guy on a bike, with no lights, running away from the cops. It's *him*, they'd have said.

It's only when the police officers stepped closer that he realised one was the female officer he had seen in the Tesco car park. The orange from the street light illuminated high cheekbones, and threw shadows in her uniform.

'You know it's an offence to ride a bicycle without lights?' the man said.

Gary nodded and shrugged. 'Yeah. Sorry. Was out earlier round at a mate's and lost track of time.' He pointed. 'I just live down there,' he lied.

The man stepped even closer, and Gary knew he was trying to detect the smell of alcohol. There wasn't any to detect. Then the policeman got his torch out and shone it in Gary's face, looking at his eyes. Obviously no drugs either.

'OK,' the policeman said. 'Off you go – but make sure you either get lights fitted or you don't go out in the dark. On a black bike with dark clothes and no lights, you're invisible. You could easily get run over.'

'OK.'

Gary pulled the pedal up and put his foot on it, ready to go once his eyes adjusted from the sudden flashlight and then the darkness. The female police officer was looking at him. 'Hang on,' she said, 'what's your name, son?'

Gary didn't hesitate. 'Malcolm,' he said. 'Malcolm McLeod.'

'And where do you live?'

'Nineteen Portal Road.' It was Jamil Sabry's address. Maybe he shouldn't have given it…

'OK. Off you go.'

And with that he pushed down on the pedal as he lifted his other leg and accelerated away, down the road and round the corner. He grinned to himself.

Back in his room – dad in the lounge watching TV – he thought back over the meeting with the police officers, and his smile faded. Would they check that address? No, probably not – they were busy investigating the murder. Would they remember what he looked like? No: the torchlight in his face would have distorted his features with deep shadows, and the guy was looking for dilated pupils. The policewoman was sharper though. She had suspected something.

They were looking for a young man on a black bike.

'Dad – where's that paint you had for the bathroom? Dad?'

After explaining what he wanted it for, and being told it wouldn't work very well, his dad let him use the paint on his bike frame, out the back of the house. It didn't stick particularly well because he hadn't prepared the surfaces, but there was enough to make it no longer a 'black bike'. He reckoned he would be invisible.

His dad was zipping up his jacket, holding his mobile to his ear. 'OK. Five minutes, doll. See you.' To Gary he said: 'I'm off. Back in the morning.' He clapped Gary on the upper arm.

Gary went upstairs to his small bedroom. There turned out to be several sites which offered him policewomen 'in hot action', and he watched for a time. None of them looked like the policewoman he'd seen: these women were porn stars with inflated breasts, unable to get into character. He closed his browser and opened a fresh Word document. They didn't have policewomen back in the Kingdom of Strathclyde of course, so he needed to start work in a totally new genre.

I watched the officers depart for the explosion on the edge of town that I set earlier, with the help of Jamil the Jihadi. Jamil is now at the site with his AK42, waiting for the police and the fire brigade and the ambulances. And the onlookers. He is about to bring terror to this complacent provincial town.

I am about to bring terror to the woman who now sits alone in the police station, at a desk behind a window.

I stand at the window and tap on it, looking nervous and excited. 'Have you heard!' I blurt out. 'The explosion.' I shake with fear.

She smiles reassuringly and stands up, adjusting her white blouse, arranging her light-brown ponytail. She comes over to the window. 'Yes,' she says. 'It's all in hand.' She smiles, still reassuring.

I gasp and stumble, then stagger sideways and collapse to the floor. As I lie there I hear the secured door open, and her footsteps. She is kneeling beside me. I can smell her perfume. 'Oh my god – are you OK?'

My powerful hands grab her forearms, and suddenly she is on her back and I am kneeling across her thighs, pinning her to the ground. 'I'm fine,' I say.

She struggles and lets out a scream.

❧ 51 ❧

The late news confirmed that a man in Clachdubh who had been helping police with their enquiries had now been arrested for the murder of a thirty-five year-old woman. DCI Paige was interviewed, and calmly gave the minimum amount of information. There was no celebration in her voice, no excitement that she'd got her man.

After a restless night, where the drugs case mixed in with the events in Clachdubh, Amanda woke very early with a mad idea in her head. Jamil Sabry had another phone and there seemed to be no way of getting to it. But if he was working with Gary McAllister, then there would be incriminating evidence on Gary's computer:

the rest of his novel, and surely other evidence that would link him to the deaths of three women. That would bring official suspicion on him. Could she get to that computer?

She slipped out of bed, showered, dressed and sat in the kitchen. She ate toast and drank more coffee, listening to Radio 2 playing quietly.

Michael could hack into computers, she thought, even though it wouldn't be 'just like the movies'. She had no idea what would be possible in real life. Could Michael sit outside Gary's house and…

No: she was thinking of scenes from TV shows and movies. Or was it actually possible?

She sat drinking more coffee until she heard the alarm go off in their bedroom and a sleepy, tousled, gorgeous Claire came through, yawning. They kissed.

'You OK?' Claire asked.

'Just thinking of a daft idea.'

Claire grinned. 'Go for it, darling. Your ideas usually work out. I'm off for a shower.'

It might work, Amanda thought. It might just work and not blow up in my face. She made a coffee for Claire.

She went into work early, and waited till around nine before calling Martin.

'Hi.' She knew he didn't do small talk, so she got straight to the point. 'This guy Gary McAllister: I need to find out what's on his computer. Can you and Michael hack into it?'

He gave a sigh. 'It's not –'

'– like the movies. Yes I know. But you've done it before. How practical is it?'

'It depends,' he said.

'Depends on what?'

'Last time we did this, we sent a USB stick with a Trojan – a virus – on it, and they put it into one of their computers and that let us in. That might work again, but it might not.'

'Is there any other way?'

He paused, obviously marshalling his thoughts and trying to make it understandable for her. 'Gary's computer will undoubtedly be on a home network with a router with a WEP2 key and a firewall. Now, the software that many routers use has a driver called

NetUSB, which has vulnerabilities which can be exploited. Basically you can steal the WEP2 key and then join the network. If this router uses NetUSB and if it hasn't been security patched, we could hack in. With me so far?'

'I think so.' She hadn't a clue what he was talking about. 'Go on.'

'Another possibility is to use a hacking system called BackTrack. This can often decrypt the WEP2 key, and again you can join the home network and probably do what you want. But it takes hours, and isn't guaranteed to work.' He sighed again. 'And it all involves sitting in a car with a laptop very close to the house where the network is, potentially for a very long time, and hoping nobody calls the police.' Another sigh. 'What usually happens is that people just keep trying to hack into different networks and systems, and they get lucky from time to time. But that's different from trying to break into one particular network. The chances of success are low.'

'So how do people do it?'

'Attachments to emails still work more often than they should. There was one last year supposedly coming from a parcel delivery company, with a delivery label attached – only it was actually a virus. But some people will actually be expecting a parcel and will actually click on the link. Unlucky.'

'Hmm.'

'The most effective viruses are delivered via what looks like a link to a video clip, especially if it suggests something risqué. Gary might open something that looked like a video file which promised to show the kind of thing he wrote about.'

'That's a possibility. Could Michael set that up for me?'

'I suppose. We have Gary's email address. But junk email filters are getting better, and it's only old people that tend to fall for this scam these days. Like phone calls from Windows offering to fix a problem with your computer.'

'Anything else?'

'Two possibilities. One, you break into the person's house and get their WEP2 key which will be printed on the back of the router or written on a post-it beside the computer. Two, you steal the computer.'

'And if I did that, you and Michael could go through it?'

'Oh for fuck sake, Amanda!'

'But you could.'

'If the drive isn't encrypted then yes, we could get information from it.'

'Thanks, Martin.'

'So what are you going to try?'

She ignored the question. 'Thanks, Martin.'

She agreed with Martin: Gary McAllister wasn't going to click on an email link, especially if the email had gone straight into his junk folder. And there was no way somebody could sit in a car in the street of a council estate without being spotted and challenged.

Which left one possibility, a variation on the idea she'd had that morning, the idea that Claire had encouraged her to try, even though she had no idea what it was. It was totally bonkers, she knew. But once she'd settled on the idea, she couldn't let it go. She was going to persuade Licker McGuire to enter Gary McAllister's house and steal his WEP2 key.

❧ 52 ❧

Licker McGuire looked a bit unsettled as he walked into the darkness of the large O'Neill's pub in the Merchant City, the main illumination coming from the large TV screens everywhere, showing the Celtic Hearts game.

Amanda watched him wander round, both looking for her and at the screens. Finally he saw her in a booth, with the glass of coke and the pint of Guinness, and sat down. He reached for the pint and glugged half of it down, then shrank into his seat, his sharp eyes looking around for any signs of anyone recognising him.

'You don't come into this part of town much,' she commented, knowing he'd be very unlucky to be spotted here.

He shook his head. 'Fucking students and middle class wankers.' He sniffed and took another drink, licking the white foam from his top lip.

'The Es,' she whispered. 'The supply that was due in at the weekend.'

'Fuckin disaster,' he said, his voice very low. 'Never arrived. Fuck up down south.'

She nodded. 'So what happens now?'

He shrugged and almost finished his pint. 'Guy makes some more and it'll be sent up. Life goes on.' He shrugged again.

'And you'll let me know.'

He groaned. 'You're going to get me killed, man. For fuck sake.'

'OK, Licker. Can I offer you a way out? A way to get off the hook?'

He finished the pint and stared at the empty glass. She pushed a ten-pound note across the table. 'Go get yourself another pint. Nothing for me.'

She waited. She'd wanted another coke, but didn't quite trust him not to add a vodka or two, just for a laugh. She watched him get served, waiting for the pint to settle and then be topped up as he pocketed the change, and then he was back. 'Cheers.' He took a mouthful, and then said: 'A way to get off the hook?'

'I'd like you to break into a house for me.'

He gave a reflex nod and then his face screwed up. 'You serious?'

'Very. It should be a doddle for you. You know what an Internet router is?'

'Aye.'

'And you know that you need a network password to log onto a network – usually the password gets stored on your computer so you only need it the first time. The password – it's called a WEP2 key – is stuck on the back of the router usually, or the owner writes it down somewhere.'

He was still frowning and nodding.

'I want you to break into a house and come back with the WEP2 network key.'

'Is that all?'

'That's all.'

'And you'll…'

'Never bother you again. Unless you really fuck up and I can't ignore it.'

'How about your sidekick DC McLeod?'

'Don't worry about him.' She'd explain it all to Pete – when it was all over and her plan worked out. *If* it worked out.

'Where is this house?'

'Town called Clachdubh.'

His eyes narrowed. 'There was a stabbing up there last week.'

She nodded. 'Nothing to do with this.'

'What kind of house?'

She assumed Gary's house would be like Jasmine's and Jamil's. 'Semi-detached council house, two storey.'

He grimaced. 'Flats are easier.'

'I know,' she said. 'But this is a semi.' Probably.

'And what if I don't find this WEP2 password thing?'

She took a deep breath. 'Then you steal the computer. It's a teenager's computer, so it'll be in a teenager's bedroom upstairs.'

He took another mouthful of Guinness, his eyes still scanning the room and pausing on a TV screen to catch the score. 'Laptop or a big fucker?'

'No idea. Probably a laptop.'

'Fucking hope so. How many people in the house?'

'The teenager, who works shifts at Tesco. His father is there too – no idea what he does.'

'I'll need to do surveillance,' Licker said. 'Over a couple of days. It'll take time.'

'I need the computer by Friday evening.' She needed to set some kind of deadline for him even though she thought it probably didn't matter when he did this.

Licker pulled out his phone. 'And the address is?'

She told him.

'Names?'

'The owner of the computer is a teenager called Gary McAllister. His father Robbie lives there too.'

'Dogs?'

'Don't know.'

Licker sighed and shook his head. 'And you stay off my back afterwards?'

She nodded. 'We meet here on Friday evening at six. You give me a bit of paper with the code, or you give me the computer. Then you'll never talk to me again.'

❧ 53 ❧

Amanda had a ton of work to do on the Robertsons, and a DI from OCCTU W was coming over to talk about what they were finding after the abortive Manchester raid. Ramesh wanted

Amanda there.

Amanda put together a summary of what she and Pete had been finding and speculating about. Then she waited for the DI to arrive.

In that vacuum of time, she phoned Clachdubh police station. Sergeant Craig Torrance answered.

'Hi, Craig – glad you answered. It's you I wanted to speak to.' She was glad because there was no one to wonder afterwards what she and he had been talking about.

'Aye, well, I do pretty much everything now. If they stuck a broom handle up my arse I could sweep the floor too.' He cleared his throat.

'It's DS Amanda Pitt here – you may have seen me around when I was up investigating that Rima Khalaf case.'

'Oh aye – that business. What can I do for you?'

'I've done my final report and everything's been squared away, so this is just for my own personal curiosity.'

'Oh? What is?'

'Completely between us and off the record.'

'Aye?' His voice was extremely doubtful.

She tried to give a light laugh. 'Retired Inspector Jones pretty much got everything sorted on the original investigation, but he wasn't what you would call thorough, was he?'

Torrance grunted a laugh. 'Jonesy's a really nice guy. I see him at the golf club – he spends all his time there these days. Shame about his wife. But no, "thorough" was never his style.'

'You would have been involved in the case.'

'Aye.'

'And Karen McKechnie – the schoolgirl who fell off the Rock a few years ago?'

His voice was sad. 'Aye, poor Karen.'

'What was she like?'

'Lovely girl by all accounts. Very pretty. A bit of a flirt, though. My theory was that she gave somebody too much of a come on and then backed away from going through with it. Teenage lassies can do that: testing their powers.'

'You think somebody could have got annoyed that night and pushed her off?'

'We couldn't establish anything. They were all pissed out of their minds – including her. One kid – Danny – admitted having a wee fondle with her away from the others, then they both came back to the group – no doubt with him grinning like a Cheshire cat – and she realised her watch had fallen off, so she went back to look for it. Nobody saw anybody else leave. When they went to search for her – well, she'd gone over.'

'There was someone there that night, Craig. Gary McAllister. You know him?'

'No – I've never come across him.'

'How about Jamil Sabry?'

'Oh, him! He's trouble, and will be all his life. Angry and stupid – a terrifying combination. We interviewed him about some thefts from the school when he was there – couple of kids' mobile phones – never made anything stick. Violent little shit too. He'll hurt somebody one day and we'll get him. It's just a shame we can't lock the little bastard up before that.'

'Do you think he could have pushed anyone off the Rock?'

'Yes – but there's no way he could have been clever enough not to have been seen and caught.'

'Right.' That confirmed everything she'd found out before, and it didn't help. Jamil Sabry was stupid – she could vouch for that – and Gary McAllister had never done anything wrong. She was no further forward. 'Thanks, Craig.'

Ramesh was out of his office, waving at her, pointing as two very tall men in suits were being shown over. She stood up, and followed them into Ramesh's office.

They were DI Colt from OCCTU W, and DS Asif from Manchester. They all sat across the desk from Ramesh.

Colt had a rough Glasgow accent. 'This is just an informal meeting, sir,' he said. 'Your team's been very helpful to OCCTU, and we wanted to bring you up to speed.' He turned to Asif: 'So, Manchester.'

'May I speak freely, sir?' Asif had a Lancashire accent.

Ramesh nodded.

'It was a complete fuck up at our end. Two of our guys were on loan from uniform, and they parked badly. Too close, too obvious. The two vans you saw leave East Kilbride were making their way round the city on the A6010, and we saw what looked like the shipment arriving at the garage we were watching, in a

Transit van. They started unloading. But they clocked our guys and started putting the boxes back in the Transit. We had no choice: we could either lose everything or get something.' He turned to Amanda. 'I'm sorry.'

She gave a small nod in return.

Colt mirrored her nod. 'But we may have got some useful material.'

Asif handed over two sheets of A4, one to Ramesh and one to Amanda. 'There are two lists there: one is the list of men we caught on Saturday, in possession, hands up, sorted, finito. The other is some names they've given us. One is 'the chemist' who is suspected of being involved in manufacturing. His name is Salah Khalaf – he's a pharmacist.' He paused. 'Are you OK?'

Amanda had sat forward. 'This man is the father of a young woman who died in a town north of Glasgow – Rima Khalaf. I knew he was a pharmacist.' And she knew from Michael's 'connections' that Khalaf was a criminal suspect. 'Is there any terrorist link here at all?'

'None that we know of,' said Colt.

Asif added: 'Khalaf would have been generating large sums of money. He's got a very big house – not on footballers' row in Heaton Park, but not a million miles away – but then he doesn't drink or smoke, doesn't party, so maybe that's his only luxury. But maybe there's more money and it's getting funnelled out to the very bad guys.'

Amanda was scanning down the list. 'Freddy Morton.'

'We're not sure about him,' Asif said. 'He's been out of sight for a year or so now, and one of these guys says he came up to Scotland. We've never pinned anything on him in the past, but we'd like to track him down.'

Colt added: 'We haven't come across him. Do you know of him? Can you find him?'

Amanda kept her features straight, her mind revving. 'No,' she decided to say. 'I've *heard* of him somewhere, but I can't remember where.' She needed to…what? Tell Michael? What would he do? Speak to Freddy Morton, tell him to get out of town?

She looked up and Colt was staring at her. She held his stare and then turned back to Ramesh. But she knew she'd held the stare for just a little too long, and she knew Colt knew she was lying. But he'd have no idea why.

'So that's where we are, sir,' Asif said. 'We've confiscated the whole delivery, so now the demand will be even higher. They'll need more supplies, and fast. And that's when they get careless.'

'Is there any other plan?' Amanda asked.

Colt pursed his lips. 'In this situation – where demand is outstripping supply – there is a possibility of setting up some kind of sting: offer Es to fill the gap in the market, see if they bite.' He shrugged. 'It's a tricky one, because it may come to nothing, and it makes the court case problematic. We're thinking about it.'

Colt looked round them all, then stood up.

Ramesh stood up and reached to shake his hand, then Asif's too. 'OK, gentlemen. Thanks for letting us know all about this.'

Colt and Asif shook Amanda's hand. Colt's eyes were boring into her. She smiled and held the stare. 'Good to meet you,' she said.

'I'll show you out,' said Ramesh.

As Ramesh took them away, Amanda went back to her computer where Pete was eagerly awaiting the story. She told him – omitting the reference to Freddy Morton – and then they talked about Salah Khalaf.

'So was the girl involved in the father's drug deals do you think?' he asked.

She shook her head. 'I doubt it. But I wonder if she suspected he was into something shady. Maybe that's why she came to Scotland to study and teach, that's why she limited contact with them.' She shrugged.

What to do about Freddy Morton, though. Or should she just let him get arrested? That would solve the problem for Michael.

❧ 54 ❧

In the quiet spells, Licker McGuire would remember the night when he'd earned his nickname, and Sookie Dixon had earned hers. Their relationship had begun and ended that one magical, drunken, stoned evening.

And his smile always faded as he went on to remember his time in prison, where they knew his nickname. The cellmate who'd made his life hell for six months there was now safely *in* hell. He'd been too big for Licker to fight inside, but back in the free world that hunting knife had evened things up nicely.

Licker let his mind roam back and forward over the years, the chances he'd taken, the ones he'd missed, the mess he was in, and then he focused on the job in hand.

A council estate wasn't an easy place to do surveillance. The houses were too close together, the gardens small. There was no wasted space. Licker did a walk past, and then walked around the streets nearby in random patterns, hoping no one would spot him and think him suspicious. Then he got his old Fiesta and parked up for no more than an hour before moving somewhere else, all in the streets round the house he was interested in. His registration plate was largely obscured by grime and mud.

It would be easy here to do a random break-in – pick a soft target and hope for the best, hope you got lucky with whatever you picked up. But if you had a specific house, and a specific thing in that house, well that was harder.

He had found Gary McAllister's house easily enough. When what was obviously the father went out for the evening, a light was still on upstairs at the back of the house, which looked like the kid's bedroom and so the location of the computer was safely established.

Gary worked at Tesco, he'd been told, and a phone call when Gary was at home established that he'd 'be in tomorrow' from ten till late shift. So the window of opportunity was clear. The building wasn't high, but all the windows on the estate looked double-glazed. So it would be through the back door then, up the stairs, and back down and away.

The father was problematic. He didn't seem to have any pattern to his life. Licker followed him on the Thursday afternoon to a house three streets away, where he was greeted warmly by a middle-aged woman, followed a few minutes later by a light coming on upstairs. That evening, Licker saw the man return to his own house, yawning but with a spring in his step. He went out again towards ten, to a different house. Licker drove to a Travelodge twenty miles away for the night.

On the Friday afternoon, Licker parked well away from Gary's house and wandered down, his jacket collar up over his face and a woolly cap on his head. He was positive Gary had gone to work, but the father was more doubtful. Licker went up to the front door and rang the bell.

The man answered. 'Whit?'

'Mr Ferguson?'

'Naw!'

The door was shut hard, and Licker went off to his car, and drove back to park – slightly riskily – where he could see the house. The man had been wiry, strong-looking. If he'd been a weakling, or a fat bastard, Gary would have felled him then and there and tied him up. As it was, Licker waited patiently, hoping this wouldn't drag on till Gary got home.

Finally, Licker thought as he saw the man emerge from the house. Finally.

As soon as the man had turned the corner, Licker was across the road and round to the back door. Tall bushes kept the small, untidy back garden nicely private. All he could do was hope no one was upstairs next-door looking out. The back door was locked, of course. His cosh smashed the window, and the key was in the lock, as in ninety per cent of cases. He was in.

Up the stairs and into Gary's bedroom. It was a laptop. Thank fuck.

But first to see if he had the easy option. He went back downstairs and found the router beside the phone. It was an old-looking Netgear router, and there was nothing written on it.

Back up to the bedroom, he looked round: unmade bed, posters from some swords and tits epic, a bucket overflowing with coke cans, empty crisp packets and used tissues. He opened drawers, looking for some bit of paper with the WEP2 code written down. Nothing.

There was, however, a ring: a nine-stone ring, probably an engagement ring. Licker held it up to the light, but he was no expert: it could be really expensive or it could be a cheap fake. He tucked it deep into his jeans pocket, and briefly wondered whether to check the other bedroom for jewellery or whatever – but Amanda had told him there was only the father, so there wouldn't be anything. He had no idea why the teenager had this ring.

Shoplifting? Minding it for someone else? Licker mentally shrugged.

OK, he had to take the laptop. He pulled out the charging cable and briefly wondered whether he should take it. Naw – he'd been asked to get the computer. He put the laptop in the ironic Tesco bag for life he was carrying. Already he was worried about how long he'd been in the house.

He went quickly downstairs again, and out the back door, locking it behind him to slightly confuse matters. Round to the front and down the path, heading for his car.

'Hoi! You!'

As he got to the pavement the figure of the man of the house was turning into the street, holding a Co-op bag. He was immediately suspicious, and he broke into a run towards Licker, who ignored him, thus confirming his suspicions. He caught Licker as he was pulling his driver's door open, throwing the bag with the laptop onto the passenger seat. Licker turned and stood upright.

'What the fuck?' the man asked.

The guy was strong right enough, Licker thought, feeling the grip on his shoulder. He whipped out his cosh, poked it hard into the man's face then hit him on the side of the head, twice, lashed out with his feet and pushed him away. As Gary's dad staggered back holding his head and face, his shopping spilling on the ground, Licker came at him, kicking his legs away and then kicking him twice in the side of the head as he lay struggling to get back up. A final stomp on his face, and Gary's dad was writhing and moaning, semi-conscious.

Licker was in his Fiesta and away down the street, hoping that no one had looked out and seen him – though they wouldn't give a good description. No one would be able to describe the car very well, and the number plates were unreadable.

He drove carefully at the speed limit all the way back to Drumchapel. At the appointed time on the Friday evening, he met Amanda Pitt in that Irish pub in the Merchant City, and gave her the Tesco bag.

'Couldn't find any code,' he said

'Any problems?' she asked.

He shook his head. No point telling her about the man he'd

felled. And absolutely no point telling her about that expensive-looking ring he'd 'found'. In a couple of days he'd show it round, see what he could get for it.

❧ 55 ❧

Kylie flicked the switch on the battery pack and placed the small wheeled robot on the floor. After a couple of seconds it raced forward towards the wall, then stopped, its green LED turning to red. It backed up a bit, looked left and then right, and decided to turn left, racing on again. Kylie squeaked with delight, and the three boys applauded, then winced as it crashed into a table leg.

'Oops.'

Kylie knelt awkwardly – two of the boys were wide-eyed – and picked up the robot, its wheels still spinning

'OK,' she said. 'Back to the program.'

They sat round the keyboard, looking at the monitor. Kylie did a ctrl-C and the robot's wheels stopped, then her finger ran down the program listing.

Amanda smiled and turned away to where Martin and Michael were exploring the contents of Gary McAllister's laptop. The laptop itself had been password-protected, leaving them several options. Michael had decided simply to take the hard drive out and attach it to another computer. Nothing on the drive seemed to be encrypted, so they could browse it easily. Amanda sat looking at the monitors as files were opened and closed, folders scanned.

This was becoming a habit, she thought, being here with Martin and the slightly odd Michael. She was still wondering when to tell him about Freddy Morton; he'd probably ask her for advice, and she had none to give.

As Michael worked through the hard drive – exploring emails, browser history, and documents, Martin turned to Amanda. 'I still can't believe what you've done here,' he said.

She agreed. 'Get over it, Martin. Focus.'

What she'd done was crazy. She'd got angry before about cases and situations, and once or twice she'd lost her sense of logic and her control. Dealing with Jamil Sabry was one such example. This was another – although arranging a burglary of someone's house was taking things to a whole new level. Still, it was very unlikely anything would be traced back to her, even though she'd seen that the burglary had been reported. An assault too, which made her frown: Licker had said nothing about that. However, if she *was* connected to those events…

'Once we've had a look at it, you can put the hard drive back in the laptop and I'll dump it somewhere,' she said. 'It'll all be fine.'

But she was thinking about that, and much depended on what they found on the laptop. She could dump it right enough, or she could drop it off at a police station where anything incriminating that was on it might be discovered afresh.

'I'm going to get a coffee,' she said, not finding it easy to settle. 'Anybody want anything?'

Michael asked for a double espresso and Martin a latte. Downstairs she queued and ordered from Taylor.

'Youse up there with the computers and that?' Taylor asked, writing 'Amanda' on the side of the cardboard cups.

Amanda smiled. 'They do a bit of work for our company,' she said.

Taylor smiled back, and gave Amanda her change.

Amanda waited patiently for the order to be made, and took it all upstairs in the standard over-sized egg box. Then she sat and tried to be patient, knowing that it was pointless to keep asking: 'Have you found anything yet?' She worried a little about Taylor, but reckoned the girl was pretty dim and wouldn't make any connections.

Amanda finished her own coffee, and went over to where the teenagers were working on the robot. Kylie showed her the program and explained what the eyes on the front of the robot really were – 'It's an ultra-sonic detector'. She pointed out the motors and the circuit board.

Amanda nodded.

'You're in the police,' Kylie asked in a suddenly shy voice.

Amanda looked round, and then nodded, wondering how Kylie knew. 'You thinking of it after school?' Shit, did Taylor know this too?

'Not sure.'

'Get yourself to university, get a degree. Work on computers, software – those are the skills we need. There are millions of clever people out there who are thieves and terrorists, using the Internet for their own ends. We need people who can stop them.'

'Did you go to university?'

Amanda smiled and nodded. No point telling Kylie about the disastrous love affair, the near breakdown and the abandonment of her studies. No point disillusioning one so young. There was plenty of time for that to happen later of its own accord: someone who looked like Kylie would be subject to sexism and harassment, and she'd have to learn to deal with it until such time as the world changed.

'Amanda!'

Amanda excused herself from Kylie and went back to Martin and Michael.

'The emails are all things to do with a writers' group, and some stuff to do with online discussion groups – notifications of posts. Sent items has been cleared out, and very little has been saved. Facebook is the same: online groups – historical discussions, sword and sandals fantasies, lots of nudity clips from TV programmes on the subject, the writers' groups.' He was shaking his head. 'Nothing connected with what you spoke about. He doesn't do Twitter or Instagram or Tinder. But his documents are fragments of historical fiction novels and short stories.' Martin swallowed. 'You might want to read through them. Some of them are worse than the extract he emailed to Rima Khalaf.'

Michael vacated the seat at the computer, and walked away across the room to the robot group. Amanda sat down, with Martin leaning over her shoulder.

She put her hand on the mouse, and scrolled through Gary McAllister's writing.

'All focused on the main character having sex with anyone he wants,' Martin said. 'Common male teenage fantasy, I suppose. And there's a theme where he murders women who have tried to reject him and he's had to rape.'

Amanda read about women being raped and thrown off Dumbarton Rock, and a red-headed woman being stabbed along with her lover, and raped as she died.

'This kid is sick,' she said, her mouth dry. 'But…'

Martin finished her thought: 'Is this fantasy or did he act it out?'

'How about his Internet activities?'

'Private browsing, I'm guessing. His Internet Service Provider will have a record of his browsing – even the private browsing – but you need legal means to get that.'

She reached into her handbag for the USB stick she always carried but almost never used. She inserted it and then hesitated.

'Here,' Martin said. 'Let me.'

He leaned across and saved the documents to her USB stick, and then closed them. 'There's some photographs as well. They were buried away.'

He opened the directory for her, and stepped back.

'They were probably uploaded from his phone. One or two match what we saw on that iPhone you acquired.'

She opened and closed them one by one, wondering what she was looking for. She recognised Crawford Ballantine and other individual smiling poses presumably from the writers' group, and Rima Khalaf whose smile was rather forced. There were other shots, in that same room that the writers' group obviously used, many of which were side views or distant views of Rima, often in discussion with an older man. Crawford Ballantine had spoken of a published author that Rima was cultivating.

Photographs of the Rock, with random passers-by in shot. She smiled as she saw the dog-walker she'd met twice up there. A couple sitting on the grass, deep in conversation, holding hands. Amanda zoomed in but lost the detail as the image pixelated, so she zoomed out and reached a compromise of size and resolution. It was Rima and a man. Amanda wasn't perfectly sure, but that didn't look like her schoolteacher lover Scott Anderson – and they would never have dared to be seen like this in public in daylight. This was someone else.

Another picture: a red-haired woman, slim and attractive, smiling and talking to a man – Kirstin the murdered woman, and, presumably, Kevin Baker, who had been accused of murdering her. A shot of Kevin Baker alone, a smile still on his lips.

Amanda went back to the picture of Rima with the man on the Rock. Martin leaned over, closer to the screen.

'What's up?' he asked.

'Is this the same man…' a click: 'as this?'

'Hmm. Might be. Hard to tell.'

'Can you enhance the picture?'

'There are things that can be done, but you run the risk of creating things that aren't there. Michael knows more.'

At the sound of his name he came back over, and Amanda explained the problem.

'Yeah,' he said. 'We can use Mathworks to process the image.' He peered at the screen. 'Maybe use a Wiener Filter to de-blur it, or do some image contrast enhancement.' He looked again at the small blurred image of the man with Rima, and the other photograph of Kevin Baker.

'Do they look like the same man to you?' Amanda asked.

He pursed his lips. 'Yeah – maybe eighty per cent probability. Clean-shaven, very similar hair, head held the same way. Maybe ninety per cent.'

'Is that a problem?' Martin asked.

'It opens up another possibility,' she said, 'and I really didn't need that right now. You checked that man Kevin Baker's Facebook stuff: there weren't any selfies with this woman, were there?'

Martin peered at the screen and shook his head. 'But if she had her settings right, she'd have had to approve any posting where she was tagged, and she might just have declined. Or maybe the affair didn't last very long.'

Amanda nodded. That sounded reasonable. 'Can you put these photos on my USB drive as well?'

✣ 56 ✣

It was getting out of control, she thought. It was too big. She'd been operating like an idiot maverick and she'd found out too much – and none of what she had found could be used as evidence. She needed to get her information into the investigation, and hope that she hadn't compromised any case against Gary McAllister. Or Jamil Sabry. Or Kevin Baker. Or any permutation of the three.

She also needed absolution for what she'd done. She'd hoped to find out something important, and she had, but it gave her a problem. A big problem.

Whatever happened, Ramesh was key, so she decided to tackle

him first to avoid pissing him off by going straight to Paige. If she got nowhere with Ramesh, then fine.

'Can I have a private word, sir?'

She closed the door and sat opposite him, with her face downcast, like the promising pupil confessing some heinous crime to the head teacher. She wondered whether Ramesh actually liked her. She'd never bothered about that before, but it mattered now. She was pretty sure he thought she was good at her job; she hoped he wouldn't want to lose her from the force.

'I've got a confession to make, sir,' she said, keeping her voice soft.

He sat back in his chair and swivelled it slightly, obviously uncomfortable. 'Oh?'

'Ideally I'd like to talk to you off the record, but I appreciate that may not be possible.'

He cleared his throat. 'Just talk to me, Amanda.'

He'd never used her first name before, and she wasn't sure whether that was encouraging or not. 'After I finished my inquiry into Mr Khalaf's complaint, which showed that nothing *significant* had been missed in the investigation of Rima Khalaf's death, I found myself compelled to look at some of what *had* been missed, to see if it really had not been significant.'

'And?'

'There was a lot, sir. There was no proper investigation into her laptop – which Mrs Khalaf had – and no search for her mobile phone.'

Ramesh nodded. 'A big oversight. But you told me all this before.'

'To cut a long story short, sir, I investigated. I probably shouldn't have, but I did. I tracked down Rima Khalaf's phone – in fact, I tracked down all three of her phones. It seems she had a habit of asking her married lovers to buy her a phone so she could communicate secretly with them. After the relationships ended, she kept them.'

'Let's park how you found the phones for now. What did you find on them?'

She swallowed. 'There are two young men living in Clachdubh: Gary McAllister and Jamil Sabry. They were both stalking Rima Khalaf to an extent, although I do not think this could be proved in court. I have Gary McAllister's laptop. On it are stories he wrote which include violent sexual fantasies towards women, involving pushing them off hills and stabbing them. As described in his writing, three of the women are identifiable as –' she ticked them off on her fingers – 'the stabbed woman Kirstin Grainger, Rima Khalaf, and Karen McKechnie – that's the schoolgirl who fell off the Rock in Clachdubh a few years ago.'

Ramesh leaned forward, his hands clasped on the desk. 'And you're about to tell me that this laptop was not obtained using a search warrant.'

'I'm not able to tell you how I obtained the laptop or the information on it, sir.'

'And I'm sure I don't want to know.' He rubbed his face. 'Let's park that as well. Anything else?'

'I have a photograph that places Rima Khalaf in a relationship with Kevin Baker, who has been charged with the murder of Kirstin Grainger.'

Ramesh sat back again, looking to the ceiling as if about to howl in anguish. After a minute he looked at her again. 'And what do you suggest I should do about this?'

'DCI Paige is in charge of the murder enquiry in Clachdubh, and she needs this evidence, sir. She has her doubts about Kevin Baker's guilt, so she *really* needs this evidence. I'd like you to arrange a meeting between me and her, and to help me tell her the story without her taking out disciplinary procedures against me. I'd like to keep my job.'

He nodded, and almost absent-mindedly said: 'So would I.' He fell silent again, and then said, 'I have three options here, DS Pitt. I can send you out of that door and pretend this conversation never took place. I can instigate disciplinary procedures against you myself. Or I can set that all aside, reprimand you verbally, and contact DCI Paige.'

'What are you going to do, sir?'

He reached for his phone. 'You've been a very naughty girl, DS Pitt. Consider that a verbal reprimand. Now go and get on with some work while I get Paige.'

Back at her desk beside Pete, he didn't pick up on her mood. 'The Robertsons are getting desperate,' he said. 'They're pissed off that their shipment was picked up –'

'As are we!'

'– and they're looking around for new ones. You said OCCTU spoke about a sting operation.'

'Yes – dangerous, though. Good lawyers would kill the case as entrapment.'

'But it would be worth a try to get the Robertsons.'

She was distracted by the thoughts of her discussion with Paige. 'We'd need a fall guy.'

'How about pony-tail – Freddy Morton?'

Freddy Morton, she thought. Set him up, get him to reel in the Robertsons, then...Then what? Lock him up? Let him go?

Would OCCTU go for this plan?

They spoke about it, and Amanda said she'd talk to Ramesh. Of course, before then she had other things to sort out.

Two hours later, DCI Paige arrived. After she'd had half an hour alone with Ramesh, Amanda was called in.

❧ 57 ❧

Ramesh was in his chair behind the desk while Paige and Amanda sat half facing each other on the other side. Amanda still intended to play the demure, apologetic role.

'OK,' said Paige. 'You have inadmissible evidence which relates to my murder enquiry, and to previous deaths in Clachdubh which have been proved to be accidental. I don't want to know how you obtained it, at this stage, because there is still a chance we can get by without it. However, there is an issue with a burglary and assault in Clachdubh.'

Amanda returned her gaze.

'The home of Gary McAllister's father was broken into two days ago. He was assaulted in the street outside by the burglar, and Gary's laptop was stolen. I assume you know nothing about this.'

'Nothing. I'm shocked, ma'am.' Amanda made no attempt to look shocked. She heard Ramesh sigh.

Paige nodded. 'If it happens that this burglary is somehow linked back to you then there is nothing I can do to protect you.'

'No, ma'am. It was nothing to do with me.'

'Right. Now, it seems to me that your evidence puts Gary

McAllister and Jamil Sabry on the trail of Rima Khalaf, and the murder victim Kirstin Grainger. Gary McAllister has violent sexual fantasies against women in general and some of his characters are identifiably these two women. And you have evidence that places my Kevin Baker with your Rima Khalaf.'

'Yes, ma'am. And the schoolgirl Karen McKechnie who fell to her death a few years ago was also stalked by Gary and Jamil.'

'So…Any of them could have murdered any or all of those women.'

'Yes, ma'am.'

'My priority is still the case against Kevin Baker. The other crimes can wait – assuming they are crimes. Your evidence implicates him further. How do you think we should proceed?'

Amanda had been ready to discuss and advise. She was taken aback by finding the ball suddenly at her feet and being told to make the run.

She took several seconds to collect her half-formed thoughts. 'I would like to sit in on an interview with Kevin Baker and ask about his relationship with Rima Khalaf. I'd then like to interview Gary McAllister about his fantasies and his photographs.'

'You can't do that – we don't officially have them.'

'Can't we find the laptop accidentally?'

Paige looked at Ramesh. 'In a skip in Easterhouse, perhaps?'

Amanda was winging it now. 'In a computer repair shop. Someone found it and brought it in because they couldn't get past the password. The staff checked it was working and discovered…'

'Obscene images,' Paige finished. 'So they called us in, and we identified it as his stolen laptop – you'll need to work out how to do that.'

Ramesh coughed. 'Which breaks the chain of evidence completely.'

Paige nodded, still looking at Amanda. 'Which was broken anyway. We can't use this in court. Go on, DS Pitt.'

'We can tell him what we know, plus the circumstantial evidence. I don't think he's resilient enough to lie.'

'You think you can get him to confess to whatever he's done?'

'Me? Eh – yes I do. I'd also like to interview Jamil Sabry, but he'll be tougher. He's deeply misogynistic, so it would actually be best if male officers interview him. I'll supply the questions.'

Paige was holding up her hand. 'Hang on: on what basis do we interview him?'

Amanda scratched at the back of her hand. 'He knew the dead women. I have an iPhone, which he originally stole from Rima Khalaf. He knows I have it, but he won't be doing anything about that, beyond wanting to hurt me if he should ever get the chance. It has compromising photographs on it.'

'But how did Police Scotland officially get this iPhone?'

Amanda grimaced. 'He can deny he ever had it – after all, it's not his phone and it's probably not traceable to him. If we interview him last, we can say that other witnesses fingered him. We'll get Gary McAllister to implicate him.'

Paige nodded slowly. 'We go with Kevin Baker first – see what he says.'

❧ 58 ❧

He was clearly confused and disorientated as he was brought into the interview room in Barlinnie prison, where male prisoners on remand normally go in Scotland. As and when he was convicted, he would most likely serve his sentence in Shotts prison. Not that it mattered very much, Amanda thought.

For a man like him, being in prison would be traumatic. Doubly so if he was innocent. If he was guilty, then he would be redoubling his efforts to maintain his innocence and get off.

Normally, once someone was charged and remanded, the police would not carry out interviews in connection with the case: that phase was over. Only if there were other crimes that the prisoner was suspected of would there be further police interviews.

Kevin Baker had obviously been advised on this by his solicitor, which was also partly why he was confused, but he was further confused by the fact that it wasn't DCI Paige doing the interviewing. Paige had thought about this in the car on the way to the prison. Amanda was sitting directly opposite Baker, the young solicitor to one side and Paige to the other.

'I'm Detective Sergeant Amanda Pitt.' Once Baker nodded to acknowledge that, she continued: 'I'm here to interview you about the death of Rima Khalaf last year.'

Maybe Paige had her doubts about his role in the murder of Kirstin Grainger, but there was no doubting the flicker of recognition and fear in his eyes now.

'Who?'

'Rima Khalaf. A schoolteacher. Lived in Clachdubh.'

He now shook his head slowly. 'Don't know her.'

'I must caution you that anything you say will be taken down and…' she gave the litany, seeing Baker pull his composure together. 'Now, for the record, did you know Rima Khalaf?'

He made a split-second decision. 'No.'

Amanda nodded, and put a print of a photograph on the table so he could see it. It was a posed photograph of Rima, part of the original case files. She looked very young and pretty in the photograph, with a slight smile on her face. A smile that annoyed Amanda.

Amanda and Paige were staring at Kevin Baker. They could see that he had trouble looking away from the photograph.

'Here's another picture of her with a man.' She placed the print of the photograph from Gary McAllister's laptop. Michael had sharpened the contrast, filtered out the blur, interpolated the pixels. It was clearly Rima. It was pretty clearly Baker with her.

'That's not me,' he said.

'Who said it was? You said you don't know her, somehow hadn't seen the media stories about her death, hadn't heard anything even though you work in the same town as she did. This is just a photograph of a man with her, on the Rock in Clachdubh. This is the man leaving shortly afterwards.' The second photograph: Baker closer to the phone camera this time, almost full face. Undeniably him. 'Is *that* you, Mr Baker?'

The solicitor leaned across slightly. 'My advice would be "no comment".'

'I'm sure it would be,' said Amanda. 'But what Mr Baker really needs to tell us is what he knows about Rima Khalaf's death. Because it's obvious he had a relationship with her, and regularly went with her to the Rock, from where she fell to her death. We need him to explain his relationship.'

Baker locked eyes with his solicitor.

Amanda said: 'Remember the bit about not mentioning something that you later rely on in court…'

'OK, OK. I knew her. I slept with her. Just three times. But she said she was in a relationship with someone and she was committed to her teaching and her writing. I broke up with her, and that was it. OK?'

Amanda controlled her excitement at getting this much of an admission. 'Did she tell you who it was she was having the relationship with?'

'No. I saw them together in a car, but I never found out who he was. I deliberately didn't read anything about it after…after her fall. It was all over between us long before then.'

Paige moved her body slightly forward. 'So, when you were suddenly stopped from having great sex with this young attractive woman, you weren't angry about it? Angry like you had been with your ex-wife?'

'The sex actually wasn't that great,' he said. 'She was pretty enough, good body, but there was no real passion there.'

Amanda wondered why Rima had gone for this man. Was she trying out a straight relationship with no strings – and did it bore her? Or did Ke Bakerin have something else to offer her?

'What did you offer her?' Amanda asked.

He frowned, unsure. 'What do you mean?'

'Rima Khalaf had several relationships in her life, all with men in positions of power or influence, who could help her career. She slept with a teacher when she was a pupil, she slept with a couple of lecturers at university, and her relationship in Clachdubh was with her head of department. Rima used sex to get on in life. So what did you bring to the party?'

He winced. 'I met her in the Clachdubh Hotel, after her writers' group meeting, and I overheard her talking to some old guy about her book. When she was about to leave, I went up to her and introduced myself. I told her I knew a couple of small publishers in London. We got to talking about the novel she was writing, and she let me read some. I said it was really good and I could help her get it published.'

'And that was a lie?'

He hesitated. 'Yes.' His voice was very small.

'Was she angry when she found out?'

'Not really. We were about to…you know, when I confessed. I was drunk, told her I didn't *have* the contacts as such but that I could *find* people who could help her. She put her clothes back on and left. That was it. We never spoke again.'

'Did you try to go after her?'

'No.'

'Did you try to see her afterwards?'

'No.'

'I think you did, Mr Baker,' said Paige. 'I think you saw her on the Rock that day and you lost it, the way you did with your ex-wife and the way you did later with Kirstin Grainger. You tried to talk to her, and then you just pushed her off.'

Tears were flowing down his face. 'No,' he said. 'No. I loved Kirstin. She was the best thing that ever happened to me. She was funny and sexy and clever. Rima was a bitch, a mistake. I wasn't sad at losing her.'

'Rima got what she deserved.'

His face was dissolving as he shook with sobs. 'You must believe me. I didn't push her off the Rock. I didn't attack either of them. Please believe me. You must believe me.'

Outside, as they drove past the secondary school that they really felt shouldn't have been built right next door to a prison, Amanda asked: 'What do you think, ma'am? You've interviewed him, you've seen him lie and you've seen him tell the truth. What do you think?'

Paige took a deep breath. 'I don't know. I'm inclined to think he could have pushed Rima off the Rock, which is awkward for Police Scotland because we've twice said her death was accidental. But I'm still not sure if he stabbed Kirstin. She had a single deep stab wound that was actually unlucky to have killed her. We don't think it was a frenzied, angry attack of the kind he could have made if he'd lost it. And there's still no clear motive. How about you?'

Amanda looked out through the car windscreen at the dark grey cloud. 'I thought his denials were different,' she said. 'So one is true and one is a lie – though it's as much a denial to himself as it is to us. He murdered one of those two women. He couldn't have had anything to do with Karen McKechnie, and her death is like Rima's – so I go for the same person for both, and it's not him.'

'I disagree,' Paige said.

They drove on in silence.

'Mr McAllister? I'm Detective Chief Inspector Paige, and this is Detective Sergeant Pitt. May we come in?'

They saw a small wiry man in his early forties. He had an aggressive rat-like face, with one black eye and bruising on his cheek, and he wore a T-shirt – muscles taut – and tight jeans.

He eyed them suspiciously. 'What's this about?' He barred the way. 'Are you here about the break-in?'

'Not completely,' Paige said.

The non-bruised eye widened.

'May we come in?'

He reluctantly showed them through to the small lounge, and they all sat down, Paige and Amanda side by side on a tiny two-seater couch.

'We've found Gary's computer,' Paige said. 'Is he here?'

'Gary!' The shout was deafening. 'Get down here!'

They waited till he appeared. He was a little taller than his father, but a bit overweight. His dark hair was carelessly cut, and his complexion was acned and pasty.

'These are the polis, Gary. They've found your computer.'

Gary didn't look overjoyed. Amanda thought he went a shade paler, and he ran his tongue over his lips. 'Great,' he muttered.

'Sit down, Gary,' Paige said.

She waited till he sat – uncomfortable on the edge of the other armchair – and she turned to Amanda, who said: 'It was recovered along with proceeds of other burglaries. We had to examine it to check who it belonged to.' She paused for a moment. 'Can you explain the photographs you have on your computer, Gary?' She felt she had nicely glossed over the details she wanted to hide.

Gary's dad was looking from Amanda to Gary and back, his face screwed in a frown. 'Gary?'

Gary had gone completely white and looked like he might faint. 'Ah…eh…'

'The photographs of Rima Khalaf, the photographs of Kirstin Grainger. Photographs of other girls you appear to have been following around.'

Gary leaned forward, almost with his knees against his chest, his arms round his calves. His toes began to tap together. He looked like he was trying to mouth sounds.

Amanda was pleased to see the effect she'd had on Gary, but she needed some kind of confession from him before they could take him away for formal interview. And she had to make sure that the exact circumstances of 'finding' the computer were never really explored. She hoped Mr McAllister would say nothing, and indeed he was sitting stunned.

'Rima and Kirstin are dead, Gary.' When Gary reacted to that with an obvious quivering of his body, she added: 'You need to tell us what you know about the murder of Kirstin Grainger.'

His head began to move in small circles, and his tongue flicked out. 'She was dead when I found her – he stabbed her.' His voice was soft, barely audible.

'You were there – ' Amanda took a deep breath, and tried to control herself.

'Right, that's enough.' McAllister got to his feet, standing between Gary and the police officers. He pointed at Paige and Amanda. 'You go no further without an arrest warrant. Now fuck off out of here.' He turned and glared his rage at Gary, and raised his arm, looking like he was about to slap him with the back of his hand.

Paige stood up and Amanda followed. 'We don't need a warrant in this situation, Mr McAllister. I have enough evidence to detain Gary, or even to arrest him. But I am asking him to come along voluntarily to make a full statement. If Gary is innocent, and cooperates with us, then we can get this sorted out very quickly. If Gary wishes, you may come along to sit with him. In the event of Gary facing charges, we will help you arrange legal representation.'

McAllister stood with his fists clenched and his body rigid, as if he wanted to attack someone. 'OK,' he said, but he didn't relax.

Paige called for uniformed officers and a car.

They re-convened in the tiny interview room at Clachdubh police station. Paige stressed that they were simply asking for Gary's version of events. This would be recorded and written down, he could check the details and sign his statement, and he would be free to go. The alternative was that he would be held on remand until they got the full picture.

Gary hummed and hawed about his stalking of Rima and

Kirstin. 'It was harmless. I was just...' and he shrugged.

'They were very desirable women,' Amanda said, 'and not interested in you.'

He nodded, a small tear in one eye.

'You'd seen Kirstin with her boyfriend. You'd been outside her house.'

'I'd been a couple of times. Thought I'd maybe see her inside...'

'Maybe see her undressing?'

He squirmed.

'And you saw her boyfriend's car there at night and again in the morning.'

He nodded. 'I thought I'd maybe...'

'Maybe see them having sex?'

McAllister looked disgusted with his son, and turned his head to face the ceiling. Gary nodded, tears sliding down his cheeks.

'You wanted background for your novel,' Amanda suggested, in an understanding sort of way – 'good cop'. 'You had Kirstin as a main character that you could have within your novel.'

'But not in real life,' Paige said. When he added nothing, she went on: 'So you went to her house on the morning of her murder. Talk us through it, Gary. Tell us everything that happened. It's the only way.'

His voice was small. 'I went round the back, tried the door-handle. The door was unlocked. I went inside. All the curtains were shut. I thought they'd be in bed. I thought I'd maybe get a look.' He squirmed unhappily. 'But she was just lying there in the hall, on her back. Her dressing gown was untied and there was all this blood.' He looked for a second like he might be sick. 'All the blood.'

'What did you do, Gary?' Amanda asked, still with a soft voice.

'I leaned over her – I think I may have touched her...'

'You pulled back her dressing gown and touched her naked body.'

'I think I must have touched her, because there was blood on my sleeve when I got home, and on my trousers. She was beautiful.'

Paige nodded. 'In your novel you murdered her, Gary.'

He nodded. 'I murdered her and her lover in my story, and then I had sex with her as she died because she'd betrayed me. And...But that was in my story!' His voice was almost a wail.

'Where was Kirstin's boyfriend at this time? Did you see him with a knife?'

He shook his head. 'I ran outside and went home.'

'Did you see the boyfriend at all?'

'I heard something in the kitchen, and a tap started running. But there was a radio on, quite loud. I just ran out as quickly as I could.'

'How did you feel when you got home?'

'I don't know. I wrote a chapter, and it didn't seem so real after that.'

'Why didn't you come forward during the enquiry?'

'I had been in her house. I'd have been arrested.'

'You said there was blood on your jumper,' Paige said.

'I binned it. Up at the landfill skip at the recycling centre. My shoes and trousers too – they all had bits of blood.'

Paige nodded. 'We need to get that all recorded formally. Factually, Gary – as it really happened. We'll take a short break.' She spoke the time and switched off the recorder.

In the tiny main office of the police station, Sergeant Craig Torrance brought them some surprisingly good coffee, and left them to speak.

'Do you believe Gary?' Amanda asked.

Paige nodded. 'But proving Baker's guilt is going to be even harder now. He can blame Gary.' She sighed. 'We'll check Gary's prints against the ones found on the door handle – I assume they'll match. None on the knife.'

'Which is good: Gary wasn't wearing gloves. If he had the presence of mind to clean the knife, then he'd have cleaned the door handle.'

'How did Baker not see him or hear him leaving?'

'Blind rage – almost literally? Why was the back door unlocked?'

'And Gary didn't see him actually stab Kirstin Grainger.' Paige sighed again. 'I'd like a psychiatric examination of Baker, to look at these rages. Meanwhile, we'll get Gary's formal statement and then you can start asking about Rima Khalaf.' As an afterthought she said: 'I need to be very careful how I play this with Baker and his solicitor. And there's still no motive.'

❧ 60 ❧

They finished with Gary in connection with the murder of Kirstin Grainger. They read his statement and questioned him about it. They went over times and details: what did he notice in the house? What exactly was the layout of the hallway? Where exactly did he stand? How did he leave the back door?' What sounds did he hear exactly when he was in the house? Describe exactly how Kirstin Grainger was lying.

They didn't shake him on any detail. Amanda thought that Paige would probably take him to the house for a walk-through at some point. Certainly they both thought he was telling the truth, but how could she break Baker's story? He couldn't now claim he'd seen Gary, could he? But his defence would be that the murder had been committed by someone other than Baker, and the jury would now believe it was Gary. Maybe.

And maybe it was. But given Gary's whole demeanour, Amanda believed he was innocent. Baker was guilty. But there was no motive other than a sudden, irrational blind rage.

Paige sat back and let Amanda take over. 'Can we talk about Rima Khalaf, Gary?' Her good-cop tone had gone.

He wiped the back of his hand across his eyes and on the back of his trousers. He looked blankly at her.

'You really liked her, didn't you?'

He nodded.

'She was pretty, and clever, and she was on the same wavelength as you with her writing – historical fiction. You saw her every month at the writers' group, and you tried to bond with her.'

Gary's dad sat slumped in his chair, hands in jeans pockets, legs spread. His bruised face was blank, stunned.

'She wasn't a nice person,' Gary said. 'Some people thought she was, because they fancied her, but she wasn't.'

'No she wasn't, Gary. She didn't want you because you couldn't help her. She didn't need you, Gary. She didn't deserve you.' Amanda took a deep breath. She didn't want to rush this. 'You knew she was having an affair with another teacher. You knew she was seeing Kevin Baker at the same time.'

188

Gary was nodding.

'So what happened that Saturday on the Rock, Gary? Tell me what happened.' She kept her voice soft, hypnotic. 'You'd seen Kevin Baker up there with her, hadn't you? You'd photographed them together. Did you know they'd broken up?'

He nodded once then stopped, his eyes far away. 'I saw her standing at the top. I went up to her to talk to her. I told her she was a selfish bitch and a whore, and she told me to fuck off – she was in the middle of texting. She turned away from me. I grabbed her arm to make her listen, take her attention away from the mobile. I wanted to tell her how we could work together, share ideas. I grabbed the mobile. She pulled it back off me. I grabbed her arm and she tugged away from me – stepped back. She got closer to the edge and I reached to pull her back, away from it, make her safe. I grabbed her mobile again. She jerked her arm away…And then she just fell backwards and turned and she seemed to lose her balance and she just tumbled down the slope. I couldn't believe it. One minute she was there and the next minute she was gone. I couldn't believe it.'

'You didn't go for help.'

'There was nobody there to help.' His voice was small, low, far away. 'I looked round but there was nobody there. I went back down the Rock and just went home. I thought she'd maybe break her leg, but she'd be down at the road and somebody would be passing.' His voice was flat and hoarse. 'I couldn't believe it when I found out she was dead. And then I was sure somebody would have seen me – but they hadn't. Nothing happened. Nobody came for me. I went up there again, to watch the ambulances. No one pointed at me. They all said it was an accident. And it *was* an accident. I didn't push her.'

'It *was* an accident, wasn't it, Gary?' Amanda asked.

He nodded, the tears flowing again. 'Yes it was. It was. Please believe me.' His voice was quiet and husky. 'Please believe me. I'm so sorry.'

'How did you feel about her death, though? How did you feel really?'

He squirmed. 'She was a bitch. She deserved something bad to happen to her. But not that.'

Amanda let the silence grow, and gradually Gary's tears stopped and his composure returned. His dad was still sitting with his hands deep in his jeans pockets, staring out at nobody.

'You had her mobile in your hand, and you kept it, didn't you?' When Gary nodded blankly, she added: 'You gave it to Jamil.' Gary nodded again.

And Jamil had passed it on to Jasmine in return for a grope.

Now it was time for her to start yet another line of questioning. 'Remember that school after-party, Gary? The day Karen McKechnie fell off the Rock?'

His body language changed abruptly, everything tightening up. 'What about it?'

He's got something to hide here, Amanda thought. 'You were there.'

'We were all there – the whole year was there. Pretty much.' He tried to shrug.

'Was Karen pretty?'

'She was a tease.'

'You fancied her.'

'We all fancied her.'

'What happened that night?'

'I had nothing to do with it!'

Amanda held her hands out to calm him. 'Tell me what happened, Gary. Just tell me. You've done very well so far. Just tell me all of it. Get it out of the way. You'll feel much better.'

He shook his head. 'I didn't see anything. We were all pissed. She went off for a snog with someone – Danny – and…And they came back. And I didn't see what happened after that. She fell. She was drunk.'

'Was she being really flirty that evening? She'd be wearing her best dress for the dance at the school. Was it low cut, showing her breasts? Did she turn you on, Gary?'

'No. Yes – yes of course. But I didn't do anything to her.'

'So who did, Gary? Who did she tease a bit too much?'

He was shaking his head violently. 'No. No. I can't.'

'Was it Jamil Sabry?'

He was stunned. He stopped shaking his head. 'How do you know about Jamil?'

'Was it Jamil?'

His face crumbled. 'He'll kill me.'

'Was it Jamil at that after-party on the Rock?'

He nodded.

'Did you see him push Karen?'

He shook his head. 'He was angry at her. When Danny came back with Karen and a big grin all over his face, Jamil said to me 'I'm next'. Jasmine McCallum said something to him – I didn't hear it. Karen had dropped something and went back up the Rock a bit – out of sight. When I looked round, Jamil had gone – I didn't see where he went.'

'But you're sure he went after Karen?'

'Yes. Neither of them came back to the party. We thought he'd persuaded Karen to go somewhere with him, that she'd suddenly fancied him. Stranger things happen with girls. But neither of them came back. We found out the next day what had happened to her.'

'Did you tackle Jamil about it?'

He gave a snort. 'No.'

Paige was looking at her watch. 'Thank you, Gary. I'm not going to put you on remand, because I don't believe you are a threat. But you are a material witness in a live murder investigation, and a possible future one. You don't talk about this, and you don't go anywhere outside Clachdubh without checking with the local police station first – here. Is that clear?'

Gary nodded.

'Mr McAllister.'

Gary's dad turned his gaze slowly to her.

'Mr McAllister, I know Gary is over eighteen, but I'm making you responsible for his safekeeping. You will be contacted within twenty-four hours about any charges against Gary that may be brought. It is very likely that we will have to interview him again, and it is almost certain that he will appear as a witness for the prosecution in the case of the murder of Kirstin Grainger. And I'm quite sure that his evidence will come under severe scrutiny by the defence.'

Gary's dad looked blankly at her. She couldn't tell whether he had absorbed any of that.

Back in the small office, with another cup of good coffee and Amanda's tummy making rumbling noises, Paige said: 'This is complicated.'

Amanda nodded.

'The inquiry into Rima Khalaf's death concluded that it was accidental, and nothing we heard just now changes that, does it?'

Amanda nodded again.

'I cannot see what would be gained by re-opening that investigation and then spending a lot of time and money to reach the same conclusion. Not to mention the damage to the reputation of retired Inspector Jones. And yours, DS Pitt.'

Amanda stilled her anger. She knew this was likely to happen: her investigation into the original enquiry had shown what everyone wanted it to show – and that was correct. There had been hideous gaps in Jones's enquiry, but nothing they'd found changed the verdict. She believed now that Rima Khalaf's death had been accidental. There was no point opening it up.

Amanda nodded. 'I'm sure the Fiscal's office wouldn't reopen the case. If they decided to prosecute Gary, there's really no evidence – there's no chance of any conviction. And it would seriously compromise the case against Kevin Baker if Gary was exposed as being involved in another suspicious death. Or two.'

Paige nodded. 'There is that. What about that schoolgirl's death? Do you think we should pursue that?' She checked her watch.

'I'd like to talk to some more people about it.'

'Including Jamil Sabry?'

'I'll leave him for now.'

'I need to get back to Glasgow. You coming?'

Amanda shook her head. 'Later.'

⤜ 61 ⤛

The working day wasn't quite over, so she drove out to Kevin Baker's unit on the business park, and parked. Jasmine's automatic receptionist smile faded when she saw Amanda walking up to her.

'Hi, Jasmine. Can I have a word?'

She looked round. 'I can't really leave my desk…'

'Let's sit over there. You can see if anyone comes in.'

The reception area had a water cooler and a coffee machine. Jasmine poured herself a cup of water, and helped Amanda to get the machine to deliver an Americano, which appeared to be a cup of hot water with a tiny splash of something black at the end. It wasn't nearly as good as the coffee at the police station.

Jasmine looked very smart, mature and attractive in her white shirt and black skirt, and full make up. 'What do you want to talk to me about?' Her self-assurance had come back. She had the practised confident style that went with her role in the office.

'I've been talking to Gary. About Rima Khalaf. And Karen McKechnie.'

Jasmine reacted to Karen's name. 'What about Karen?'

'Rima and Karen. Two very pretty girls – young women – who attracted a lot of attention. Rima had an affair with a married man and also your boss here.' No flicker – Amanda couldn't be really sure whether Jasmine had known this. 'Karen was a bit of a tease, especially when she'd had a drink. Some would say they got what they deserved.'

Jasmine sipped her water, her face impassive.

'What did you think of Karen?'

Jasmine shrugged. Her fingers shook as she drank some more water and then stood to refill from the cooler. 'She was all right.'

'Was she prettier than you?'

'What's that supposed to mean?'

'Or were you both a bit of a tease?'

'Look, what has this got to do with anything?'

'Who pushed Karen off the Rock, Jasmine? Danny went out of sight with her and came back – word is he was looking pretty pleased with himself.'

Jasmine's lips turned into a sneer.

'So who went next?'

'She was a slut that night. Boys were all over her at the dance, and after. She was lifting her dress and pulling down the neck. Showing them what they could have. Slut.'

'So you didn't get too much attention?'

Jasmine arched her back. 'I got enough.'

'So who followed Danny?'

'I didn't see.'

'Yes you did. Who were you talking to?'

'I was near Jamil.' Her voice was reluctant. 'He was coming on a bit, giving me more vodka, trying to get inside my dress.'

'Did you like Jamil?'

'In a way. He was mad – still is. Dangerous in an attractive way, you know? But that night he was way out of control.'

'So how did you get rid of him?'

She looked like she was fighting an internal battle. 'I told him Karen was up for it. I said she'd told me she secretly fancied him. So he went off up the Rock once Danny was back. She'd said she'd dropped something up there.'

Amanda nodded. 'I need you to make a statement about this.'

'Why?' she wailed. 'It was three years ago!'

'You need to put it right. You need to make sure Karen McKechnie gets justice.'

'That slut doesn't deserve justice!'

Amanda took a very deep breath and drank her coffee. 'Tell me about Kevin Baker.'

She took a moment to catch up with the turn in the conversation. 'You know all about him.'

'Did he fancy you?'

She gave an instinctive toss of her hair, and her back arched slightly more. 'Probably.'

'Did he ever come on to you?'

She thought about that and gave a slight shake of her head. 'Kept checking me out, looking down my front when he got the chance, but he never tried anything on. Never asked me out or anything. Never tried to touch me.'

'Did you ever see him angry?'

She shook her head firmly. 'No, never.'

Amanda thought that was honest, which made it a surprising answer. But maybe Kevin Baker didn't fancy someone so young as Jasmine. 'I want you to type out what happened that night of the after-party, print it, and sign it. Now.'

With Jasmine's statement in her handbag, Amanda went out to her car and sat there wondering what exactly she might do now. Had she enough evidence to arrest Jamil Sabry? Dare she tackle him herself? He wouldn't be taken by surprise again – unless he was really stupid.

She'd left Jasmine her card with her mobile number on it. 'If you want to talk more, Jasmine, then call me. You know you can't rest till all of the past is out in the open, till you've done what you can to put it all right. If you keep a secret, you'll be haunted for the rest of your life.'

Now Amanda yawned. She really couldn't be bothered going back to Glasgow and then back out here tomorrow, but she had things to do with the real case she was working on. Jamil Sabry could keep.

And then there was Freddy Morton.

❧ 62 ❧

Michael had put his phone on silent during the lecture. As the students filed out he did the same as every other student: switched on the ringer and checked for messages.

'Hi, Michael.'

Shawna was Indian, and usually stayed quite close to Michael. He'd never been good with girls, but he was slowly learning that they were just people like him. But he still blushed and got scared whenever one showed any interest in him. Like now. Especially if they were pretty. Like Shawna.

'Hiya,' he said, still checking his phone, his ears slowly turning red.

'You going to eat?'

'Ah – ' He glanced down at the time on his phone. 'I'm going to this computer club I'm involved with. I help out – earn some money. I'll probably eat later.'

'OK.' She smiled, showing very white teeth, and started to move away.

He watched her for a second then blurted out: 'Would you like to come along?' His face turned bright red now: she would laugh at him and shake her head, and he'd feel stupid.

She stopped moving away and turned, still with the smile and the questioning dark brown eyes.

He backtracked. 'It's – ah – probably not very interesting. It's a makerspace kind of idea. School kids…some old guys too. Hackers. If you like. Probably not interesting.'

'Sure. I'd love to come.'

He swallowed and nodded. 'OK. It's not far. Byres Road.'

As they walked down the hill, he tried to explain what the club did, tried to make it sound interesting but not too interesting – nothing about Shala. Once above Roasters, she was genuinely in awe: 'I've often had a coffee in here: I'd no idea what was upstairs! This looks brilliant, Michael.'

He watched her walk over to a group of kids and crouch by their table, and they immediately began to talk to her about what they were doing.

'I just need to check something,' he said. She turned briefly with a huge smile, and he went to the computer in the corner.

Shala had sent him a WhatsApp, saying she needed to speak to him. Once he had the computer up and running, he started the encrypted message program they used – easier than using the phone to text.

'I spoke to my FBI contact,' Shala wrote. 'They're getting increased traffic from a group called B, and that sounds like there's something being planned. They can't decipher the messages, but they can see where they're coming from. One source is in Clachdubh. It might be your guy Jamil Sabry.'

'What kind of something?'

'Any disruption. Could be coordinated terror attacks, could be random one-off killings.'

'I take it the FBI has warned the UK?'

'He doesn't know. They don't know anything about groups like B, what their capacity is. And there is no timescale.'

'Has Jamil got weapons of any kind?'

'No idea.'

'What should I do?'

'You might want to tell your police contact.'

Shawna was still over by a group of kids, and they were listening to her talk about things she'd done. Kylie was particularly fascinated.

Michael called Martin. 'Martin, I've had a call from my contact. She says there is a high probability that Jamil Sabry is planning something – she doesn't know what, where or when.'

'Something big?'

'I don't know, Martin.'

'Hmm. I'll tell Amanda. I don't know what she'll do, but I'll tell her.'

Michael finished the call, and smiled across the room to

Shawna. She came over to him. 'This is fascinating. You help all the time?'

'Yeah, I help out. Mainly it's Martin McGregor. He owns B&D Software Solutions in town. A couple of schoolteachers set this up and Martin's company helped with money for equipment. Martin comes down when he can.'

'So do you work with Martin?'

'I help him out from time to time with odd projects.'

She grinned. 'I really am hungry, you know. Do you need to stay here?'

'Ah – no. No – I can take you…come with you…have dinner with you.'

'Let's go, Michael.'

Michael shut down his computer while Shawna spoke again to Kylie and the others, then she followed Michael out of the door and down the open wooden staircase. On the way they passed Taylor, who gave them a smile.

'Where shall we go?' Shawna asked.

'Ah – you decide.'

✤ 63 ✤

'That's him coming in now,' Pete said very quietly, and trying not to stare. He lifted his pint.

Amanda sipped her glass of tonic, calculating that she'd catch sight of Freddy Morton in the pub mirrors as he walked to the bar. And she was right. Quite tall, fit, good-looking. In his late thirties. She'd barely registered him when she'd seen him as they'd left Patterson's bar before.

She was nervous about being here, because the girl Taylor was behind the bar again, and had been looking over at her. Amanda had smiled at her whenever their eyes had met, and got a smile in return. Would it be worth trying to flirt with the girl, she wondered.

Freddy had an easy smile as he ordered a pint of special from Taylor, and stood leaning his elbows on the bar. Amanda saw him speak quietly to Taylor, and saw the response: a small shake of the head, and a shrug. The words were inaudible, but she could read her lips: 'Anything?' And a shake of the head from him.

The pint was paid for, change given, and the first third gulped down. Taylor went off to serve others. Freddy leaned sideways on the bar, looking round: smiling and nodding to acquaintances, and then freezing for a second when he saw Pete and Amanda. Then he recommenced his 360 of the bar, and focused on his pint and the gantry.

'He's got an eye for a stranger,' Pete commented. 'And a cop.'

Amanda finished her tonic. 'I'll get this round.'

Standing at the bar, she barely came up to Freddy's shoulder, and she could smell clean sweat from him. She ordered, and he turned his head to her. She sensed his confidence and the aura of dangerous excitement, and could see how some women would be attracted to that type.

'Haven't seen you around here before, darlin'. How you doin'?'

'I'm doing really great thanks,' she said, exaggerating her Scottish accent to contrast with his London one.

'Tell you what, darlin'. You let me get you this drink and you tell your boyfriend to fuck off, eh? Then we can have a chat.'

'I'll pay for it thanks,' she said.

'Does he get jealous, then?'

Taylor was back, and Amanda ordered her tonic and a pint of Special for Pete. Taylor looked from Amanda's smile to Freddy's gaze, and she frowned as she poured the pint. The drinks were set down and Amanda handed over a ten-pound note. When she collected the change, she took a sip of her drink but didn't move, staring straight ahead at the mirrored gantry.

Freddy's eyes narrowed, and the cocky cockney mask slipped. He realised she had a particular agenda here, and it involved him. He seemed to sense personal risk.

'Shortage of Es around this week, Freddy, isn't there?'

He took a deep breath and then a deep drink.

'You struggling?'

'No idea what you're on about, darlin'.'

'I've got some.'

'Yeah, right. Locked up in some evidence vault somewhere. Save it up for party nights, do you? Big fuckin' orgies down the cop station, all of you stoned off your tiny tits.'

Taylor was glancing back from serving another customer, obviously hearing parts of the conversation and looking very confused.

Amanda sniffed. 'Thought you were a man we could do business with, Freddy. Or are you exclusive with the Robertsons?' In the reflection in the gantry, she saw him give a sneer that was part admiration, part contempt, part discomfort.

She turned to beckon Pete, and then back to face Freddy. Pete came and stood just behind her, putting his empty pint glass down on the counter and lifting his fresh one, taking a healthy drink. He stared at Freddy.

'Thing is, Freddy, we haven't come in here just for a cheap pint.'

Their voices were low. The other barman was half listening in, but he was busy. No one else around seemed interested, and the pub was noisy.

'We came here because you're a man we can do business with, Freddy. Now my friend here is an exceptional lover but he's also absolutely crap with money. In our police station there's boxes of Es, lifted from a Manchester warehouse the other weekend. They were destined for Glasgow. And they can still make it onto the streets here.'

His eyes narrowed, registering that he knew about the shipment. 'This is bollocks.'

'We got part of the shipment for our experts to analyse and trace – cooperation with Greater Manchester cops. I'm sure there's somebody down there you could check this with.'

That last bit was pure bluff. All of the confiscated shipment was safely locked away in Manchester.

She could see Freddy wasn't sure, but he wasn't about to walk away from this.

'Two grand,' she said, and saw him flinch. 'I can get you six hundred pills for two grand. Do the maths, Freddy. At current street prices you can double your money. Even selling on in bulk, you'll make a big profit.'

'Fifteen hundred,' he said.

She shook her head. 'Two grand.'

'Seventeen hundred.'

She turned to Pete, who shrugged and nodded. Then to Freddy, she said: 'OK, Freddy. Now, we'll be in here at ten tomorrow night. Be here with the money, and I'll have the box. We can do the trade outside – there's an alley round the back. You check the pills, I'll check the cash.'

'How do I know you're genuine?'

She smiled. 'You'll have to trust me, Freddy.'

She and Pete went back to their table and sat looking at Freddy while they drank. He finished his pint and left. They gave him ten minutes, then went outside and up the road to Amanda's car, checking around the whole time for anyone following them.

'You think he'll go for this, boss?' Pete asked.

'I think so. He looks pretty desperate. We'll tell Ramesh the idea seems to be a runner, and he'll talk to OCCTU W. They'll plan the sting.'

Her mobile rang. It was Martin: 'I need to talk to you.'

❧ 64 ❧

She locked her car again and left Pete to get the underground from Hillhead to St Enoch, then his train home from Central Station. She walked up to the Oran Mor at the top of Byres Road, and inside.

She found Martin at the bar, with a fresh pint of St Mungo lager. She declined a drink, and they found a table as isolated as it could be in this big, dark, busy place.

'I got a message from Michael,' Martin said, speaking quietly. 'The FBI have intercepted increased traffic from a group they're watching – called B – and it's highly likely that your guy Jamil Sabry is in that group.'

'What does that imply?'

'Some kind of incident being planned. Nobody knows where, when or what. But it looks very like something is being set up.' He drank some of his lager. 'And your guy is probably involved,' he repeated. 'I think that's why he's kept the iPhone off most of the time: it was mainly for these special messages, and he hoped he wouldn't be picked up as being part of the traffic. Now he's having to use another phone and it's probably on most of the time.'

'I need to tell my boss,' she said.

Martin nodded. 'I would assume the information will have been shared and will come to him, but you need to make sure. And you need to keep me and Michael out of it. Especially Michael.'

'Thanks, Martin.'

She got up and left him with his beer, and went home to have a rather restless night, her mind teeming.

In the morning she had a meeting with Ramesh, where she told him about the meeting with Freddy Morton, and her assessment that he would buy the Es from her at the planned rendezvous. Ramesh nodded, and she watched him as he emailed OCCTU W – probably DI Colt.

Then she partially reprised the guilty schoolgirl impression, and tried to look as humble as she could as they talked once more about Clachdubh.

'DCI Paige told me about what happened,' he said. 'Retired Inspector Jones completely screwed up the investigations, it seems. Paige says it isn't a problem with the Khalaf girl, because that does seem to be completely accidental – though not for the reasons Jones thought. However, there seems to be an issue with a previous 'accidental' death. Karen McKechnie. She says you have a possible suspect. One Jamil Sabry.'

She nodded. 'Yes, sir. I have two witnesses who put Jamil Sabry alone with Karen McKechnie the night she fell off the Rock in Clachdubh. I need to interview him.'

Ramesh nodded. 'You want him arrested and brought to a police station for questioning? Or do you want to interview him at his home?'

'There is a complication, sir.'

He closed his eyes briefly and sat back in his chair, hands clasped in his lap. 'Go on.'

'I have a confidential contact who has links with people.'

'Everybody has links with people. Except for hermits. Who are these people?'

'People in the US, sir. I haven't been told myself by my contact exactly who his contacts are, but there is reliable information that Jamil Sabry is implicated in a possible terror plot.'

'Whose "reliable information"?'

'The FBI, sir. I would imagine it has been shared with our security services.'

Ramesh sat forward and tapped on his computer. 'I can't see that information,' he said after a minute. 'But it may be above me.'

'I don't know how that all works, sir, but I'm guessing that senior police officers will only be alerted when there is an imminent threat.'

'So Jamil Sabry is not an imminent threat?'

'Not imminent, sir. But there is information that he is planning to commit some kind of event. He is connected to some group but I have no information of who they are or what they are planning, except that they are called "B".' After a pause, she added: 'My information *is* reliable, sir.'

Ramesh tapped on his keyboard again, and read something from the screen. Then he sat back with his hands loosely clasped once more. 'I'll need to take advice. It may be that Jamil Sabry is being watched, in which case the security forces may want him left alone until he's about to do whatever he is about to do.'

'Or until afterwards.'

Ramesh gave her a grimace.

'So what do I do?'

He spread his hands and his eyes opened wide. 'You do nothing. You don't go near him. This information you obtained about him, the people who told you this: are they still connected with Jamil?'

Amanda thought of Jasmine and Gary. But to tell Ramesh the details of their contacts and feelings about Jamil would be complicated. So she said: 'No, sir, they don't see him.'

He nodded. 'Very well. Leave him alone.'

'Yes, sir.'

❧ 65 ❧

OCCTU W came up with the operational plan for the Freddy Morton sting, but Amanda had the lead role. She knew the key players and had made the first contact.

She got parked near the bottom of Byres Road, and picked up the plastic carrier bag containing the box – half the size of a ream of printer paper but much lighter. She called DI Colt to confirm she was all set: he was parked up with his team in Ashton Lane, out of sight of the pub. Two uniformed officers would be doing a pretend foot patrol, watching for Amanda, Pete and Freddy leaving Patterson's and going round into the lane behind it to do the trade.

It was ten to ten.

She really could have used a stiff drink, but it would have to wait. Once in Patterson's, she ordered a coke, and Pete took a pint but stood just sipping at it. Again, Amanda exchanged smiles with Taylor, and noted the suspicious look: the cover story about Pete was looking untenable, but that was OK – if Freddy and Taylor worked together, then he'd probably have told her what was going on anyway.

The bar was very busy, and they barely had a square foot of floor space to themselves. They stood near the bar – but not at it – and looked round.

Amanda saw Michael, sitting in a corner, with a pretty Indian girl. She froze, thrown by both aspects of this. He looked up and saw her and smiled. She smiled back, but gestured 'No' when he beckoned her over. She shook her head, and turned away.

'Someone you know?' Pete murmured.

'Yes,' she said.

'Nice looking friend he's got. How do you know them?'

'He's a kid who helps Martin McGregor out from time to time.'

The main door opened and Freddy Morton was there. He eased through the crowd to the bar and bought a pint from Taylor, then pushed back to stand next to Amanda and Pete.

'OK,' he said, 'impress me.' He didn't look at them.

'Cash up front.'

'Fuck off. Pills up front.'

'Show us you've got the money at least.'

He indicated the brown envelope bulging from his jeans pocket, and teased the flap aside to show notes: lots of them, all looking well used.

'Show me yours.'

She opened the carrier back and reached in to pull back the lid of the box, showing the small clear plastic freezer bags crammed with white pills.

'Let's get outside to swap.'

He finished his pint in one impressive long draught, and pushed the empty glass onto a nearby table. Amanda and Pete left their almost full glasses beside it. The three of them squeezed through the crowd and out of the door, through the smokers and the vapers. Amanda didn't look towards Michael as they went, didn't want to see his reaction to Freddy being here and with her.

As they turned right to go round the corner, she glanced across the street, through the streaming cars and taxis. She couldn't see the two policemen, which was good. She just hoped they could see her.

Round the corner into a quiet residential side road, then into the lane that ran along the back of the pub and the shops. It was damp here, a clinging lingering dampness that made Amanda shiver. The pub had been like a tropical rainforest.

She handed the box to Freddy, and he pulled out one of the packets from near the bottom. Amanda watched: Pete had predicted this, so most of the fake pills were in bags at the top. Freddy selected a pill at random from the packet and nibbled the edge of it. Then he licked the surface. Finally he rubbed away some of the pill and turned to check his fingertips under the light of the nearest street lamp. They stood for a heart-stopping moment and then he nodded. 'Seems OK. I need to check with the proper test kit, though. Can't give you the money till I've checked more.'

'Sorry?' Pete asked.

'This one looks genuine, mate, but that could be just down to luck. No, I'll need to take this away with me and get back to you.'

'I don't think so,' Pete said.

Freddy's half-grin – teeth bright – widened. 'You fuckin' gonna stop me, mate?'

Pete pulled himself up to his full height.

'Well. Are you?'

'No,' said Amanda, 'but these guys will.'

The two cops were amongst the tallest Amanda had ever seen, and wide with it. Before he'd fully registered what was happening, and had a chance to aim a kick or a punch, Freddy was down on the ground with one guy handcuffing him. The cops pulled him to his feet.

DI Colt was there, nonchalantly watching. The cops restrained Freddy, pointing him at Colt.

'OK,' Colt said. 'This is not as bad as it looks, Freddy. We still want to make a deal with you, but it's a different kind of deal now. The game's changed.'

'Fuckin' bastards. Cunts. This is fuckin' entrapment.'

Colt shook his head. 'Here's the deal, Freddy,' he said. 'We can do various things here with you. We can proceed with the charges and maybe they'll stick and maybe they'll be dropped. My colleagues here can harass you endlessly. Either way, your life as a middleman drug dealer in Glasgow is over. And it's over wherever you go in Scotland. Or we can negotiate a deal and you can get a one-way Virgin rail ticket south, out of our lives for ever.'

'I've got relationships here,' he said.

'You can form new ones,' Amanda said.

'So what are you after?'

Colt deferred to Amanda, and she said: 'We want the top dogs, Freddy. You're not important to us.'

'You want the fuckin' Robertsons, don't you?'

'Spot on.'

'You want me to get them for you. You're mad.'

She nodded. 'You tell them about a shipment you're organising. You say you've seen a sample and it's all genuine stuff. You arrange where and when, and tell us. You'll turn up with the goods, hand them over, and then we'll arrest them.' She dropped the box back into her carrier bag, his eyes following it longingly.

'Bang to rights, guv,' Pete said.

'Fuck off!' This was to Pete. To Amanda, he said: 'And what do I get out of it?'

Amanda turned to Colt, and Freddy's eyes followed hers.

'Freedom,' Colt said.

'If they find out, they'll kill me.'

'So get packed and buy your ticket first, Freddy. One way remember.'

Freddy strained, and tried to aim a kick at Amanda. 'I'll fuckin' have you for this.'

She smiled. 'I don't think so, Freddy. You do this for us and then you get out of town.'

❧ 66 ❧

She was back in Ramesh's office as he stroked his beard.

'So we just wait for Freddy Morton to contact the Robertsons? Amanda nodded. 'Pete and I will go out and about and sow the seeds about a big shipment coming it – maybe mention "some English guy". We'll ask for people to let us know.' She fought a yawn. 'Can't do anything except wait.'

'Do you think Freddy Morton will hold any kind of grudge against you?'

'Oh, he undoubtedly will, but it's not *that* big a deal to him and he won't be around much longer. He'll keep this small embarrassment to himself, I think.'

Back at her desk, she unlocked her computer and sat looking at the screen, suddenly incapable of switching her mind to other tasks – and god knows, there was plenty to do.

She sat looking at her emails, then phoned DCI Paige. 'Good morning, ma'am. DS Amanda Pitt here. I was just wondering…' Her voice tailed off. She had no right to be wondering anything, no right to be asking Paige anything. Paige would be entitled to get irritated and tell her to get lost.

'Nothing new,' Paige said, in the tired voice that Amanda recognised. 'We're finalising the evidence.'

'Have you spoken to Kevin Baker about Gary McAllister?'

Paige was hesitant. 'No. No I haven't. I'm trying to hold off for as long as I can, but there's a danger of jeopardising the whole trial if I don't tell the defence what we know soon.'

'Have you spoken to Gary McAllister again?'

'My DI did. He repeated his story – no inconsistencies. The only scenario I can visualise is that Kevin Baker lost his temper – massively – and stabbed his girlfriend, then wiped the knife handle clean, called 999, and went into emotional meltdown and maybe even extreme denial. We can believe that he lost his temper – though it's on a totally different order of magnitude from what he did before with his wife – but we can't see why. They were a loving couple, he'd spent the night with her – there's evidence of a whole heap of sex going on. So what made him lose it like that?'

'No chance of a third person – Jamil Sabry? Have you spoken to him?'

'Not yet.' Paige suddenly realised she was being quizzed about her investigation by a sergeant. 'Anyway, DS Pitt, that's not for you to worry about.'

'I was given information that Jamil Sabry may be planning some kind of event. I told CI Ramesh. Did he contact you?'

'No.' Her voice was curious. 'What information?'

'A confidential informant, ma'am, who has a source in the FBI.' That sounded dramatic, and she winced, but it was true nonetheless.

'OK. I'll check on that. Thank you.'

Paige hung up, but twenty minutes later she was back on the phone. 'I'm going to interview Jamil Sabry. Given you have background information, I'm asking you to sit in on the interview with me and my DI. I've been told it doesn't compromise any security issues – as long as we don't breathe a word about them or ask; no mention of IS, OK? How soon can you be in Clachdubh?'

'Hour and a half at this time of day, ma'am.'

'OK. Get going. Come to the police station – we'll interview Jamil there.'

Amanda shut down her computer, and briefly told Pete what she was up to. He wasn't happy at her bailing out on him again. She placated him as best she could, not happy herself with all this driving up and down to Clachdubh, and went out to her car.

As she started the engine, her mobile rang. The female voice was soft and surprisingly contrite. It was Jasmine McCallum. 'I need to talk to you.'

'OK.'

'Not at work, though. Can you meet me on the Rock – around five?'

The timing worked for her, so she didn't hesitate. 'See you there, Jasmine.'

She put the mobile down and wondered what Jasmine might tell her.

❧ 67 ❧

She thought Jamil could not have looked angrier if he tried when he saw Amanda sitting there beside Paige and the DI whom Amanda had met twice before – now introduced as Helen Mackenzie. His eyes blazed and he bared his teeth. Amanda remembered the description the head teacher had given: *feral*.

Sergeant Craig Torrance sat Jamil down and then stood with

his back to the door, eyes focused on Jamil. The room was too small for this number of people.

Jamil sat back, legs open – manspreading – thumbs hooked in the belt-loops of his jeans. He glowered at the three women, and then his eyes slowly surveyed each in turn, faces and busts. He decided DI Mackenzie was the best looking of the three, and slightly adjusted his position so he could look straight at her.

They'd all faced this many, many times before. They found it irritating, but didn't get angry – there was no point. In fact, the more blatant the looks and the sexism, the more they smiled, though it depended on the context.

Amanda was prepared for Jamil to start shouting about her taking the iPhone from him. Her plan was to deny it straight out – she had no other way of dealing with it.

Paige introduced them all, and told Jamil he was not under arrest. Nor was he a suspect in any investigation. She simply wanted a statement from him on what he knew about Kirstin Grainger and her boyfriend Kevin Baker.

'I don't know nothin about them,' he sneered.

Paige smiled. 'Well that's exactly what I want to know, Jamil. So let me just write that down.' She spoke slowly and deliberately while she wrote: 'I have never met Kevin Baker or Kirstin Grainger.' She looked up. 'Did you ever see them around the town? In the pub? Tesco?'

'No.'

She did the slow speaking as she slowly wrote that down too. 'And where were you the morning of her murder?'

He shrugged. 'In bed.'

'Any witnesses?'

He recognised the trace of sarcasm in her voice. 'Not that day. No.'

'Thanks for that, Jamil. Now, you know Gary McAllister, don't you?'

'That pervy cunt – yeah.'

'When did you last speak to him?'

Jamil shifted his position, and sunk his hands completely into his jeans pockets. 'Bout a week ago.'

'Not since then?'

'No.'

Paige turned to Amanda, who asked: 'When did you last see Jasmine McCallum?'

His tongue flicked out over his lips. 'Can't remember.'

'Think again. You must remember Jasmine. When did you last see her?'

'Can't remember.'

'You knew of a teacher at the High School. Miss Khalaf. Rima Khalaf.'

He didn't seem sure whether that was a question or not. 'I left before she started.'

'But some of your pals stayed on and knew her, talked to you about her.'

Her tried to shrug. 'Maybe.'

'She was Muslim. She taught about the history of Islam, putting it in context.' When he offered nothing, she added: 'So what did you think of that?'

'Stupid cow.'

'Oh? In what way?'

'Trying to promote Islam like it was better than the West. Pointless. Fuck the crusaders – we'll fuckin wipe them out. We got nothin to apologise for.' His face was an angry sneer.

Amanda kept her body and face still, and was conscious that the others were doing the same. Craig Torrance's eyes were hooded, his fists clenched as he folded his arms. She could feel Paige looking at her: she hadn't been supposed to mention this stuff.

'Did you try to talk to Miss Khalaf about this?'

'Like she would have been interested. Like she was brave enough to join the cause.'

Amanda looked at Paige and raised her eyebrows. Paige gave a small nod: carry on. But there was an accompanying frown.

'Did you ever meet with Miss Khalaf?'

'No.'

'Did you ever see her around?'

'Suppose.'

'Did you think she was pretty?'

He snorted. 'She was shaggin that teacher.'

'Did you fancy shagging her yourself?'

It was an outrageous question to ask, and Amanda almost heard a sharp intake of breath from the others, but Jamil answered it.

'I could have given her a good time.'

'The same as Karen McKechnie?'

Jamil froze and his face paled. Both eyelids dropped slightly.

'You were there on the Rock that night. You saw Karen go off with Danny, come back with him grinning all over his face.' Every word she spoke generated a small but perceptible physical reaction in him. 'Then she went back up the hill and you followed.'

He tried to swallow, and then tried to move his legs. He sniffed.

'Did you show her a better time than Danny had – or did she tell you to get lost?'

'Couldn't find her.' The voice was almost inaudible.

'Are you sure, Jamil?' She knew she'd lost the interview. She'd tried to rattle him with all the information that he didn't know she had, tried to shake him into bragging about having Karen, but she hadn't expected him to admit to stupidity. 'It's not a very big place.'

He sniffed again and met her eyes. 'Couldn't find her. Didn't fancy the party after that. Went home.'

Amanda could have leapt across the table and grabbed him by the throat, forcing a confession out of him. Somehow he'd regrouped, got himself together. She'd given it her best shot, and it hadn't come off.

Of course, there was always the chance that he was telling the truth.

Paige waited for a few seconds, then said: 'Well, thank you for coming in, Jamil. Sergeant Torrance will take you home.'

'I'll walk. Can't stand the smell of pork.' He stood up, leaning forward to try to intimidate them, but Paige stood up also, and she was taller than him.

'Thank you again, Jamil.'

They sat in silence, listening to Sergeant Torrance lead Jamil to the front door, and then a distant shout of 'Fuckin crusader dyke pig cunts'.

Paige looked at Amanda. 'Where does that leave us?'

Amanda shook her head. 'Sorry, ma'am. That didn't help at all.'

DI Mackenzie said: 'He definitely caught up with that girl Karen McKechnie, didn't he? What happened to her? Was she raped?'

Amanda shook her head. 'The official story is that she fell off the Rock, but I think Jamil lost his temper when she rejected his advances and pushed her off. I have circumstantial witness reports, but it was three years ago and there's no corroborating forensic evidence. The enquiry into her death was half-hearted at best.'

'And,' Paige reminded her, 'you've no forensics linking Jamil to Rima Khalaf either.'

'Nor to Kirstin Grainger, ma'am. But I do have the iPhone that Jamil had that once belonged to Rima Khalaf.' Both iPhones, she thought. One had been taken from Rima as she fell to her death from the Rock and passed along to Jasmine McCallum. Gary hadn't known the PIN this time, Amanda realised now, so it had been just given away to Jamil who gave it to Jasmine in return for a grope but probably in expectation of more. Gary had known the PIN for the other phone, the one that had been stolen from Rima at school, and Jamil had kept it and used it sparingly, to stay undetected as much as possible.

Paige grimaced. 'All we have is Jamil's denial. If anything does arise, though, that denial may play well during interviews. But he had nothing to do with Kirstin Grainger's death, had he?' She was looking at DI Mackenzie, who shook her head sadly.

'We're no further forward, ma'am,' DI Mackenzie said. 'My money's still on Kevin Baker.'

'So's mine,' Paige said. 'But I need a motive.' She turned to DI Mackenzie. 'Let's go. We've wasted enough time.'

❧ 67 ❧

She had to remind herself that the Rock was less than two hundred feet high, but the climb up the zigzag path – towards the figure silhouetted at the top – was tiring. Amanda was depressed and frustrated that she couldn't quite close it all off.

She was growing ever angrier at Jones's incompetence over his two enquiries. Stating that he knew it was accidental before starting the enquiries at all. Not seriously investigating Rima's laptop. Not connecting the deaths. Not investigating the missing mobile phone – three of them, after all.

But what exactly had *she* achieved?

She reached the top and stood with the surprisingly strong – and cold – breeze whipping at her jacket.

'Hello, Jasmine.'

Jasmine was wearing a long jacket that was being lifted and thrown about by the wind. 'Have you arrested Jamil?'

News travels fast, Amanda thought. It had only been an hour. 'We questioned him – that's all.'

'Do you think he pushed Karen off the Rock?'

'Do you?'

She was fighting to keep her hair off her face. 'Yes,' she said.

'So do I. But I've no evidence. Have you?'

'No.' She turned away to look northwards, into the wind.

'So what makes you think he did it?'

'The way he behaved the next day. He was quiet. Nervous. Just for that day, then he was back to normal.'

'Did you ask him about it?'

'No. Nobody did.'

'How about Gary, Jasmine?'

Jasmine turned to face her, hair tossing all round her face. 'What about him?'

'Gary was fascinated by Rima Khalaf. He followed her around. He was fascinated by Kirstin Grainger and he followed her too. He wrote them into his novel – he was obsessed by them.'

'Gary couldn't hurt anyone.'

'What makes you so sure?'

She laughed a short humourless laugh. 'We all used to tease Gary. Karen did, and I suppose I did too. Sometimes we went a wee bit too far. One night he was in the pub, really trying to come on to me, and I was encouraging him. I told him I was going to the ladies and to follow me in five minutes. I said I'd make sure no one else was there.' The laugh came again. 'He did it, and when he was there and he thought it was just me and him, I took him into a cubicle and said I'd show him mine if he showed me his. When he dropped his trousers, the others shot up from the cubicles on each side, snapped him on their phones.'

'Pretty cruel.'

'Yeah. Suppose. Anyway, he was angry, but he didn't lash out. He wasn't violent.'

Amanda saw what she was getting at. Gary would never have murdered Kirstin Grainger, not in real life. He murdered her in his novel, and Karen, who had rejected him, Jasmine, and the rest. And most of all Rima Khalaf, who had ignored his main obsession – his writing.

'If Gary didn't murder Kirstin Grainger,' Amanda said, 'then your boss Kevin Baker must have.'

She turned away again, face into the wind.

'He told us about his relationship with Rima Khalaf,' Amanda said. 'And he said he wasn't bothered that it had ended. Did he ever mention her to you?'

'No.' The word was almost whipped away by the wind.

'And you say he never tried it on with you. Is that really true?'

She turned to face Amanda once more, and she was either crying or the wind was stinging her eyes.

'What is it you wanted to tell me, Jasmine?' Amanda's voice was as soft and persuasive as she could make it. Almost seductive. 'Just tell me, Jasmine.'

Jasmine took a deep breath. 'He told me he had contacts in modelling, said he could take some snaps and send them down.' She stopped, as if fighting to get the next words out. 'He took some pictures – he had a nice big camera – an SLR, or whatever, yeah? – so it looked like it was a serious hobby for him. I went round to his house one night, wearing my best dress, all made up, and he took some poses. He gave me a few vodkas. Then he showed me pictures of other girls he'd taken, and told me how he'd helped their careers. Some of the girls were topless – one was nude, full frontal. He said that every model had to 'get their tits out' – it was part of the job. Full nudity was preferable, he said, but there was no pressure.'

'So did you get your tits out?'

Jasmine hesitated. 'Yes.' The word was barely audible. 'I stripped down to my underwear at first, and he took some pictures. Then he persuaded me to take my bra off, but he just took some photographs of me from the back, or with my arms folded across my boobs.' She swallowed. 'Then he gave me another drink, and his voice was just so soothing, so I put my arms down and let him photograph me like that. He said I had the most beautiful breasts he'd ever seen. And then he got me to turn my back to him and take my knickers down…and then off, and then he asked me to turn to face him.' She wiped tears away from her eyes. 'I almost did it, and he kept saying, 'Come on,

213

Jasmine – you're gorgeous – come on – let me see what you've got.' And I started crying – stupid of me. I pulled up my knickers and put my bra back on, and then I sat there and just cried. I was so ashamed.'

The silence was only broken by the wind whipping round them.

'He sat beside me and put his arm round me, and he said, 'Hey, what's wrong – you're beautiful – so sexy – you've got a great body – people will want to see it' and he pulled me close to him, and he said, 'They'll be horny as hell – come on, let's get them out again – just for me'.'

Amanda breathed slowly, enraged at Kevin Baker. 'What did you do?'

'I just cried and cried. I was so ashamed.'

'And what did he do next?'

'He stood up, and then he was crying too. He said, 'I'm so sorry – I'm so sorry. I forgot – you're just a kid. I'm so sorry.' I got dressed and he just kept apologising, over and over again. He took the memory card thingy out of the camera and smashed at it with a glass, and gave the pieces to me.' Jasmine sniffed and gave a short laugh.

'And what happened afterwards?'

'He called a taxi for me, and the next day at work it was like nothing had ever happened. He still flirted a bit, and it was creepy when he looked down my top because – well, he'd seen my tits. He'd seen everything.'

'Did you feel you were in danger that evening with him?'

She shook her head. 'No. I didn't think he'd hurt me.'

Paige needed to know about all of this, but it didn't help her case. Not at all.

'Was that all you wanted to tell me?'

'No.' She took a deep breath. 'I heard what happened at Jamil's house the other day. You took his iPhone off him. Our neighbour saw you, heard him screaming after you drove away.'

Shit, Amanda thought. If anyone wanted to organise a complaint then the evidence was there. Stupid.

Stupid stupid stupid.

Jasmine took a deep breath. 'Jamil gave me the iPhone you were asking about, the one you took off me.'

'I know.'

214

'He said Gary gave it to him.'

Amanda nodded. 'And you let Jamil kiss and grope you in exchange for it.'

'Yes. Just a feel.' She looked at Amanda. 'That was all.' She hesitated. 'I've never been with anyone. Never met anyone I wanted to do it with.'

OK. Too much information, but Amanda could relate to that. 'Do you know anything about the other iPhone – the one Jamil kept for himself?'

She shook her head. 'No. Not for sure. I heard a story that Miss Khalaf had had a phone nicked from her room at school – there were a few went missing around that time. That might be the one Jamil has – had…the one you took off him. Jamil has a rubbish old HTC that he uses most of the time, but now and again he'd flash the iPhone. He never said where he got it or why he didn't use it much.'

Amanda was seething. If retired Inspector Jones had done his job even half-properly they would have explored all these loose ends at the time, and things might have been resolved. As it was, Jamil Sabry was free even though he was almost certainly the killer of Karen McKechnie. And Kirstin Grainger might never have been murdered…

No. Kirsten was doomed the minute she fell for Kevin Baker: all it had taken was the trigger, though no one knew what that was.

'Anyway,' Jasmine was saying, 'they say Jamil is very angry with you. You should have arrested him. He's going to find you and slit your throat. That's what he says.' She paused. 'He says he'll kill you after he "fucks your brains out".'

Amanda instinctively looked around. Martin's contacts had suggested that Jamil's group was planning something. Well, she thought, murdering a police officer would be something, and also satisfy his hurt pride.

'You better take care,' Jasmine said.

Amanda smiled reassuringly. 'I will.' She'd call Paige, who would check up the line and across to the security services. This should be enough for them to arrest Jamil under the prevention of terrorism act, get him safely out of the way.

Taylor waited till the front door of the flat closed behind Freddy Morton, and then got out of bed and dressed. She put the used condom onto the side-plate with the remains of the joint they'd shared, and went to the bathroom to flush it all away. Then she opened the bedroom window to let out the smell of smoke and sex.

He'd said he was going away for a few days. He'd been away for 'a few days' before – in fact, he spent several evenings a week away from her with another woman, he said. She never queried this, never wanted exclusivity. He was happy, he kept her happy.

But the way he'd said it earlier was different. She sat on the bed looking out at the grey sky. She had the feeling he was going for good this time. And he'd borrowed forty pounds from her, which she couldn't afford: that was this week's share of the rent.

The front door opened and closed again. She recognised her cousin Jimmy's footsteps, and then his shout: 'Taylor?'

'In here, Jimmy.'

He opened the bedroom door and stood looking at her. 'You OK?'

'Fine.' Her voice was flat. She wasn't fine at all.

He sniffed the air. 'You been smoking in here?'

'Aye – sorry.'

He looked at her, and sank his hands deep into the pockets of his jeans. He was taller than her, just a few years older, slim and fit like her.

'How's mum?' she asked.

He shook his head. 'Just a matter of time, they say.'

She nodded. This had been the story for over a month now. The attractive forty-something had shrivelled to a near skeleton with the breast cancer that she'd ignored for too long, but she wouldn't die.

'She was asking for you.'

'I'll see her tomorrow. I'm working tonight.'

'She's still mumbling stories.'

Taylor wiped tears from her eyes. 'Oh aye?'

'She's talking about your father.'

She grunted a bitter laugh. 'Does she remember who he is yet?' Taylor had never known her father. Snippets had emerged from her mother's ramblings as the morphine ebbed and flowed through her system, but nobody had made sense of them.

'She's no makin sense.' He shrugged. 'Some computer guy, she says. She mentioned names: Davey, Martin. Charlie.' He shrugged again.

Taylor nodded, flinching at the sound of 'Martin'. Her mother had spoken to her about Martin, who had used her and dumped her, left her pregnant.

Jimmy coughed. 'You got this week's rent money, Taylor?'

'I – eh – I had to lend it to somebody.'

He looked at her, his breathing growing deeper, and he checked his watch then glanced over his shoulder. 'Usual deal, then?'

She nodded, and began to unbutton her shirt.

'I'll just check the front door's locked.'

❧ 69 ❧

It was the following evening.

Michael let himself in, listened to the silence, and then went upstairs to his room. Now he could hear faint giggling from his mum's bedroom, and then a loud, drawn out moaning sigh and the cockney voice: 'Phew, darlin', fuckin' best ever that was. You Scottish women ain't half bad at that. Now go and brush your teeth and I'll give you a kiss.'

His mum giggled again, there was a slapping sound, and Michael shut his own bedroom door just as hers opened. 'Hi, mum,' he shouted, to make sure she knew he was home.

'Oh – hi, Michael.'

The bathroom door closed and the tap started running.

He sat at his desk. This, along with the single bed, the wardrobe and the old bentwood chair, was all that fitted into the room. He opened his MacBook and messaged Shala to say he was back on line. The toilet flushed, and his mother pounded back into her room, to more guffaws and giggles. The door closed firmly, but her voice came through the wall: 'Stop it! I have to get to work!'

Michael resolved yet again that he had to leave home. He had no idea how he could manage it, but he guessed Martin could give him regular work – and pay him. He was enjoying seeing Shawna. He didn't have any close friends as such, just like-minded people at school and University, people he could talk to about gadgets and software. Shawna wanted to talk about other things, asked about his parents. That had been awkward at first for him, but he was starting to get the hang of it.

But overshadowing that had been seeing Amanda and that other guy in Patterson's the other night with Freddy, and then all three disappearing together. He knew that was something to do with him telling her that he thought Freddy was doing something with drugs, but neither Amanda nor Martin had told him anything and that was making him anxious.

'Bye, Michael!'

'See you later, Mikey boy!'

The voices floated back to him up the stairs, and the front door closed.

Michael got on with some tasks from his study – a program just wasn't working as it should, and he couldn't see the problem. He worked away, adding output statements to check the changing values of variables, stepping through it, and time slipped by as it always did when working on a computer.

The front door opened and closed again, and there was the unmistakable gait of Freddy bounding up the stairs and into Michael's mum's bedroom. Michael listened as drawers were opened and closed, wardrobe doors rattled.

Finally curiosity got the better of him, and he opened his bedroom door. Freddy was emerging, his leather jacket and waterproof on, a bulging holdall in his hand. Michael looked down at it.

'Hi, Mikey. Just heading off for a bit.' He started down the stairs.

'Where are you going?' Michael called down.

'Down south. Back in a few days.' The front door closed behind him.

Michael went into his mum's bedroom, and saw the note lying on the pillow.

Didn't we have ourselves a ball, girl? This afternoon was just the best. Got to go, though. Maybe back in a few days, maybe not. Don't wait up!

Won't forget Glasgow in a hurry, though. Or you. Freddy.'

Michael thought again about the pub the other night, Freddy and Amanda, the serious chat they had had, going outside together. Now Freddy was leaving. Michael didn't like the guy, but his mum obviously did. This would break her heart. She'd had the occasional brief fling before – some one-night stands – but nothing as intense as this, nothing as long lasting.

Michael felt anger. And then he started to think logically about what he might do.

He had Freddy's mobile number.

He logged onto the mobile tracking website, still on Martin's free trial. Freddy wasn't far away. Then the screen refreshed, and he was closer to the city. Again, on his way, parallel to the Great Western Road.

He must be on the train, heading for Glasgow Central.

Michael put his MacBook in his man-bag, checked he had his phone, wallet and keys, and headed out the door. It was dark outside, cold.

There were direct trains every half hour into Central. He got his ticket from the machine, and had only five minutes to wait before the long train silently rolled in then halted with squealing brakes. It was almost empty.

As it glided off again, Michael checked Freddy's progress on his phone – there was no Wi-Fi on this ancient electric train, and 4G was patchy. Freddy was stationary, somewhere along Dumbarton Road.

The train came into Partick and Michael got off.

Down into the surprisingly large station concourse, and outside, trying to orientate himself. He walked up Dumbarton Road, until he saw the pub, The Scarba, and realised Freddy must be in there. Michael stopped, not sure suddenly what he thought he was doing.

As indecision teemed through his mind, he phoned Martin.

'Eh – hi, Martin.'

'Michael. What can I do for you?'

'Have you been in touch with Amanda?'

'Not recently. Why?'

'It's – eh – it's about that guy I told you and her about: Freddy Morton. I know where he is and I think I know what he's doing.'

'Oh?'

'He's in a pub on Dumbarton Road – the Scarba. I think he's up to something big – probably doing a drug deal.' Once Michael had articulated that, his thoughts ran away with him: 'You need to tell her, Martin. You need to tell her to get down here and arrest him.'

'Woah woah. Hang on, Michael. Look, I'll call her and tell her what you've said. Now you sit tight – don't do anything silly, Michael.'

Michael had been walking slowly in the direction of the pub, and now he stopped and waited. Then events unfolded in front of him and he watched open-mouthed.

A police car pulled up and four uniformed policemen got out and rushed into the pub, a tall man in a suit following. At the same time, two men followed by a woman were running across the road to the pub too, and in through its doors, scattering the smokers. The smokers at the door held the door open and stared inside, silhouetted by the lights, still smoking, and trading comments and laughing.

Michael watched. Nothing happened for a few minutes.

Then a figure burst out of a different door, through another group of smokers, almost knocking two of them over. He carried a large holdall and a brown parcel under the other arm. The smokers shouted and laughed after him: 'Run, white boy, run!'

He was running towards Michael. It was Freddy Morton.

❧ 70 ❧

DI Colt had set it all up, and asked Amanda to be the contact with Freddy Morton. He also asked her and Pete to be there for the sting, because they knew the Robertsons.

Freddy had arranged to meet the Robertsons in the Scarba pub. Amanda was to meet him at Partick Station beforehand and give him a box of six hundred MDMA pills – all genuine.

After the handover – noting his holdall – she shadowed Freddy along Dumbarton Road to the pub, and then broke away. Pete was already inside, trying to drink a pint very slowly.

Two plain-clothes cops from OCCTU W were lurking across the road, chain-smoking. Four uniforms, with Colt, were further up the road in a car.

On her way back to Glasgow, Amanda had called Paige to tell her what Jasmine McCallum had told her about Kevin Baker, and Paige reckoned that might be enough to interview him again and maybe not. She also told Paige about Jamil, but Paige said that wasn't her call. If Jamil was being monitored, then it was up to the security services whether they made a move or not.

Amanda joined the two smoking detectives across the road from the Scarba, doing a reasonable impression of arguing while keeping warm outside a café She discreetly showed her warrant card and lurked by them, accepting a cigarette and pretending to smoke it. She hated the taste, but it reminded her of a previous lover, and for a moment she was transported back in time.

'There's the Robertsons,' one detective said.

The BMW had paused at the kerb, and the Robertsons – small, slight guys wearing nondescript waterproof jackets – headed for the door of the pub, with a bigger, stronger looking minder behind, his eyes flicking everywhere. The BMW drifted away to find somewhere to park.

'And who's that?'

He was looking down the road to a thin figure, slightly stooped, who was staring at the pub. 'Not a minder, not a punter. But he's interested, that's for sure. Who the fuck is he?'

Amanda's phone rang and she stepped away to answer it. It was Martin.

'Michael phoned, said he knows where Freddy Morton is, and that he's doing some kind of drug deal. Have you any idea what he's talking about?'

'Yes,' Amanda said.

One of the plain-clothes smokers was looking at his mobile, then putting it away and dropping his cigarette. 'We've to go in.' They began to move across the road, dodging a taxi, and a car sped towards them, braking hard at the door of the pub, four uniforms and DI Colt spilling out, heading straight inside the pub.

'Got to go, Martin.'

She was looking left at that lone figure: shit, that was *Michael* down the road. What the fuck?

She put her phone away and headed through the traffic across to the door of the pub, following the two detectives. She glanced again at Michael, but he wasn't moving, thank goodness.

Inside, as ever, it was hard to predict exactly what was going to happen, what the customers would do. But the pub wasn't busy. The Robertsons were at the bar beside Freddy. They looked shocked, and Freddy was doing his best to look shocked too. Colt was showing them his warrant card, and going through the formalities of arrest. The customers sat watching, like this was an episode of Taggart in the round. None of them, it seemed, felt the urge to intervene on the Robertsons' behalf. They were more interested in the traditional music trio playing on the raised area at the far end of the pub.

The minder stood with his fists clenched, but before he could do anything, the other detectives were at his side. 'Don't even think about it, pal,' one said. He obviously did think about it, but then he thought better of it.

Amanda stood with Pete as the three suspects were cautioned by DI Colt. The Robertsons were grinning like they didn't have a problem, but Amanda knew this was bravado.

That was when Freddy made a break for it. He grabbed the box of MDMA pills out of Andy Robertson's hands, and slipped between everyone and out of the side door up near where the band were. A few customers cheered him on his way.

One detective immediately set off after him, and Colt told one of the uniformed cops to go too, and then turned to Amanda: 'You as well: you know him.'

She heard a voice: 'Is that your fuckin evidence just gone oot the door?' as she headed outside. She grinned: Pete had been recording the deal, so there was plenty of evidence.

Amanda ran in the direction of Partick station, and stopped as she got to Michael, who was standing stock-still and staring. There was no sign of Freddy or the cops who were chasing him.

'What are you doing here, Michael?'

'I saw Freddy with his holdall. I knew he was leaving my mum. I knew he was dealing drugs. I traced him.'

'You can go home now, Michael,' she said. 'Go and see your mum.'

'What do I tell her?'

'I don't know, Michael. Was Freddy good to your mum? Will she miss him?'

'They had a lot of sex,' he said. 'But she was out working in the pub most evenings. They didn't do anything together. Not really. Except for sex.'

'He was bad news, Michael. He would have left her sooner or later anyway.'

Michael was looking round, seeming to only just become aware of his surroundings. 'Will they catch him?'

'I'm sure they will. Look, I need to go, Michael.'

Her mobile rang: Colt. 'They've caught him. Nearly at Partick station. He says he wants to talk to you.' Colt's voice was doubtful.

'I'm on my way down,' Amanda said. 'I take it we let him go as per the deal.'

'I'm in two minds about that – talk to him first, see what he's got.'

'OK.'

She stared at Michael. 'Can I give you a lift anywhere?'

His voice was small. 'It's OK. I got a return ticket.'

She hesitated to ask: 'Have you heard any more about Jamil Sabry?'

He shook his head. 'Want me to check?'

She shrugged. 'When you can. It's not urgent.'

She walked with him down to Partick station, past the two policemen holding tightly onto Freddy Morton, one of them with the box of MDMA pills under his arm. Michael walked past, his head bowed, and into the station. Freddy looked at him, but said nothing.

'You wanted to talk to me.' Amanda said.

'I thought you were going to let me go,' he said. 'I've got my ticket out of here.'

'Your evidence in court would be better.'

'We had a fuckin' deal, darlin'.'

She sniffed. 'Did we?'

'You going to stitch me up?'

'For fuck sake, Freddy – you're not in an episode of the Sweeney.'

'Look, I've got something else I can give you. If you let me go.'

'Oh?'

'I can give you Craig Steele.'

Amanda stared at Freddy.

'You know of him? He was a big Glasgow villain.'

'Yes,' Amanda said. 'I know of him. What about him?' Craig Steele, who had slipped away from all of them, including Amanda of course. Could she really be about to find out where he was? 'What about him?' she repeated.

'I know where he is. I can give you him. If you let me go.'

Amanda looked. The two policemen were obviously all ears. 'So where is he?'

'You let me go, yeah?'

'Where is he?'

'Malaga. I've met him in a cafe on Calle San Telmo. He's there every Wednesday morning. You can pick him up any time you like. He was helping to fund this whole operation.'

Amanda nodded. 'OK.' To the two policemen, she said: 'DI Colt says to let him go as we agreed.'

They cautiously let go of Freddy's arms, and he straightened himself up and grinned. 'Good boys.' With that, he turned away from them and sauntered towards the station.

It was after midnight before she got her evidence recorded to Colt's satisfaction, including what Freddy Morton had said about Craig Steele, and Colt told her that was the end – for now – of her involvement in the case. But he thanked her, and thanked her especially for the information about Craig Steele: 'We'll check that out.'

She'd briefly phoned Claire to tell her not to wait up, but she had. Amanda told her some of what had happened, and then they went to bed. Amanda dropped into a deep sleep, but woke around four with her brain worrying her: all the issues in Clachdubh, DI Paige's case…

In the morning, she got in late to Stewart Street. The Robertsons were out on bail, Ramesh said. Amanda was philosophical, not least because Ramesh had said that OCCTU W were officially very pleased with what Amanda had done – and, by implication, with Amanda herself, Pete was angry, though. 'All that fucking work, boss, and they just walk!'

'Relax, Pete. It takes time.'

Then Jasmine McCallum phoned her. 'It's about Jamil,' she said. Her voice was tense.

'What about him?'

'He's definitely going to do something. He called round last night, brought me a bottle of vodka. My mum was out. He said he was going to be dead by the end of this week, and he deserved a martyr's send-off.'

Amanda shook her head. 'An original approach,' she said.

'Yeah, well. I believed him.'

'Oh for fuck sake, Jasmine. You really need to wise up about men.'

'I believed him.' Her voice was a little girl whine.

'OK.' What she didn't want to hear was what she'd done for Jamil, though her mind ran along the whole range of possibilities. 'What did he say afterwards?'

'He said he was going to kill a cop. Said he was going to kill that 'dyke MILF'. Is that you?'

Amanda gave a laugh. 'A bit of an oxymoron, but probably that is me. He'll still be pissed off at me.'

'Anyway, look out for him.'

'He's nowhere near me,' Amanda said. 'He doesn't know where I live.' But he knows what car I drive, she thought, and the registration. She shook her head. No chance of him spotting her car. What else did Jamil know about her? Nothing. He didn't even know which police station she was based in. He didn't even…'Jasmine, you didn't give him my mobile number, did you?'

'No, of course not. But I let him look at my phone. It's better than his, but we both miss the iPhones.'

'Do you think he saw my number on your phone? Did you save me as a contact?'

'No – but he might have noticed my recent calls. He didn't ask though. He just wanted me to walk around a bit more, you know? And then he wanted me to lie down and – '

'Jasmine, I don't need to know about that. You gave him a martyr's send off, and now he's out there wanting to kill me, and he's got my mobile phone number.' She deliberately let her anger show.

'I'm sorry!' Jasmine laid on her little girl tearful voice even thicker. 'I'm sorry. He couldn't find you, could he?'

'Of course not. Look, I need to go, Jasmine.' She tried to make her voice nice again. 'Let me know if you find out any more. I appreciate it.'

She sat back in her chair. How technological was Jamil? Did he know there were ways of tracking mobiles? Could he find her here in Glasgow? Could he find her home?

Or could the group he was in contact with find her? Who were they anyway? A group of sad disillusioned kids like Jamil, or something much more serious?

That thought was dispelled by her police mobile ringing.

'Sorry to disturb you, ma'am. This is PC Dunbar from London Road. We were called to a jeweller's in the Argyle Arcade an hour ago. A suspicious character was trying to sell a very expensive engagement ring – worth around two thousand pounds, we've been told.'

Amanda heard a distant growl from near the PC: 'I'm not a fucking suspicious character.'

'We have him in the back of the car as you can probably hear, ma'am. The man has previous convictions for burglary and reselling, so we planned to take him in for questioning about this ring, but he claims that you will vouch for him.'

Amanda closed her eyes. Oh no. She had recognised the voice and knew the answer to her own question: 'What's his name?' She looked at her watch.

'John McGuire, ma'am.'

Fuck, it was Licker. What had he done? She opened her eyes and then closed them tight again, and rubbed her temple. 'Put him on, could you – and could you exit your vehicle and let me talk to him in private? He's a registered informant of mine.'

'Very well, ma'am.'

She heard the clunk as the phone was handed over – Licker's voice: 'Should fuckin think so too' – and car doors closing.

'DS Pitt.'

'Licker. What's going on.'

'I need your help to get me out of this.' The voice was pleading.

'I told you, I couldn't help you if you did something big.' She was prepared to resist any blackmail demands from him: she'd determined that right at the beginning of this whole business with the break-in. 'I can't get you off a charge of reselling a two grand engagement ring.'

'I think you need to, DS Pitt. I – eh – picked up the ring during that little job for you in Clachdubh.'

She gasped. 'You what?'

'When I was looking for that code thing, and I lifted the laptop for you. I saw this ring and took it. Figured they'll claim the insurance.'

'Where was it?'

'In the kid's bedroom.'

Amanda struggled to make sense of it. The McAllisters had never mentioned the ring. Gary had never asked about it when she and Paige had gone to his house to talk about his computer. OK, he'd been distracted by subsequent events. But even so.

She could sort that out later, but meanwhile she needed Licker out of that police car. 'Call PC Dunbar back.' She heard Licker tap the car window.

'Yes, ma'am.'

'Hi. It's complicated with McGuire, PC Dunbar, so I need you to trust me. I want you to let him go: I know all about him and I know where he lives.' She grasped at a cover story. 'He's currently crucial to a drugs operation we're involved in, so I don't want him in custody. Understood?'

'Yes, ma'am. What about the ring?'

Yes indeed, she thought. What about…

And suddenly she realised exactly what had happened with Kirstin Grainger. Bloody hell! It suddenly made perfect sense!

'Bag it as evidence and bring it to Stewart Street. Careful handling it – we may get contact evidence or fingerprints from it.' Her voice was quick, urgent.

She found Paige's number in her recent calls. But she forced herself to wait, to test her theory.

Yes, it had to be right. It was the solution. She made the call.

Paige sounded distracted. 'DS Pitt, what can I do for you?'

'It's about Kevin Baker, ma'am. I know what happened between him and Kirstin Grainger, and I think I can prove it. But you'll need to talk to Gary McAllister again to cross-check, and you'll need forensics too.'

❧ 71 ❧

Kevin Baker looked exhausted. Amanda suspected he hadn't slept much, and who could blame him. The young solicitor listened patiently while Paige took Baker through his story again.

'Look, I must protest,' the solicitor interrupted. 'You should not be questioning my client like this. He's been charged and is awaiting trial. So unless there is something new…'

'There is something new,' Paige said. 'More evidence has come to light and we need to share it with both of you.'

Baker looked at her, his eyes red with bags under them, his face white.

Paige reached out her hand, palm down, and then opened her clenched fingers and let the small plastic evidence bag drop to the table. Inside was an engagement ring. It was the one Licker McGuire had picked up from Gary McAllister's bedroom and tried to sell.

Kevin Baker stared at it, and then his face crumpled and he started crying. 'Oh god,' he said. 'Oh god.' His shoulders were shaking.

The solicitor was about to speak but Paige raised her hand.

'This ring has your fingerprint on the inside surface, Kevin,' Paige said. 'Tell me about it. Tell me what happened.'

He cried and wailed for some time, and they waited patiently until he began to speak. They had difficulty making out some of the words as he held his hands to his face. 'I knew she was the one. I knew we could be happy for ever. We'd had such a wonderful time together, and that night had been so good – so magical. I'd bought the ring days before, and that morning I just decided to ask her. Ask her to marry me. I knew we could be happy together. For ever.' The voice choked. 'I knew we could be so happy.'

'And…?' Paige prompted after a few seconds.

'She shook her head. She laughed. She actually laughed at me. She said we hardly knew each other. It was too soon. I said it wasn't. I told her we were perfect for each other. And then she said she didn't think she'd ever want to get married again.'

His body racked with sobs, and his fingers reached towards the plastic bag. 'I don't know what happened. I'd been doing something…in the kitchen…I followed her into the hall, I wanted to shake sense into her. I wanted to make her understand that we could be so happy together. I pressed the ring into her hand.' His sobs stopped abruptly. His eyes were far away, and then his voice went cold. 'She said no. She dropped the ring. I was angry. I grabbed her and she pulled away. The next thing I knew she was lying on her back and I had the knife in my hand. And she looked at me and she took a deep breath and she was gone…'

'So you went into the kitchen and washed the knife handle clean and came up with a story that someone else had killed her.'

He was nodding and sobbing.

'Can you clarify for the recording that no one else was present when you stabbed Kirstin Grainger, Mr Baker. Please.'

'There was no one there. I did it. But it was an accident.' He turned to face his solicitor. 'The balance of my mind was disturbed.'

'Not so disturbed that you didn't manage to try a cover up. But you couldn't find the ring.'

His sobbing began again and he covered his face. Paige picked up the evidence bag with the engagement ring. Amanda could tell she was happy that she had the motive for Kirstin Grainger's murder. It all made a kind of tragic sense now.

'Hang on a minute,' said the solicitor. 'How did you come by this evidence? Where did you find the ring?'

Paige smiled at the solicitor and turned to Amanda, who cleared her throat before saying: 'Someone tried to sell it to a jeweller's shop. The owner grew suspicious because the man trying to sell it didn't look like someone who could afford a two-thousand pound ring, and he called us. The seller panicked and ran, leaving the ring. Our boys did a routine check for fingerprints and matched Mr Baker's.'

The solicitor was frowning. 'But how did it get out of Miss Grainger's house? There was only a short period of time between her murd…her death and the arrival of the police'

'Indeed,' Paige said. 'Mr Baker, can I just ask you to confirm the details of what happened between you and Miss Grainger that morning.'

He went through it all again for them. Amanda thought he was even more exhausted, and yet he seemed like a man who'd had a weight lifted from his shoulders. This was often the way, she knew. Confession was good for the soul.

Afterwards he sat back.

Amanda said: 'There is a young man in Clachdubh called Gary McAllister, who had seen Kirstin Grainger around. The night before her death, Gary had come past the house hoping to get a glimpse through the window of the couple making love. He came back in the morning, knowing that Mr Baker had stayed the night. Again, he hoped to see them in bed together. He's a lonely teenager, a fantasist. He tried the back door handle, and found it was unlocked.'

Baker sniffed. 'I'd put the empty wine bottles out…Must have left the door…'

'Gary entered and saw Miss Grainger lying dead. He heard Mr Baker in the kitchen, with the tap running. He also saw the ring, and he took it.'

'Hang on, hang on,' the solicitor was saying. 'You're telling me you have another suspect at the crime scene.'

'Not a suspect. A witness.'

'No no no. I think we can claim that this Gary murdered Kirstin Grainger.'

'I don't think you can.' Paige turned again to Kevin Baker, her voice low. 'Because you stabbed her, didn't you?'

He nodded. 'Yes. It was an accident. A horrible accident. She laughed at me. She turned me down. She dropped the ring I gave her. She threw it down. She didn't want us to be together and happy. And we could have been so happy.'

The solicitor was open-mouthed in despair at his client. 'So what happened with the ring? How did it come into police possession?'

'Exactly as I described. Gary McAllister's house was burgled. His laptop was stolen – we subsequently recovered it. We only recently established that this ring was stolen too.'

'I think you'll find the defence will be challenging the chain of evidence, and the exact role played by this Gary McAllister in the death of Kirsten Grainger, in court. This investigation has been very badly managed. We will robustly challenge everything.'

'Fair enough,' Paige said. She looked at Kevin Baker.

'I'm sorry,' he said. 'Her death is my fault. I didn't mean it. We could have been so happy together. Forever. Me and Cordelia.' He frowned and gave a slight shake of his head. 'Kirstin.'

Paige and Amanda shared a look. 'Interview terminated.'

They sat in Paige's car outside the prison.

'Gary could get a tough time in court,' Amanda said.

Paige turned to her. 'And you're bloody lucky you're not going to be questioned under oath. Thank Christ we've got his confession.'

Amanda swallowed. 'Yes, ma'am.'

Paige calmed herself. 'Anyway. I think he'll stick to his confession and they'll go for mitigating circumstances. Probably a psychiatric review. If he changes his plea, well it's going to be a bastard of a court case.'

'Yes, ma'am. Sorry about…'

Paige shook her head. 'You got the result, DS Pitt. I'm not sure about your methods, but you got your result. Anything still to be done about your cases in Clachdubh?' She started the engine.

'No, ma'am. That's all done and dusted.'

❧ 72 ❦

Yes, Clachdubh was all done and dusted as far as Amanda was concerned: there was no way in to reopening the Karen McKechnie death. The Robertsons' case was rumbling on, of course, and would be for months, but it was all nothing to do with her now. She wondered about Mr Khalaf in Manchester, and the exact relationships in that tragic family.

Amanda and Claire decided to go out for dinner on the Friday evening, for a celebration of sorts. They managed to get a table in a bistro near their flat, and went to the pub up the road to kill the hour they had to wait. It was good to have her mind clear of all the stuff that had been going on.

They talked about young girls like Jasmine McCallum who had no focus in their lives except how they looked, and who fell for someone like Jamil Sabry. Claire knew all too well about situations like that. They talked about Kevin Baker, who had so wanted a wife to replace the one who had left him, and had been so obsessed about it that he couldn't handle Kirstin's – perfectly rational – rejection of him.

'He was fine when Rima left him because at heart he knew she wasn't the one. Jasmine was just a blip – very attractive, so impressionable and fixated that he persuaded to get her clothes off for him, but she wasn't what he really wanted. Then Kirstin Grainger, so like his first wife, and such a great relationship. But he pushed too hard, too fast, and he didn't stop to consider what *she* wanted.'

Claire reached and put her hand on Amanda's.

231

'And Gary McAllister – he's a weird one. I wonder if he'll actually get anywhere with his writing.' She shook her head. 'Anyway, I have been neglecting you massively and I want to make it up to you. How's your week been?'

They arrived at the bistro and were shown to their table, declining pre-dinner drinks and going straight for a bottle of Chilean Malbec. The waitress gave her normal customer smile for Amanda, and then frowned quizzically. 'Amanda?'

Amanda looked up. A woman of her own age, a bit taller and fuller figured, with long brown hair tied back from a pretty, smiling face. Amanda recognised her but couldn't place her.

'Denise. Denise Williams. Denise Grant now.'

'Oh my god.' Amanda stood up and embraced her. 'Denise.' She turned to Claire. 'Denise and I were friends at Uni.'

Claire raised her eyebrows and Amanda knew what she was thinking. And she was right.

'So,' Denise said. 'What did you do when you graduated?'

'I didn't finish my degree. I left and joined the police. You?'

'Went into teaching. Married, had kids, didn't go back to it. My DH part-owns this place and I help out when I must. Look, I should take your order.'

Amanda and Claire quickly checked the menu and ordered, and Denise went off to put the order in. They poured the wine and chinked glasses.

'Hmm,' Claire said.

Amanda smiled. 'Denise was experimenting when I met her,' she whispered.

They ate their meal and drank the wine, and lingered over a couple of large gins just to finish off. As they were about to leave, Amanda told Denise that they must catch up some time and said she'd give the restaurant a call and arrange it.

'You know where I am,' Denise smiled to them both. 'Goodnight.'

Amanda walked arm in arm with Claire round the corner towards their flat.

'Will you call her?'

'I don't think we've anything to talk about,' Amanda said.

The night was cool but dry, the street almost empty. As ever, cars lined the pavements. Amanda held Claire close.

Up ahead was a slim figure, walking purposefully towards them. Amanda frowned as the figure got closer, and then she saw he was wearing a balaclava, and she saw the long knife in the right hand. She stopped and pushed Claire behind her, and reached into her bag for her mobile. Where the fuck was it…

She turned to Claire. 'Run,' she said. 'Run back to the main road, find someone, get them to call the police.'

Claire was drunk and confused, but Amanda had instantly sobered up.

'Get help! Run!'

And Claire was off, awkward in her heels. Amanda could have run as well, but that would have left this man with the knife to find other targets.

Amanda turned to face the approaching figure, who stopped six feet from her. 'Fucking dyke MILF,' he shouted.

Shit, she thought. Oh fuck. Jamil Sabry had found her. She didn't know how he'd done it – her car was near her flat, unusually, so maybe he'd just waited for her. Maybe he'd got her address somehow, maybe traced her phone.

But that wasn't really the point at the moment.

Could she outrun him? Possibly – but what would he do then? Who would he hurt instead? He might run amok on one of the busier streets. She made a decision: she had to stand up to him. She tensed and braced herself.

Jamil stepped forward, the knife pointing towards her face. Up the road, over his shoulder, she thought she saw small flames. Had he set fire to a wheelie bin?

Jamil took off his balaclava and grinned. 'Hello, MILF. What a fucking surprise, yeah?'

'What do you want?' She tried to keep fear out of her voice, but it sounded to her like she failed. And from the manic look in Jamil's eyes she didn't think it mattered.

'Now, MILF, where did we get to last time? Oh yes, you were just about to show me your tits and give me a blow job.' He laughed. 'One big bang before another, eh, MILF?'

She was standing with her hands in front of her. She wondered whether she could jump for the long knife, but she was tired and had lots of gin and wine inside her: her head felt clear, but her reflexes would be poor. And if she did jump, he just needed to turn his wrist and he could sever an artery or a tendon and she would be useless.

She remembered well the training she'd had for dealing with people with a knife, because in the police working in Glasgow that's what you mostly faced when things got bad.

The first rule was to wear a stab-proof vest and have lots of colleagues with you so you could rush the guy and put him down. An alternative was to have a Taser or a gun and shoot him.

Clearly neither of these was an option right now.

So she stood her ground, eyes locked with Jamil. She wondered whether he'd ever stabbed anyone before. She wondered whether he was capable of just murdering her. Jasmine had said he'd wanted to 'cause a stir', and murdering a policewoman would achieve that, put him at the top of the news.

But it seemed he didn't want to kill her right away. He wanted sexual gratification first. Afterwards...Well. Shit, hadn't Jasmine satisfied him last night? Jasmine: younger and prettier, with a much better figure. But he had unfinished business with Amanda. She'd humiliated him. Like Karen McKechnie had – and she'd been thrown off a hill by him. He wanted to humiliate Amanda in return, then kill her too.

Had Claire called 999 yet?

Amanda decided to go for the second option in the training manual. Distract them, then try to inflict an injury: turning and smashing a foot into a knee was recommended.

'OK then,' she said. Stall for time, certainly.

His eyes lit up, then narrowed suspiciously. 'OK. Let's see them.'

She put her handbag on the pavement, slowly took off her jacket and laid it on top, kicking both to one side, out of her way. Then she very slowly unbuttoned her dark shirt and took it off, and reached behind herself to unclip her bra. She held it in place for a few seconds then let it drop away. She arched her back to try to make her small bust look more impressive to him. He was grinning, focused on her nipples, thinking no doubt that they were erect in lust for him rather than with the cold and fear.

She watched him stare at her for a full minute. 'Want to see my pussy?' she asked, starting to slowly unbutton her trousers and taking a step closer to him.

He nodded, licking his lips.

'Get your trousers down, then. Get ready for me. Get your cock out. Come on. Let me see how much you want me.'

His laugh gurgled in his throat. He moved the knife to his left hand and started undoing his belt, looking down as he fumbled with it.

She hadn't practised this manoeuvre for months, and could only hope it would work. He had the knife in his wrong hand, he was as distracted as he was ever going to be, the distance looked about right, so this was it. She didn't even pause to take a breath.

She half-turned and dropped onto her side, her hand hitting the rough pavement hard. She hooked one ankle round his leg and kicked at his other knee with her other foot. It connected right on the kneecap: textbook. He howled and staggered, and the leg gave way. She levered herself up and kicked at his other leg. All the while he waved the knife in her general direction and she felt something burn across her left leg and arm.

But he was down now, and she was getting to her feet. She kicked at the side of his head, allowing fury to take over, the knife still waving. She stamped on his wrist and he let go of the knife and she bent to take it as he groaned and writhed on the ground.

That was when she suddenly felt incredibly dizzy and fell to her knees. She had no energy, the knife was loose in her hand. She felt wetness trickling down one arm and under her trousers.

She realised he was coming to his senses, and she was losing it. She saw his eyes open and glare at her.

'You fucking bitch. I'll slice you into pieces for this. You're fucking dead.' He was half-up on one knee.

No, she thought. I've too much to live for. I'm not going to die like this.

She gripped the knife two-handed and thrust it upwards into his lower stomach. He screamed and fell back, pulling his legs up. She leaned over him and got another stab in, not knowing what damage she was doing to him, but his screams had turned to moans now, and he had rolled away, clutching at his stomach.

Away in the distance came the sounds of police sirens. Too late, she thought, as she lay back on the hard pavement. She couldn't breathe, and she was so tired. Her eyes closed.

Her eyes opened, and logic told her she was in hospital and something had happened to her. There was this *thing* over her mouth and nose. Despite the fact that she was clearly able to breathe, she panicked and tried to reach for it.

She'd almost made it when the young nurse by the bed, waiting for her to wake up but distracted by her phone, caught her hand. 'It's OK, Amanda. You're safe now.'

Amanda's eyes looked round, and the nurse saw the panic.

'You're in QEH. You'll be OK. I'll get the doctor. Don't move now.' Her voice was strangely dull, echoing like she was talking from another room.

Amanda could see other beds with patients, other nurses. This must be post-op, she thought, where they all came to wake up. The thing on her face still bothered her, but she could breathe. She tried to remember what had happened, but all she remembered was having a meal with Claire, and a former lover serving them. That was weird.

The nurse came back with a young man in jeans and a shirt and tie. He looked about twenty.

'Hi, Amanda. I'm Doctor Foster – I know, try not to laugh. Now, I'm not sure how much you remember of what happened to you, but you have two long knife wounds in your thigh, one on your arm, and we've glued you together again – not *too* much blood loss, luckily.' He coughed. 'You'll almost certainly – well, you have a very good chance – of mending as good as new – pretty much – we hope – but you will have to take it very easy for quite some time. Any questions? No? Good.' He gave a wide smile. 'Well, I'll come back and check on you later. Meanwhile I need to let your colleagues know that you're awake.'

Amanda had no concept of what he was saying. How had this happened to her?

He left, and someone else – he was just as young and said he was the anaesthetist – came by to tell her exactly the same stuff. They took the thing off her face and checked she was fine. Then she was wheeled to a lift and up, and into a ward with six beds in total, but only two of them occupied: a mass of grey hair was visible on pillows as she passed. They pulled the curtain round her and transferred her to the bed, putting the clip on her fingertip, the ECG pads on her chest.

The nurses were smiling and chatty, but Amanda found she couldn't speak. Finally they gave her a tiny plastic cup of morphine to drink and left her. Tiredness washed over her, and her eyes closed.

A hand was gently touching her, and she opened her eyes to see Claire, smiling bravely with tears running down her face. 'How are you, darling?' Claire asked.

Amanda said 'Fine', but her throat was dry and very sore so the word was almost unrecognisable. She coughed and wet her lips. 'I'll be fine.'

'They say you'll be OK.' And Claire broke into sobs, and buried her face in Amanda's neck, her red curls spilling everywhere.

Ramesh interrupted them five minutes later, and Claire reluctantly went for a coffee. Ramesh sat by the bed.

'Can you remember it all?'

'I can't remember anything,' Amanda croaked. 'I was having a meal with Claire and then…nothing.'

'You don't remember Jamil Sabry?'

It was like the knife slashing at her again. The humiliation of what he'd made her do, the horror of what he might have done. She felt ashamed.

And she'd…What had she done to him?

Ramesh reached to hold her hand, seeing the trauma and the tears. 'He came looking for you, no doubt to rape and kill you. We don't know how he found where you lived, but he must have seen your car there. He waited for you to come home. He'd soaked a rag in petrol and stuffed it into your petrol cap. It burned out inside the tank – he obviously expected an explosion, like in the movies, but we know that doesn't happen.'

She remembered it all now. 'He wanted to 'see my tits'. So I showed them to him, and suggested I was up for giving him a blowjob. That was enough to distract him and I did the standard hook and kick. What happened to him?'

Ramesh took a deep breath. 'You don't remember stabbing him? In the lower abdomen?'

She did now. She felt again the fury of holding the knife and plunging it into him.

'Self-defence obviously,' Ramesh said.

'How is he?'

He took a deep breath again. 'He's dead, Amanda. You hit his abdominal aorta with your second stab, caused massive bleeding. You don't come back from that unless you're very lucky.'

They sat in silence, Amanda eventually feeling that lying there with Ramesh holding her hand was a bit creepy. But she wondered what would happen now: there would be an enquiry into Jamil's death, of course, the whole events of that evening would be laid out.

And then the story of her previous contacts with Jamil. Shit, Jasmine had said the neighbour had heard her stealing Jamil's phone. That could look bad.

She felt vaguely sick. This was awful.

'Pete McLeod sends his regards. He'll come and see you tomorrow.'

'Thank you, sir. I think I need to rest now.'

'Of course.'

By the time he'd stood up she was asleep, but not calmly. He let Claire back in as he left, and she sat by the bed, holding Amanda's hand and crying silently.

❧ 74 ❧

They met at Logan Airport, in a corner of Legal C Bar, landside in terminal B. Grosvenor had just flown in and was flying straight back to La Guardia.

Natasha gulped her double espresso and he ordered her another.

'That thing with Jamil Sabry didn't work out so good,' Grosvenor said. 'Did you hear?'

'He attempted to kidnap and rape a female police officer but she got the drop on him and he got killed and she was badly injured but she's OK now.' She took a breath. 'Do you know anything about the rest of the group?'

He shook his head. 'I haven't heard – certainly no outrage, and nobody's told me if a cell was caught before it could do anything.

They're downplaying it, saying it wasn't a terrorist incident, just attempted murder of a police officer who was trying to arrest him.' He shrugged. 'You had asked about Khalaf.'

She blinked at him.

'He's supplying money to them. Raising it by manufacturing illegal drugs – MDMA. Please leave him alone. We're on him.'

She nodded. 'Is there anything else?'

'We're still recruiting, Natasha. We need good cyber people – people who are better than the criminals out there. I know your views, but if you have any contacts, then let me know.'

'I'll be sure to do that, Mr Grosvenor.'

'I gotta go.'

'So do I.'

❧ 75 ❧

Claire sat in the small room with the two male doctors across from her. She didn't understand what they were saying. She heard the words, asked them to repeat them, then shook her head with her eyes closed. 'I'm sorry. What do you mean exactly?'

'It's important we tell Amanda that she's going to make a full recovery,' Dr Foster said. 'It's essential that she believes that.'

'Of course. Why wouldn't we?'

The two men looked at each other, and then Foster spoke again. 'Because it's unlikely that she will. There's serious muscle and nerve damage to her left leg and her left arm. We'll work on it – physio – further operations – but we can already tell that the damage will be long lasting.'

Claire stared at them.

'Her life is not in danger, but it looks unlikely that she'll recover the full use of her leg and arm.'

'Will she walk?'

'Oh yes. But maybe with a stick. Certainly with a limp.'

Claire nodded. That didn't seem so bad. Then she understood. 'She won't be able to go back to her old job, will she?'

The two doctors exchanged glances, and Foster said: 'I don't know how Police Scotland works – whether there would be some kind of desk job – maybe intelligence – ' He shrugged. 'I don't know. But she won't be running around chasing criminals.'

Claire stared at them.

Our lives have changed, she thought. Completely. What have we lost because of that mad, angry young man and Amanda's relentless curiosity? She continued to stare at the young men, watching them look increasingly helpless in the face of her plight.

The End

About the Author
BRM Stewart

Brian RM Stewart was born in Rutherglen and grew up in Grangemouth. He attended Glasgow University and Jordanhill College of Education, taught in Edinburgh, then moved to Nairn where he and his now-late wife Jan raised their children.

Brian now lives in Broughty Ferry with his wife Sally, where he is a member of the Angus Writers' Circle and an active member of Rotary.

Brian spent much of his working life teaching mathematics and computing, but is now partially retired and lectures for the OU.

When not writing, Brian attempts to play golf and the guitar (though not at the same time), and is a keen Bridge player.

He has published two previous movels, *Digital Circumstances* and *Digital Investigations*.

More Books From ThunderPoint Publishing Ltd.

The Last Wolf
David Shaw Mackenzie
ISBN: 978-1-910946-39-8 (Kindle)
ISBN: 978-1-910946-38-1 (Paperback)

'So what is the novelist's duty then?'
'Oh, to tell the truth of course.'

But what is the truth when there are at least two sides to every story?

Brothers Maurice and Christopher have not spoken to each other for over 40 years, despite living on the same small island. And nobody talks about Maurice's first wife, Hester – until an apparently unconnected act of vengeance reverberates across the generations and carefully guarded secrets begin to unravel.

Moving from 1930s Capri to Paris, London and the Isle of Glass off the Scottish coast, *The Last Wolf* is a subtly crafted tale of lies and betrayals.

'*The Last Wolf* is an intimate tale of lies and betrayals lightly and deftly told by a master storyteller.'

Mere
Carol Fenlon
ISBN: 978-1-910946-37-4 (Kindle)
ISBN: 978-1-910946-36-7 (Paperback)

'There's something about this place. It's going to destroy us if we don't get away.'

Reclaimed from the bed of an ancient mere, drained by their forbears 150 years ago, New Cut Farm is home to the Askin family. Life is hard, but the land and its dark history is theirs, and up till now that has always been enough.

But Con Worrall can't make it pay. Pressured by his new wife following his mother's death, Con reluctantly sells up.

For Lynn Waters, New Cut Farm is the life she has always dreamed of, though her husband Dan has misgivings about the isolated farmhouse.

As Con's life disintegrates and Dan's unease increases, the past that is always there takes over and Lynn discovers the terrible hold that the land exerts over people – and the lengths to which they will go to keep it.

'...a well-written and engaging novel about marriage, genealogy and attachment to land' – Anne Goodwin

Toxic
Jackie McLean
Shortlisted for the Yeovil Book Prize 2011
ISBN: 978-0-9575689-8-3 (eBook)
ISBN: 978-0-9575689-9-0 (Paperback)

The recklessly brilliant DI Donna Davenport, struggling to hide a secret from police colleagues and get over the break-up with her partner, has been suspended from duty for a fiery and inappropriate outburst to the press.

DI Evanton, an old-fashioned, hard-living misogynistic copper has been newly demoted for thumping a suspect, and transferred to Dundee with a final warning ringing in his ears and a reputation that precedes him.

And in the peaceful, rolling Tayside farmland a deadly store of MIC, the toxin that devastated Bhopal, is being illegally stored by a criminal gang smuggling the valuable substance necessary for making cheap pesticides.

An anonymous tip-off starts a desperate search for the MIC that is complicated by the uneasy partnership between Davenport and Evanton and their growing mistrust of each others actions.

Compelling and authentic, Toxic is a tense and fast paced crime thriller.

'...a humdinger of a plot that is as realistic as it is frightening' – crimefictionlover.com

Shadows
Jackie McLean

ISBN: 978-0-9575689-8-3 (eBook)
ISBN: 978-0-9575689-9-0 (Paperback)

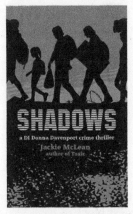

When DI Donna Davenport is called out to investigate a body washed up on Arbroath beach, it looks like a routine murder inquiry. But then the enquiry takes on a more sinister form.

There are similarities with a previous murder, and now a woman connected to them both has also gone missing.

For Donna, this is becoming personal, and with the added pressure of feeling watched at every turn, she is convinced that Jonas Evanton has returned to seek his revenge on her for his downfall.

Fearing they may be looking for a serial killer, Donna and her new team are taken in a horrifying and unexpected direction. Because it's not a serial killer – it's worse.

Moving from Dundee to the south coast of Turkey and the Syrian border, this is a fast paced novel about those who live their lives in the shadows, and those who exploit them.

'...a frank and unapologetic depiction of the ways human trafficking affects societies worldwide' – The Lesbian Review

In The Shadow Of The Hill

Helen Forbes

ISBN: 978-0-9929768-1-1 (eBook)
ISBN: 978-0-9929768-0-4 (Paperback)

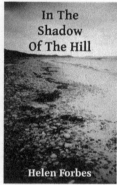

An elderly woman is found battered to death in the common stairwell of an Inverness block of flats.

Detective Sergeant Joe Galbraith starts what seems like one more depressing investigation of the untimely death of a poor unfortunate who was in the wrong place, at the wrong time.

As the investigation spreads across Scotland it reaches into a past that Joe has tried to forget, and takes him back to the Hebridean island of Harris, where he spent his childhood.

Among the mountains and the stunning landscape of religiously conservative Harris, in the shadow of Ceapabhal, long buried events and a tragic story are slowly uncovered, and the investigation takes on an altogether more sinister aspect.

In The Shadow Of The Hill skilfully captures the intricacies and malevolence of the underbelly of Highland and Island life, bringing tragedy and vengeance to the magical beauty of the Outer Hebrides.

'...our first real home-grown sample of modern Highland noir' – Roger Hutchison; West Highland Free Press

Madness Lies
Helen Forbes

ISBN: 978-1-910946-31-2 (Kindle)
ISBN: 978-1-910946-30-5 (Paperback)

When an Inverness Councillor is murdered in broad daylight in the middle of town, Detective Sergeant Joe Galbraith sees a familiar figure running from the scene.

According to everyone who knows him, the Councillor had no enemies, but someone clearly wanted him dead.

The victim's high profile means the police want a quick resolution to the case, but no one seems to know anything. Or if they do, they're not prepared to say.

This second novel of Highland Noir from Helen Forbes continues the series with a crime thriller that moves between Inverness, North Uist and London, reaching a terrifying denouement at the notorious Black Rock Gorge.

'Top notch crime fiction – a gripping and satisfying read'
– Ann Stormont

The Birds That Never Flew

Margot McCuaig
Shortlisted for the
Dundee International Book Prize 2012
Longlisted for the Polari First Book Prize 2014
ISBN: 978-0-9929768-5-9 (eBook)
ISBN: 978-0-9929768-4-2 (Paperback)

'Have you got a light hen? I'm totally gaspin.'

Battered and bruised, Elizabeth has taken her daughter and left her abusive husband Patrick. Again. In the bleak and impersonal Glasgow housing office Elizabeth meets the provocatively intriguing drug addict Sadie, who is desperate to get her own life back on track.

The two women forge a fierce and interdependent relationship as they try to rebuild their shattered lives, but despite their bold, and sometimes illegal attempts it seems impossible to escape from the abuse they have always known, and tragedy strikes.

More than a decade later Elizabeth has started to implement her perfect revenge – until a surreal Glaswegian Virgin Mary steps in with imperfect timing and a less than divine attitude to stick a spoke in the wheel of retribution.

Tragic, darkly funny and irreverent, *The Birds That Never Flew* ushers in a new and vibrant voice in Scottish literature.

> **'...dark, beautiful and moving, I wholeheartedly
> recommend'** scanoir.co.uk